TALES OF
WEEPING HOLLOW

& THE CURSE OF THE

HOLLOW
HEATHENS

• BOOK OF BLACKWELL •

ALSO BY
nicole fiorina

www.nicolefiorina.com

HOLLOW
HEATHENS

nicole fiorina

HOLLOW HEATHENS
Book of Blackwell

Tales of Weeping Hollow Collection

Copyright © 2020 by Nicole Fiorina
Original Publication Date: October 13th, 2020

Written by Nicole Fiorina; Published & Formatted by Nicole Fiorina Books, LLC
Map Illustrations by Frederick Kroner; Stardust Books
Interior Illustrations by Surovi Bain
Character Art by Pandy Als Art
Cover Art by Okay Creations

www.nicolefiorina.com

BEFORE YOU *read*

Hollow Heathens: Book of Blackwell is the first book in the Tales of Weeping Hollow series. This book can be read as a standalone, but for a better reading experience it is recommended to read books in the order they are published.

This is the original, new adult edition. If you are interested in the Young Adult Edition, hardback is available at nicolefiorina.com

The Audio edition of this book will be available on Audible & iTunes.

Hollow Heathens Playlist available on Spotify
https://spoti.fi/30bzg5C

For book club info, topics, & discussions,
please read on at the end of the story.

Thank you, and I hope you enjoyed this world I created!

For my daughter, Grace.

I always said you were my mother in another life.
My tenacious girl, I'm ashamed to admit
That you make me forget
who is parenting who.

Thank you for being uniquely you, with a steadfast soul,
a thirst for knowledge, & living without fear.
You're a lethal combination, baby, and
I don't think this world was prepared.
But, you're moving way too fast.
Slow down & take notice of the world around you.
Even the smallest, inconsequential moments
that don't seem important now,
but will be one day.

Thank you for helping me plan and plot this story.
Thank you for bringing Fallon to life.
Sharing my dream with you has been
my favorite part of Hollow Heathens.

Always remember,
you are not *just* a girl.
Stay humble & be your own lover first.

xo, *mom*

welcome to

WEEPING
HOLLOW

don't look behind you.

Weeping Hollow

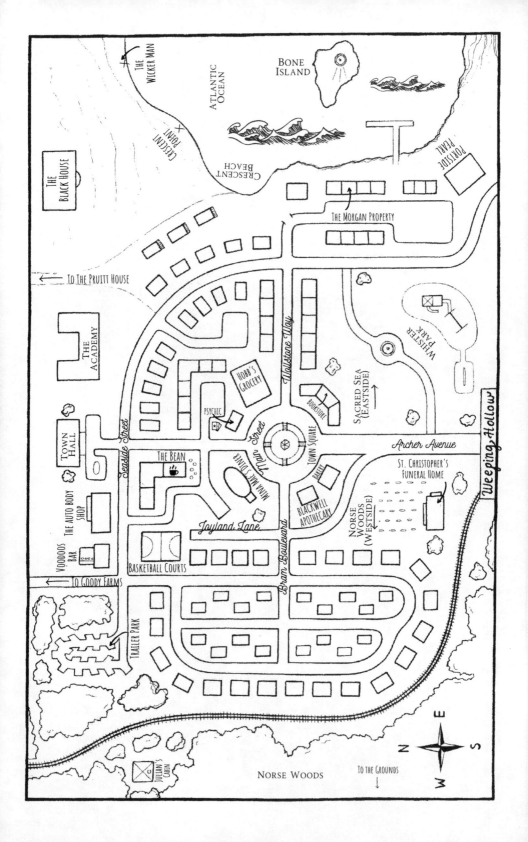

GLOSSARY

From away: This is an expression used for people who are not from town.

Flatlander: What the town calls the people from away. Those who do not belong to either coven and have no ancestors from the original founding families.

Ayuh: Used to express agreement. Originated in Maine.

Right out straight: Maine expression meaning very busy.

The Summerland: The name given by Theosophists Wiccans and some earth-based contemporary pagan religions to their conceptualization of an afterlife.

Sawa: Kenyan – meaning "fine" and/or "all good"

GRAMP'S GLOSSARY

Fopdoodle: A stupid or insignificant fellow; a fool.

Whooperups: A term meaning "inferior, noisy singers"

Wandoughts: A feeble, puny, weak creature; a silly, sluggish, worthless man; another word for impotence.

Rantallions: A person whose penis is insufficiently long, in its 'relaxed' state, to exceed the length of the scrotum.

Dunderhead: A stupid person.

Arfarfan'arf: A lazy drunk.

Off his/her kadoova: Crazy

Bedswerve: Jumping from one person's bed to another; ie: cheating; a promiscuous person.

Maffickin': To celebrate with boisterous rejoicing & hilarious behavior.

THE FOUNDING FAMILIES

NORSE WOODS COVEN

HIGH PRIEST: *CLARENCE GOODY*

BLACKWELL

Element of Spirit – Origin: Vættir

Current: Julian Jai Blackwell

Brother of Jolie Blackwell; son of Javino Blackwell (deceased) &
Agatha Bianchi Blackwell; ancestors: Horace Blackwell & Bellamy
Blackwell

GOODY

Element of Air – Origin: Njǫrd

Current: Zephyr Blue Goody

Brother of Winnifred Goody; son of Clarence Goody & Beatrix
Ricci Goody (deceased)

WILDES

Element of Fire – Origin: Loki

Current: Phoenix Loki Wildes

Brother of Wren Wildes; son of Hayden Wildes (deceased) &
Amelia Ander Wildes; ancestors: Kyden Wildes

PARISH

Element of Water – Origin: Ægir

Current: Beckham Brooks Parish

Son of Earl "Drunk Earl" Parish & unknown flatlander (deceased)

DANVERS

Element of Earth – Origin: Jörð

Current: N/A; Last known Danvers; Foster Danvers (deceased);
husband of Clarice Woolf Danvers (deceased)

SACRED SEA COVEN

HIGH PRIEST: *AUGUSTINE PRUITT*

PRU*ITT*
Current: Kane Kos Pruitt
Brother of Koraline Pruitt; son of Augustine Pruitt & Ginevra De
Luca Pruitt (deceased)

CAN*TINI*
Current: Cyrus Olen Cantini
Brother of Camora, Kaser, & Cillian Cantini; son of Darnell
Cantini & Viola Conti Cantini; ancestors: Matteo Cantini

SULLI*VAN*
Current: Ivy Amaya Sullivan
Adora Oria Sullivan; non-member; pending initiation
Fable Hazel Sullivan; non-member; pending initiation
Daughters of Ronan Sullivan & Marcelline O'Connor
Sullivan

THE ORDER OF WEEPING HOLLOW

FROM SACRED SEA
Augustine Pruitt
Viola Cantini

FROM NORSE WOODS
Clarence Goody
Agatha Blackwell

FROM THE FLATLANDERS
Mina Mae Lavenza

I believe this world is filled with nothing of the normal, that we are all monsters and freaks, and if my beliefs are true, we can escape the shadows to find one another.

I believe something more hideous and cruel has put us there, in the dark corners of our minds. Something that isn't normal itself. For normal is the *lie* to keep all the monsters and freaks tamed.

part
ONE

once upon
A TIME

T HINGS LURK IN THE DARKNESS; MONSTERS, GHOSTS, GHASTLY supernatural beings tethered by bottomless energy to keep them there, pinned to the earth and walking without direction. Without purpose. A growing gaping hole feeds hastily on their dark soul, and most cannot understand why. Pain, anger, sorrow, grief … emotions bleed into one another over the years, causing spirits to forget why they were left behind.

And the cruelest is love. Long after death, love has the power to turn us all into the darkest of monsters.

I WAS BORN WITH ONE FOOT IN THIS WORLD AND ONE IN THE NEXT. "You're a Grimaldi," Marietta would always tell me. *I'm a Grimaldi*, yet no matter how many times I repeated the mantra, the young man in the corner of my room refused to go away. He was curled up in my reading chair with his knees pressed close to his chest. During the cold months, I'd leave my window open to allow the chilling breeze to slip through the crack, but he couldn't be shaking because of the cold. Spirits only felt the hungry emotions eating away at them. Yet, he was shaking. There was something different about him.

"Don't cry," I whispered under the paper white moonlight streaming between us. I'd learned not to fear the ones who would come to me, and kept them as my secret. But there was something different about this one, fading in and out like a poor picture on a TV. His lips were glacier blue and his hair as white as an Arctic wolf. And his eyes … his eyes were demonic. Cold. A starless galaxy. And terrified.

I pushed the thick quilt off my legs and slid my feet to the cold wooden floors. "What's your name?"

His frosted brows pulled together as he looked up at me under thick wet lashes, trembling. Most were surprised I could see them and was unafraid by their presence, but h seemed more confused about my question. He didn't remember his name, which only meant he was new.

But he seemed so real, blurring between dimensions.

He wasn't like the rest of them.

The floorboards creaked as my feet inched forward, and I paused halfway to him when Marietta's footfalls echoed off the hollowed stairs.

"Y-y-ou have to help me," he said through a desperate plea. "F-f-find me."

My bedroom door creaked open, and I rushed back to bed and under the quilt. As the sound of her footsteps crept closer, I slammed my eyes closed to pretend to be asleep. My hair covered my face. I pulled my arms and legs and fingers and toes, every part of me hiding beneath the thick, hand-made quilt.

"I know you are awake, moonchild." Marietta's voice was silky. My bed dipped as she sat at the edge. She pulled the quilt down, and I turned to face her. "You cannot be up all hours of the night, or you will sleep all day," she added with a light tap on my nose.

I pushed my hair from my eyes and peeked to the chair where the ghost was sitting.

But the ghost was no longer there.

My gaze slid back to my nanny. "I can't sleep. Will you tell me a story?"

"*Ah!* A story is what she wants to hear." Marietta's purple lips pulled into a slight grin, and the bracelets lining her arm banged together as she tucked the blanket around me. "I tell you a story, and then you will sleep." Her brow peaked into the shape of a crescent moon.

I nodded eagerly. "Yes, I promise."

"Oh, I do not know," she replied with demise. "I do not think you are ready for this one."

"I am, Marietta. I am."

"Oh, child, all right. But, you see, I will need to start from the beginning." Marietta dragged in a long breath and shifted beside me...

"Once upon a time, far, far away, mysterious land was discovered. This land became a town, but the new town cannot be seen by people from away. Many know the name and have even set out to find it, but this town can only be discovered when it wants to be seen. No barriers exist between worlds. Strange happenings. A town of magic and mischief, where superstition and the stars in the sky are the only guides, yet just as unpredictable as the Atlantic tide.

"You see, centuries ago, two separate and very different covens founded this land, yet the stars aligned when they crossed paths. A boat sailed in by sea, escaping cruelty from their country. At the same time, outcasts from the New World came up from the south, running away from the same torment, trudging through dense woods while harsh sleet slammed against their chapped faces.

"Neither would leave upon arrival, both marking their claim on the land, casting this very spell, an invisible shield, to hide and protect their people, making the town unseeable to all outsiders. Little did either coven know, something else had already lived in those woods.

"Branches from birch trees whispered, ravens sang their darkest tale, and with every crackle of fallen leaves beneath their heavy boots, secrets of the forest unraveled, spinning words together like a web from a black widow spider. And this was just from the forest because the sea, child, *oh!* the sea, it roared with prophecy, waves crashing against the imperishable cliffs, the moon's transcendent phases glimmering over the eternal waters.

"And one day, the town will call upon you, my moonchild. But hear me when I say, you will always have the freedom to choose. You will never be forced to return. But if you do, there is no escaping. Not until the town lets you go—"

"To return? Return to where?" I asked with my fingers clutched around the quilt, ears perked and hungry for more.

"The town of *weeping* HOLLOW."

ARCHER AVENUE, WEEPING HOLLOW

FALLON
chapter one

BOUNCING OFF THE REFRIGERATOR'S GLASS DOOR, WHICH HOUSED numerous caffeinated drink options, I caught myself staring at my ghostly reflection. My white hair and pale blue eyes looked opalescent, almost as if my doppelganger was stuck between the glass of the chilled door. The more I stared at myself, the more I wondered who was really looking into who.

"Excuse me," a man said, opening the glass door and snapping my detached gaze. In an unbuttoned red plaid shirt and dirt-stained jeans, his grimy hands, with black sludge permanently under his fingernails, grabbed a twelve-ounce cold-brew coffee. He turned to face me. "Made up ya mind?"

A heavy question. It was apparent I'd made up my mind. Otherwise, I wouldn't have been standing in a rundown Shell truck stop half past midnight where the "S" was broken and dangling. It just said *Hell*, my last stop before reaching the small town I'd only heard of in stories told under star-filled skies in the middle of restless nights. A town I'd never imagined myself returning to.

Dirty-Trucker-Man lingered, awaiting a response. My gaze remained locked on to where my reflection had lived moments ago, my thumb swirling my mood ring around my ring finger over and over. The glass door freed from his hold and fell back into place before the man walked away, mumbling under his breath, "Okaaay then. Whatta freak."

Freak.

I opened the refrigerator door, and the frosty temperature brewing inside flared goosebumps up my forearm, raising every white hair on my skin. I wanted to climb inside and fall asleep with the icy current. However, I snatched up the last hazelnut coffee and made my way to the checkout counter, keeping my head down, but my attention on my surroundings.

Hell, past the midnight hour, was a lighthouse for pedophiles and serial killers, and I was the perfect prey.

Loner. Young. Odd. An acquired taste. A freak.

A girl no one would search for or miss.

On the other side of the checkout counter, behind a cabinet filled with lottery tickets, a guy lifted his elbows from the counter and clicked off his phone before tucking it into his pocket. Straight black hair fell over one eye before he tossed it to the side. "Anything else?" he asked through a forced sigh, dragging the chilled can across the counter.

"Yeah …" Reluctance dripped from my voice. I pulled out my iPhone to open my GPS app. "I'm a little lost. Do you know the way to Weeping Hollow?"

Dirty-Trucker-Man from back at the refrigerators hobbled behind me as the cashier looked up from his register with a blank stare. Then the cashier's gaze moved past me to the Dirty-Trucker-Man. "Yah can get heyah from theya, but yah can't get theya from heyah." His Maine accent was thick as he half chuckled, shaking his head.

Dirty-Trucker-Man muttered to move it along. I dropped my phone-holding hand and shifted in my black and white saddle oxford shoes. It was past midnight. I was tired. I was lost. I didn't have time for riddles. "What's that supposed to mean?"

The cashier tapped the top of the can with a forced smile. "It'll be three-fifteen."

"Thanks for nothing," I grumbled, slapping a five-dollar bill on the counter and scooping up my drink.

The little silver bell above the exit chimed on my way out, and the mild ocean air slammed into my eyes as I headed back to my car.

I'd been on the road for about thirty-five hours, only stopping for gas and eating at the closest drive-thru. With every passing mile, my lids had grown heavy, and I had to shake my head to keep myself awake. I'd always been stubborn like that. I'd always challenged myself to carry every grocery bag from the car to our Texas home at once. Lining my arms, using my teeth, anything to avoid a second trip.

Caffeinated and back on US-1, a few cars scattered along the highway as I followed the coastline up the state of Maine, remembering the directions Gramps had jotted down in his letter. GPS didn't recognize the small, secluded town of Weeping Hollow, and the farther I drove, the spottier the reception became until the exit off Archer Avenue appeared.

The dull sign was hardly visible from the narrow, empty road. The dim headlights from my silver Mini Cooper turned into my only flashlights as I slowly drove past the faded sign. Rain had rusted the sharp metal edges that read the town name, and under it, POPULATION 665.

As I passed, the last number transformed, blurring into 666.

I rubbed my eyes. I was tired, seeing things. *Right?*

I continued onward, creeping along the eerie dark road tunneled by looming trees. Famished vultures littered the path like roadwork, fighting over a dead carcass and painting the street in blood and black wings. Ruthless with hunger, the birds hardly moved out of the way nor seemed threatened by the Mini Coop crossing their path. I crawled forward, and for the next three miles, the trees dwindled on both sides, dissolving into tombstones on my left and a rundown children's park on my right.

The translucent moon hung high above, illuminating a rusted iron sign arching over the only way in … and the only way out.

Weeping Hollow.

My Mini Cooper sputtered from the exhausting journey across numerous state lines, and I paused at a stop sign before the roundabout to canvas the small town I'd only heard of in stories. It didn't look like it belonged in the beautiful state of Maine. It was as if the Devil handcrafted Salem's Lot with a black-feathered quill and ebony ink on a tattered canvas, then blindly dropped his creation in amusement to see what could come of it—how the people would accommodate. And they did.

The engine stalled, but I was too focused on what laid before me to care. Antique lamp posts glowed from every corner of the sidewalks. And under the midnight sky—where watercolor-gray clouds smeared before a galaxy of stars like a sheer veil—townspeople walked through the heart of Weeping Hollow, casually up and down the gloomy streets as if it were completely normal at this hour. At almost three in the morning. At the start of August.

A chill slithered through my veins. After twenty-four long years, I'd finally returned to the place I was born, and the very place my mother had taken her last breath.

I twisted the car key, praying to hear the single most delicious car sound of the motor being brought back to life. The engine stuttered a few seconds before it finally took, and I slapped the steering wheel before circling the gazebo. "That's right, baby. We're almost there. Just a few more miles."

Gramps lived along the coastline, the sea cliffs and open waters a backdrop for his historic blueish-green coastal home. I'd seen the house before from an old dusty box I'd found in our attic back in Texas. Marietta, my nanny, had caught me sitting on the aged hardwood floors in the attic, sifting through the old photos. I'd once asked her if we would ever return to the town in the photos—the town from the stories.

"You can't go back unless it needs you, moonshine," she had said, crouching down in front of me and taking the photos from my fingers.

Marietta was a crazy old hag; velvety skin, eyes black and beady, with thick Kenyan accent. She had spent her evenings on the porch, rocking in her chair and sipping from her Moscow mule mug with a dark omen in her eyes.

Marietta and I were frightening to most, rumored to cast spells on boys who dared to come near me. In high school, it was better to be on my good side than bad, fearing my witch of a nanny would prick her hand-made fabric dolls if anyone caused me harm. I never spoke out against the rumors, not after what they had done to me. And also, a part of me believed they were true.

Like Gramps had written in his letter, a lone key was left for me in the mailbox. I parked the car along the side of the street, leaving my baggage behind for the morning. The sound of waves crashing against the sea cliffs filled the eerie silence as I walked up the front porch steps. My feet froze when a hair-raising glare landed on me. I felt it first, then reluctantly turned my head.

A tall woman, thin and fragile, stood on her front porch next door in a raggedy white nightgown. Her wiry gray hair poured over her shoulders, and her long boney fingers gripped the railing. Dark eyes pinned to mine, and my muscles flinched beneath my skin. I forced my hand up and offered a small wave, but the old woman didn't remove her intimidating gaze. Her grip on the railing only tightened, blue veins popping beneath her ethereal skin, keeping her frail body from being blown away by the slightest breeze.

I fumbled to get into the house. The wind through the keyhole iced my fingers, and the key jammed perfectly into the lock when another cold wind blew, whisking my white hair all around. Once inside, the heavy front door shut behind me and I fell back against it, closing my eyes and sucking in enough air to fill my lungs. The old musty scent seeped up my nose, coating my brain.

But I'd made it. I'd finally made it to Gramps, and it felt as if I'd stepped onto Duma Key—some fictional place you'd only read about in a book.

It was colder inside the house, too. My knobby knees shook, needing more than a thin layer of black stockings under my pleated shorts to keep me warm. But despite my body's reaction, the cold felt like home.

I reached behind me and locked the door.

Clang! Clang! Clang! Sudden striking bells pierced the quiet, causing me to flinch. My eyes popped open, and my gaze fell upon a cherry-wood grandfather clock casting a monstrous shadow across the foyer. Over the deafening song ringing in my ears, I dropped my head back against the door once more and tucked my tangled hair behind my ear, laughing lightly at myself.

The bells died down, and the old house came to life.

With a few uneasy steps down the foyer, the old planks screeched under my shoes and up the inside of the walls until harsh, labored breathing slid through a cracked bedroom door just beyond the foyer. I tip-toed across the wooden planks to peek inside the bedroom before pushing open the door.

There, sleeping with his mouth wide open, was the man I'd only known through letters passed back and forth over the last twelve months. Before a year ago, I had no idea I had a living grandfather. When I received the first envelope postmarked from Weeping Hollow, I'd almost tossed it. But curiosity was my kryptonite, and once my eyes landed on the first word, *moonshine*, everything changed.

Moonlight spilled from the window, casting a sliver of light over the old man and his bedroom. Gramps was lying on his back, slightly slanted upward against his headboard. His skin, like worn-out elastic bands, hung from his bones. Aged and wrinkled, he glowed in the dimmed room surrounded by antique furniture and deep-green damask wallpaper. Fedoras and newsboy hats decorated the wall facing his bed. Dentures floated in a glass cup on the nightstand beside a pair of tortoise-rimmed bifocals. I sank against the doorway to take him in.

His burly brows were a shade darker than the gray wisps randomly poking from his head. Gramps let out a loud snore, the kind to gurgle in your throat. After a full cough, he returned to the gravelly breathing, his gummy mouth wide open. I didn't really know him all that well, but with every struggling breath he took—like it was the hardest thing he had to do—my jaw tightened, and my heart constricted.

It wasn't until the sickness took a turn for the worst that he'd confessed his condition in his final letter, which led me here. He didn't have to say it, but the last letter seemed off—like a cry for help.

Gramps was sick, and he didn't want to do this alone.

What Gramps didn't know was that I was alone, too.

"I'm here, Gramps," I whispered into the darkness …

"*i'm finally* HOME."

FALLON
chapter two

A BOOMING AND AMBITIOUS DEEP TONE BOUNCED THROUGHOUT THE old house. *"And these are your Sunday morning Hollow Headlines. Happy August third. Keep safe out there, and remember, no one is safe after 3 AM."* Then the intro of *Haunted Heart* by Christina Aguilera followed, pulling me sluggishly from the squeaky iron bed.

Outside the French doors of my new bedroom, the clouds, dusty shades of gray, moved lazily across the dewy sky. I rubbed my eyes and took the stairs down at the same pace as the clouds, following Christina's lusty voice as if her haunting was calling me.

Husky coughs moved fluently throughout the home and down the hallway. When I turned the corner, Gramps was sitting at the small breakfast table nestled in the middle of the butter-yellow kitchen with a steaming cup of coffee. A newspaper was scattered before him. He was already fully dressed, wearing a wrinkly ivory button-down shirt under suspenders and khaki slacks. Green and tan argyle socks covered his feet inside a pair of slippers.

The granddaughter thing to do would be to kiss his cheek, throw my arms around his softened muscles, and shed a few tears at finally meeting my grandfather for the first time. But I'd read the letters. Benny Grimaldi was moody and not the most affectionate.

"You shouldn't be up and about. You should be resting," I said casually, stepping into the semi-lit kitchen overlooking the sea. Scratchy tunes replaced Christina's voice from the old radio sitting beside him on the table.

Gramps flinched, raised his head, and dropped the tissue-holding-hand from his chapped lips as if I'd frightened him. He looked up at me from under the rim of his tan fedora for a long moment, surely finding pieces of my mother—his only daughter—in my appearance. His glassy brown eyes froze like he'd been transported back to twenty-four years ago. As if he'd seen a ghost.

Then his eyes fell to the newspaper. "Six lettah word for neithah dead nor alive?" he grumbled, readjusting his giant, round bifocals and going back to his crossword puzzle.

It was stupid to believe he would ask about my travels or thank me for coming. In his letters, he'd complained about the paperboy tossing the latest issue of The Daily Hollow beside the mailbox instead of by the front door, or the reckless teenagers leaving broken liquor bottles at the rocks behind his house, or Jasper Abbott falling into a rage during Bingo night at Town Hall. Gramps made fun of the absurd superstitions and traditions of the town and the people in it, and each week I'd looked forward to receiving his letters. Somehow, his prejudices fulfilled my mundane days.

I spun on my heel and faced the tiled countertop that stored homeless dishes, cookware, and vintage gadgets, and touched the side of the coffee pot nestled in the nook to see if it was still warm.

Six letter word for neither dead nor alive. "Undead." I opened the yellow cabinets in search of a mug.

"Tha coffee's shit," he warned, following a few more coughs. The wet ones that come up from your chest. "Yah bettah off headin' uptah town. Don't go inta tha dinah though, they put somethin' in tha coffee. Go to tha Bean. But bring yah own mug. They don't like people from away. Ordah a few stacks while yah at it. No pukin' it up eithah. Yah all bones."

My head turned in his direction. "I'm not—"

"What-ah-yah doing heyah, moonshine? I didn't ask yah to come!" he snapped, interrupting me with a bite in his words. A cough left him, and he brought the tissue back over his mouth before continuing, "I don't want yah heyah."

My brows raised—a punch to the gut.

The old man had told me he wasn't doing well, left the instructions to Weeping Hollow, and put a key in the mailbox for me. If that wasn't asking me to come, then why go through all the hassle? Maybe he'd forgotten about the last letter he'd sent. Maybe he regretted sending it in the first place. Maybe he was worse than I'd imagined, like *going-senile* worse.

"Well, I'm here now, and I'm not leaving you. It's just us two. We're the only family left, so let's make the most of it, alright?"

Gramps mumbled through another coughing fit. "How long? I'll call Jonah, get yah a job ovah theya at tha funeral home to keep yah outta my hair. I don't know why yah inta dead bodies ... Sick if yah ask me ... Yah need to keep ya-self busy ... Jonah will get yah tha job ..." he rambled on.

The plan had always been cosmetology, but once Marietta died, the plan changed. Marietta's funeral had been an open casket, and even though I was the only one who attended the intimate ceremony, she was there with me. Her spirit stood right next to me as we stared down at her corpse, which looked like someone else entirely. The makeup was all wrong. It was the first time I'd seen a dead body, and the only thing I wanted to do was wipe the bright-red lip color off with the pad of my thumb, retrieve the Mac matte lipstick from my snakeskin purse, and paint the Del Rio shade on her heart-shaped lips. It was then I knew what I should do with my life.

To be a mortician was a calling.

And there was beauty after death, like a wilted rose, petals stiff and fragile. Timeless and enchanting. A casted spell and oldest tale. Stories frozen in time within the ruins.

Just like the stories Marietta had told of Weeping Hollow.

"Tell him I don't deal with the families." My awkwardness around grief made me seem insincere. It was terrible for business and best this way for both parties involved.

"Yea, yea. Yah have to work that out with Jonah," Gramps replied.

At the back of the cluttered cabinet, I finally found a mug and pulled it off the shelf. "Thanks, Gramps."

31

The old man shook his head and grunted, "Call me Benny. Everyone around heyah calls me Benny."

I smirked. "I'll call you Benny when you stop calling me *moonshine*."

Gramps' burly brows pinched together. "I'll call yah whatevah the hell I wanna call yah."

There was a hint of a smile in his words, an extra wrinkle beside his lips. Though I was still trying to figure and feel the man out, maybe he was happy to see me after all.

"I'll talk to the funeral director. Now, tell me, what did the doctor say about your cough?" I poured my coffee into a mug that read, REAL WOMEN MARRY ASSHOLES. It must have been my late grandmother's.

Gramps snatched the pencil off the table and leaned over the newspaper, filling in the black and white checkered boxes. My tailbone hit the counter, and I crossed my ankles, pulling the steaming hot coffee to my lips.

"Please tell me you saw a doctor …" I said, my authoritative tone spilling into the cup. He tapped the eraser on the wooden table a few times, avoiding the question as a child would. When he peeked at me from the corner of his eye, I shrugged. "Fine. I'll just call them myself."

Gramps fell back against the wooden chair, pointing the tip of the pencil at me. "Yah have to know somethin' about us, moonshine. We do things differently heyah. We go 'bout things our own way. This virus, it's outta tha doc's control. Theyas nothin' they can do. Yah wanna piece of advice? Mind yah own. Just do yah"—he waved his wrinkly hand out in front of him— "mortician thing. You'll stay busy with all tha death goin' 'round."

"Mind my own?" I laughed. "You think you're just gonna get me this job to keep me off your back? That I'm just gonna stand back and not help?"

Gramps dropped his elbow on the table and went back to his puzzle.

"Fine. I'll take this coffee outside and enjoy the view." I kicked off the counter and passed by him. "Oh, and I'm heading into town later. Try not to die while I'm gone."

He grumbled under his whiney breath. "If yah go inta town, don't take tha cah. Only stiff-necken snobs and hooligans drive a cah around here. Theyas a scootah in the garage."

I nodded, holding in a smile, and before leaving through the side door that led outside, I grabbed a wool blanket off the couch and wrapped it around me.

There wasn't much of a backyard. I passed by a detached garage and walked the stone steps to the cliff's edge. The deep blue waters of the Atlantic stretched far and wide, fading into the sky. The salty sea mist brushed across my cheeks, and my eyes closed under the somber song of the sea, the air twirling in my hair as I took another sip of coffee.

Gramps was right. The coffee was shit.

When I opened my eyes again, down below, where the waves met the rocks, there was a guy. He was alone, wearing a black coat and a hood pulled over his head, staring out into the blackish-blue ocean under gray clouded skies. Content and at peace, he had one arm hanging off his bent knee, the other leg stretched out in front of him. He stared out into the horizon as if he was seeing something so much bigger than the sea, like he wanted to be a part of it.

Waves crashed against the rocks, and ivory foam fizzled at his feet when the water spilled over but never touched him. Nothing could touch him. I looked left then right, wondering if anyone else was out at this hour. The sun had just risen. But it was only us two, gazing out into the same vast ocean, under the same smeared sky, only a short distance between us.

He picked up a small stone from beside him, examined it between his fingers, then threw it far past the waves. I took a step closer at the top of the cliff when loose rocks rolled down the sharp drop behind him.

The guy looked over his shoulder at me.

A black mask covered his face, only his eyes—the same color as the silvery skies—fell over me like snow on a cold wintry night. Light and gentle. A shiver swept across my skin. Neither one of us moved a muscle or spoke a word. He was looking at me as if I'd caught him in an intimate moment, like he was making love to the morning. Turning my eyes away would be the right thing to do, yet it felt impossible. I should've glanced away and given him the space he came out here for. Perhaps a normal girl would have.

But, instead, I called out to him. "What are you doing down there?"

The hand hanging off his bent knee lifted in the air. If he had replied, his words were washed away by the crashing waves. The mask stretching across his face prevented me from seeing his lips move, too. But his gaze never faltered. It held on.

My mouth went dry, and I tried to swallow.

"I'm Fallon. Fallon Morgan," I shouted, hoping he could hear *me* and not the nerves leaking into my voice.

He hung his head for a moment before peering back up at me. Seconds passed as we shamelessly locked eyes, and my fingers drifted over my smiling lips. I wondered if he was smiling as well behind the mask. I needed to get closer.

My eyes followed along the edge of the rocky cliff, looking for a way down until I spotted one.

The blanket fell from around me. With one hand gripping the hot mug in my hand, my coffee seeping over the rim, I balanced the other on the sharp edges, heading down barefoot.

When I reached the same lower level as him, he watched me with raised brows as I teetered on the rocks. Nerves skipped up my spine to the back of my neck as he stood tall, rubbing a stone between two fingers. His body twitched as if he might bolt from the scene at any moment, but something was keeping him rooted in place.

I walked around him and stepped up on the higher side of the rock. "I couldn't hear you."

"And you took that as an invitation?" He turned, keeping his attention on me, watching my every move.

When my bare feet found balance, I looked up at him, and his cold eyes froze any warm thing left in me. The chill rushed from my head to the tips of my fingers, probably chilling my coffee too. His stare fixated on me, probably trying to figure out this strange girl who disrupted his peaceful morning.

"What's your name?" I asked. His eyes flicked skyward then down as he faced the water again, shaking his head. "Okay ..." I sipped from my coffee, and a wave came and splashed over the rock and onto my bare toes. The glacial temperatures pricked my skin like a thousand needles, but I didn't jump back. My eyes steered to him, noticing the way his were distant, uninterested, locked on to the horizon of the black waters. "You always come out here in the morning?"

"Not always." He bent down and picked up a handful of stones. They jumped in his palm, and one slid between his pointer finger and thumb.

"You like the water?"

A vein in his neck popped. He darted a stone far past the waves, and it skipped along the smooth surface, past the choppy whitecaps. "I despise it."

"Then, why come?"

His shoulders lifted, and my gaze slid over his profile. He was tall, possibly six foot two. He chucked another stone against the water's surface. "If I tell you, will you leave?"

"Depends. Will you be real with me?"

His chin dropped, and his chest expanded before looking back up at the water through thick lashes. "You wouldn't know the difference."

"True. But I'm a stranger. You have no reason to be anything but real."

He finally looked at me—really looked at me. We were only a few feet away from each other, but he still managed to collect my breath with the one sweep of his gaze. His eyes, dispassionate as bullets, traveled over my features with unnerving thoroughness, unearthing me, studying me, learning me.

Then he let go as if he'd dropped me from his arms, and returned his gaze to the ocean. "Okay. If I said that when I throw the stones, they'll make ripples, and that these ripples are like sound waves," he pitched another stone, "and these sound waves can cross to the other side and send a message, would that be real?"

"Yes." Another wave splashed over our rock, and the foam sizzled at the toe of his boots. "Can I help?"

The stones popped up in his palm again. "It's a one-person job."

"Well," I started to say, looking down and around at the rock we were standing on. I bent over, placing my mug behind us. "Maybe, between the two of us, we'll reach whoever you're trying to send a message to. Plus," I continued, balancing myself beside him again, "I'm a pretty badass stone skipper." I offered a smile and the palm of my hand. I couldn't tell if he was smiling or not. His eyes remained distant and as lifeless as the bodies that passed over my table at the morgue back in Texas.

"Alright," he dropped a single stone in my hand, "Let's see it."

"You give me *one?*"

"Make it count."

"Whoa, the pressure. Okay." I popped the stone in the air, and my foot lost balance when I went to catch it. The guy snatched my arm, keeping me from falling into the ocean.

"The stones aren't toys," he scolded. His eyes darted to his hand on my arm, and he cleared his throat, releasing his grip just as quickly as if he'd touched something that burned him.

I steadied his conflicting reaction, and whispered, "My bad."

He straightened his shoulders. "Rookie mistake."

Seagulls squawked above. I rubbed the stone between my fingers, feeling the smooth surface, feeling his eyes watching me, his chilling stare sliding over my body like a blanket of something cold and fierce and familiar, like home. It flared goosebumps across my flesh. I tried to shake it away, and with a flick of my wrist, I threw the rock.

It only treaded a few feet out, plopped into the water, and sank.

"You're right. That was … badass," he stated dryly.

"Hey!" someone shouted in the distance. I turned to see a woman in a robe and rain boots, curlers in her hair, waving a newspaper high in the air from a few houses down. "I thought I told you to stay off our land!"

Following the cliff's edge, she marched toward us, looking down to the rocks and shouting threats about taking his trespassing to the next Town Hall meeting.

I snapped my gaze to the guy. He nudged his head with a crinkle in the corners of his eyes before he turned and swiftly moved across the rocks. The lady shouted again. My gaze bounced up to her, and when I looked back to the guy, he was already gone.

I TOOK A COLD SHOWER AND SPENT THE REST OF THE MORNING UNPACKING, then made up the full-sized poster bed I'd slept in the night before.

My large bedroom was on the second story with its own bathroom and views of the coastline. Oakwood planked the cathedral ceiling with low beams running above. Through the French doors and out onto the balcony facing the sea, a staircase curved to the ground below.

I took the stairs and walked across the overgrown brush to the garage, where Gramps had said the scooter would be.

After a few tries, the single garage door lifted, and clouds of dust ballooned out as it folded at the top. Boxes stacked one on top of the other, lining the walls inside. I walked past a covered vehicle, and sitting behind it, a white scooter.

It looked as if it hadn't been used in quite some time, the key still resting in the ignition. I ran my white fingernail across the frame. Beneath the thin layer of dust, the remnants of a faded silver emblem branded the side. The same emblem embossed on the cracked leather of the photo albums I'd found in the attic back in Texas.

A five-pointed star with five symbols all inside a circle.

I turned the key, and the little thing backfired before it purred to life. With my hair tucked inside the helmet, I rode the white scooter up and down the neighborhood streets before taking it into town.

There had been more souls walking the streets at night than during the day in Weeping Hollow. Circling the gazebo were tiny shops; a bookstore called The Strange & Unusual, a post office, Hobb's Grocery, a doctor's office, The Corner Store, and The Bean coffee shop Gramps had mentioned, to name a few.

The grim town was decorated in dull oranges, yellows, and browns as if it weren't summer. As if the town was trapped in fall, even at the beginning of August. Artificial autumn leaves wrapped around the spindles of the gazebo, and hay bales and pumpkins decorated the storefronts. The depressing scent of dying leaves was laced in every fierce breeze, unlike the warm and playful winds back in Texas.

I parallel parked in front of Mina Mae's Diner and pocketed the key. Inside, the atmosphere was a drastic change from the somberness stirring just outside the doors. Cushioned bar stools lined the long counter space stretching from one end to the other, and in front of the hungrily awaiting patrons, the kitchen. The staff and waiters—wearing black and white pinstripe shirts with food-splattered aprons—moved swiftly to accommodate the morning rush without looking up to see where they were going. Somehow, no one ran into each other through the hustle and bustle.

Upon my arrival, everyone stopped to stare in my direction. But just as quickly as they looked my way, they looked away, going about their work, meal, or company, as if realizing I was nothing special.

I plucked a menu from the sleeved-pocket of a standing sign that read *Seat Yourself* and spotted an empty booth beside a window. My gaze roamed over the diner as I slid across the bench.

Mina Mae's seemed to be a melting pot for Stepford wives, judging eyes, and regulars who most likely came here every day for the last fifty-plus years. Three elderly ladies in fancy hats stared at me, lowering their voices to a whisper. I returned my attention to the menu, feeling their gazes move to the back of my neck.

"Let me guess," a voice said, causing my head to pop up. "Fallon Morgan."

A guy in his mid-twenties was standing in front of my table, wearing beige slacks and a newsboy hat.

"Yes," I confirmed, looking around to make sure he was talking to me, even though he'd said my name. "I'm Fallon Morgan, and you dress just like my grandfather."

"Cranky ole Benny?" He sat across from me, dropping a pile of books and papers between us, and rested his elbows on the table. Nodding, I leaned back, thinking he was mistaking me for another Fallon Morgan. No one ever willingly sat with me before. "I'll take that as a compliment. You see," he lifted a finger, "that man is a legend."

My brow arched. "Is that so?" I asked, and the guy nodded. "How do you know my name?"

"Word gets around. I'm Milo, by the way. Where did you come in from? New York?" He lifted off his newsboy hat to reveal soft-brown, side-swept hair, naturally curling at the ends. The guy was slender with honey-brown, soulful eyes and a million stories to tell in his smile.

I lifted my head a little. "Why New York?"

"You stick out like a sore thumb," his finger moved in a circular pattern in the air over my wardrobe, "with all your fancy clothes going on here."

I bit my lip, looking down at my boxy silk blouse, which was the cheapest thing I owned, suddenly feeling self-conscious. "No, San

Antonio," I corrected, looking back at him.

"Mhm … Never would've guessed."

An elderly lady approached our booth, a long braid of gray hair hanging off one shoulder. She shrieked with her hand over her mouth, staring at me with a twinkle in her eyes.

"Oh-my-word. Yah Benny's granddaughtah." The sweet-faced waitress laughed without belief. "I'd hug yah, but I don't wanna freak yah out." Her eyes steered to Milo. "Milo Andrews, give tha girl some room, would yah? Can she be heyah more than five seconds without the paparazzi swarmin'?"

Grinning, I waved away the intrusion. "He's fine. It's a nice change for once, talking to someone who doesn't have a stick up their ass."

"Oh, Benny?" She clicked her tongue. "Don't let that man fool yah, he's gotta heart somewhere … Deep, deep, in there."

Milo flashed me a side-eye and a crooked smile. "Mina Mae and Benny go way back if you know what I mean." He wiggled his brows.

Mina slapped Milo upside the head. "Don't be spreadin' rumors, boy."

"Hey, now … a good reporter only states the facts," Milo said in defense with his palms up in front of him.

Mina shook her head, returning her eyes to me with a pen pressing against a notepad. "Whatarya havin', dear?"

Milo was quick to speak up. "Two orders of hotcakes and. Let me treat the outsider."

Mina closed the pad and dropped it with the pencil inside her apron. "Fallon Morgan is no flatlander." With certainty and a single nod, she took off in the opposite direction.

"That lady scares me sometimes," Milo admitted, watching her walk away. "But she makes a mean hotcake."

AFTER BREAKFAST, MILO CONVINCED ME TO GO WITH HIM ON A STROLL through Town Square. Side by side, we walked the herringbone-patterned pavers, Milo standing at six feet and carrying the pile of books between his arm and hip. I kept up with his long strides as he went on about Weeping Hollow and the residents.

"We don't get many flatlanders. Ya know, people from away. And forget about trying to get information about the outside world. This town is trapped in time. The founders made it that way, cutting us off, protecting us from societal manipulation. We only know what we know from the flatlanders, and if by some miracle ya find an internet connection." When we reached a crossing, he paused to face me. "There's no point in trying to use your cell. Your only hope is at The Bean, but be careful what you're looking into because someone's always watching."

Milo turned his eyes away and resumed walking. "Weeping Hollow is off the grid and ran by the two covens. And you're a Morgan and a Grimaldi, so that makes you extremely important around here. It's only a matter of time …"

Without looking, Milo took a step off the curb and walked across the street to the other side. I looked both ways before catching up to him as quickly as I could in my black ankle boots. "Matter of time for what?"

He halted and spun to face me in the middle of the road. "For your initiation, of course," he said, matter-of-factly, as if I'd asked a stupid question. A pair of brown eyes scanned over my confused expression. "That is why you're here, right?" His brows drew together. "You don't know?"

I threw my palms up at my sides. "Know what?"

Milo continued walking, his smile just as baffled as he shook his pointer finger in the air. "It's all making sense now, the *reason* Tobias Morgan took you away." He was clearly talking to himself, but the mention of my father stole my attention. "Two witch covens caught in a tangled web, but the Grimaldi and Morgan families—"

"Witches?" The balls of my feet burned in my boots, and I gripped his bicep to slow him down. "Speak English."

He paused, shifting his body to face me, his tweed cap casting a shadow over half his face. "Yeah, your mother, Freya Grimaldi, is from Norse Woods Coven." He pointed toward the woods. "The Norse woods is like the waste lands, where the lower-class is from. But your father?" Milo's finger steered toward the sea. "He was from Sacred Sea Coven. They're the upper class who control the east, all the way up to Crescent Beach. You just drove into a town feud your father started before he left." Milo patted the top of my head. "Sooner or later, you'll have to join Sacred Sea where you belong."

Witches?

Milo continued up the sidewalk, leaving me behind with a blank stare.

His mention of witches transported me back to Marietta's unique behavior, like when she used to lock herself in the attic at the strangest times, whispers spilling down the steep wooden steps, her tangible storytelling about the gods and goddesses of Weeping Hollow. I thought they were all just bedtime stories—midnight tales.

Norse Woods and Sacred Sea, I hadn't heard those names in so long.

But there was no way Dad could have been a part of a coven. Tobias Morgan had been in the Air Force, a man who served God's country, brave and loyal until he died in war after I'd turned fifteen.

And yet, Weeping Hollow was real. Could all the stories be real too? Had Dad chosen Marietta, my nanny, bringing her from this town to Texas to take care of me for a reason?

"Hey," I called out, catching up to Milo, who was ten feet ahead. "But I'm not a witch. I'm just here to take care of Benny and see that he gets better. What if I don't want to be a part of any of … that?"

Milo's pace slowed, but he never met my gaze. Then he shrugged. "I don't know, but nothing good can come of it. You belong with Sacred Sea." Milo's eyes dipped down to my wary ones, then his features softened. "It's a lot to take in. Let's just forget I said anything for now. I know a place that'll help with Benny's cough."

The dense clouds, drab and jaded, slid over the skies above town square as we stopped in front of a fall-decorated storefront. BLACKWELL APOTHECARY was written on a swaying black sign jetting out from the brick above us. Up the cracked steps toward the door, antique lanterns, pumpkins, gourds, and pinecones lined the way and fanned out in front of the grid-style windows on each side.

Milo opened the door and pinned it still with the heel of his brown leather shoe to wave me inside. The door closed behind us, and I scanned the small store with curious and eager eyes.

Hanging from the ceiling, live plants crawled down the aged shelving that housed jars with hand-written labels. Herbs, flowers, spices, and essential oils filled the apothecary jars lining the walls. Milo rang the bell at the front desk as I walked to the oils and began smelling each one, from sandalwood to chamomile to frankincense.

"These are incredible," I hummed, closing my eyes as the warm and woody scent consumed my senses.

"That is my grounding blend," a woman's voice replied. "Spruce leaf, ho wood leaf, frankincense, blue chamomile flower, and ..." A distinct *snap!* pierced the air. I quickly screwed the cap back on. "Oh, yes, the blue tansy flower. Brings harmony to the mind and body."

She had raven-black hair and stubborn gray wisps framing her delicate features. She was a tiny lady, easily in her forties or fifties, but you could only tell because of the wrinkles and age spots on her hands.

Her surprised eyes drifted over me. "It can't be," she whispered through a gasp, then in a frenzy, transferred the items from her arms to beside the cash register before scurrying closer. Her gentle fingers threaded through my long white hair. "Freya?"

I froze under her hopeful eyes as they scanned my face. "Freya was my mother."

"Of course," her hand dropped, and her features transformed into embarrassment, "I'm so sorry, dear. It's like ... looking into the past." She offered a weak smile laced with lost memories.

"You knew my mother?" It was strange, being here. The woman who birthed me most likely had eaten at Mina Mae's Diner, visited this apothecary, and walked these streets. The people of Weeping Hollow would have known her, whereas I, her flesh and blood, couldn't. They had something I would never have—memories. And I was suddenly jealous of a town cut off from society because, at one point in time, they weren't cut off from my mother.

The lady nodded. "She was like a sister to me. Thick as thieves up until—" she paused, shook her head, "Well, you know...but you couldn't tear us apart, your mom and me," she said through a light-hearted chuckle. And her laughter quickly faded when her eyes turned glossy. "I think about her every day. And you, Fallon, she loved you very much."

She wiped at her eyes and sucked in a breath, gathering her composure. "Anyway, are you here for Benny? I can put something together to help with that cough of his."

"Yes, ma'am," Milo interrupted. "Each time that old man coughs, the entire town shakes. We're all gettin' dizzy."

There were so many questions flying around inside my head as my feet glued to the floor, only able to watch her pace back and forth across the shop to gather jars from the shelves. The lady returned to the front counter and began twisting open each lid, sprinkling a concoction into a marble bowl before crushing and grinding the leaves into a blend.

"This tea will soothe his throat. The taste is sweet like honey, but the aftertaste will feel like bitter molasses on the tongue. Benny is a stubborn man, so you have to stay on top of him."

Milo leaned on the counter with one elbow and turned to face me. "You hear that, Fallon? Ms. Agatha knows what she's doing. Better than that dull and dumb Dr. Morley." I unglued my feet from the floor and walked up beside Milo as Agatha Blackwell hid her amusement with a tight smile. "You know I'm right," Milo lifted his palm toward Agatha, "No reason to be gracious when it comes to the truth."

"You're one of a kind, Milo," Agatha sang, shaking her head while sifting the new mixture into a separate mason jar, then slid the jar into a gift bag.

"How much do I owe you?" I asked, finally able to find my voice.

Agatha peered at me with endearing eyes. "First one's on the house. I'm just so happy that after all this time I finally get to see you again. The last time I saw you, you were only a baby … I just never thought this day would come, quite honestly. Will you be staying long?"

"Thank you, and no, only until Benny gets back on his feet." I didn't know what else to say.

Her smile seemed more forced this time, and she folded her arms on the counter. "In any case, we're happy to have you back. Let me know how that works out for Benny."

After farewells, Milo and I left the apothecary and stepped outside onto the paved sidewalk. The fog only thickened, hovering the slick streets as we headed back in the opposite direction, toward my scooter. Though it was only afternoon, the sun had already burnt out as if it had spent the day attempting to break through the clouds but failed to do so.

When we reached the crosswalk, Milo stopped, something catching his attention. I followed his gaze down the street, and the road disappeared into the fog, the black outline of the woods in the distance.

Coming through the damp mist, four silhouettes walked through the murkiness. One by one, they gradually appeared. Four men, all wearing dark coats, worn slacks or jeans, and boots. Their faces, pinned straight ahead, were hidden and masked from the world around them. One wore a bandana, one a Halloween bunny mask, and another a plain black mask. But the one front and center wore the skull of an impala, long ash-brown horns pointing toward the clouded skies.

"Who are they?" It came out in almost a whisper as I watched the pack of guys draw nearer.

Milo laid a hand on my shoulder and pulled me closer to him. "Beck, Zephyr, and Phoenix. Those are the last four of the five original descendants from the Norse Woods Coven."

"Who is the fourth one?" Less than fifteen feet away, the man in the animal skull hesitated his pace. Familiar silver eyes struck mine, steadfast and binding, holding my breath in their clutches, my gaze in its grasp. Only for a moment before he turned his head away, releasing me.

"The one in the middle? That's Julian Blackwell. Agatha's son."

Julian. The man from the rocks.

They continued past us, neither one of the other three acknowledging us or paying us any attention. They walked with purpose. They walked with certainty. They wore a shield, callous and unaffected.

Milo's grip tightened on my shoulder. *"Those are the*

HOLLOW *HEATHENS.*"

FALLON
chapter three

At the front, near the entrance of Weeping Hollow, where winding trees, tombs, and mausoleums dusted the rolling burial field, St. Christopher's Funeral Home was tucked away. The deserted train tracks cut across the main road and disappeared behind the building and into the forest.

It was Wednesday, and I followed Jonah St. Christopher IV through the dwindling hallway until we reached a spiral staircase. Jonah was much younger than I'd expected, mid-thirties, wearing fitted jeans and a crisp white button-up with a slim black tie. His hair was cut short, professional and stylish.

"Your office is down here in the cellar," he explained as we took the spiral staircase down. Jonah paused mid-way, gripped the curved railing, and jiggled it back and forth. "Careful, this still needs to be fixed."

My foot let off the last step just as a girl bounced up from her desk. The office chair on wheels rolled back until it hit the cemented wall behind her, and she greeted me with a broad and welcoming smile.

"Oh, yay!" she exclaimed, walking closer in bright yellow Vans. A pink pen with a rainbow pom-pom rested behind her ear. She was the most colorful creature I'd seen since arriving, wearing a tight neon long-sleeved shirt with yellow, hot pink, and electric blue stripes under her black overalls. Her fiery-red hair bounced as her hand jetted out. "Monday Mitchell. You must be Fallon. And don't worry," she leaned over, her cheery voice hardly turning into a whisper, "Jonah told me yesterday that you don't deal with families. I have you covered."

Jonah shoved his hands into his jean pockets. "Yeah, I was relieved when Benny called. We could really use an extra hand around here." He faced Monday and nudged his head. "Monday will train you on how things work around here. You'll be responsible for dressing, cosmetics, and casketing the LOs."

I arched a brow, turning my attention from Monday to Jonah. "LOs?"

"Loved ones," Monday answered, winking at Jonah.

He pressed his lips together in a fine line, adding, "And keeping the equipment and preparation room clean, which is upstairs."

"Of course, everything sounds good." I took one last look around the basement.

Monday's desk was filled with photos of the deceased and a shrine to bobble-heads and figurines. An empty desk with an ancient computer sat at the opposite end of the basement, and pushed against the back wall was a bunk-bed and dresser.

"This is a twenty-four-seven, on-call job," Jonah reminded me as if I'd never done this before. But over the last five years, being a mortician was all I'd done. I was aware of the late nights, spur of the moment calls and having to drop everything to arrive and take care of the deceased.

Jonah walked to the desk and picked up a black object. "You have to keep this beeper on you at all times."

He handed me the beeper, and I looked up at Monday and raised a brow. "A beeper?"

Back in Jonah's office, I filled out the non-disclosure agreement as he went on about how paperwork and reporting for the deceased were completed differently in Weeping Hollow.

He put me to work right away, and I spent the rest of my morning cleaning the preparation and display rooms, which showcased the coffins and different linings the funeral home had to offer. I didn't mind and had always respected every job, big or small, even if it meant scrubbing toilets or mopping bodily fluids off the tile.

The rainbow-colored stationary taped to the refrigerator in the kitchen read *Help Yourself* in loopy letters. Monday had stocked the fridge with deli sandwiches from Mina's Diner. I grabbed one marked *Italian*, deciding to tour the cemetery and get some fresh air.

The morning fog had cleared and fallen leaves crunched under my work shoes through the maze of tombstones. Branches from the trees twisted overhead, almost as if the limbs were reaching out to grab whoever passed. The air was damp. It smelled like history.

It smelled like death.

And somewhere under this sacred ground, my mother was buried. The thought never left my mind as I continued my aimless stroll between the headstones, cracked and tilted from the earth's shifting planes. I forced my eyes away from reading the engravings, not ready to come across hers yet. Her spirit had never visited me, and a part of me always believed it was because I was the one who took her life.

I bit into the cold sub when fire-engine-red hair peeked from behind a large beech tree. As I walked closer, I spotted Monday, who was sitting on dead grass with a sugar skull lunch box at her side. A carrot stick was poking out of her mouth.

"So, this is where you ran off to." Aside from the two of us, and the gravedigger a few yards away, the cemetery was vacant. "Typical mortician, eating in a cemetery ..."

"Sounds like the start of a bad joke." Smiling, Monday patted the ground next to her and shifted her lunch box to the other side, scooting over. "Come, sit," she insisted. "This is the best seat in town."

I plopped beside her and crossed my legs.

Monday's gaze slid to me, and I felt her eyes scanning my features. When I looked back at her, she quickly looked away.

Growing up, kids had only been nice because they were afraid of my ghostly traits. My natural platinum-white hair, my bone-white skin, my faint-blue eyes; two crystal balls no one would look into for more than a second. Kids had only been kind because of the rumors. I hardly had real friends. However, all those problems seemed trivial once high school ended and real life began. A time when more significant problems took over, like money, career choices, shelter, and a social status one would have to build solo, without one given by parents.

I finished my sub, watching the gravedigger shovel mounds of dirt. A black bandana was tied around his face. Monday's knee nudged the side of my thigh, breaking my stare. "You arrived just in time, ya know. With Defy Superstition Day, Mabon, Samhain ..."

I stretched my legs out in front of me and crossed my ankles. I knew Mabon was the equivalent to Thanksgiving in the Wiccan community, and Samhain was during Halloween to celebrate the dead. But ... "Defy Superstition Day?"

"Ever heard of it?"

"Can't say I have."

"It's a stupid holiday if you ask me. You can't trust a holiday that was invented in 1999. You can't trust the same year LFO made the charts. You saw what happened to them..." she paused and turned to see my lifted brows hanging in the air. I shook my head, oblivious to anything she was saying, and her jaw dropped. "You're kidding me, right? Rich died, dude. And that's not even the freaky part. The band split up, then after they got back together again, *bam!* another one bites the dust. I'm telling ya. Su-per-sti-tion." Monday shook her head and bit into her carrot. "You don't believe in that sorta thing, do you?"

"I think it's bad luck to believe in superstition," I said through a laugh.

An awkward silence landed between us. She looked at me. I looked at her, waiting for her to find the hole in my joke. Then her lips quirked. Monday was a three-second-delay girl. I loved three-second delay girls.

"I got it now." She nodded with a slow-forming smile.

"How do you know all that stuff? I thought Weeping Hollow was cut off from what's going on out there."

"I have a thing for nineties music," she shrugged, "and when you have a thing, you find a way. But back to Defy Superstition Day. The festival is at night, and the whole town will be there."

I immediately thought about Julian, the man on the rocks from the day before. A Hollow Heathen, as Milo had called him. I'd returned to the cliff's edge this morning to see if he was there, but he wasn't.

"Maybe I'll go." There was a vacancy in my tone. My head was somewhere else: rocks, crashing deep blue waters, an animal skull, and silver-gray eyes.

Monday's head whipped to the side, eyes widened. "Oh, you gotta go. You need to get out and be a part of this town, or everyone will think you're a flatlander." She snapped the carrot in half without looking. "My friends wanna meet you, too. I told them you were starting here today."

It seemed everyone already knew who I was, and I wasn't used to this kind of attention. Sure, people always noticed me, but they kept their distance. They waved and smiled and treated me as an acquaintance. But for Monday to form a conversation with me, ask me questions, and invite me places was all surreal. I'd spent most of my life keeping to myself, focusing on nothing but my career for the last six years. I'd become a workaholic. My only friends were the dead. I'd prepared the corpses while confessing all my bizarre dreams to spirits. How the screams from the couple in apartment 7901 kept me up at night, fighting over infidelity. How beer pong shouldn't be considered a sport. And the time Netflix had dropped my favorite show … Then it hit me.

Shit. I was Gramps.

"Sacred Sea …" Monday went on. "Well, the Sullivan sisters, Milo, Maverick, Cyrus, and Kane. You're bound to meet them before Defy Day, and you'll totally fit right in. It's not like you don't already belong there, anyway. Oh," she bounced in place, an idea popping into her head, "we can go shopping after work sometime next week and find you a dress and a mask. You have to wear a mask."

"If I'm still here, I'll go," I agreed upon hearing Milo's name. At least I would know two people there, and maybe going out wouldn't be all bad either. Milo had said Dad was once a part of the Sacred Sea Coven. My curiosity had me on the fence about diving into this world and seeing where Dad had come from, where I'd come from, and if Milo's word about my parents being witches held merit.

My relationship with Dad had been long-distance due to his obligation to our country, and I'd respected him for his dedication to the Air Force. Maybe he kept me and his past at arm's length for a reason, but did I want to know why?

I leaned back and slid my gaze to the gravedigger. He was drinking from a water bottle slipped under his bandana. He was slender but in shape with a shaved head. He glanced in our direction, reminding me of Julian and the Hollow Heathens.

"What about the Hollow Heathens? Do they go?"

Monday's eyes drifted to the gravedigger as well. "They really don't do events. But you want to stay far away from them." She nudged her head toward the gravedigger, watching us.

He was one of them. I peeled my eyes from him and back to Monday. "Why's that?"

"Beck's quiet and will leave you alone. They'll all leave you alone if you leave them alone." Monday leaned in. "But everyone knows they practice dark magic. The kind you never want to mess with and the shit we don't touch. Sacred Sea is wholesome, but not them. River Harrison's convinced it was them who put an evil hex on Jasper Abbott, making him go mad."

"An evil hex," I repeated, a humorless grin following. And the grin wasn't because I didn't believe in magic or witchcraft, because I'd always been open to what couldn't be seen since I'd seen more than most, knowing the supernatural lurked behind layers of the world. But I also understood what it was like for people to see you as something different than what you were, to be the center of a town's sickest rumor.

"Did you ever stop to think it could be just what it is...him losing it? What reason would they have to do something like that anyway?"

"To punish him for having loose lips, or at least that's what they say." Monday suddenly stopped there when I was expecting more of the story. She bit into a carrot, and it crunched between her teeth as she hazily looked out into the cemetery. "Meet me behind the cemetery tonight at midnight. I want to show you something."

"Why at—"

She waved her hand out in front of her. "Just meet me. You'll see for yourself."

IT WAS THIRTY MINUTES BEFORE MIDNIGHT, AND GRAMPS HAD FALLEN asleep in the blue and green plaid recliner. After leaving the funeral home earlier, I'd stopped by the corner store to grab a few things, then cooked a large pot of chili, hoping the cayenne pepper would cut through his congestion and reduce his flu-like symptoms. I paired it with sweet and crumbly homemade cornbread. It had been Marietta's go-to whenever I was sick, which was often since I never had the best immune system.

I stood over a sleeping Gramps, wearing black leggings and a large gray sweatshirt under my oversized denim jacket, ready to meet Monday behind the funeral home out of curiosity. I re-heated his unfinished tea and placed it on the side table for him in case he woke. Atop the same table, a black and white candid picture of me caught my eye. It was on this morning's issue of The Daily Hollow. A welt formed in my chest, and I read the headlines.

FALLON 'MOONSHINE' MORGAN RETURNS TO WEEPING HOLLOW
AFTER TWENTY-FOUR YEARS, POSSIBLY HOARDING SECRETS.
Article written by: Milo Andrews

"You've got to be kidding me."

Milo? I lifted the loosely folded-up newspaper, rolled it, tucked it into the back of my leggings, and dragged the wool blanket over Gramps before taking off to the garage.

Houses on the east side of town were beautiful, traditional coastal homes, all distinct in shades of corals, sea-foam greens, and Gramps' egg-shell blue. Except at the end of the street, which was the highest point of the cliff. It was there where a deteriorating mansion stood; a deserted black house plagued by nature and neglect, with broken shutters, overgrown brush, and vines crawling up the bone-like structure like poisonous veins.

I circled the square's roundabout going ten miles per hour as townies raided the sidewalks under the polished half-moon. At this hour, all the shops were open. Candles flickered inside lanterns behind the glass storefronts, and jack-o-lanterns smiled from atop the rails of the gazebo. Residents drank from silver goblets, and little girls wearing colonial dresses with ribbons in their hair frolicked to eerie tunes spilling from speakers rooted under the gazebo's eaves, the heart of it all.

People laughed and mingled as if it wasn't an ordinary Wednesday night.

Milo sat on a bench with a girl at his side. She was running her long fingers up and down his collarbone inside his stretched shirt, and seemed younger, eighteen maybe, with dark brown hair.

Seeing him caused the lump inside my chest to reappear, reminding me of the newspaper headline tucked at my back, inside my waistline. I had to confront him, and with ten minutes to spare, I turned the scooter around and didn't stop until the wheel bounced off the curb in front of the gazebo. A group of tipsy teenagers jumped back as if I was going to run them over. I kicked the stand free.

"Milo!" I shouted with the newspaper clenched in my fist, my temper flaring. "What the hell is this?"

Dad never had one, and I blamed my mood swings on the mother I never knew. Or the moon. *You phase with the moon, child,* Marietta's words swam in my head.

Either way, the lump turned into a pumpkin and dropped into my stomach, knowing these people may have already made a judgment call about me.

Townies watched as I marched across the lawn surrounding the gazebo, heading straight for Milo, who lifted off his back and shooed the girl's hands away. I halted at their feet and shook the newspaper out in front of me until it laid flat in my hand.

"The only descendent of Tobias Morgan returns, but what does this mean for Weeping Hollow …" I read off, then flitted my eyes to deliver a menacing glare. Milo took off his newsboy hat and pushed his hand through his fluffy curls, his lips pressed firmly together. I continued, "If there is one thing I am certain of, no one is as innocent as they seem."

"That's a fact," the girl beside Milo pointed out, and my domineering gaze shifted to her. "What?" Her matter-of-fact voice turned into a whisper as she looked away. "No one really is innocent."

"River, not now," Milo mumbled.

My glare narrowed. "This is *slander*."

Milo dropped his hand on his stretched thighs and sat back. "I didn't think you'd be upset about it. It's just an article."

I threw the newspaper at him, and he caught it before it hit his face. "Find someone else to write about." I'd made my point and didn't want to hear more. I turned and stormed back to my scooter with my skin heated and my mind in a frenzy.

"People want to know about you," Milo shouted at my back. "I only give the people what they want."

A PAIR OF RAVENS SAT SIDE BY SIDE ON THE GIANT BLACKWELL mausoleum, their high-pitched squawking shattering in my ears, tiny black eyes following my movements as I walked deeper into the cemetery to meet Monday. The slithering fog returned and blanketed the gravestones. Tombs disappeared into the damp void, and I shivered inside my jacket.

I rounded the corner of the funeral home to find Monday leaning against the brick wall in a black terry cloth tracksuit. The bottoms of her pants were tucked inside red hunter boots, almost as if she refused to wear all black. A ray of color in this depressing town, Monday was easily likable. So easy, it almost seemed as fake as the girls back at Johnson High School, which made me wish I had more experience in the friend department—the ability to tell the difference.

"I didn't think you were going to show," she admitted through a sigh.

I wrapped my jacket around my chest and crossed my arms to keep it pinned. "I said I would come. What are we doing here?" It was dark and late. What could we possibly be doing back here, isolated and far from the gathering going on at Town Square?

Monday lifted off the wall and started a casual trek toward the woods. "I want to show you something, and after you see this, you'll never want to go near those Hollow Heathens."

There was no direct path, but Monday seemed to know the way as I followed close behind. Twigs broke beneath our boots as we wandered past the train tracks and deeper into the woods. The trees swayed like a Danse Macabre ballet, their branches dancing over our heads. The only light was the burnished moon filtering through the twisted limbs, and if you listened closely, you could hear the trees talking, their restless leaves spilling the secrets of the night. I kept my eyes in front of me, following the bright red ribbon neatly tied in Monday's high ponytail.

Off in the distance, a vast, circular object curved above the tree line to my left. "Is that a Ferris wheel?"

"A Ferris wheel?" Monday twirled and looked to where my finger was pointing, the moonlight casting over half her face. "I don't see anything."

"Right there," I nudged my finger, "What's a Ferris wheel doing in the middle of the woods?"

"*Shh*, we're almost there." Monday faced forward again, her steps slowing.

After a few more yards, an orange glow flickered between the trees. Deep red and orange sparks flew up past the branches and into the night sky. Smoke billowed between the branches above. Monday grabbed my wrist and yanked me behind a fallen tree trunk. She crouched, taking me down with her.

Two men stood before the fire from this angle, their bare chests glistening against the embers and flames as the wood crackled. The fire reflected off their callous eyes within the two holes of the black masks over their heads, dress pants hanging loosely off their hips. I raised from behind the log and kicked my leg over, needing to get closer. I needed to see more.

"No, don't! Where are you going?" Monday whispered in a panic.

"I can't see." I raised my hand behind me, gesturing for her to stay put. Hunched over, I crept to a closer tree, and the hot blaze from the fire licked my face.

The other two men came into view, all four of them in a complete circle with their long torsos bare and heads covered by the drop cloths, except one.

An animal skull secured to the fourth member's face, his mouth partly visible. Flickering flames and distance were the only barriers between the Hollow Heathens and me—between Julian Blackwell and me.

My eyes fixed on the way his mouth moved under the shadow of the skull, slow and precise and bewitching as the raging fire drowned out his haunting words. White clouds from the icy night slipped from my parted lips with every breath I released, obscuring my view of him.

A rope was tied around Julian's wrist. He turned slightly, gently tugging on it, when a goat appeared at his side. Beads of sweat rolled down his chest and the valleys cut into his stomach. My eyes followed its path to the black pants hanging off his hipbones.

Julian ran his palm along the goat's back and whispered into the animal's ear. He paused for a moment with his lips parted, then tilted his head in my direction.

Though I couldn't see his eyes behind the skull, I was certain he saw mine. I felt them on me like they were his fingers. Sweat raced down my spine as I froze in place behind the tree. My breath caught, a bubble of air begging to release from my lungs as he continued to whisper into the goat's ear, his long fingers drifting up and down the copper brown fur, bringing calmness and releasing the goat's fear.

Chanting grew louder, picking up like the thrashing heartbeat in my ears. Julian reached behind him and pulled out a long sharp blade, and the hellish flames reflected off the metal.

Then he brought it to the goat's throat. I wanted to scream. I wanted to cry. But nothing materialized. My senses went numb. The only thing I could do was dig my nails into the trunk.

Julian glanced once more at me, and I knew what was to come.

"No …" It came out as a breathy gasp as I shook my head and slammed my eyes closed.

The *thump!* against the earth didn't happen for a long time. With my lips sucked in and fingernails embedded deep into the tree, I waited. It was only seconds but felt like forever, which was sometimes how long forever could last, especially for the goat.

And the chanting stopped, but I refused to open my eyes. I refused to believe what had to have happened from only feet in front of me, what Julian had just done, the life he'd taken.

A cool wind swept across my face.

The tips of my loose strands tickled my cheeks.

The fiery and anarchic night was chilling and peaceful again.

The heat from the fire was gone.

I opened my eyes and became paralyzed by a bone-white skull and a broad chest only inches away. At first, my eyes latched onto a silver pendant hanging from his neck. Then I looked up, seeing the Heathen towering over me. He was tall, solid, and sculpted as if created by Michelangelo. His pale skin was flushed and slick and glistening from the fire, and I hadn't noticed until now the countless white and pink scars slashing his torso like the trunk of a tree, his sides, his chest. Blood dripped from the tips of his fingers onto the forest ground. I heard every *drip, drip, drip* as his scarred chest violently heaved. Familiar, cold steel eyes locked on mine through the skull's hollow openings.

Julian Blackwell—the kind of presence that could leave cold spots in the places he had been.

And I should have been scared. Maybe a part of me was. But the other part, the side wanting to reach out and touch him, to make sure he was real and not an illusion, kept me rooted to the ground.

His lips parted slightly beneath the bottom of the skull, a vibrant and delicious red. The forest fell silent as fear and fascination warred. Thoughts raced. What happened to him? What was he going to do to me? Did he still have the blade?

But it all summed up in one word.

"Why?" It had come out as a breathy whisper, and his muscles flinched at my response. Behind him, the other three walked to where we were standing, closer and closer and closer ...

They were closing in on me, and fear lodged itself in the empty spaces between my bones, chiseling into my marrow, crawling up my spine. Oxygen was thinning, and panic constricted my throat, making it harder to breathe. Faceless, their masks suffocated the moon above, shutting out the light.

Instinct kicked in, and I turned and took off through the woods.
A second pair of footfalls echoed behind me, possibly Monday, possibly
the Hollow Heathens, so I ran harder. My lungs burned, and twigs snapped
under my boots. The black of the forest contorted into a mirage of skull
faces taunting me, but I didn't dare turn around or go back for Monday. I
didn't stop until my feet ran past the railroad tracks and my palms hit the
BRICK OF THE *funeral* *HOME.*

ST. CHRISTOPHER'S CEMETERY

FALLON
chapter four

THE GRANDFATHER CLOCK CHIMED FROM THE BOTTOM OF THE STEPS. I shoved more clothes into my suitcase, pacing back and forth from the armoire to the creaky bed. I lasted three days, cornered by the town, the headlines, the Heathens. It had been seventeen years since feeling so...trapped, and the only way to break free was to break out.

I wrote a note for Gramps and left it beside the coffee machine. By the time he would see it, I would be halfway through Connecticut. But he would be happy I was leaving. He never wanted me to come, anyway.

In the dead of night, I tossed my bags into the Mini Coop. I didn't have much and didn't bother changing. After a few attempts and pleads, the engine kicked, and the car roared. *"I put a spell on you,"* crackled through the old speakers as I plugged the charger into my iPhone and waited for the screen to light up again.

The townspeople's eyes followed my car as I rolled through the foggy streets and around the gazebo. Milo stood from the park bench, children paused their dizzying dancing, and Mina from the diner held a hand to her chest beside a disappointed Jonah.

They were all out and about. I tore my eyes away, driving at a turtle's pace. Agatha Blackwell pushed open her apothecary shop door. Winds ripped her silky black hair from her bun as she stumbled upon the steps with a pained look in her eyes. She shook her head, hurt on full display.

It shouldn't have come as a surprise after what Milo had said about me. The townies *should* have been happy to be getting rid of me so quickly. Instead, they looked as if they were hurt, insulted. Was it because I was leaving Gramps? A man they loved and respected? They all knew him better than I did, why was it up to me to be there for him?

I reached the arched sign of Weeping Hollow, and my car crawled under it. I pressed my foot onto the gas and sped down the narrow and winding road, only able to see ten feet in front of me with my birthplace in my rearview mirror.

My gut whispered to turn back around. My head screamed to move forward. Instead, I turned up the volume on the radio to submerge my thoughts in music.

The same metal sign appeared, this time reading, *You are leaving Weeping Hollow. Don't look behind you,* with a pair of ravens sitting on the sharp edges, crowing into the night.

On both sides of me, the trees turned dense, skeleton-like figures tunneling Archer Avenue. They were white against the black backdrop of the night and seemed as if they were twisting and turning and ... moving!

I shook my head, certain it was my imagination.

But after a few miles, I couldn't believe what was in front of me.

I slowed the car to a stop, staring at the entrance to Weeping Hollow.

The arched sign hovering the road.

"What?" The single word came out like fog.

I turned to look behind me, seeing nothing but a road fading into darkness.

I faced forward again, the town's radio station pumping a new eerie song through my car speakers. A chill skated up my spine. I gripped the wheel tightly, pressing on the gas to maneuver the car around in a three-point turn.

"You can't keep me here," I whispered, straightening the steering wheel. With hesitance, my gaze moved to the rearview mirror. I didn't know what I was expecting. The town couldn't be moving! I was surely losing my mind.

My foot lay on the gas. My eyes darted back and forth from the rearview mirror to in front of me when a sharp static broke through the radio. The engine stalled, the steering wheel locked, and I'd lost control of the car as it veered off the road.

Panicking, I turned the key, spewing curses, banging my palm against the locked steering wheel, trying anything as the car rolled off the pavement, heading straight for the woods.

My car went headfirst into a tree. Metal crunched and smoke rippled from under the hood, floating lazily toward the stars.

Defeated tears pooled at the corners of my eyes, and I dropped my head back against the headrest.

Marietta was right.

Weeping Hollow wouldn't let me leave.

Not until it was done with me.

Having no other choice but to go back, I sucked in a breath and pushed against the car door. Metal screeched as it opened, and I planted a foot onto the pavement.

I reached for my bags on the backseat. Behind me, a pearly-white cat pounced from the woods and sat in the middle of the street. One green eye and one blue eye fixated on me, the Weeping Hollow sign behind it.

"You must be in on this too," I said to the cat, and dropped the suitcase onto the street with a thud. "And I'm talking to a cat." I'd lost my mind.

The ravens mocked me as I trotted past with my suitcase rolling behind, the white cat in tow—the long walk back to Gramps' house.

"Good morning, Wiccans. It's Thursday, and September is closing in on us, celebrations already igniting the streets at midnight. But, in the midst of celebration, the body count is rising. Please keep the Gordon family in your thoughts, and let's give thanks for the good fortune we have received. This is Freddy in the Mournin', and remember ... no one is safe after 3 a.m.," the broadcaster announced solemnly from the kitchen radio.

I grumbled, taking the stairs down in a sluggish manner.

It had been close to five in the morning by the time I'd returned to Gramps', and I barely got any sleep. Flashbacks of the night before—the Hollow Heathens, the fire, the woods, the goat—had kept me up the remainder of the night.

"*Great*, yah still heyah?" Gramps mumbled with sarcasm from his chair in the same butter-yellow kitchen with the daily crossword puzzle laying across the table in front of him. "I thought yah got fed up and left. Just like Tobias, leavin' me heyah with a lousy lettah. Didn't have tha guts ta tell me ta my face," he growled, pinching a pencil between his fingers.

"Please, Gramps, I've had a long night." I massaged my temples and moseyed to the coffee machine.

The cat from last night weaved between my legs, having not left my side since we'd met.

He'd followed me to Gramps', and when I didn't let him inside the house, he'd climbed the outdoor staircase to my bedroom and cried on the other side of my French doors with the neurotic wind.

I'd caved. I'd named him Casper.

Static crackled through the old radio, and Gramps pounded his fist on the top.

"This damn thing," his husky voice rattled, cut short by a coughing fit. I turned to see him pull a tissue out of the box and cover his mouth. His shoulders lurched forward until he cleared his lungs. "What happened to yah? Yah look like roadkill. And wheyas yah cah? It's not out theya on tha street."

I ignored him and was more concerned about the subtle shivering he was trying to hide. I marched over to him and pressed the back of my hand against his clammy forehead. "*Oh, my god*, Gramps. You're burning up."

Gramps pushed my hand away. "I'm fine."

"No, I'm taking you back to bed."

He cursed under short breaths and shook his head.

"If you don't go to bed, I'll get Mina over here," I threatened.

Gramps' eyes bulged out of their sockets, staring blankly at the newspaper.

I knew Mina's name, the elderly lady with the braided hair from the diner, would get his attention. There was a reason he didn't want me to go there and had recommended The Bean instead. He didn't want me talking to her.

"Come to think of it, the bed doesn't sound so bad aftah all, moonshine," he muttered, standing to his feet. "Make me that tea, will yah? I can walk on my own, no need ta coddle."

A slow smirk formed on my face, and I pulled it back as Gramps used the table to balance himself, preparing to walk.

After getting him situated, I retreated to my bedroom and pulled my suitcase off the floor and onto the mattress before zipping it open. Casper watched from the top of the armoire, his long white tail swaying across the wood while I grabbed clothes and headed to the bathroom.

The shower cried out as the water sprayed my hair and back, my long locks sticking to my skin. Once dressed, I swiped the beeper from the top of the armoire and noticed I'd missed an alert.

I'd never been fired before, and Jonah had every right not to give me the job back after he had watched me drive out of town the night before. But if I was staying here, I needed this.

I glanced at the clock on the nightstand. It was already late in the morning and way past the time I was supposed to be there. I'd have to explain myself to him.

The sun had risen over the sea cliffs, and my chapped skin soaked up the warm rays as I drove the scooter through the quiet town. Bulbs inside lamp posts had faded out, music had died, and evidence of last night littered the gazebo. Goblets cluttered the rails, and candy wrappers blew in the wind.

I paused the scooter once I reached the town exit sign and peered down the winding road where my car had crashed.

Except, my car was no longer there.

It was gone.

The scooter skipped forward, a part of me wanting to drive down Archer Avenue to make sure I wasn't seeing things, but I gripped the handlebar and turned the wheel toward the funeral home instead.

Jonah gazed up from his computer with surprise in his eyes as I pushed open the funeral home door. He rested back into his chair and crossed his arms.

"Before you say anything," I immediately started, closing the door behind me, "I *am* cut out for this job. I never partied, I never had friends. I never even had a boyfriend. I devoted my life to school and my apprenticeship. This is all I have and all I want to do. Being late this morning and not answering the call last night isn't me—"

Jonah's sigh cut me off. "Fallon—"

"You have to give me a second chance. I can't stay here in this town without doing this. It'll drive me crazy. I need this."

"Fallon," Jonah repeated, and this time I stopped rambling. "I thought you left."

"Truth is, I tried to leave. But then I crashed my car on Archer Avenue."

"You okay?"

"Yeah, I'm fine. I just had a long night."

"And now ... what? You're staying?"

I nodded. "I'm staying. I got freaked out, but it won't happen again. I'm usually not like this. My mind's all ..." I lifted my hands to my head and imitated a bomb going off. "Can we just forget this morning happened? Like an Etch-A-Sketch? Slate clean?"

Like an artist had to paint or a singer had to sing, I needed to do this. This... this passion of mine, this calling, it was the only thing that didn't leave or die on me.

Jonah tapped a finger on his chin, pretending to be in deep thought. I flashed a pouty lip, and he dropped his elbows on his desk. "Fine, but only because I need you more than you need me right now." He rose from his chair, walked around his desk, and sat on the edge. "I'm not too cocky to admit it."

"Thank you, thank you, thank you!" I lurched forward and wrapped my arms around him. The smell of his rustic cologne filled my senses before it clicked inside my brain how unprofessional this was, hugging him. "Shit," I said through a breathy exhale, slowly releasing him from my tight hold. "I'm sorry. That was..."

"Like an Etch-A-Sketch," he cleared his throat, standing, "Never happened."

We exchanged a tight smile. I took a step back. "Are we good?"

Jonah smoothed down the front of his black button-up shirt and fixed his blood-red tie. "Yeah, we're good. Why don't you take the day off, get some rest and restart tomorrow?"

"Will Monday be able to handle everything? I feel terrible. I noticed the alert on the beeper," my words trailed as Jonah walked back around his desk. Then it dawned on me that I'd left her in the woods last night. "Monday is here, right? She's okay?"

He lifted his tie as he sat back down. "Monday's here. She can handle it."

A relieved breath escaped my lips. I never had to consider anyone else before. I was so used to it just being me. "You sure? I don't mind, really. I got a few hours of sleep. I just need a few cups of coffee—"

"Fallon, please," Jonah interrupted through a chuckle. "Get out of here."

"Got it," I turned, then spun back around with my finger in the air, "And one more thing. If you left a car on Archer Avenue and it disappeared, where could it have gone?"

Jonah's face wrinkled from behind his desk, making him look twenty years older. "Well, the first place I'd check is the body shop next to Town Hall." The hesitation in his voice was undeniable. "It's on the opposite side of town, near Voodoos Bar."

"Thanks."

"Get some rest, Fallon," he added authoritatively.

"Yes, sir."

Town Hall was north of the gazebo, the two locations that split the town in half. Facing the large white building, I peered left down Seaside Street off Main and spotted the auto body shop right next to Voodoos, just as Jonah had said.

I drove the scooter up the empty street until it jumped the curb of the hole-in-the-wall brick building. Inside the garage, my Mini Cooper was lifted in the air while someone worked underneath.

I leaned the scooter on the kickstand and hopped off. "Excuse me," I announced myself, walking closer. The man under my car had his back to me, wearing a backward hat. He paused at the sound of my voice, the muscles in his arms flexing. "That's my car."

He dropped his head, dusted his hands, and lifted himself out of the hole. "I know," his indifferent voice said, staying in the shadows as he walked to the front of the car. He turned his cap around before he came into view.

Liquid gray eyes pierced through me, and I stumbled backward as he took another step forward.

"Don't come any closer," I said with my hand out between us.

Julian tilted his head, wearing a stretchy black cloth over his mouth and nose. "You shouldn't be walking the woods at night." He continued his trek toward me, wiping his grease-stained hands across the front of his shirt. "You could end up hurt," his brow arched, "or worse."

"Are you threatening me?" I asked, but it came out all wrong and fragile and breakable. I narrowed my eyes, mustering the Grimaldi strength. "I hear the things they say about you, but none of that scares me."

The cloth stretching across his mouth puffed out as he released a breath. "Yet, you ran from me."

I wanted to say it wasn't from him. I ran because I had been caged in by them as a whole. But I didn't. The close proximity of him pulled an unwanted desire straight from my heart down to my core, making my tongue feel swollen. It was only the night before he'd slit a goat's throat, and now, standing only inches away from him, unable to muster a steady breath, I'd felt as if he were holding me and slowly slitting mine.

He took another step closer, and gravel crunched beneath his heavy boots. "Why did you come back?"

"W-w-what?" The only thing keeping me upright was our locked eyes.

"You left twenty-four years ago and just decided to come back? Why?" The bill from the hat cast a shadow over his eyes, the sun no longer hitting them like before. Still, behind the stone-cold and chilling color, there was a gentleness hidden behind the reserved and potent shield.

My brows pulled together. Had he read the article? Did he think I was hiding something? "Benny needs me."

"Is that all?"

"Yes."

Julian's eyes dropped to my hand, where I was twisting my mood ring around my finger. Then he ripped his gaze away, taking off for the garage. "Your car should be ready in a few days." He grabbed a tool from a shelf and threw a rag over his shoulder. "I'll see that it gets returned."

The connection snapped, but I wasn't ready to let it go. I wasn't done yet. I had so many questions.

"Wait, what was that last night? What were you guys doing in those woods?" I followed after him up the hill, into the garage. "Why did you kill that goat?" *And how did you get all those scars?*

He readjusted his cap, ducked under the car, and hopped into the hole, going back to work.

I stood there for a few moments to see if he would turn around and acknowledge me again, but he continued working, hands moving swiftly, oil staining the fingers where blood once dripped from.

"Julian?" but

NOTHING.

FALLON
chapter five

TOM GORDON DIED OF HEART FAILURE.
Heart failure. The organ I would follow anywhere, without question, without reasoning. When lost or confused, it was our hearts we were told to trust completely. The speaker of desires, deliverer of feelings, and giver of hope. Yet it still had the audacity to fail us.

Like I had almost failed Gramps, if the town would have let me.

Yesterday, Monday embalmed Mr. Gordon, and today his skin was firmer under every stroke of my thumb, his frozen flesh refusing to soak up the color of life, a golden beige with a smudge of pink.

Working on a corpse wasn't much different from working on the living, but with different techniques used. Some preferred to airbrush, but I preferred the pads of my fingers. I slid my eyes back and forth to the picture of him when he was alive, the picture I'd requested Monday to collect from his grieving wife.

"What's your sign?" Monday asked from the opposite side of the room, but I was distracted, and her words slipped through the faulty cracks of my mind. She had easily forgiven me for leaving her behind in the woods, but made me work harder for attempting to leave Weeping Hollow.

"Fallon?"

"Cancer." I ran my hand through Mr. Gordon's hair to naturally sweep it to the side, like in the picture when he was dressed up in a suit and tie and twenty years younger. In the photo, his dashing bride stood beside him with a bouquet clutched in her hands, their bare feet in the sand.

The girl who loved Tom Gordon.

He had given his heart to her that day.

A heart that was no longer his to fail.

"You seem to be caught between the devil and the deep blue sea today, moonchild. You have intense feelings that have you uptight and fearful, but you are keeping quiet about it all. It may involve a relationship that hasn't quite manifested yet, or someone in your line of sight you haven't seen. You do not want them to see you in anything but a position of strength and control. The day's planetary constellations beg the question as to who you are kidding. Being vulnerable is a part of trusting another," she read off, blindly bouncing a yellow stress ball off the concrete wall. Catching it in her fist, she turned in her chair. "Well, that's a load of shit."

"Horoscopes are vague on purpose." But as soon as she'd said it, I couldn't help but think about Julian.

I left Mr. Gordon's side and walked to the sink to wash foundation off my hands, an attempt to wash away images of Julian from my mind, too.

"Tom's ready," I said, changing the subject. "I'm going to head home for the night." Gramps' breathing had only gotten worse, and he hadn't made it to the kitchen this morning.

"But it's Friday night."

"So?"

"So, come out with us. A few of us are heading to Voodoos."

"The bar?" I'd once drank alone. It was my twenty-first birthday. I'd driven to Gabriel's Liquor store for a bottle of something. Inexperienced and naïve, I'd grabbed the first bottle my determined eyes came across, a pre-mixed Carlo Rossi Sangria because the bottle was pretty. Dry red wine and tart fruit, the taste of red apples kept me going back for more, searing my tongue and staining my lips until I'd passed out in the early hours of the morning. And when I'd opened my eyes and my gaze followed around the uniquely shaped, half-empty bottle with a thud inside my head, I'd never felt so pathetic and alone.

I sighed at the memory. "I must warn you, I'm not an experienced drinker."

"Then that, my dear, will make tonight all the more fun."

On my way back to Gramps, I stopped at Mina's Diner to pick up minestrone and baked bread. When I returned, I heated it up on the stove. Casper sat on the windowsill, eyeing the broken birdhouse hanging from the garage eave, his green and blue eyes searching for life.

Gramps' sagging jowls vibrated, and his eyes popped open when I walked into his bedroom with the tray of food and tea.

"Freya," he whispered. The moon cast slivers of light through his dusty window over the bed, outlining the silhouette of his thin legs and boney knees. His brown eyes shifted from recognition to doubt to disappointment to the undeniable pain at the memory of a father losing his only daughter. The darkness swept across his face like a broom sweeping away all fragments of light from his past. A clean and tidy floor of truth, and his features turned cold. "Moonshine," he grumbled.

"Maybe I should stay home tonight." I dragged the tray closer to the bed and set down the plate of food.

Gramps sat up, and a cough caught in his chest. He turned on his side until it ceased, his lips trembling in the aftermath. "I'd rather yah go."

"Gramps..."

For twenty-four years, Gramps had been trapped in a house he'd never considered a home—alone—and the emptiness had slowly clawed away at the rest of him. I didn't blame him either. The Morgan house had a way of creeping over your skin, pushing anyone into a madness. Or maybe it was the town.

I'd learned his wife, my late grandmother, died when my mother was born. It seemed history had repeated itself when I came into the world, my mother dying from childbirth as well.

Milo had said the Norse Woods Coven cast both my mother and Gramps out of the west side after my mother married my father, a man from Sacred Sea. This forced them both to move into my father's family home off the coast—the Morgan Property.

"I don't have tha energy ta argue with yah. Just go." Gramps swung his legs over the edge and refused to look at me, keeping his gaze outside the window. Silence filled the awkward space between us. His hand shook, lifting the spoon and scooping it into the soup.

MONDAY STOOD OUTSIDE THE DOORS OF VOODOOS WITH ANOTHER GIRL, passing a lit cigarette back and forth. Her eyes widened when I pulled into the parking lot under a buzzing streetlight. She crushed the butt against a brick wall, and the two of them headed over.

"Fable, Fallon, Fallon, Fable," Monday introduced, and her eyes snapped to me. "What. A. Mouthful. Quick, let's go inside, it's gettin' chilly out here." She was already sparkly-eyed with a glistening smile, leaning to one side as she strolled across the parking lot in a flowy skirt to match her flaming-red hair.

When Monday turned her back to us, Fable held up three fingers, indicating she'd already had one too many.

Naturally wavy, golden-brown locks hung down to Fable's waist, bouncing off her maroon leather crop top. She had a witchery beauty about her, like a Victoria Secret model on the runway. The kind of beauty you were allowed to gawk at, slowly putting you into a trance until it suddenly hit you all at once, and you weren't quite sure how much time had passed—the bewitching beauty kind.

The doors opened to Voodoos, turning the outside cold to dust. It was dim and dark with masculine details and a nostalgic vibe. All the tables were occupied, and regulars lined the stools around the bar.

A haunting twist to "Black Hole Sun" played by a band on the stage. The eerie and penetrating female voice slithered in the air as I took in the atmosphere, waiting by the door.

Across the room, the Hollow Heathens were gathered around a pool table.

Three sets of eyes pinned to me, and my gaze circled their stares until it met Julian's. He was there, leaning against a brick wall with a pool stick in one hand, a drink in the other. His hair was black and glossy, yet thick and disorderly. In all black, even the black mask covering his face, his chrome-colored eyes zoned in on me from across the room.

The chill from his stare was like a hit of menthol, cooling my insides and freezing me in this spot. The music dropped into the background of his gaze, and my entire body felt like a single pulse, thumping in hard-hitting beats.

I didn't know why, but my foot stepped forward, wanting to go to him. Then Monday wrapped her fingers around my arm, yanking me in the opposite direction.

"Meet my friends," I think she said between the words of the song drifting. One of the Heathens smacked Julian's chest, and he tore his eyes away.

Monday wedged us between people at the bar. "You already know Milo. This is Ivy and Maverick, and the rest should be here soon." She snapped her fingers high in the air to get the bartender's attention.

Milo threw up a thumb from down the bar, making sure it was okay between us after what had happened with the article. I nodded.

Forgiveness always came easy to me. I'd seen what holding grudges could do, how it ate away at the souls of the spirits who'd visited me.

Ivy had shiny black hair cropped at the shoulders and bangs cut evenly across her forehead. She was tucked inside Maverick's arm, paying me no attention. Monday explained she was one of the three Sullivan sisters, along with Fable and Adora.

Maverick lifted his head in a careless greeting, shaggy blond hair and a private school upbringing style about him.

"Ignore them," Monday whispered. "Maverick's just cranky the other guys aren't here yet and the Heathens are."

The bartender chuckled as he turned, wearing the same black mask as the other Hollow Heathens. I glanced back to the pool table, counting three Heathens, so this must have been the fourth.

The bartender leaned over the bar, gripped the edge, and winked at a sour-faced Maverick.

Maverick shook his blond head and grabbed his glass, emptying it. "I'm going outside. The place reeks of a dead body, and I need fresh air," he stood and slid the glass down the bar, then turned to Ivy, "You guys coming?"

Ivy and Milo agreed, and the three took off.

"See what I mean?" Monday sighed.

An impala skull hung high above the shelves of liquor on the back wall of the bar, its long brown horns twisting up.

"What can I get ya?" the bartender asked, and all that stared back was a pair of golden eyes. A bit of curiosity stirred inside them as he studied my features.

"She'll have what I'm having," Fable interjected.

A long pause passed as the Heathen's eyes dragged from mine to Fable's, and he pushed off the bar and walked away. Fable's face fell, and Monday twisted her neck to deliver a warning glare. Fable waved her hand dismissively. "Don't look at me like that."

"He's one of them?" I questioned in a whisper.

"Yeah, Phoenix Wildes," Monday leaned closer, "He owns the bar and can't turn us away. I think it drives him crazy."

"Why come at all if you know you're not welcome?"

"This is the only bar aside from the Portside Pearl. There're not many places to hang out." She shrugged and pulled away when Phoenix returned, setting a drink in front of me.

A loud crack rang out as billiard balls slammed together on the green felt of the pool table. The sounds of the balls falling into pockets mixed with the music. I sat between Monday and Fable as they chatted back and forth about Defy Superstition Day and Mabon.

I'd tuned out, scanning the room and running my fingers along the lines of the detailed wood of the custom bar.

Julian was bent over the pool table, and the pool stick slid between his fingers when another *crack!* rang in my ears. He faced me, straightening his posture, paying no attention to his double ball drop-in as his gaze locked on mine.

"Yoo-hoo, Fallon," Monday snapped in my face, and I turned my head, "Was what we saw in those woods not enough for you?"

"It's not that," I said, trying to deviate whatever assumptions she had going on inside her head about Julian. "There's something … about him. Something different."

And there was, or maybe it was the alcohol. Light-headed, dizzy, spellbinding. Either the liquor was poisoning my brain, Julian was getting inside my head with his so-called dark magic, or the town was making me sick. But when I should be scared after seeing him slaughter a goat, I wasn't.

Monday crossed her legs and swung on the stool to face me. "Different? And the masks didn't give that away? I get it—the fascination. The wonder." She wiggled her fingers between us with wide eyes. "Who are the mystery guys behind the masks? But trust me, it's a dead end. They're cold. They have zero personality. They're hardly even human. And they don't talk to anyone unless they have to, as if *we're* the wasted breath."

My gaze found Julian's again. He'd talked to me on the rocks, but I didn't tell Monday or Fable that.

I swallowed and skated my eyes back to the girls. "What's up with the whole mask thing, anyway?"

The girls exchanged glances before Fable leaned closer. "They're cursed."

"The Curse of the Hollow Heathens," Monday added and took a sip from her straw.

Fable flipped her long brown locks off her shoulder and rested her elbow on the bar. "Julian is a member of the Norse Woods Coven and a Hollow Heathen."

"Yeah, Milo told me about them, and how they are the last four of the five original families from that coven."

"Right," Fable continued, "Supposedly they wear the masks because if you were to see their faces, all you'd see are your fears staring back at you. Their face sucks you in, and just like that"—she snapped, and I flinched—"your heart stops, scared to *death*."

I arched a brow, eyes narrowing. "You can't be serious ..."

Fable pursed her lips and shrugged. "No one really knows for sure, not like anyone's lived to say if it's true or not. It's a shame, really. Their coven is dying. Not like they care." Her eyes turned sad, and she stared at the back of Phoenix's head, drilling holes as she spoke, "They don't care about anything."

"Fable used to crush hard on Phoenix," Monday explained through a whisper. "Thought she could get through to him."

"Not *get through to him*." Fable rolled her eyes. "You know what? Forget it. I'm not telling you shit anymore."

"How come it's only them who wear the masks?" I haven't seen any other's keep their faces hidden.

Another quietness swept through the two of them.

Fable flicked her eyes to where Phoenix was standing then back to me. "Only the first-born sons of the original five. Death always follows their family. Julian's dad murdered seven people twelve years ago, so the Order had him executed. Beck's dad stays inside, no one has seen him in years, and Phoenix ... both his parents ... gone," she continued, and my eyes slid to Phoenix, who had his back to us at the other end of the bar, his brown hair tied into a low bun at his neck. With one hand on the lever, he poured beer into a tilted glass, and the muscles in his shoulders flexed as if he heard what we were saying. "They're a dying breed."

"You forgot about Mr. Goody," Monday jetted in.

"Oh, yeah. Well, Zephyr's dad is the High Priest of the Norse Woods Coven right now. Has been since Julian's dad was executed. You'll see Clarence Goody around sooner or later."

Executed? She'd said it so casually.

"Which one is Zephyr?" I asked, sliding my eyes back to the pool table.

Fable lowered her mouth to my ear. "The tall one with the blond hair. Can't miss him."

Beside Julian, there was Zephyr, standing taller than all of them with slicked-back dirty-blond hair. Dark circles rimmed his deep-set eyes, the color of glowing emerald chips. He and Julian seemed to be in a controlled disagreement, and where their gazes were anchored, it had nothing to do with the game of pool. Both pairs of eyes were fixed in our direction.

Phoenix dropped two mugs on the bar in front of two customers sitting beside us, and the three of us flinched as foam sloshed over the lip of the glasses. Without a word, not even a skim of eye contact, he walked away and assisted the next customer.

"I'll need another drink after this," I said for the first time in my life.

As the night carried on, so did the music and drinks. Maverick, Milo, and Ivy had reappeared with a few others, the group growing in numbers. It was hard to keep track of all their names and faces, especially since I was seeing double inside the swaying room.

"The Tobias Morgan is your father?" A guy named Kane asked, sitting on the stool beside me. I nodded, my eyes drifting from his charming features to where the Hollow Heathens were seated. The pool game had ended, and they were all grouped at the other end of the bar. "I want you to meet my father," Kane added, but his voice fell into the background. Julian was looking at me from the corner of his eye. I mindlessly twisted my mood ring around my finger as our gazes connected and tangled and...

"Fallon?"

My head snapped forward. "Yeah?"

"My father, I want you to meet him," Kane repeated.

"Aren't you supposed to take me on a date first?" I joked, and his blank eyes blinked. "Calm down, I'm kidding. I'm not much of a comedian and just spit out words when I'm uncomfortable."

"Right ..." Kane's face scrunched.

"I don't like talking about my dad," I admitted, but the truth was, I didn't like talking about this secret side of Dad everyone else knew. It made me feel as if I didn't know him at all.

"Well, Tobias was my dad's best friend growing up. He'd love to meet you, minus the date." He pulled a glass to his lips, then lifted a shoulder. "Sorry."

I nodded absentmindedly. "It was a joke. I didn't mean it." An uncanny attempt to backpedal my way out of my outburst. They were the first group who'd ever shown genuine interest in wanting to get to know me, and I didn't want to scare them away with my social awkwardness.

Kane shook his head and stood from the bar, swallowing the last of his drink. "It's okay, I'm used to it. But the truth is ... you're just not my type. It doesn't mean we can't be friends, or that you can't meet my dad."

You're just not my type, my brain repeated. Another term I'd heard many times before without asking for it. No matter how many times I'd heard it, it still hurt all the same.

"Sure, yeah," I agreed with a forced smile.

The first beat of a remake to "Sympathy for The Devil" dropped, and Kane raised his brows the same time the crowd went up in a roar. Drink-filled hands shot high into the air, and alcohol slapped the floor. The crowded bar turned into a frenzy.

Monday shrieked and climbed over the stool and onto the bar, and the three Sullivan sisters joined her.

"What's going on?" I called out to Kane as men snatched their drinks from the bar, clearing it for the dancing girls.

"You gonna go up there?" he asked without answering me, then lowered his soft-brown head, his nose brushing my hair. "Or has the town not gotten to you yet?"

"Gotten to me?" I glanced to Phoenix, who threw a towel over his shoulder and leaned against the back wall, watching Fable as the music and stomping shoes vibrated the bar.

Julian's silver gaze latched to me, his elbows on the bar and drink secured in one hand, as if waiting for me to make a decision.

"What are you going to do, Fallon? Are you a flatlander or one of us?" Kane edged on.

Fable reached her hand out, and my brain went fuzzy.

"Okay," I said, not thinking, half nodding, half laughing.

Already committed, I linked my hand with Fable's. Kane gripped my hips and hoisted me up on the bar, and once I was high in the air, I glanced around the room. The crowd looked up at me as the music pumped through the speakers, everyone waiting for me to do something.

"I'M A TOWNIE," I screamed, throwing my arms high in the air. "AND I'M REALLY, REALLY DRUNK!"

The entire room hollered at my declaration, and everyone went back to dancing to the unique cover of the song, including me.

The crowd turned into a blur when I twirled in place with my arms out at my sides, my hair soaring all around. Fable grabbed my hand and pulled me to the center of the bar. She and Monday began to teach me their stomping dance. I had no idea what I was doing and was too drunk to care.

And perhaps this was why people drank, to not think.

To forget. To feel free.

My face burned from the candid smile stretching across my numbed lips. My limbs moved as if they had a mind of their own, and when I looked to where Julian was sitting, he was already watching me from down below with a mysterious wonder in his eyes.

A wave of gravity lifted inside me, the feeling of weightlessness after

driving over a small hill. A free-fall. A tickle in my stomach.
But then my

FOOT
slipped.

JULIAN
chapter six

I REACTED.

I wasn't supposed to react, but before I could stop myself, I'd already slid across the bar and caught her before she had a chance to hit the ground. Fallon Grimaldi was in my arms, and it was as if the entire world had stopped. The music had stopped playing. The crowd had stopped dancing. All horror-filled eyes flared in our direction. Everyone had stopped except me.

I couldn't stop my damn self from reacting.

She was in my arms, and I couldn't undo this.

Fallon swam in her smile.

She wasn't the least bit afraid of me. Tipsy, but unafraid.

"Hi again," she whispered, her voice like an incantation.

I wanted to say something but couldn't. They were all looking at me, looking at her. I scanned the clarity in her eyes, her diamond-shaped face. I was holding her, and it felt as if I were holding a bomb or the colors of a sunset—a thing I shouldn't be caught with.

"Blackwell!" someone shouted, snapping me from her spell. My eyes slammed closed as the rest of the world fell back in tune. Then I opened them again, bounced to my feet, and Fallon tumbled from my arms to the ground.

If only I could've watched her fall.

"What do you think you're doing?" Kane barked, his fist slamming against the bar.

Ignoring him, I fixed my sleeves, keeping my attention on what my hands were doing.

The room was hushed. The energy was loud.

Phoenix threw his arms up at his sides, question marks in his fiery eyes.

I pushed past him and jumped back over the same wet bar girls were dancing moments before. Where Fallon was dancing, swaying her hips in those little shorts with the seven seas in her eyes.

"I know you're not looking at that freakshow," Zeph had said only an hour before. *"She's one of them."*

A reminder before my reaction.

But she was dancing, and I was watching her dance.

Zeph's gaze drilled into me.

"Let's go," I ordered, shrugging on my coat as my blood ran black, my darkness about to spill across Phoenix's bar for everyone to see.

"Hey, I'm talking to you!" Kane roared behind me, testing my patience.

My muscles twitched. I surveyed the room.

Everyone was watching me, waiting for me to react. For me to go mad as my father had, as if the rumors were true—as if the same mania ran in my blood. They wanted to prove the shadow in the Blackwell bloodline was incurable, that I'd inevitably end up like him. Mad and deranged like the men of my past.

And perhaps I was.

I shifted my eyes to Fallon. She was standing behind the bar where I'd left her, staring straight ahead as if she were lost or stranded or wondering if time had swallowed her whole.

"We were just leaving." I nodded to Phoenix, who couldn't afford another brawl in his bar like the one that had happened six Samhain seasons ago, when Sacred Sea ended up here after the moon filled out. Its light had soaked into our veins, driving us to do the craziest of things.

"Keep your demented hands off her, Blackwell," Kane spat, courage seeping from his drunken pores. "She's with us. Morgans are Sacred Sea territory."

Kane was braver when he had an audience. We'd been down this road before, but it didn't take much to see the urchin recoil. He was just as afraid of us as the rest of them because he knew there was truth in the curse. Everyone was afraid of something, even Kane Pruitt.

"Thank *fuck*, here I was thinking the freakshow was a flatlander," Phoenix's deep voice vibrated in the room behind Fallon. I cocked my gaze to him, not surprised he spoke out but endlessly wished he wouldn't. It was impossible to control myself, let alone him.

I shot him a knowing look. One that said, *contain yourself*. Phoenix ignored my narrowed eyes and took a step forward. My gaze flicked to the ceiling. *Here he goes…*

"Now it makes sense. The thing's with you."

I turned my attention to Beck, who began counting his fingertips with his thumbs at his sides as he had always done since we were kids. *One, two, three, four, one, two, three, four …*

Kane chuckled in his khaki slacks and pressed shirt. "Take off your filthy mask and say it to my face."

Phoenix growled, taking another step forward from behind the bar, his muscles jumping in his skin.

Patrons inside the bar found cover, terrified. Kane's friends whispered in his ear, no doubt trying to talk sense into him.

I locked eyes with Phoenix in hopes he'd keep his mouth shut.

My arm shot across Beck's chest to keep him steady. I was more worried about Beck at this point. He hadn't said a word, but his heartbeat was slamming against my palm.

"Beck," I gritted out, a caution-filled whisper—or a threat. One of us had to be the calm one, and I was already on edge because of Fallon. Her presence wrung me out, hung me to dry, made me weak.

I darted my eyes around the bar. There were too many people.

To my left, Zephyr watched with amusement in his eyes. To my right, Beck's veins protruded in his neck like a rabid dog. He was going to lose it right here in front of everyone.

Kane's chuckle rattled in my ears, making it worse. "You should really listen to your boyfriend."

The comment rushed straight to my brain. I cocked my head, sliced my eyes back to Kane, my feet ahead of my restraint, flexing my fingers to control the rage. The transformation within me felt like a cycle of the werewolf.

Kane's smile vanished. He stumbled back against the bar stool.

Everyone froze, ceasing all sudden movements with terror in their eyes. My chest heaved and my hands shook from the feeble attempt to control myself. But I felt the darkness filtering, the brazen energy vibrating inside me, and I clenched my hands into fists.

A roar quaked in my chest and vibrated in my throat. I couldn't stop it.

An animalistic scream thrashed in the air with winds of different seasons. The windows convulsed, and both entry doors flew open with a loud *bang!* against the walls. Violent winds swooshed through the small bar. Gasps and whispers went off like fireworks. The scream rippled like the very soundwaves I made across the sea. Bottles fell from their shelves, shattering when they hit the floor. Papers ripped from the wall, carried away by the strong winds. Phoenix jumped out to catch another bottle that had slipped from the shelf, calling out to me, but his voice was not pulling me out of it. Someone yanked on my stiffened shoulder. I knew it was Beck, but nothing would give.

The front window shattered. Townies cried out, clinging on to one another as glass flew into the cyclone inside the bar. But I was too far gone inside this daze for it to stop. Nothing could stop me.

Not until my gaze fell over Fallon's long hair tangling with the storm.

Through the thrashing white war of her hair, her clear eyes locked on mine. I inhaled, the sound of her breathing in my ears as if she were standing beside me.

Then everything stopped, and the doors swung to a standstill.

Quietness. Stillness.

Kane's eyes narrowed to crinkled slits.

The crowd looked around, baffled, searching for answers to what just happened.

One last flicker of a glance at the girl who returned home, and I walked forward through the crowd and out of Voodoos, Zeph and Beck close behind.

THE THREE OF US SAT AROUND A FIRE IN A SMALL CLEARING IN THE WOODS just off the deck of my property.

"Seriously, Jules. What were you thinking?" Beck asked with a lazy grip on the mouth of his beer bottle, letting it swing between his bent knees.

Hours had passed. The fire crackled between us.

I drank from my bottle, considering my words. "I wasn't." My gaze lingered to the cabin, where the oil lamplight flickered from inside on the window sill. "Something's not right." Or perhaps something wasn't right within me. I'd never done anything like that before, out in the open. I'd never put any of us in a position to be prodded. I fell back against my chair and balanced the bottle on my knee. "Something's off."

"Obviously." Zeph cocked his head, and his hair fell over one green eye. "It's the girl. Since she arrived, you've been different," he said with such disdain.

If they knew I'd picked her car up from the side of the road just so I could have a way to see her again, they'd ask questions—ones I didn't have the answers to because I didn't know what the hell I was doing. I had to keep my thoughts about Fallon to myself. "Fallon has nothing to do with it."

"Since when do you call her by her first name?" Zeph dragged out.

I flipped him the bird.

"Either way, the goat slaughter isn't good enough," Beck added with a slight slur as if those thoughts hadn't already crossed my mind. Eventually, he would pass out on my couch and be gone to work at the cemetery by morning, avoiding the troubles inside his home—avoiding his father. "There's gotta be a different way to break the curse."

A raven perched nearby, two condescending eyes staring at me from inside the deep forest. Its squawk made my blood curdle.

Since I was born, the death omen had been following me, but only worsened since Fallon's arrival—since her car drove under the Weeping Hollow sign.

The raven squawked again, reminding me I didn't have much time. Death was coming, and I had no idea who it was going after next. Or by whose hands.

"The mutant was looking at you, Blackwell," Phoenix declared, appearing suddenly from the dark shadows of the forest, a pointed finger directed at me.

I could see in the dark, those who didn't cast shadows often did.

Spite swam in Phoenix's gaze. He was a firestarter, and his internal battles were written in his glowing irises because he had a hard time holding back, but it was the only way the cursed had survived this long.

Stay hollow, stay detached, do right by the coven.

"And I have a feeling that whatever is going on is mutual," he added.

She was dancing, and I was watching her dance. Fallon was falling, and I couldn't stop myself from reacting. "You misread that entirely."

Phoenix shook his head and sank into a wooden chair. "Breaking this curse comes first—"

My jaw clenched. "I said it was nothing. A mere reaction, now drop it."

The forest blinked under the harshness dripping from my words. The rest of them silenced. All that was left was the forest waking in the night. Roots groaned beneath the cold soil, branches and leaves rustled. The forest was alive and moving, and I closed my eyes in its constant stability.

If not my loyalty to the Heathens, my shadow-blood coursing through my veins was enough to never question my priorities. After watching how the curse had destroyed our families, there was nothing I wanted more than to break it.

Twelve years ago, after Johnny's death, we'd made the pact in the woods and sealed it with our blood. I ran my thumb across the scar in my palm as a reminder.

It was different than the rest of our scars.

This one meant something.

For the last twelve years, we've laid low, earned the town's trust, became model citizens, played nice, gained access, sacrificed relationships. We did what our fathers couldn't. And we were so close.

"What was that, Jules?" Beck finally asked as the fire burned at our feet, the four of us sitting around it in a circle.

The incident at Voodoos. The door had swung open. A fury-filled storm made of magic and intimidation had blown through the bar, and Fallon's gaze had frozen with mine, covered me, comforted me, pulling me out of it somehow.

I dropped my head back and opened my eyes to the starless sky, watching as smoke and embers from the fire climbed the darkness to the moon. "I don't know," I said through an exhale, the lie scratching at my throat.

"Let's just let loose tonight. There's something inside you, and you need to get it out." Phoenix wanted to release his magic, release his anger. And he was using me as an excuse. "Be free like you used to, it's been too long."

"No one's going anywhere," I said.

I haven't run the woods in twelve years. I wasn't running now.

The others were quiet. Phoenix threw his bottle into the fire. The flames spiked into the sky between us, and the gold in his eyes studied me through the blaze. "You don't control me."

"Someone has to," Zeph told him.

Beck shook his head. "We can't. Jules is right."

"No." Phoenix laughed, standing and pointing at me. "That isn't Jules. Jules left twelve years ago. I don't know who the fuck that is anymore." He shook his head and took off.

Beck stood, facing his retreat.

"Let him go. He'll forget by morning," I said, bringing my beer to my mouth. I tipped the bottle

and closed
MY EYES.

the protection of
THE ORDER

Under the Full Cold Moon, in the last month of the year 1803, snow blanketed the newly found land. Those who sailed through the choppy December waters were seasick and dehydrated from their strenuous journey across the Atlantic. An anchor of hope kept them forward, finding a place to be free. It wasn't but a few miles back where a woman was forced to let go of her child, her coven ripping his dead body from her arms and tossing him overboard, his remains now belonging to the ocean. Her cries traveled along the sea, sank in its waters, and if you closed your eyes, you could still hear the mother's weeping interlaced with the waves over two centuries later.

"From the west, Norse Woods Coven appeared from the forest. Tiresome, their boots made drag marks across undisturbed snow. Five men, front and center, carried the weight of their coven, their deceased on makeshift cots, with a hollowness in their eyes.

"It had been days, weeks since they detached themselves from those who they were carrying. It was the only way to get by—the only way to save those who were remaining.

"With their strength depleted, living off partridgeberries and the berries of wintergreen, they continued onward, putting more distance between them and the witch trials in the home they had left behind.

"And it was there, under a marble moon, when Sacred Sea and Norse Woods crossed with no fight left in them.

"Women tended to their children as men built a fire in the center, which separated the land. They learned they were the same, both escaping a brutal fate. The two covens made a pact around the blazing fire and cast a spell that would forever protect this new land and shield it from their enemies around them—their peace treaty, their bind under the law of the Order. The elements were balanced, the covens were balanced, bringing harmony and peace. A haven to practice their beliefs.

"It took all night into morning—the Full Cold moon's kiss lit a pinkish glow across the sky on the coldest night of the year—when leaders of the Order were assigned, and the shield was complete.

"Both covens rested their heads, the fire a hot breath across their trembling flesh. The only sounds were the snapping of firewood and water breaking across the rocky edge.

"Yet unbeknownst to the covens, already hidden in the woods lived two scared and pregnant women.

"These women watched from the trees as these strangers scattered across their home, sleeping around a fire under their sunrise, afraid of what their arrival might mean. So, in the woods, they would stay.

"Until sixteen years later, when a curious and stubborn young girl who lived among the forest, white hair made of snow flurries, aquamarine stones as eyes, decided to step out …"

FALLON
chapter seven

ANY DAY ABOVE GROUND IS A GOOD ONE, I'LL TELL YA. BUT THERE'S *something in the air that's giving even me the heebie-jeebies around here. Maybe it's the storm rolling in, so careful out there on the waters today, salty dogs. I know, I know, no storm will hold ya back. But hey, whatever floats your boat,"* —he paused to chuckle— *"And these are your Hollow Headlines with Freddy in the Mournin'. Let's kick Saturday off with some good music ..."* Freddy announced, interrupting Gramps and my conversation.

Gramps mumbled, his jaws chomping at his dentures that were barely holding on. "It's because tha window in yah room is facin' east. Maybe yah should move to tha othah room down tha hall," he replied, but I hardly believed my nightmare from last night had anything to do with the direction my window faced.

"I thought you didn't believe in all that mumbo jumbo nonsense," I playfully said as I sat across from him with the warm mug between my palms and the nightmare still sticking to my mind.

Gramps' eyes hit mine above the rims of his bifocals. "I'm done talkin' to yah today."

"Yeah, yeah." I stood when the bread popped out of the toaster. I plucked the toast at the hot edges of the crust and dropped it on a plate.

Last night I'd left my scooter at Voodoos and walked the rest of the way home. Kane's words of *"Morgans are Sacred Sea territory"* lodged itself into my brain. Morgans were someone else's territory?

Territory.

When Kane had said the word, it felt as if he had bound my arms together. A shiver jumped up my spine to the back of my neck. *Territory.* The single word had stayed with me the entire way home, and last night I'd dreamed of the night I'd desperately wished I could erase. Blood and blackness and the blistering cries—what those kids had done to me seventeen years ago. My thumb anxiously twisted my mood ring around my ring finger.

"Moonshine," Gramps' voice broke apart my thoughts. "My toast."

I dropped my gaze to see the toast already on a plate waiting for me to spread the butter.

I let go of a breath and pulled a knife from the drawer. "Do you know anything about Dad's side of the family and Sacred Sea?" I asked casually, spreading the creamy butter over the toast.

Gramps leaned back in his chair and dropped his pencil, the crossword puzzle far from finished. He would never leave the table until it was. "I know-a lot about a lot around heyah. Why ar-yah askin' about Sacred Sea?"

I licked a splatter of butter off my thumb and rested the fork on the sink. Walking to him, I continued, "I met some people last night. One said something about Morgans being Sacred Sea...*territory,*" the word wouldn't roll easily off my tongue. It clung to the back of my throat as if my mind refused to say the word aloud.

Kane had gone from uninterested to overprotective in the blink of an eye. He'd rather see me hit the ground than have a Heathen come near me.

I retook my seat and leaned over the table with one elbow propped near the edge and blinked up at him. "What does that even mean?"

The old man looked out the window into the sea, his jaw grinding and jowls shaking. Inside those tired eyes rested a museum of history, secrets, and conspiracy theories. When his gaze returned to me, his brows furrowed. "What do yah know already?"

My lips moved faster than I'd intended. "What do *you* know."

"I asked yah first."

His stubbornness was uncanny, comical even, but this was hardly the time to laugh.

We stared at one another in a standoff, neither one of us Grimaldis backing down. But after a few seconds, I cracked first.

"When I was a little girl," I started to say then paused to find the right words, to think it through. I dropped my gaze from his and pinched the seam of my oatmeal-colored cardigan draping across my knees. "I would sleep all day and stay up all night. Marietta called me her *moonshine*. I thought that was the reason why, too. Because I would '*Wake and sleep with the moon*,' she'd say." I returned my eyes to his. "She would tell me stories, Gramps. About Weeping Hollow and Norse Woods and Sacred Sea. Some I still remember, some are so vague it feels like a dream. But I thought they were just stories. I didn't believe any of it until I started getting your letters. Then I get here, and Weeping Hollow is *real*. Dad was part of a coven. And my mom … my mom … I still don't even know anything about her, but this town knows. Everyone seems to know everything but me. All I have are vague memories of these bedtime stories my nanny used to tell me."

Gramps' hard eyes locked on mine, and a long pause dragged between us.

"Tell me what it means," I pleaded.

"Yah shouldn't be hangin' around fopdoodles who have the handshake of a wet sock," Gramps spat, red replacing his pale cheeks. "Yah shouldn't even be heyah at all! Yah ask too many damn questions, just like yah mothah. And I'm gonna tell yah the same thing I told her. Theya's a burden that comes along with knowin' the truth. It's heavy and cripplin' and comes at a price. Don't ask questions yah not ready to heah."

"You never talk about my mother. You never wanna talk about anything important," I pointed out, and I hated how my voice sounded like a child's. "Why do I feel like everyone's keeping a secret from me? You and Dad, no one wants to talk about—"

"Yah have no ideah what yah talkin' about!" His voice was harsh and his eyes were wide. "Tobias took yah away to protect yah. Best decision that dumbass evah made!"

My face cringed from the blow, the way Gramps had spoken ill of my dead father. A father who never visited the daughter who could see the dead when his spirit was the only one I looked for in every room I walked into.

I bit the inside of my cheek and let the *dumbass* comment slide. "What does it mean I'm *Sacred Sea territory*, Benny?" I repeated, sterner this time—more adult than child. I'd realized this was my last hope of getting anything out of the man.

"It doesn't mattah anyhow!" he shouted. "Yah wanna know why?"

"Why?"

"Because even though yah a Morgan, yah a Grimaldi too! Yah *my* blood, *my* granddaughtah," Gramps finally said for the first time with a glimmer of compassion in his features, his cheeks and finger shaking. "Yah no one's territory, moonshine!"

My Mini Cooper passed by the living room window facing the street, stealing my attention.

"What is it?" Gramps asked, disturbed.

I got up from the small table in the kitchen when Gramps shifted in place as if he were to get up, but we both knew he didn't want to. The crossword puzzle wasn't finished yet.

"I think someone's here."

I walked through the living room, craning my neck to see outside the window. My car was parked in the gravel driveway. Barefoot, I shuffled down the porch steps. Black clouds were rolling in from the east over the Atlantic, and the air was dew-like and misty. A storm was coming.

I narrowed my eyes, my hand shielding them to keep my hair from my view. The Mini Cooper idled in the driveway for a long time before the door swung open.

Boots landed on gravel, and my eyes scanned up the black pants and coat. Thick icy-black hair waved with the oncoming storm when he turned to face me. With liquid smoke in his eyes, Julian's gaze met mine through the threatening winds.

Julian Blackwell was in my driveway.

An arctic chill breezed past me, and I pulled my cardigan closer around my chest, trying to cover my tank and midriff.

"What are you doing here?" As the words left me, I felt stupid for asking them. He was only returning my car. The car *he* had fixed.

Julian walked up the path with one hand in his pocket, the other grasping my keys in his palm. Each step he took, his eyes remained on mine and never veered down my body or past me or around me. A deadlock.

He stopped only inches before me, and I had to lift my head to see his covered face. He could easily reach out and touch me, but he didn't have to. His intense eyes cut through my skin, grabbed hold of my soul, and gently caressed it. There was a serenity lurking behind the walls of his madman illusion—a false imprisonment of a wonderland I wanted to wander in. A place I could get lost in.

"Your keys," he stated, holding them out between us with a stone-cold stare.

I held out my palm when he dropped them into my hand, physically not touching me and making sure of it.

A faded song of breaths counted the next few seconds, neither one of us saying anything or making an attempt to move.

Then a loud clatter came from inside the opened door, sounding like glass shattering, and Julian's eyes blinked once before they ripped away from mine.

My heart dropped when it dawned on me. *"Oh my god*, Gramps!"

My feet moved quickly, up the steps and through the front door.

Gramps laid motionless on the kitchen floor. A broken plate surrounded him, and his hat had slid across the floor from his balding head. My eyes bulged, a panic struck my chest.

"Gramps!" I cried out, running to him. I collapsed to my knees near his body.

His eyes were closed. Mine were burning. He wasn't moving.

What do I do, what do I do, what do I do ... my mind was in shambles, my heart left somewhere outside, probably gone with the wind.

Julian appeared and crouched down near Gramps' head, pressed two fingers against his neck.

"Get away from him!" I shouted, pushing against his shoulder. "Don't touch him!"

Julian caught my wrist in his hand, and I froze. "He's still breathing," he spoke evenly, his voice coarse and detached. "I'm going to walk over there and call the doc." His fingers remained firmly around my wrist, his gaze holding mine.

Julian bounced his eyes between my panicked ones, then moved my hand to Gramps' neck and placed my fingers on his pulse. "You feel that?"—A gentle tap of Gramps' pulse hit my fingers, and I nodded, tears streaming down my face, my lips trembling— "He'll be okay. Hold on to his heartbeat."

Julian jumped up and disappeared behind me, grabbing the house phone from the wall.

"I'm right here, Gramps. Don't you dare die on me, you hear me?" Tears sputtered through my words. I sucked in a more stable breath as his pulse thumped against my two fingers beneath his paper-thin skin. "It's all my fault," I cried to whoever was listening. The spirits who followed me, Gramps, Julian. "I shouldn't have pushed you so hard. I shouldn't have upset you. I'm so, *so* sorry." All my words tumbled out, one right after the other. Gramps was sick, and I'd made him so angry because I'd asked too many damn questions. "This is all my fault."

Gramps' eyes blinked open, and a gurgled moan escaped from his lips. I scrambled closer.

"You're okay." I sighed in relief as he came to, another tear falling from the corner of my eye.

Gramps shifted on the floor, and his startled gaze darted around the kitchen.

"Don't move, Benny. The doc is coming," Julian stated from behind me.

DR. MORLEY TOOK HIS TIME CHECKING GRAMPS' VITALS AND HIS HEAD. Gramps sat in the dining chair, glaring at Julian, who hadn't moved from the counter.

The doc removed the thermometer from Gramps' mouth. "Your temperature is at a hundred and two. I told you to stay in bed. You keep overexerting yourself, you'll never get better."

Dr. Morley was oddly tall. He stood close to seven feet at full height, making him the tallest man I'd ever seen—a large frame of bones. His knee caps bulged even as he stood, his elbows too even when his arms were straight. The bottoms of his slacks hit right at his calves, his sleeves at his forearms.

"*Clowns.* I got dizzy, is all," Gramps mumbled. "No need for all the dramatics."

"For once, listen to him, Gramps."

Winds howled around the house as rain pounded against the kitchen window. The storm was here, the skies black in the late morning. The house's lights flickered.

"Tomorrow," Dr. Morley started, towering to his feet, "Come see me so we can do more testing at the office. I'll be better equipped." He looked down at Gramps, whose brows were pushed together and downward. "If there's something I can do to help, better now before it's too late."

Gramps kept his lips pressed together in a hard line, not speaking a word.

Not until after Dr. Morley left.

As soon as the door closed behind the doctor, Gramps couldn't keep it in any longer. "Duke of limbs is nothin' but a moron."

"Gramps!"

"I should be on my way," Julian muttered.

"Damn right, yah should go," Gramps seethed through his veneers. "And you, yah Heathen. You stay away from my granddaughtah."

Julian pushed off the counter and walked past me.

The rattle of the front door closing behind Julian echoed, and I jumped to my feet to run after him.

"Where yah going, moonshine?" Gramps called out. "You better stay away from those Heathens ... Stay away from Blackwell ... Yah hear me? ... *Stupid girl.*"

My feet moved fast. I swung the front door open and ran off the steps as rain pounded into me, soaking my hair and my clothes, the strong winds beating me from every direction.

I spotted Julian walking down the driveway with his head down.

"Hey, wait!"

Julian turned at the sound of my voice. "What are you doing out here?"

he shouted over the rain, walking back up the driveway. My eyes locked onto the cylinder pendant hanging from around his neck as it swung back and forth. "Go back inside!" He pointed at the house behind me, his thick black hair soaked and sticking to his forehead.

"You're going to walk all the way home in this? No, let me drive you!"

The winds were forceful, threatening to rip our clothes from our bodies, our hair from our scalps. Rain drove into us, intending to pierce through our flesh. There was no way he could walk home in this.

Thunder rumbled, the sound vibrating my spine. I licked rain from my lips, stepping on soggy grass to him where he stood like a statue. The shirt under his soaked coat clung to the sharp ridges of his torso. Rain dripped from the tips of his hair over his eyes.

"Please, let me drive you. It's the least I can do."

Julian shook his head, erased the distance between us, and dropped his mouth to my ear. He hovered there for a moment. I could hear the sound of his breath in my ear, playing along with the slapping of the icy rain. "I'd rather walk home in this than be seen with you." His hollowed eyes lifted to mine, and rain dripped from his long black lashes.

I stared into the grey storm, unblinking and still processing his words.

Julian shook his head, turned, and descended the hill back to the street.

The rain beat on me as I WATCHED HIM *go.*

FALLON
chapter eight

T HE RAIN HAD LASTED FOR THREE DAYS, AND ON THE FOURTH DAY,
the town worked together to clean up the aftermath in Town Square
and the surrounding neighborhoods. A limb from the giant beech tree
near the gazebo had gone straight through the front window of Hobb's
Grocery. Agatha and a few other townies stopped to help the grocery store
owner board it up.

Mina passed out coffee since her diner hadn't lost electricity as most of
the town had. I worked alongside Jonah and Monday, my gaze searching
for Julian.

I hadn't seen him since he'd walked home when the storm first started.
I hadn't seen any of the Heathens out and about, helping the town. But
why would they? From what Monday and Fable had told me, they didn't
care about anyone or anything. They were cold creatures with a cutthroat
blood type, Heathens who stayed hidden in the woods and only came out
at night.

Once the phone lines were back up, I'd made a call to Dr. Morley and
forced Gramps out of the house and into the Mini Coop.

"What is this? This isn't a cah, this is a hearse for midgets," Gramps had
commented, rambling the entire way to Dr. Morley's office as he looked

over the buttons on the console. *"I'll show yah a real cah, moonshine. This,"* he had tapped on the dash at all the buttons, *"This is a toy. Does it even take gas or yah gotta buy a powah pack? Plug it intah a wall? Is this what it feels like when yah pickin' up dead Bahbie?"*

Dr. Morley said that Gramps had a mild heart attack, and the lack of blood flow to the brain caused him to get dizzy and pass out. We'd left with a bottle of aspirin and strict orders to keep stress at a bare minimum. As far as the virus, it had to run its course.

That night, Casper cried from the foot of the bed, pacing back and forth. But it hadn't been the cat to pull me from my unconscious state in the middle of the night.

There was always a flickering moment behind closed eyes when the feeling of a ghost watching me from the shadows slithered over my skin. It was a sinister lull. In those fleeting moments, I had no earthly—*or unearthly*—idea what was waiting for me once my eyes were open, but it was there. I could feel it in my bones. In my soul.

I'd always imagined the worst. A contorted face, ripped skin stitched from the center of the forehead and across the eye, disfigurement from a car accident, part of the head missing from a gunshot wound, the most gruesome of death.

A skin-prickling breeze skimmed over my face. Whatever it was, it was here with me. I was not alone, and a lazy terror crawled through my veins as it always had just before I acknowledged the spirit—the ones who found me.

I opened my eyes. Both balcony doors were ajar, creaking back and forth with the wind. The Atlantic Ocean's colors were one with the night sky, endless depths of darkness. The grandfather clock chimed from the bottom of the stairs, and I held my breath until it was over.

The light giggle of a child carried in from the balcony, and my eyes darted to the sound.

A small boy with cropped dark hair and a striped red and white shirt appeared behind the billowing curtain. His little voice drew me from the bed, and I planted both bare feet onto the wooden floors.

The small boy laughed and darted from the balcony, disappearing at the top step.

I pushed back the curtains and stumbled onto the balcony. My hair slid off my shoulders and hung over the railing as I looked down.

Our eyes met, and my breath stopped in a gasp.

The boy was hardly a child, three or four at best guess. My fingers moved across the railing to the stairs, and I descended, keeping my gaze locked on his. He stood there, hands fisting the bottom hem of his shirt at his thighs. He had pale, iridescent skin, and dark shadows painted around his sad brown eyes.

When I let off the bottom step, another bone-cracking giggle released from his dry lips, and he jumped in place before taking off around the house toward the street. I followed him out of the neighborhood, across Town Square, and to Norse woods on the opposite side of town, but not to my own accord. I walked willingly, yes, but I had a feeling if I hadn't, the little boy wouldn't leave me alone otherwise.

He skipped and jumped and walked backward in the empty streets under the night sky. A cracked smile greeted me with every spin, a childish game as his arms swung out at his sides. He sang and laughed and pulled me deeper into Norse Woods territory. *How did we get here so fast?*

The blue rubber boots he wore were muddied and too big for his little feet. They dragged across asphalt until we reached the start of the woods. Leaves crumbled beneath my bare feet, and he sped up, zigzagging between white birch trees and leaping over fallen branches.

"Wait up," I whisper-shouted, trying to catch up to him in only a thin pajama tank and matching cotton shorts. The temperatures had dropped to the mid-fifties, and the forest groaned in the dark as if the trees were growing around me, stretching.

"... *Ashes, ashes,*" I heard the chanting song from the little boy. I continued to follow the young and playful voice deeper and deeper and deeper into the woods.

Until the ghost came into view.

My running turned to a standstill at what laid before me.

Julian was sitting on the forest floor, his head hidden between his bent knees. He rocked back and forth, blood sticking to his flawless bare skin as dead ravens scattered around him.

My gaze jumped up to the little boy who began to fade quickly with his hand on Julian's shoulder.

"*We all. Fall. Down,*" were the ghost's last words, then he disappeared like how an old television would turn off, flickering then all at once.

I dragged my hand down my throat to my chest, partly to make sure I was still breathing, partly having no control over my own actions. Julian's gaze lifted from his knees, and his eyes, the color of two lethal swords, pierced me. And at that moment, I knew I was no longer breathing. I'd known once my lungs ached.

Dark circles painted around Julian's eyes. A knife trembled from his fingertips that was hanging off one knee, and blood dripped from the sharp point of the blade.

"Death is here," he whispered, his mask absent and only the shadows of the woods shielding his face. "It's here, and I can't stop it. *Why can't I stop it?!*"

"Julian?" The single word left upon a panicked breath.

He slowly rose to his feet, head down, black slacks hanging off his hips. Bare-chested, barefooted, and rooted to the forest ground like the pale birch trees. Their branches moved with him, casting a shadow over his face, protecting him, adoring the man who was more woods than flesh.

Black and red invaded my senses. Dark crimson blood stained his hands. Dead ravens blanketed the forest ground at his feet, a pile of twisted necks, broken wings, beaks, and lifeless beady black eyes.

Then Julian's hollow gaze met mine. Inside his eyes, all the lights were out. There was a deep void, empty rooms, uninhabited planets—the dead zone. At that moment, I knew. Whatever it was he wanted or needed, it had turned him into a monstrous thing.

"Go home," he seethed as if it pained him to say, his empty hand clutching at his chest where silver chains hung over his scars. Blood smeared across his heart.

The ghost wanted me to be here, to witness this, yet for what reason? To help him or to be his next kill. It could have gone either way. And still, despite all odds, I took a step forward.

"Julian …" I pressed again, trying to get through, and something stirred in the depths of his eyes—life, panic, fear, a delusional thought, confusion, or something else entirely. I wasn't quite sure. But he was shaking, why was he shaking? Better yet ... why wasn't I running away?

Ca-caw! another raven warned. It flapped its glossy wings in front of the moon, settling on a branch above us.

Julian's eyes twisted with the song of the raven, and his fingers tightened on the blade, his chest heaving without rhythm. The rustling of leaves blew around us, a nursery rhyme of Norse woods. It played along with the thrusting of my heart.

Ca-caw, rustle, pound!

My hair blew around me with every step I took to him. I kept my arms at my sides. Bones cracked under my feet, fresh blood slipped and oozed between my toes, and feathers stuck to my heels.

Then we were only inches apart. My fingers trembled as they reached out between us, and I laid them on his forearm. He was so cold, and Julian flinched under my touch. His eyes pinned to where I was sliding my fingers down the length of his arm to the knife.

"Do you want to hurt me?" I dug my teeth into my lip to deter the response awaiting me.

His wild gaze lifted to mine, and his brows bunched together. "*What?*" Then his eyes softened. "*No.*" He'd said it as if he couldn't believe he had to convince me of the same.

A long exhale escaped from my nose, and the knife fell onto the pile of death.

His trembling relaxed in my hold. The raven squawked again above us, causing Julian to slam his eyes closed. I pressed my other hand to his bare chest, and his eyes opened. His hand covered mine.

"The ravens won't leave me alone," he bit out the words through his teeth. "Why won't they ever leave me alone?"

The trees moved again with him, casting shadows along his face. I was so close, yet unable to see anything but the dark tower he was, the smoking gun in his eyes.

I lifted his bloodied hand and pulled it up to my neck, then pressed his slippery, cold fingers against my pulse, the same way he'd shown me to calm after Gramps had passed out. It was the only way I knew how to calm in such terrifying moments, because of him. And his stiffened posture relaxed, breathing steadied.

Julian wrapped his fingers around my throat, his thumb resting under the base of my chin. I closed my eyes. He pulled me forward. A cool breath fanned across my lips. Then they quivered.

Julian's forehead fell to mine. "Don't look at me," he whispered into my mouth, clutching the side of my face. His lips coasted over my parted ones. "Whatever you do, don't look at me."

As soon as he'd said the words, my eyes blinked open.

All oxygen sucked from my lungs, and darkness devoured me whole. Terror cut me open, slicing through wounds that had been scabbed over but always there. A scream ripped through my throat as I clawed at the walls that suddenly circled me. "Julian!"

The well. I was no longer in the woods.

Julian was gone.

My eyes darted around in a panic.

Trapped, trapped, trapped.

My palms hit brick. All around me was brick. This panic exploded within me, and I clawed frantically at the walls on every side. The full moon beamed through the small opening at the top. Water sloshed around at my knees. I continued to claw and scratch at the walls, trying to climb my way out. My nails broke as tears rushed down my face. My throat was hoarse. My fingertips were raw and bloody. But I had to get out.

"HELP ME!"

My teeth chattered, my limbs convulsed, my entire being desperate to escape the hot well in the dreadful heat of the summer night.

"JULIAN!" I screamed again, my throat on fire as if shards of glass lodged in my windpipe.

"*... an emergency Town Hall meeting will be held at eight a.m. As always, all are welcome. Except you, Jasper Abbott. You are not welcome.*" —Freddy paused to chuckle— "*And these are your Hollow Headlines with Freddy in the Mournin'. Let's kick Thursday off with some good music. And remember, witches, no one is safe after 3 a.m. ...*"

I startled from my bed, shaking and terrorized. A cold dew covered my slick skin. The bedsheets had been tossed to the end, halfway to the floor. A sunrise swirled and smeared across the sky over the blue waters.

Casper pounced on the bed from the armoire and laid beside me at my hip.

My head hit the pillow. "It was only a dream," I convinced myself, one hand protecting my racing heart. *"it was all a* DREAM."

FALLON
chapter nine

T OWN HALL WAS THE BIGGEST BUILDING IN TOWN SQUARE, SITUATED behind the gazebo. It had large white pillars, black plantation shutters, and a curved door off to the side of the main entrance. This led to a spacious room, where folding chairs lined up in front of a podium.

The town's people filed in, one after another, filling the room with some familiar faces, such as Mina Mae, Dr. Morley, Agatha Blackwell, and those I haven't met yet, seen only in passing.

Jonah had said it was mandatory for Monday and me to be there. The three of us sat at the end of the row in the center of the room. Chatter echoed off the low ceilings. I turned in my seat, noticing the Hollow Heathens standing against the back wall with their arms clasped firmly in front of them.

Julian's eyes never faltered and stayed pinned ahead, but the veins in his arms popped as he tensed with my gaze as if he struggled to remain still and focused.

Each time I closed my eyes, the dream would come back to me. The ghost—*Julian*. The color of black ice and currant—*Julian*. Death omens and trees—*Julian*. Blood and black feathered wings sticking to our skin in the dark and wicked woods—*Julian, Julian, Julian*.

It had been as real as real could be in a dream—or as real as a dream could be. And as the nonsense crossed my mind, it somehow all made sense to me.

I could still feel his cold fingertips against my neck, his breath against my lips, and the horrifying terror that had ripped me away from him.

There was no stopping it, no ridding myself of the memory. Julian lived there now, in my malefic imagination, and he had no idea. Whatever had walked in my mind, I'd walked with it alone.

A distinct *bang!* of a gavel grabbed my attention. Standing in front of the podium was an older man with a chestnut-colored toupee combed perfectly to the side.

"We will begin," he announced with blinding authority. The chatter ceased at once before him. "This meeting will be handled maturely and with respect. I will not have a repeat of last month."

Jonah dropped his mouth to my ear. "That's Augustine Pruitt, one of the four in the Order, which governs the town. Think of them as the regulators."

Nodding, I kept my eyes forward on Mr. Pruitt as he continued, speaking of upcoming events, news within Weeping Hollow, and the aftermath of the storm.

A collection of groans, oohs, and aahs see-sawed in the room, reacting to his every word, whether the people agreed or disagreed. The man stood with unfathomable posture and wore a sweater vest under his navy-blue blazer. He was a handsome man with wise lines crinkling in the corners of his mouth and eyes.

Agatha Blackwell stood beside Mr. Pruitt. Alongside him was a woman I'd never seen before with a man who wore a white plastic mime mask. His stringy blond hair hit his knobby shoulders.

"Who is that?" I whispered to Jonah, nodding to the odd creature beside Mr. Pruitt.

"That's Clarence Goody. He's also in the Order, along with Agatha Blackwell and Viola Cantini."

The conversation had changed to smaller issues between townies. The owner of Hobb's Grocery stood from the crowd after being called upon by Mr. Pruitt.

"What ar-yah gonna do about my shop window?" he called out angrily with a fist in the air. "It should come outta the town's expense! That storm blasted through my window and soaked a quartah of my inventory! What yah gonna do about that, Pruitt?"

Jonah's shoulders shook next to me as he silently chuckled. "Gus Hobb is a cheapskate. Always finds a way to get the town to pay. You know, since the market is *essential*." He chuckled again while the rest of the town lost interest in the argument, rolling their eyes and looking around the room at each other.

"Sit down, Gus," Mr. Pruitt drew out, annoyed. "Need I remind you that you're behind on the town's dues by two moons? You will pay for back dues and the broken window. Until you can get caught up, the market will be closed. The truck coming in next week will be set up in the East wing. The town will cover the food cost, and the money received will go back into the town. My best advice for you, *Gus*, is to get your business together, or this arrangement will become permanent."

Gus' face turned red. "You can't do that!"

Pruitt ignored him. "All in favor, say 'Aye.'"

The town collectively said "Aye" with smiles and a few laughs.

"Next order of business," Pruitt moved on, and Gus walked with a limp out of Town Hall, mumbling empty threats in his wake.

"A Heathen was at the coastline!" a woman shouted from behind me. "One of them is always hangin' around the cliffs in the early mornin'."

Julian. I turned to see behind me, and one of Gramps' neighbors was standing with a finger pointed at the Heathens posted at the back of the room. Not one Heathen showed a lick of emotion or faltered in their poise. Julian remained aloof.

Augustine Pruitt stepped aside and allowed Mr. Goody, the tall man in the painted mime mask, to take the stand.

"Which one?" he asked, his tone like a bass guitar.

"I don't know which one, for cryin' out loud. They all look the same!"

"If you don't know which one, are you certain, without a shadow of a doubt, it was a Heathen at all? It could very well be Augustine's son, Kane"—Mr. Pruitt took a step forward, and Mr. Goody shot up his hand—"or Dolores Claiborne or Jasper Abbott or the mysterious Freddy in the

Mournin'?" The people collectively laughed as if the names he'd listed off were ludicrous. "Irene, you know that unless you can identify your trespasser, there is nothing I can do."

"How am I supposed to identify 'im?" the woman, Irene, shot back. "Norse Woods was on our coast! *That,* I'm certain of!" The crowd looked around, the calm before the storm. "Probably coming to hex our land on the Eastside or take women from *our* coven. Like that Norse witch, Freya, took our Tobias. *OUR HIGH PRIEST!*" she spewed through clenched teeth, and the crowd began reacting, nodding, and agreeing. My stomach fell, my gaze darted in a frenzy. "They're coming! They're desperate, and we should all be worried! They'll only take and take and *take* like the hungry wolves of the Calla!" The woman dragged her rage-filled eyes around the room, warning her people. "Mark my words, chaos will erupt, order will crumble, and the shield will fall. We will *all* be doomed!"

The woman's voice carried throughout the room and fueled the townspeople. More than half the room fed her fire, voicing their worries and theories like gasoline and torches. The rest who were from the Norse Woods sat still and motionless, unaffected by their taunts and threats.

"Sit down, Irene!" Mr. Goody shouted, repeatedly banging the gavel as turmoil arose amongst the crowd. "Order!" he screamed this time, his blond hair shaking over his shoulders. No one listened.

Half the room was standing and pointing fingers in all directions, at the Hollow Heathens, at the people on the left side of the room. But the people of Norse Woods remained stoic, blank features pinned to their faces.

The mention of my mother and father suffocated my mind. I was unable to think, unable to concentrate. All I could do was bounce my eyes around at the fear in the eyes of half the people, the hollow in the eyes of the rest.

"It was me," Julian's voice boomed within the room as he took a step forward. The room quieted, and arms dropped to the people's sides, surprised. The rest of the Heathens' gazes glued ahead without a tell as Julian fixed his attention on Irene. "Rest assured, we do not want your women," he said flatly, bouncing his eyes to me, then snapping them back to Irene. "We stay true to our own. As far as the ocean, it called out for me, and I listened."

"Lies, you monster," Irene spat.

Kane jumped up from the front of the room, dressed as if he were at a church service, and faced the crowd. "Julian Blackwell went after Fallon Morgan," he added. "And used his shadow-blood against me when I intervened."

The room roared with whispers, and all eyes fell on me.

My heart pounded in my ears.

I looked to Julian, not understanding the big deal.

Julian's posture remained unchanged and collected.

Augustine Pruitt, who I'd learned was Kane's father, stepped up beside Mr. Goody with knitted brows.

"Is this true?" he asked, eyes sailing between Julian and me.

"I ... I ..." my words were lost in the scuffle of banter as everyone looked in my direction.

"Say what you will, but the accusation is weak at best," Julian scoffed, venom in his tone. "The girl is a flatlander, is she not?" Kane growled, and Julian continued, "Not to mention the absurdity in desiring a Morgan. If you must know, Norse Woods embodies morals, and I—*a monster*—a certain taste. The girl is hardly worth Norse Woods' time or attention. And, yes, I'm guilty of chivalry. Couldn't bear to see the helpless girl hit the ground since Kane's ego weighs him down."

And a knife sharpened by his words twisted me open in places unknown, unfelt. It was a different hurt than the rest. *Why did it hurt like this?*

Kane took a hasty step forward. "You—"

"Mr. Goody," Julian interrupted, cutting off Kane. "There is no need to cause panic over a misunderstanding. Let's get back to more important matters, like the food rations the residents will have to savor this week until the truck arrives."

"I agree," Mr. Goody stated, then his gavel slammed down on the podium, the topic closed for discussion.

Mr. Pruitt shook his head, visibly disturbed on how the matter was handled, but after a few moments, he straightened his shoulders and swallowed his thoughts back down. "This meeting is adjourned."

People stood unsatisfied with the meeting's outcome, and I stayed seated as they swarmed around me, heading for the exit.

I'd learned two things during the meeting. One: I couldn't bear to be around Julian after the dream I had, the moment we had shared. In my mind, he was vulnerable to me, yet still the very dark soul who controlled the dark forest and the dark things that haunted it. But the Julian who'd appeared today was someone else entirely, aloof and impenetrable.

Two: hearing how Dad was Sacred Sea's High Priest. The older generation cared for him deeply, respected him, looked up to him once upon a time. A time before I'd come into this world. And my mother ... What was so terrible about falling in love with my father? Why did they hate her?

Dad had rarely talked about my mother. He had barely been home enough to even speak to me.

Dad was a handsome man with a strong Italian nose, glossy black hair, and bright blue eyes. When he was home, he would spend most of his days in the garage, tinkering with model airplanes. Almost daily, we would get boxes full of ordered parts for his beloved hobby. Marietta and I used to stack the boxes outside the garage door, and for months they would wait for his return, as did I. Then after he would come back, he would disappear even longer.

Once he was done building them, he'd take me out into the field. It had been the only one-on-one time we would spend, out there with the tall grass tickling at my legs. No trees or people, only land for miles and looking up into the clear Texas skies. Together, we would fly the plane far after the sun had set. He would keep his words to himself, locked away. He was barely ever present, but in times when he was flying, he was present—the only time I'd ever seen a spark of life in him. All other times, he was trapped in distant memories, his mind always somewhere else. A place I didn't exist.

On a rare occasion, he'd come into my room at night smelling like sawdust and motor oil and sit beside my bed. It was the only time he had talked about Freya, my mother. He hesitantly pushed locks off my forehead as he cried, apologizing for his misery. He'd said it was his fault he couldn't climb out of it. That this slow and painful death of living without her was unbearable, but he had to go on because he'd made a promise.

Monday broke apart my daze when she said, "Jonah let us off the hook for the day but said to keep our beepers on us. Let's go shopping."

I scanned the room. Jonah had already left. Julian had already left. The room was nearly empty, only a few stragglers gossiping at the doors.

"Fallon, hey," she snapped her finger in front of me, and our eyes locked. "Defy Superstition Day, remember? It's in like three weeks, and if we wait any longer, everything will be sold out."

"I need to check on Benny first, make sure he's alright." I hated to leave him alone just as much as Gramps hated me hanging around, but if something were to happen, and I wasn't there to help, I didn't know if I could forgive myself.

"Yeah, sure," Monday nodded, "Go on and check on him then meet us at the gazebo in thirty. We'll wait for you."

IT WAS LATE MORNING. GRAMPS WAS HALF ASLEEP WITH THE FINISHED CROSSWORD puzzle and an empty coffee mug on the bedside table. The sun settled high in the sky, beaming across his wrinkled face. I pulled the curtains closed and turned to clean up the table.

"Just leave it, why don't ya," he muttered under his shaky breath.

"Are you hungry?" There were still leftovers in the fridge from the soup Mina had dropped off after the storm passed, and word got around that Dr. Morley had made a house call. "I can heat up that chowder."

In deep, dark circles, the moon phase calendar printed in the newspaper was circled so hard the pencil had pierced through the paper.

"If I wanted chowdah don't yah think I woulda gotten up by now?" he argued. "I don't want the damn chowdah, moonshine."

I bit the inside of my cheek and cleared off the table, tucking the newspaper under my arm and holding the coffee mug in one hand, the used tissue bundle in the other. Before I reached the door, I turned back around.

"You know, Benny. I don't ask for much. I came all the way out here, more than willing to take care of you, no questions asked. The least you could do is treat me with respect."

"I don't know how many times I told yah, I nevah asked yah to come. Nevah wanted yah heyah in the first place!" His eyes brewed with indignation, a coldness.

My heart slammed inside my chest as a thousand needles poked behind my eyes. But I would not cry in front of the man or increase his stress. Instead, I closed the door, fell back against it, and held back the tsunami inside me.

The empty mug shook in my hand. I looked down, forcing my hand to steady. *Calm down, calm down, calm down …*

Whenever Gramps had the chance to remind me he didn't want me here, I had to remind myself he was the only family I had left, and the same for him. Past the cruel exterior, I knew he wanted me here too. Why couldn't he admit it?

I placed the cup in the sink and went to stack the newspaper on the windowsill with the others, when a circle around a specific date grabbed my attention.

TWO FULL MOONS FOR THE MONTH OF OCTOBER
STARTING WITH THE 1ST.

Based on how the year has gone, expect this October to be filled with magic, murder, & madness. The full moons could show kindness, a cursing, or unveil truths that have been buried.

FALLON

chapter ten

OH MY STARS BOUTIQUE WAS LOCATED ON THE EAST SIDE OF TOWN SQUARE. When I'd visited Voodoos Bar, Fable and I clicked instantly, but I hadn't gotten to know the other two sisters, Ivy and Adora.

All three sisters were a year or two apart in age, all three beautiful and bewitching in their own, opposite ways.

Ivy was the oldest, with the coal-black hair that angled sharply at her shoulders. Fable was the youngest, with fawn skin and chestnut-colored hair that flowed to her waistline. Adora was the middle, tendrils the color of honey dripping down her tanned skin, and she'd been the most distant from me since I'd arrived.

The glossy floor had been hand-painted into a swirling galaxy of purples, blues, and blacks, whereas the walls and ceiling a crisp white. Clothes and dresses hung from silver rods, stretching up and down the walls. Circular tables showcased shoes, masks, and costume jewelry.

The heels of my boots sent an echo off the tile. "The floor is gorgeous."

"It is, isn't it?" Adora sighed, pulling her joined hands to her chest. "Fable doesn't take compliments well, but she's a true art*iest*." She kissed the tips of her fingers.

Fable rolled her eyes from behind the counter, having to work this shift. "I just don't respond to compliments well," she corrected. "Doesn't mean I don't take them."

"What do people wear to this Superstition Day anyway?"

"It depends on whether you will defy or not. If you defy, you wear a mask so the universe can't see you," Monday said, holding a black leather jacket out in front of her with studs and spikes at the shoulders. Her head fell to the side, a lollipop stick poking from between her lips. "If you're not defying, you're basically just drinking and avoiding superstitions. But the people in masks will be out to get ya, try and force ya to break 'em."

"I'm wearing a mask," Fable added. "I'm not having a repeat of last year."

"Oh, last year was so good," Ivy joined in with a laugh. "Remember that?" She turned to face Adora, her straight black hair slapping her cheek like a dark storm. Adora absentmindedly nodded as she draped another shirt over her arm. I hadn't found one thing yet.

"Those who don't wear masks, you try to push them to defy superstitions. Fable..." she paused to calm her laughing fit, "By the end of the night, Fable was so drunk, she ended up toasting with a shot of water after I'd switched out her glass. And the worst part? It was with crazy Jasper Abbott."

Monday, Adora, and Ivy all lurched forward with a loud cackle.

Fable did not.

"'*I'm so sorry, Jasper. It wasn't me. I didn't mean to,*'" Ivy mocked Fable and what had happened the year before.

"And look at him now," Fable pointed out, a finger pressing the air.

"Oh, stop. The man's still alive," Adora said.

"I don't get it."

"You don't *cheers* someone with water unless you're wishing death upon them," Monday explained. "Just grab a mask. You'll be better off. No one will mess with you." She picked up a Greco Roman mask from the center table and handed it to me. "This one suits you."

It was silver with a beaded design around the edges and eyes. "Guess I'm wearing a mask then."

If I'd told myself a year ago I would be in Weeping Hollow, taking care of my grandfather and picking out a mask for Defy Superstition Day, no way would I have believed it.

"Oh, wicked." Adora gasped with a devious smile. Her long blonde hair piled over one shoulder as she shifted the clothes that were lining her arm.

"I have the perfect dress to match that."

Adora waited outside the curtain of the dressing room. I gazed at myself in the mirror with the black leather dress glued to my skin. It was a scoop neck, the hem hitting at my upper thigh, with capped sleeves. It was something I'd wear, but never to a small-town festival. I turned and reached for the zipper at my back.

"Won't I be overdressed?" I called out from behind the curtain.

Adora pushed it to the side and pulled it closed behind her. She walked behind me in the mirror and pulled my white hair off one shoulder and draped it onto the other when it cascaded down to my waist.

I felt the zipper tug at my back. "You know, Fallon," she started, keeping her green eyes on me in the mirror. "I have a feeling you're going to be trouble. Especially in this dress." But there was no smile on her face, no humor in her tone. The zipper slowly slid up my back as her breath hit my neck.

"Hardly," I tried to say, and I wanted to say more, but the air grew thicker in the room. It was too small for the both of us. Too enclosed. My lips pressed together when her pointed red nails dragged down the length of my arm.

A weak and unbelieving smile embraced Adora's pouty lips. "As much as I hate it, you have to become one of us."

I swallowed. "Why do you hate it?" She didn't know me. Out of the three sisters, Fable was the only one who took any interest in getting to know me. Adora hadn't talked to me until today.

"Because I was supposed to be with Kane."

"But I'm not Kane's type, he said so himself." I turned to face her. "You have nothing to worry about." I was hardly competition, and Adora was beautiful. Plus, I didn't have space in my mind for anyone else when Julian Blackwell consumed most of my thoughts.

I couldn't shake the dream. It was so real—too real. And tonight, I was going back to Norse woods to prove it.

Adora's fingers dug into my hips, pulling me back to the moment, and she pinned me forward as she stayed behind, pressing her chest to my back.

"It doesn't matter. He'll choose you. All I'm asking is for you to keep all the flirting and closeness away from me when he does. I don't want to see it." Her words were like an iceberg. Hard and cold, yet slowly melting under the waters of her emotions. She embodied the same kind of heartbreak I'd seen mar many faces of the ghosts who would come to me.

"Adora, you have the wrong idea about me," I assured her, still trying to process the fact she saw me as being something a man could want.

"No, sweetheart. *You* have the wrong idea about *us*."

And with that, Adora disappeared behind the curtain, leaving me alone in the dressing room.

I WAITED UNTIL AFTER GRAMPS FELL ASLEEP IN HIS RECLINER WITH STEPHEN KING'S *Lisey's Story* resting on his lap.

It was a quarter after midnight. I quietly locked the door behind me, walked to the garage, and rolled the scooter to the street. I didn't want to wake him.

If my gut was correct, the dead birds would still be piled somewhere in those woods, proving whatever had happened the other night wasn't a dream, and I couldn't let this go until I knew the truth.

The streets were busy, all the shops were open. Lamp posts gleamed a dim yellow over the square. Children played in the grass and high-schoolers sprawled out in the gazebo, watching as I drove past on the scooter.

Through the diamond-paned window of The Bean, the Sullivan sisters, Monday, and the guys from their coven were gathered around a table, drinking from their mugs, smiling and laughing and … belonging.

I parked behind the funeral home and entered the woods, desperate and on a mission to find answers. To prove I wasn't crazy.

An eerie hush fell over the woods and shadows contorted sluggishly, compelled by the wind. Leaves and pine needles crackled under my boots with every step into the dark. The only light were the constellations in the black sky. I hadn't been walking long, but as I drew deeper between the trees, the lights from inside the houses lining the Norse Words faded.

A hoot from an owl ricocheted in the canopies and shuddered across my skin, but I kept walking. *I could find my way back*, I thought, underestimating the nighttime as it pressed on me from all sides. I breathed in the cool air more rapidly, quickening my steps.

An orange glimmer appeared off in the distance. As I drew nearer, voices from a group of guys grew louder until they came into view. Four of them sat around a fire behind a cabin. I sank against a tree, hoping none of them could see me.

"—and when you said you have a certain taste, I almost died, Jules." One laughed.

"Morgan's all right," another said. "If you're into a hit of anthrax …"

"You could lay her across the table and snort the freakshow."

Freakshow. And my heart caved inside my chest.

"Snort her? I wouldn't touch her with a ten-foot pole."

Laughter bounced into the night.

I didn't want to hear any more, but I was stuck at a standstill. I took a careful step backward, and a twig snapped, causing a bird to fly from the branches. A stir within the woods. I held my breath.

Four Heathens jumped up from their chairs and peered into the woods in my direction. I braced myself against the tree, making sure none of my limbs were sticking out.

"Who's out there?" one of them called.

"You see anything, Jules?"

"I'll go check it out."

This was my shot. I could run now, and they couldn't catch me. But I couldn't move. I was frozen here behind this tree, willing my feet to do something, but nothing would come of it. I threw my head back against the bark and bit my lip, breathing slowly in and out of my nose. Footsteps followed the silence. I'd lost my chance because if I were to run now, they could tackle me to the ground.

Someone was nearing. My heart pounded, his every step foreboding on the damp earth. Then he walked past me, wearing black slacks and a black coat, black hair styled as if he'd woken up like that.

It was Julian, and he stood there for a moment with his head fixed straight, his back to me. I watched how his shoulder blades moved inside his coat, the subtle tilt of his head, listening to the secrets sewn into the trees.

"What is it?" a voice called out from behind.

Julian turned, and his gaze slammed into mine.

For a moment, his empty gaze stared into my scared one. Then his eyes filled with something I didn't recognize. A mixture of something familiar and fearful.

He pressed his pointer finger to his mask in a *quiet* gesture as he stepped closer until the tips of his boots touched the tips of my oxford shoes.

"It's nothing," he called back to the others, then his voice fell to a whisper, "You can't be here."

"Was last night real?" I begged quietly, needing to know. "Tell me it was real. Tell me I'm not crazy."

"You're crazy." Julian's eyes squinted. "There, I said it. Now leave."

He took a step away, and it cut me open. My head slowly shook as it didn't make sense. If he was right, and it was all a dream, he wouldn't hide me like this. He wouldn't have lied to his friends about me being here.

My hand darted out and latched on to his.

Julian froze under our joined hands.

Beats passed, and he hung his head.

"Please, Julian. Be real with me." My thumb grazed his skin. He clutched on to mine tighter, and the silence of the night shaped us into one for a few shallow breaths. Then he turned and walked me back against the tree. He grabbed the back of my neck and tilted my head back.

The lump in Julian's throat bobbed. His eyes sailed over my features as I was arrested in his hold.

"I'll come to you, but you can't tell anyone," he whispered. I nodded, and his gaze moved past me to the others before hitting mine again. Then he let me go, disappearing and leaving me with a pounding heart.

"Let's head to Voodoos," he called out to the others, giving me a way out of the woods.

The fire clicked off in an instant, erasing heat and light all at once.

I waited long after their voices faded and I was certain they were gone before darting back through the woods.

I couldn't remember how long I'd run between trees, over grooved ruts, no distinct way out, every turn seeming the same. Was I running in circles? The woods seemed to morph around me, taunting me as my legs burned, but thoughts of Julian kept pushing me farther.

"I'll come to you," he'd said ...

My foot caught on a protruding root, and I was thrown face down against the hard earth, something crunching beneath me.

Dried, crusted blood, velvety wings, and bone fragments painted the forest floor. A scream caught in my throat as I shuffled back to my feet, swiping at my hands, my arms, my legs, my hair, trying to get the stench and remains of death off of me.

My gaze darted around the raven graveyard. The birds' eyes had turned white like cataracts, and their bodies were shredded apart in pieces and scattered.

It was all real. Julian had killed them all. The wild and desperate look in his eyes, his crazed pulse in his fingers beating against my neck, the blood, the way his lips skimmed across mine, then the dark void in his face.

The terror.

It had all been real, and memories of it slammed into my skull. *"Death is coming..."* he'd said, and it was his voice that followed me all the way out of the woods. "... *and I can't* STOP IT."

FALLON
chapter eleven

FOR HOURS, I PACED MY BEDROOM AS THE COLD
nightly breeze played upon my cheeks, which braced
my already startling nerves. I sat on the edge of the bed,
talked to Casper, pulled a magazine from my bag, tried to read, but nothing
could calm my restless mind. In a few hours, the sun would rise without a
sign of Julian.

Casper sprawled out at the foot of the bed and watched as I walked
about, the planked floors creaking under my bare feet.

One green eye and one blue eye remained fixed on my every move as
Casper listened intently with his ears twitching to my voice.

"It was real," I said through a sigh, then sat beside him and ran my
fingers through his soft white mane. "A dream would have made things
easier."

Casper meowed, as manly as a boy cat could meow, then arched his
back against my palm.

"No, it wouldn't have," a voice said, and my head snapped to the sound.

Behind the thin veil of the woven curtains, Julian stood on my balcony,
away from the railing, looking out into the ocean. Though the moon's light
illuminated him, he cast no shadow.

"You saw me kill all those birds, and you still went back to the woods
to find me." He turned, and through the shadows of the night, his cold and
silvery eyes assaulted me. "I told you—*crazy.*"

A shot of adrenaline forced my muscles to flinch under my skin, and

Casper jumped from my bed to his favorite spot on the armoire. My throat went dry as he walked closer, and a turbulent desire tumbled to the tips of my fingers down to my toes.

I cleared my throat. "I had to make sure what happened was real."

Julian stood over me—the night sky through the opened French doors behind him—and my palms began to sweat from gripping the edge of the mattress.

"Did you tell anyone what you saw? What I did?" Only his eyes were visible. Two slits above the mask line.

"No, I wouldn't do that," I clipped out, and my shoulders slacked in defeat. "But what *did* happen last night between us? And why did you kill those birds?" I had so many questions.

Another quietness swept the room. I grew impatient, but just when my mouth opened to speak, Julian crossed his arms. He looked at me with hollow eyes, the light color popping against his thick black lashes.

"I snapped," he said, resolved, remembering as his gaze remained distant. "No matter how many I—" his words stopped there, and he shook his head, "—more come, more sing, more haunt me. It doesn't stop. It only gets worse."

"The ravens, they're some kind of death omen?" I asked, remembering Marietta's folklore about ravens, black beetles, and white moths. The deliverers of fate.

Julian dropped his head in a somber nod.

Another question surfaced. My chest ached from the mere thought of it, and I couldn't understand why. I pulled my bottom lip between my teeth, but the words still escaped despite my fight. I had to know. "Are you going to die?"

Julian's brows pinned together. "You see me kill birds because of a death omen, and you ask if it's *me* who's dying?"

"What is that supposed to mean?" I felt my heated flesh turn into a white chill as if the blood drained from my feet. I tried to swallow down the unsettling panic. "Is it Benny? Me?"

"Someday, yeah. We're all slowly dying." He was blunt, a quick jab to the gut. He ran his hand through his black hair, probably noticing the horror on my face. "I don't know who it's for," Julian finally admitted, then looked behind his shoulder and shifted in place before sliding his gaze back to me. "It doesn't matter, it's not the reason I agreed to come."

"Then why did you come?"

I took notice in the way Julian took his time responding. It was as if I could see the words scroll rapidly in the cracks of his careful mind through his eyes.

"I'm not a fan of making assumptions until I'm sure of something. I'm the same way with people. But, based on your unwelcomed drop-ins lately, I can see you're the type who doesn't stop until you have all the answers, and in Weeping Hollow, there are no answers. Reality bends here. Same with time. Some days it's hard to tell the difference between what's real and what isn't. This town can make you go mad the harder you try to figure it out. So, don't. You have to stay away from the woods. You have to stay away from me."

"And if I don't want to?" *If I can't now?*

A steel storm stirred in his intense eyes. "Haven't you witnessed enough? I am the dark, cursed stranger they all warned you about," he mocked, his chest rising and falling heavily, and he slapped his palm to his chest. "I could kill you. I *should* have killed you," he said with a battle in his eyes. "It's who I am."

"I don't know what exactly happened last night, but whatever happened, it wasn't your fault ..." I started to say, and he dropped his head, shaking it as if he was refusing to hear it. "I saw you. You were scared, and it was almost like..."

Julian looked at me from the corner of his eyes. "Like what?"

My mouth went dry. "I don't know, like you needed me..." The words sounded strange outside my head. "And something tells me you would never intentionally hurt me or anyone, and maybe I can help." I paused to catch my breath. "I don't see you the same way they do, Julian. I'm not afraid like the rest of them."

"Don't be stupid. You're afraid of *something*, and that's enough." Julian raised his brows. "Do you have any idea what I can do?" I snapped my jaw shut. "Whenever you see my face in its entirety, all you'll be able to see is your fears. And when you looked at me last night, I was there with you in that dark place you're so afraid of. I felt your terror. I heard your screams.

I felt it in my own throat! Whatever happened between us in the woods," he leaned over, looked me in the eyes with my head in the palms of his hands, "Whatever *that* was, it was torn away as soon as you looked at me. You should have died."

Oxygen froze- in my lungs, and my heart raced as if all the stars had died and shot across the skies of my chest.

Realization dawned in Julian's eyes at how close we were, and he pulled his hands away and ran one through his hair, gripping the back of his neck.

Everything Fable and Monday had told me about the Hollow Heathens were true. They were cursed, and I witnessed it first-hand. I had looked at his face and was thrown back into the well of my childhood.

The reality of it all crept along my spine. "How did I get home? I don't remember going home after that."

"You passed out, and I brought you home." Julian released a heavy breath. "I can tell the difference, and your fear seemed more like a memory. How did you end up in that place? Is that why you are afraid of the dark?"

"The *dark*?" There was an unintentional bite in my words, and I didn't mean for it to come out that way. I shook my head. "It's not the dark I'm afraid of."

"Then what is it?"

"Does it matter?"

"Yes," he snapped.

"Why?"

Julian sat beside me at the edge of the mattress and dropped his elbows to his knees, hanging his head between his shoulders. A heavy exhale left him as I held mine, waiting for a response.

When he lifted his head, his gaze slid to mine. "You're the only person who's looked into my face that I haven't killed. You survived, and it doesn't make sense. No one has survived me before."

For some reason, I trusted the stranger in my room who had the power to pull me back into my fears. I had no reason to trust him, but I did. If all this was true, Julian had experienced that terrible night from when I was a kid right along with me less than twenty-four hours ago, and he was the only one who could understand it.

We were connected in some kind of way.

My entire body shifted on the mattress to face him.

"Confinement," I spilled, my fingers fidgeting in my lap. I'd never told anyone before, and it felt as if a burden lifted with my confession. "Small places, walls, confinement, my freedom taken away ... being trapped. All of it. If I can't escape..." I couldn't finish the sentence. I couldn't think more about it, so I let it die off there. And it was as if the world had gone silent with my declaration.

Julian turned too, giving me all of his attention. His hand came over my naked thigh. "Tell me what happened."

It felt so new and familiar at the same time, and a shudder ripped up the ladder of my spine. He was here, making places tingle that had never been touched, gazing at me with a fierce tenderness. He was here, making me feel things I'd never felt before.

I scanned the room, questioning if I was even awake.

Maybe I'd never woken up at all.

Reality bends here. "Is *this* real?" I think I asked aloud, the sound of the clock sitting on my nightstand ticking, playing behind the silence.

Julian caught my eyes with his. "Do you want it to be?"

"Yes." I'd said it so quickly, not having to think. *Yes, I did.*

"Tell me what happened," he insisted.

Casper meowed from the armoire, watching our exchange closely. Julian removed his hand and leaned back, bracing himself with his palms on each side of him.

The man was gentle and intense. How was it possible? The moonlight dragged a shadow across him, and his light eyes punched through the layer of darkness, probing for me to continue. So, I did, but not without a shaken breath.

"I was only seven. The kids on my street constantly teased and harassed me, followed me all the way home from the bus stop. They used to call me the spawn of Satan, an evil witch ... *freakshow*. Whatever evil thing you could imagine, that's what they called me. *'Don't look into her eyes,'* they'd say," and my words broke at the seams of my childhood.

I paused to contain my emotions, to keep them at bay. Julian's posture turned rigid, but his eyes never left me, even when I had to look away.

"One day we were walking home from the bus stop, and they wouldn't stop. They pushed me around. They stole my backpack. They pulled my hair. They mocked me. They taunted me. Then they pushed me inside a well because *that's where witches belong*. In Hell. And at first, I couldn't get up. My whole side hurt so bad … but at some point, I did. And all night long, I tried to get out. I tried so hard that my nails ripped from my fingers. I was bleeding, hurt, alone, and convinced I was going to die. It was the longest night of my life."

I shuddered at the mere thought of going back there. And I knew for certain, if I'd ever see Julian's face, I would be back there in that well, and my chest tightened. I continued so he wouldn't notice, "My nanny, Marietta, she found me. For thirteen hours, I was in there," I shook my head, "Jaxon Jenkins lost his sight the next day. Brady Matthews went mute a week later … and … after that, no one would come near me or touch me or talk to me. They were *nice*," the word tasted bitter on my tongue, "because they were scared of me and the things I could possibly do."

"The Order was right. Nothing's changed," Julian mumbled, his brows pinched together in deep thought. "The world is still the same after all these years." He peered at me. "But you didn't do those things to those kids? After everything they did to you?"

"No. Even if I could, I wouldn't," I shook my head and pinched the edge of the mattress. "But, now I'm thinking it really was Marietta, and if she *could* do those things, she'd only do something like that to protect me. She wasn't evil." I looked up to Julian. "I've never told anyone that before. Not even my dad."

Julian's glazed and tormented eyes dwelled on me with all their madness; I noticed the wrinkle between his brows deepen, an understanding or a sorrow. I noticed these things, and it did something crazy to my heart.

The silence between us was comfortable yet loud. I couldn't understand what he was thinking, so I shredded the silence with my voice. "But then I get here, and it's as if everyone wants to be my friend. Usually, I'm the girl everyone is scared of, the one who everyone avoided, but not here. It's different here."

"Because they all want something from you," he answered. "They want you in their coven."

"Except you," I pointed out, focusing on keeping my voice steady. "You don't care. In fact, if memory serves me correctly," I started, remembering what he'd said at the Town Hall meeting, "You have a certain taste. Wanting someone like me would be absurd."

His gaze froze on me. "I was—"

"'Cause I'm a *freakshow*, right?"

Julian's eyes turned to slits. "Fallon—"

"No, I heard you guys in the woods. I heard what you all said about me. I've heard it my entire life. I always hear what they say about me as if I'm not there, as if it doesn't hurt. But it does hurt! You said so yourself, you saw my memory. Do you think I enjoyed what they did to me? What I had to listen to from your friends? You think being no one's *taste* doesn't hurt? God forbid anyone took the time to actually get to know me."

Julian's posture stiffened, his gaze ran cold. A growl thundered inside him, holding back the same turmoil he released at Voodoos.

He jumped up, snatched my arm, and yanked me across the room to the full-length mirror standing in the corner of the dim room until I was confronted with my reflection. My heart hammered as he stood behind me, his chest slamming against my back.

He looked down at my confused expression. My eyes fell to the girl in the mirror with no makeup, bright white skin, and even whiter hair. Colorless, the scary glass blue eyes in the mirror stared back, and I turned my head away.

"No. Look at yourself," he commanded, his voice like sandpaper.

Julian wrapped his fingers around my jaw and forced my head forward until my eyes slammed into my own again.

"What are you doing?" I tried to maneuver my way out of his hold, but his grip tightened, one hand locked around my jaw, the other on my hipbone.

"You *are* a freak," he said slowly into my ear. I closed my eyes, and he squeezed my jaw until they popped open. "You're an insecure freakshow. Anthrax. Powder. The spawn of Satan. Ghost. Mutant. A strange fucking thing. Look at you!" His voice grew louder with every word.

My vision blurred as I tried to fight against his tight grip. He pinned me against his chest to keep me still. "Are those tears coming? That's ... what?" He tilted his head, mockery in his eyes, and I wished I could squeeze mine shut. "Twenty-four years of listening to them? Of letting them define you? Because you care so much about what everyone else thinks, right?"

"Stop," I gritted through clenched teeth, tears pooling and shaking in the rims of my eyes. I tried to shake my head from his grasp.

Julian had turned into something else. Something screaming. Something raw. Something candid and cruel. The shape of a passionate shadow, the color of cutthroat. Was it something I said? "Why are you doing this?"

"Me? You're doing this to yourself," he insisted, breathing hard, chest beating against my back. "And it's sad. Acceptance is a ten-letter prison we're all eager to be locked in." His glossy eyes wild and alive. "You let everyone else tell you who you are, and you listen. You let what's out of your control, control you! And look at what you've become—locked in your personal hell surrounded by the bars of these insults. This is *your* fault. At the end of the day, the only person to blame is you. And now that's all you are. A little. Fucking. Freakshow. Still left inside that well all those years ago. You never left."

My eyes narrowed, and I pushed back against him. Julian forced my head forward again and curled his hand into my waist, bringing me back to his front as he continued, "I bet these words haunt you. You wear the very mask those hypocrites made every day, and I bet it's heavier than mine."

Silent tears slipped down my numbed face and spilled over his fingers.

Julian paused as his eyes zeroed in on them. Then he flipped up his mask only to reveal his mouth, his vibrant scarlet lips.

His tongue darted out and licked my tears from his knuckles. "Tastes like a salty little freakshow, too." His eyes sailed to mine. "People will always have something to say, but it's your fault you become it. At least you can fight back. Some of us don't have that luxury."

My bottom bucked against him, and Julian's right hand came over my throat.

I froze.

Julian froze.

My scared eyes locked on his eyes that were thrashing in conflict.

Then the confliction snapped, and all that was left was a weak and vulnerable man who couldn't catch a solid breath. And time slowed. His movements slowed. His touch slowed. His breathing slowed.

Julian gathered my hair and pulled it off my shoulder. The grip around my throat became gentle as he tilted my head. And my heart was beating so fast. I couldn't feel anything aside from his hands on me, and his finger dipping into the hem of my cardigan over my shoulder. They grazed my bare skin as he slipped the material off one side, and goosebumps flared across my flesh.

Then he kissed my shoulder so softly it felt like wings or a whisper. I didn't understand, couldn't conform to a single thought.

I watched his mouth, his soft lips trailing my skin, and felt myself slipping and heating and falling as my lashes fluttered, having no idea what was happening; how I went from angry to sad to … this. But what was this? This feeling I never wanted to go away? What was it called?

His tongue licked the length of my shoulder to the crook of my neck. His hot mouth covered my flesh. My knees weakened, but his hands on me, his mouth on my skin, all kept me bound to him. It was torturous yet not enough as the same heat rocketed to the space between my legs. His lips were shaped as if cut by a sharp blade yet felt so delicate against my flesh when he landed one last kiss on my neck.

Julian lifted his head and blew an icy breath across my throat where his mouth had just been.

"There," he said, finally calm and collected, admiring his work before his silvery eyes snapped up to mine in the mirror. "This time, when you wake up in the morning, you'll see this and know tonight was real." He pulled my cardigan over my shoulder and released his hand from around my throat. *"And you'll* REMEMBER TO *STAY out of the woods."*

FALLON
chapter twelve

THE SOUND OF MY BEEPER GOING OFF WOKE ME THE NEXT MORNING. The balcony doors swung slightly back and forth, and I rubbed my eyes to see the sun coming up over the horizon. An indigo blur burning across the Atlantic Ocean.

I ran my fingers across the hickey he left me. It pulsed in my neck as if it were a thing with a heartbeat of its own.

I jumped to my feet, scurried across the wooden floors, and looked in the mirror. The bruise was deep purple. A mark of where his mouth had been. I closed my eyes when the memory of last night flashed behind them.

He'd arrived so abruptly and left all the same. He'd left me with a warning, with a craving, with a demand to stay out of the woods. And I would stay out of the woods, but I knew he wouldn't stay out of my mind.

Especially not with his mark pulsing under my skin.

After quickly getting ready, I called Jonah from the house phone in the kitchen as I put on a pot of coffee for Gramps. Jonah had said to meet him at a trailer in a Norse Woods neighborhood. He'd said he couldn't wait for me, and that he would drive the hearse for transport and wait for my arrival.

A trailer park was tucked away in the woods past Voodoos Bar. The black hearse sat in front of a single-wide hoisted up on cinder blocks, a broken lattice fencing wrapped around the bottom.

A small crowd gathered behind yellow tape blocking the home's perimeter. I spotted Jonah trying to calm down a neighbor with a police officer and Monday at his side.

"What took you so long?" Monday asked, pushing her way through an enraged mob.

The scene was utter chaos. Curses and accusations filled my ears as she pulled me through the crowd. *"The Parish should perish!"* some chanted. *"Murderer!" "Our town isn't safe anymore!"*

Milo was there too, carrying a notepad glued to his hand with another girl holding a tape recorder, interviewing and searching for an exclusive. I scanned the trailer park, noticing people watching the scene play out from their porch steps. Some from inside their homes, peeking through blinds or behind curtains. My gaze bounced around the street, seeing cars lined up along the curb.

It dawned on me.

The angry townies weren't neighbors at all.

The attire, the hair, the shoes. They were all upper class from the east side.

My eyes widened. "What the hell is going on?"

Monday shot me a wide-eyed look as she lifted the tape and pulled me underneath.

Beck was sitting on the trailer steps with a cigarette between his tattooed fingers. He had his hood up and his head down, smoke rising from the dark void of his face. He looked up with a distant gaze, his knee bouncing uncontrollably.

I'd only known it was Beck Parish because I'd seen him in the cemetery digging graves countless times now. I recognized his build, his demeanor, and the way he carried himself, with icy waters lurking in the irises of his soul.

Monday ushered me past him and into the mobile home. Cigarette smoke and a stale breath of booze loomed in the air like a shadow.

We walked straight into the living room where a man was sitting on a beaten couch with his head in his hands. Faux-wood vinyl sided every wall. The carpet was dingy and stained. The home, if one could even call it that, was an ashtray and graveyard for empty beer cans and take-out boxes.

Brown work boots peeked from behind a coffee table where a body was lying.

"This is Earl Parish. Beck's dad," Monday introduced the man who was sitting on the couch, and he glanced up from his hands with a shirt tied around his face. An elixir of anger and agony boiled in his glossy blue eyes. *Beck's father.*

Monday knelt beside the body that laid face down on the floor, and I followed her. There was no blood, and rigor mortis had already set in, which only meant he'd been lying here for at least three to four hours. The body was trapped in a death chill, and his skin was pale with purple blotches at the underside where the body met the floor.

"Ready to talk, Earl?" someone asked, and I turned to see another officer standing under the opened doorway. "Beck, Julian, no one's talking, and I'm getting answers today. I'll take you all three down to the station if I have to."

Jonah pushed through the front door. "Officer Stoker, a word, please," he insisted, gripping the officer's elbow.

And that was when I saw it. A dark outline of a figure cowered behind the front door that was hung open. The spirit yanked at his thinning hair behind the door, spewing curses only I could hear. Shocked and scared eyes fixed on his dead body—the body he'd inhabited only hours before and only a shell of what he used to be—as everyone else moved about the trailer as if he weren't there.

But he was there. I saw him, enraged, scared, and powerless.

The officer went on again, threatening Earl.

Jonah was growing impatient, steering Officer Stoker away from Earl.

"What ar-ya thinking?" Monday asked.

Another officer came into the house, requesting for more backup to control the mob outside.

The ghost stepped out from the corner screaming for someone to hear him.

A ringing hummed in my ears as the room swayed, my knees weakening from the chaos unfolding around me. My breathing turned hollow. My palms were sweating.

Too many people. Too many voices.

I slapped my hands over my ears to erase the noise. "QUIET!"

Everyone, including the ghost, studied me from where they froze with piercing scrutiny. Even the shouting outside dimmed by my voice. My palms dropped from my ears.

"Take it outside," I announced. "Let me do my job in here." What I really wanted was to see if I could get through to the ghost. The spirits came first. They *always* came first.

"Yeah," Monday added.

I looked at her. "You too, Monday."

"Wait, what?"

Either I had to admit how strange I indeed was, or I'd have to leave the ghost of this man here to fend for himself, to be lost and unsure of what had happened to him. Because I had this gift, I'd always felt it was my responsibility to help them, talk them through it.

Some spirits wanted nothing more than to make sure their death was avenged. Others wanted to watch karma play its part in a slow and torturous manner. For some, it was worse and more fun that way since their pain tethered them here, allowing them to stick around and watch. But watching turned them into the maddening and crazed kind of spirits—the ones who could never find peace.

"Please," I stated in a calmer voice. "I just need a minute."

The officer took Earl out of the room and down the steps where the angry town's people awaited him, Jonah and Monday close behind. As the door was closing behind them, I caught a glimpse of Julian, who was standing in front of Beck, and my heart skipped inside my chest. Julian lifted his eyes to mine just as the door shut, closing me inside alone with a dead body, a ghost, and the aftermath of a harrowing incident.

I sucked in a breath and turned my attention to the ghost in the corner of the room. "What's your name?"

"What happened to me? How is it that I'm standing here? Put me back in! I'm fine! You make this go away." His enlarged eyes looked over his hands, his shirt, grasping at himself frantically. "Fix me!"

"I can't, you're already dead," I said slowly, hoping to soothe his energy. They had never physically hurt me before, and I didn't know if it was at all possible. "Can you tell me what happened?"

"I-I-can't remember," he stuttered, then his stutter turned into a roar, and he banged his palm repeatedly against the side of his head. "Why can't I remember?!"

"Because you haven't accepted what's happened to you yet. You need to accept it, then your memories will come back."

"How do you know this? Who are you?"

"Fallon. Fallon Grimaldi." *You're a Grimaldi,* Marietta had always told me, and I didn't know why I'd said Grimaldi at that moment, but it felt right, as if it would answer all the burning questions inside him. I was a *Grimaldi.* A girl who could see and talk to ghosts. A girl whose father was a witch, and a mother I still knew nothing about.

Yes, I was a Morgan, but I was a Grimaldi, too, and maybe that meant something.

I didn't know how much time had passed as I watched his expression twist into different phases, almost as if he was trying to accept, trying to remember. He stared at the walls, the door, and the floor like the room was speaking to him.

"Jury." Then he looked at me. "My name is Jury Smith."

I nodded, keeping silent to not break his train of thought.

"I was out of it ... I don't know how I ended up there, but I was *so* mad. I came here to confront Earl about something, and he was just as surprised to see me. But it had to be about something. *Kill Earl ...*" His eyes darted behind him to the door. "There was another man! He ... he jumped me from behind!" He looked at his hand, and his face transformed as if a light went off with a memory. "I was holding something in my hand, but it was knocked to the ground." His eyes slid to the couch.

I followed his gaze to the couch and looked underneath. There was a knife, but there was no blood anywhere. The knife couldn't have been used.

"His face," he continued, "I'd never seen something so ... so ..."

"Scary?" I asked on my knees beside the couch, my heart slamming

137

inside my chest as I looked up at the ghost who held a world of terror in his deadened eyes.

His jaw slammed shut, and he shook his head vehemently, gripping the ends of his hair.

"What did you see?" I probed further.

"Would you believe me if I told you a clown is hiding in there? In that face of his?" he asked, coming from the dark corner of the room with wrinkles in his drooping forehead. "The clown, it choked me with one hand. I couldn't breathe." The ghost clawed at the shirt covering his stomach, lifting it and exposing his hairy gut. "He stabbed me! I remember the pain in my lungs!"

We both lowered our gaze and examined his stomach as he twisted in place, but there were no lacerations or knife wounds. The ghost dropped his shirt, his body shaking.

Then he looked up at me through strange pale eyes. "But I felt it. It fucking stabbed me."

"It? Do you mean Earl? Beck?" My stomach dropped. *Julian?*

"No!" he screamed. "THE CLOWN!"

JULIAN
later that night

I'D TOLD HER WHAT I SHOULD HAVE TOLD MYSELF ALL THESE YEARS. I'D told her all the things that I couldn't face.

Fallon Grimaldi carried the same stain on her soul as mine from the weight of rejection and insults. The fear rimming her eyes reflected my own, and perhaps that was why I noticed it—why I cringed in the way she couldn't see that she was the most real thing in this town of deceit. She carried the same lies I'd carried for twelve years, but Fallon Grimaldi wasn't enslaved by a mask. Fallon Grimaldi didn't have to hide, isolate, or become someone she wasn't.

Fallon Grimaldi was kind, not a killer like me.

Pure, not cursed like me.

She was everything I wasn't, yet looked at me—*to me*—as if we were stitched by the same string.

She looked at me, and it drove me crazy, it drove me calm. *My god*, I was at peace when I didn't deserve it. Just being around her felt as if she took a knife to my chest and sliced me open to let my darkness bleed out. Being around her felt like I crawled into myself and confronted my soul. *Being around her?* It made me feel naked, burdens on display, scars ruptured, making everything intense like an open wound. And I had snapped. *Snapped!*

I wanted to punish her and kiss her at the same time for the way she was making me feel.

I had tried to keep my cool, to keep my distance. I had promised myself I would, but how could I when she was looking at me from across the bar, powder blue eyes both challenging and filling me with her moonlight. As if I didn't kill a man less than twenty-four hours ago. As if I deserved it.

And as if her innocence wasn't already messing with my head, she had to wear a slinky black dress on top of it. The girl couldn't be taller than five-foot-two but all legs, wearing her white hair piled on her head with the hickey I gave her on full display.

I wanted Fallon Grimaldi to never forget the cursed Heathen who had shown up in her room with a warning to stay out of the woods. It was for her own good.

Hate me, moon girl. Hate me like the rest of them. Hate me as I hate me.

Because if you don't, one of us will kill you, and it will probably be me.

"Jules, you're up," Zeph sang at the corner of my eye as he walked around the pool table. I downed the rest of my drink and placed it on the shelf.

We'd come to Voodoos every Friday night since we were kids, just like our dads with their fathers. The torn green felt on the side was from when I was four, and I'd snagged it while running my 1968 Brown Custom Camaro Hot Wheels toy car across. To hide the car, I'd shoved it down the side pocket and into a hole, and it has been stuck there ever since. The car was now worth at least three thousand dollars, and the only way to exhume it was to take apart the pool table. And we loved the pool table.

The dent on the right corner happened when Beck was thirteen. I'd stolen a bottle from Earl's trailer. Drunk Earl had marched up here, grabbed the back of Beck's head, and slammed it against the corner because Beck refused to give me up. Two scars that day, which was the last time Drunk Earl was allowed inside Voodoos.

My thumb grazed the crack in the pool stick, the time Maverick smacked Zeph's sister's ass when I was sixteen. Maverick has had a lean in his stride ever since. The chip in the solid three-ball? The first time Phoenix Wildes snapped in public, and none of us really knew why he threw it across the bar six years ago. The hole was still there, an empty wooden frame around it.

He dated it and tagged it *The Gunslinger*.

We'd learned to walk around this pool table and have been walking around it every Friday night since.

We only had two rules when we played the game: no magic and no one else.

The pool table belonged to the Hollow Heathens.

I glanced back at Fallon, seeing Kane's hand drifting across her thigh under the bar. The pool stick slid between my knuckles too hard, slamming the eight-ball in behind the solid. Fallon adjusted in her seat, clearly uncomfortable, and my jaw clenched.

"You think she knows?" Beck asked, and I heard him but didn't. "You know she was in my trailer for a while after she kicked everyone out. That was strange." Beck was concerned about someone finding out I killed Jury Smith. All I was concerned about was Kane Pruitt touching Fallon's thigh when I shouldn't be. "We should have just burned the body like last time."

I caught all the words he'd said, but Fallon's eyes were on me, Kane's hand on her thigh.

Beck shoved my shoulder. "Look at you, man. You're here, and you're not."

"I am," I insisted, throwing a glance at him. Zeph re-racked the balls as I stood beside Beck, my focus back on Fallon and my grip tightening on the pool stick. "She can't prove anything."

I killed Jury Smith. Jury had shown up at Earl's trailer with a knife, crazed and out of his mind as if he'd been compelled or hexed by someone. It wasn't Earl or Beck's fault for what had happened to Jury, and there was no other way but to kill him. Jury Smith had gone to the trailer with no other intention than leaving with blood on his hands, so I'd made a decision. Everyone depended on me. And the safety of the Norse Woods Coven came first—always.

"You and I both know the dead can talk," Beck continued. I looked at him as his eyes flicked to Zeph, then back to me. His voice lowered to a whisper, "Everyone seems to forget she's a Grimaldi too. Her mother knew those woods better than you, and that's saying a lot, Jules. Freya always wandered in our woods and talked to the dead," he said. I wanted to laugh. No one knew the woods better than me. Freya Grimaldi may have walked the woods, but I slept in them. A twilight sleep-walker, curled in the womb of Norse woods as if I'd been born from her cold, hard ground. "What if she's just like her mother? Am I the only one who thinks we should corner her? See what she knows?"

Zeph's green eyes bounced up to us. He'd heard.

Over my shadow-blood would I allow Zeph or any of them near Fallon. "Cornering her would only give her reasons to pry, and quite frankly, I'm not worried about it. I did it. I killed Jury, not you. Plus, there's no proof. Let the dead sing their song. Fallon still can't prove anything."

Zeph fisted the pool stick. "If she interrupts the plans—"

I forced a laugh. "You think a flatlander with the brain of fish could screw the plan? The same plan that's been years in the making?" I clicked my tongue, faking my feelings. "You give the girl way too much credit." I wrapped my hand around the back of his neck and pinned his focus to Fallon. "Look at her. Back straight, white-knuckling her drink, can't even look her new friends in the eyes. She's hardly comfortable." *She never looked out of place with me.* "She's just a scared, insecure girl. She doesn't have the nerve to cross Kane, let alone us."

I couldn't believe my own words as they were being said. Why was I protecting her from my own?

I released Zeph, and his eyes hardened. But my attention remained on Fallon as she stared out into nothingness in deep thought. I dropped my back against the brick. She did that often when she was around them.

141

Gone, but still there. *Where are you going when you do that, Fallon?*

After another round of Zeph kicking my ass, we huddled in the corner as the DJ pumped a song through the speakers. Phoenix's rush had slowed, finally pouring us a round of shots. Fallon stood on the sidelines, shaking her head as the redhead pulled her to the dance floor. I downed the shot under the flap of my mask, wiped the corners of my mouth with two fingers, and dropped my elbow on the bar, watching her as the guys talked around me.

"Hi," a girl said over music, approaching nervously with her two friends close behind.

They were standoffish and scared of us, as they should be. Usually, no one talked to us—no one approached us—but now and then, we would get the brave soldiers who came over as a dare or mission to see if they could be with a Heathen for the night. Curious to know what it would be like, to see if we had a heart at all, or to try and change us. Monsters could have hearts too, and the truth was, we had a heart just like every other living thing. But we couldn't let anyone get close enough to feel it, see it, take it, shape it.

We had to push them away to protect them.

Because when people get close, they die.

Beck's eyes were glued to the drink in his hand. Phoenix kept his attention on the bar, and I returned mine to the dance floor, watching Fallon sway awkwardly in place with her straw between her teeth.

"My friends dared me to come over here," the curious girl continued, but neither one of us opened our mouths to speak to her. She would walk away eventually.

The rest of the silent and awkward rejection fell into the background when Kane pulled Fallon deeper into the crowd, her drink splashing down her legs. I tensed in my chair. Fallon pushed against his chest, shaking her head as her eyes darted around until they landed on me. She didn't want to. I gripped my drink.

"Not one dance?" the curious girl tried again.

Kane's hands slithered down Fallon's sides. The white shirt she was wearing under the slinky dress bunched up at the sides, revealing her smooth white skin. I lifted myself over the bar and blindly reached for a bottle.

"Not interested, now move along," Phoenix caved, annoyed, waving the flatlanders off until they scurried away. "For fuck's sake, I'm not a piece of meat," he hissed under his breath.

I chugged from the bottle as Kane used his ways on Fallon, getting her to relax.

The Pruitts were Sea Witches, having the ability to manipulate the weather, the sea, and little freakshows too, if that was who they wanted. Kane could trick and influence minds and, on his worst day, enter the unconscious, give wet dreams, lust-filled fantasies, and make anyone fall for him. Thanks to Kane's grandfather, we were all forbidden to use our magic out in the open—especially since the flatlander population had increased—but Kane was childish, a one-upper.

And his move on Fallon was all a show for me.

Kane's manipulation worked on her, too. His hands slipped into the dress's openings at her sides, and her ass grazed across his Khakis. His eyes bounced to mine, a look of victory while Fallon's lips pulled into a drunken smile—drunk on him and under his spell.

"Don't," Beck whispered all-knowingly in my ear, gauging the tell of my gaze. I could never hide anything from him—could never pretend with him. "He's seeing how you'll react."

"I don't play games."

"I know, man. I'm just saying."

Kane flashed me a cocky grin, his hands gripping Fallon's bare flesh, and I flung the empty bottle into the trash on the other side of the bar. "I'm ready to go."

Zeph cocked his head, watching me slide on my coat. "The night's still young."

Adjusting my waistband, I looked up at Fallon, an anger-induced dizziness simmering just below my surface that I couldn't quite understand. If Zeph or Phoenix noticed how much she was already getting to me, they could do something stupid. They could harm her, get rid of her. I couldn't take that chance. The reason I'd warned Fallon to stay away from the woods, away from them, away from me.

"I have an early morning at the shop."

nicole fiorina

On my way out,

THE *DARK*
pulled me
UNDER.

144

FALLON
chapter thirteen

WINDS COMBED MY HAIR AND CARESSED MY CHEEKS AS I walked home from the bar in a daze. Rolling clouds—the color of wet ash—crawled across the black sky, and a breath of dampened death lingered in the air. Fat raindrops fell like a leaky faucet, splashing my face and soaking my clothes. Water sloshed in my leather saddle shoes, and the bun in my hair had fallen, hanging off me like deadweight.

Both Kane and the girls had offered me a ride home, but I'd told them I needed to breathe.

I needed air, space, and to be away from them, but the silence was deafening, the night was whispering, and the paranoia was prickling behind my neck as my feet stumbled down Seaside Street.

I didn't know what time it was either. Time passed fast and slow here. Time passed here as if it didn't exist at all, a place of the in-between. Maybe this was where I belonged all along. Weeping Hollow, the hidden town left in limbo.

As I turned the corner to Town Square, the wind howled around me and the hickey on my neck thumped under my skin. Julian was in my head. He was everywhere and nowhere. I couldn't escape him.

Then that was when I heard it.

Small whimpers rose and fell and diffused into the air. I turned, scanning the pathway behind me. My gaze touched all of Town Square's emptiness until my eyes landed on a silver outline.

Sitting on the gazebo's steps was the little boy in the red and white striped shirt, hugging his knees that were pressed against his chest. At first, he was no more than a shimmer of mist. The staircase appeared behind him, like a poorly taken photograph from times beyond my existence.

My breath held in my lungs. My pulse sped. I should be used to situations like this, but the adrenaline was all the same.

It was the same ghost who'd led me to a distraught Julian in the woods only nights before. He was so young, merely a toddler, and so lost, it was slowly tearing at my heart. My posture turned rigid as I stared into his sad eyes that were brimming with tears. His tiny hands curled into fists.

And the ghost jumped to his feet! *"Jai,"* he cried. *"Jai, stop! Stop it! Jai, no!"*

He flickered across the lawn, coming closer, the winds swirling.

The strength of his wind pushed me back against the brick of the apothecary store when he appeared before me. His face was pale and blotchy, his hair wet, his eyes swirling with a mixture of pain and anguish.

"JAI, NO!" he screamed, and I felt his heartache bury itself inside me.

Another cold wind blew. It was the kind to trap itself in my bones. A haunted house was living inside me.

And the spirit fizzled like static to nothing. He disappeared.

"Jai, stop," his eerie whispers continued, and I followed the sound down the path.

This spirit needed me. The little boy was so strong, so ruthless, so determined, and I had to help.

My feet picked up when his cries did, and I turned frantic as the echoes faded. I reached the alleyway and bolted into the shadows, having no idea where he was leading me.

I ran and ran, my feet numb and heels blistering, until my palms hit a chain-link fence behind the shopping center. Under a single buzzing streetlight, Julian was standing in the middle of a basketball court with his bare back to me. His shoulders and muscles flexed as he held a girl in the air by her throat. She had short black hair, but it wasn't Ivy. It was someone else I didn't recognize.

"JAI, NO!" the spirit cried in my ear.

A scream ripped into the air and all around me. An earsplitting sonorous scream. Julian's scream.

I tried fighting through it, and my fingers gripped the fence as I yanked back and forth. *"Julian!"*

He didn't hear me. He didn't even flinch. *"Julian!"*

Panicked, my gaze begged for an opening. There was one at the far end. I moved quickly, passing a man who was sleeping against a dumpster, or dead. I didn't have time to check.

"JULIAN!" I tried to scream over him. It was impossible. *"STOP!"*

The girl's face was turning blue. Blood seeped from her ears as he held her high under the dim, humming light. He was locked in another world, a daze. With all my strength, I bulldozed into him, knocking Julian to the ground and the girl from his grasp.

HOURS SEEMED SHORT. SECONDS SEEMED LONGER, BUT IT HADN'T BEEN hours that passed.

The girl coughed life back into her as she stumbled to her feet and took off across the basketball court. My head pounded and my face was pressed against the cold concrete. I couldn't hear anything. It was as if an atomic bomb had blasted inside my head. But Julian's screaming had stopped. I knew that much.

I blinked, watching her half running, half screaming for help. Julian was lying beside me, his pant-leg grazing my bare one, his arm pressing against mine, looking up into the midnight sky as if he wanted to be one with it. It was cold. It was wet. I was breathing. Julian was breathing. The girl he almost killed was breathing, too. She was alive.

I closed my eyes and opened them again, unable to move from his side as if we'd become one.

There had to be a reason why I was being pulled to him, whether it was me, this ghost, or something else entirely. There had to be a reason why I hadn't succumbed to my death from seeing his face as the rest. It all had to mean something …

The fog in my ears was slowly dying away. Julian's chest expanded, and I noticed the sadness expel in a dull breath behind his mask. "What's happening to me?" he croaked into the night, the light from the moon and stars touched his outline. His form, his shape, his edges, his colors. Julian was dark and bright like a morbid black sun.

"I don't know," I told him, rolling onto my back and staring at the sky with him. The clouds crawled over the star-freckled canvas, ribbons of ink and eternity. "What do you remember?"

For a moment, Julian didn't speak. The night didn't speak either. It was as if the world had been turned upside down or we'd been transported somewhere else where no worry lived. Everything was calm.

"Nothing. I was lying in my bed. Now I'm lying here. Now I'm with you. And it's nice. I don't want to leave."

I don't want to leave either. "Does this happen a lot?"

"I don't know. I don't know anything anymore. It feels like something is controlling me … I have no will. I'm not me … I'm something else. Something dark. And Darkness doesn't have fingers to pierce into me or legs to chase after me. It doesn't stalk or prey on me. It can't drag me under anything because Darkness is already here. Everywhere … All the time … It lives inside me. It's all I am. I am Darkness." His shoulder relaxed beside me. "And you're still here. Why are you still here?"

Why am I still here? Had he meant in Weeping Hollow? At this basketball court? With him?

I didn't have the answers. Even if I did, none of them would have made sense to anyone, but it all made sense in my heart. I was still here, lying beside the Hollow Heathen because it felt familiar and normal. If I weren't here with him, the mere thought of *that* wouldn't make sense to me.

So, I wrapped it all up in six words: "Because I want to be here."

Julian released a breath. Everything he did was so loud and in my atmosphere, no matter how far away he was. His breaths rattled like a drumline in my ears, and every flutter of his long black lashes was like notes bouncing off a cello. He was loud and filling me, dragging in heavy breaths and letting them go.

"Okay," he told me. "Can we just lay like this for a while?"

A fistful of his words wrapped around my heart, pumping a new beat inside my chest. My gaze followed the angles of his silhouette and his thick black hair and the hardness in his form as he lay beside me. He was all backward, wearing his soul like skin—and his soul was beautiful. Not beautiful like a rose but beautiful like a Black Velvet petunia.

Never in my life had I come across a more captivating man than him. His eyes generally held a madness. His muscles had a way of tensing, perhaps from burdens he may be carrying. But there were moments, such as these, when they beamed of nostalgia and wistfulness of equal proportion—a sweet blend of melancholy.

And Julian's burdens must be deranged and disturbing considering the town and the curse, turning him into this nightmare who lurked in the shadows. But despite all these things, he was capable of such a glacial gentleness, and I wanted to wrap myself inside it and fall asleep in his chill.

I inched my hand closer until my fingers touched his. I watched as his eyes closed for a moment before they opened again, probably trying to make sense of this strangeness that lived within me. The *freakshow*. The creature who looked like a ghost—something not ordinary. But I didn't feel his distance, a sign he may have found and accepted it.

Julian turned his head and looked into my eyes as he ran the tip of his finger down the length of my palm. He interlaced his fingers with mine.

As we lay there on our backs with our hands tied together, we returned our gaze to the starry midnight sky.

There was no longer a need to figure him out or ask him questions.

Only to be around him. To be with him. To be real like this.

JULIAN BLACKWELL WAS *CURSED*,

and now, SO WAS I.

JULIAN
chapter fourteen

AFTER WHAT HAD HAPPENED DURING THE TOWN HALL meeting and the death of Jury Smith, I knew it would only be a matter of time before I was called here to the Order's Chambers. This wasn't the first time I had been invited. Yes, the Order had *invited* me by a formal invitation postmarked and hand-delivered to my mother's house, complete with the Order's seal stamped on the flap enclosure.

Thankfully, Ocean, the homeless man who slept behind Mina's Diner, had been passed out and didn't witness my attempt on the flatlander at the basketball courts when I'd blacked out. The girl I'd almost killed had been drunk, her story hardly credible. Officer Stoker had shown up at the auto shop for questioning. I'd told him she came on to all of us at Voodoos, and we turned her down. That I went straight home after I left the bar. A heap of half-truths, which only turned a monster into a coward.

But, as I stood before the Order beside a smug Kane Pruitt, I realized it had nothing to do with what happened at Earl's trailer or the basketball court. We were all gathered here for a different reason. And I suddenly wished it had to do with me killing Jury Smith or my assault on the girl because I knew it had everything to do with Fallon.

The Chambers were located in the tunnels under the gazebo. Augustine Pruitt, Viola Cantini, Clarence Goody, and my mother, Agatha Blackwell, sat atop the stairs behind their long table, making up the four within the Order. Two cherished symbols hung on the stone wall above the Order to protect the Chamber. The five-pointed star pentagram represented the Norse Woods Coven, the five original families from the elements of earth, air, fire, water, and spirit—the Hollow Heathens.

On the other side, the Celtic knot, representing Sacred Sea Coven—the Weeping Witches.

Candles lit from within various pockets in the walls of the room, along the floor, and up the stairs leading to the Order. No matter the time of year, the room remained damp and cold and maintained the same stagnant temperature.

The atmosphere was unlike a monthly Town Hall meeting. One could not speak without first being spoken to. The flatlanders weren't welcomed—aside from Mina Mae. And the punishment against a member of a coven was far worse than those the flatlanders would receive. We were hardly favored in our own town, but I understood the reasoning.

We had magic. We held an advantage. They did not.

Hence the reason Mina Mae sat in the corner of the room, always the mediator. Mina's ancestors had been among the first flatlanders to arrive in the late 1800s after we'd already claimed the land. As we learned from history, our covens had been appalled as to how they'd found the town and were able to pass through the protective shield—we still couldn't make sense of it to this day.

After their first arrival, a new family, couple, or solo flatlander would mysteriously arrive and take residence every passing decade. Some had learned of our ways, our beliefs, and chose a side. Some had kept to themselves yet thrived in the small town of Weeping Hollow, with their talents and occupations, making the town what it was today.

Mina's family was well respected within the community, becoming the voice of the flatlanders and making sure every decision the Order made was in all fairness and for their safety as well. The town's very own fairy godmother, if you will.

I stood tall with my hands behind my back. Viola Cantini's son, Cyrus, sat behind us. We looked alike as if we had been bred from the same family line, both tall with jet black hair and light eyes, but we were from two different worlds within the same town. I never had bad blood with Cyrus. He kept to himself, never giving Norse Woods or the Heathens problems. But I had no idea why he was here, what he had to do with Fallon, or why this group was gathered. In this small chamber, I was outnumbered by sea witches.

I kept my statue-like posture, hiding all weakness I had toward Fallon.

In the center of the table sat Augustine Pruitt with a stack of books before him. I immediately recognized the Book of Blackwell's silver foil. We'd learned passages from each of the books in our schooling at the academy, only approved copied passages. However, resting before the Order were the original books, inaccessible to the rest of us. These books undoubtedly contained history of our home, our families, spells and curses placed on the town, and the shadow-blooded Blackwells.

Mr. Pruitt adjusted his glasses on his nose and sucked on his teeth, flipping through the battered pages. "First, we will discuss the careless magic at Voodoos. Kane, what is your claim?"

"It wasn't magic harnessed from the elements," Kane stated in his fucking boat shoes and polo, sure of himself. "It was the kind of magic we haven't seen in town since ..." he paused, turning his eyes away from his father and looking to the ground, "Javino Blackwell."

If Agatha was offended, she didn't show it. It would be no surprise if her heart were forged by the toughest of iron with a blend of gold by the blacksmith of her soul. She was kind and empathetic to those who deserved her compassion, but she concealed her emotions and vulnerabilities like a cloak ever since she lost her husband and son.

"We get it, the Blackwells are shadow-blooded," Mr. Goody spoke out in the Chamber, always defensive of my family. "Let this be a history lesson, shall we? Their element is spirit, containing all four other elements, and this includes the dark void. This isn't brand new information. Everyone knows this." He turned to Augustine. "Julian has been a remarkable citizen."

"Julian?" Mr. Pruitt abruptly said, his perfectly cut brows pinched together above his glasses. "Could you tell us what happened?"

"There were over sixty people in the bar that night, including both covens and flatlanders. It could have been anyone." How much longer could I hide behind these half-truths? It had been my fault, though it couldn't be proven. "In spite of what happened, no one was hurt, and there is no solid proof on either side."

At the corner of my eye, Mina nodded, pleased.

Mr. Pruitt cut his eyes to Cyrus. "Cyrus, you were there. Could you please tell me the events of what happened?"

Kane turned to face Cyrus. I did not. I was somewhat familiar with the dynamics of Sacred Sea. There was a reason Fallon's father appointed Cyrus's mother, Viola, to take over his position before he left twenty-four years ago. The Cantini's were known for their brutal honesty and trustworthiness and lived by the Law of Return: whatever energy a person puts out into the world, positive or negative, will be returned to that person three times. Norse Woods lived by that law as well, or at least, we used to. I had no doubt Cyrus would be honest about the events.

Kane's teeth clenched at my side as Cyrus spoke loud and clear of what had happened that night at the bar, including Kane's outburst and ill actions. Word after word, Cyrus betrayed his friend, as I knew he would. What he hadn't mentioned were his thoughts on where the mysterious storm had come from.

"I see, this all stems from Fallon Morgan," Mr. Pruitt uttered under his breath, bothered by the facts and sorely disappointed, if not embarrassed, of his son. "Let me be clear, for the shield to stay intact, the laws we set forth tonight must be followed," he reminded all within the Chamber, which caused my chest to tighten. "The Order and all under the dome must remain balanced."

Then Viola Cantini's voice filled the room. "Tobias had entrusted Sacred Sea with Fallon's safety if she ever returned for reasons I cannot disclose. From this point forward, she is under Sacred Sea protection."

Zeph had told me this after hearing the whispers amongst the covens since the night she had arrived. Kane had spat the same words at Voodoos after I'd caught her when she fell from the bar. That she wasn't a flatlander—not free—but with Sacred Sea. Even my conscience had warned me, but it seemed nothing else inside me wanted to hear it. As I stood solid, appearing to be unbroken by the news, I was fucking falling apart on the inside.

My head pounded. My jaw flexed. My eyes closed.

Fallon was able to calm me in ways I had never expected, straightening a broken chord in my heart, and plucked it, bringing it to life in a soothing song, like a nightingale of the Norse woods.

A part of me knew this would happen after I first met her on the rocks. I tried to ignore it, but it was too late. We'd connected, a kind of connection that seemed as unworldly as this very town and the residence it beheld. And it was just as surreal to try and explain this to the Order, the reasons for my erratic behavior lately.

How do I rid myself of her, and fast?

"There was a reason Tobias took her away," my mother spoke up, surprising everyone. She'd never spoken up against Mr. Pruitt, and I was eager to hear what she had to say, if she had a say. "Neither he nor Freya wanted her to be a part of this. I spoke with Fallon myself. Her only purpose is to see that Benny gets well. I doubt she will take an interest in being a part of a coven, let alone stay."

"She cannot leave. The town won't let her," Mr. Goody argued.

He was correct. Without knowledge, Fallon had driven into town under the weight of the Blueberry Moon. It had taken a great measure of unity and magic to allow her and Tobias to leave twenty-four years ago, which remained a mystery to most as to who had been involved in their escape. I'd watched her from the woods the night she'd tried to leave again, waiting for the town to stop her, hoping she wouldn't get hurt in the process.

Though neither the mystical town nor the Order would allow her escape again, the thought of Fallon leaving tensed every muscle. Having her leave could make it easier for me, but I didn't know which was worse. At least if she were here, being able to see her would sing to my masochistic soul.

"Fallon Morgan belongs to Sacred Sea," Mr. Pruitt ordered in finality as the book slammed closed. Dust clouds exploded from the pages the same time my heart did. "Kane, do you have any interest in the girl?"

I could not stop my muscles from flexing—a weak attempt at holding this anger in, this bubbling loudness in my spine.

Kane's eyes drifted to mine. "No, I honestly have no interest in the

155

Morgan girl," he looked back to his father, "but you will remember that I'll do this anyway for the sake of the coven, and I'll make sure she feels the same for me in return."

And the wild thing in my chest splintered and peeled apart, unable to make sense as to what was happening around me.

"Very well," Augustine Pruitt announced. "The Morgan girl is under Kane's protection. And, son, do what you need to do to make sure she initiates into Sacred Sea by Mabon."

Make sure she initiates into Sacred Sea? They're forcing her?

"No, this isn't right!" I yelled out inside the Chamber. "What's so different about her? Why does she need protection? Why doesn't she get a choice like the others?!"

My vision obscured, and I looked to Agatha, who stared back with horror in her eyes. Perhaps she thought the same as the rest of the town, that I was going mad. That my shadow-blood would take over, and history would repeat itself. But this decision was clearly against what we stood for, and Fallon's freedom was being taken—her greatest fear. Agatha had to feel the same and understand these outbursts I could no longer control.

But Agatha slowly shook her head, begging me not to cause a scene. I narrowed my eyes, and my teeth gnashed behind my mask, silently *begging* for her to speak up—to do *something*.

"Why do you think, Blackwell? Protection from the cursed Heathens. From you!" Pruitt roared. "We've made the decision. This was what her father wanted. It's final. You will not go within twenty feet of Fallon Morgan. You will not talk to her, coerce her, touch her, or as much as release a breath in her direction unless we order it. She is Sacred Sea, and you and the Heathens will keep your distance."

My eyes narrowed at the man. "You're taking away her free will. How far are you willing to take this?" This was sick. Fallon had been gone for twenty-four years, and now they were assigning her to a man and passing her off as property. "She should have a choice whether or not to join a coven."

Mr. Goody and Agatha exchanged glances. Viola cocked her gaze to Pruitt. And Pruitt rose to his feet, his cheeks reddened. "Are you questioning the Order within the Chambers, *Blackwell?* Considering your bloodline, what your father has done, and what we all know what *you* are capable of, it would be wise to back down now, or I will take action."

I stepped forward, but Agatha jumped to her feet before I could speak my mind. "It's the right thing to do, Julian. It's what her father wanted. I know it doesn't seem just, but it's only one girl." She looked at me as if I'd lost my mind, and perhaps I had. I'd never questioned the Order before, never brought heat upon myself, but it still didn't make this right. "Please, *Jai*," Agatha pleaded through her barred teeth. "Step down."

LATER THAT NIGHT, I FOUND BECK IN MY ROOM SITTING ON THE EDGE of my mattress with a steaming mug in his hand next to Jolie, who was sound asleep in my bed. The heated scent of white jasmine and honey from the tea filled the small bedroom, carrying flower petals on its steam. It was Jolie's favorite.

"What's my sister doing here?"

More times than not, if Beck wasn't working, he was here. Beck didn't have siblings, much less a father. His mother, a flatlander, died soon after Beck was born. She was a one night stand and hadn't believed Earl when he'd told her about the curse or why he had to cover his head, and when she had looked into her newborn's face, her fears took her.

Beck cared for Jolie as if she were his own sister. He ran a palm across his shaved head and lifted his gaze. "She and your mother got into it earlier. She came here to find you. I was already here, so we were going to talk. I've never seen her so upset, man. I was only gone for five minutes to make her tea. Guess she cried herself to sleep."

Sweat dewed Jolie's forehead and cheeks as she slept in the corner of my bed, curled under the heavy blanket. Her damp black hair clung to her face as she snored lightly.

"What was it about?" I asked, and Jolie stirred inside the covers with our voices. I nudged my head toward the door, and Beck glanced back once more at Jolie before he stood and followed me out.

"Not sure, she passed out before I could get it out of her," he said at my back as I walked to the fridge. It probably had to do with the other kids at the academy. The Heathens' siblings had it the hardest at school, and

157

this wasn't the first time Jolie had shown up at my house upset because of them. She had a mouth on her, and it got her into trouble more times than not. Though behind closed doors, she was only a fifteen-year-old girl with a heart too big for her mouth.

Agatha didn't put up with her dramatics.

Beck and I fell for it every time.

I opened the fridge and leaned in to grab two beers from the back as he continued, "There's gotta be a way, man. Maybe the Order—"

"No." The fridge door swung shut, and I wedged one beer cap on the counter and pounded my fist on the top. The cap popped off, and I handed the bottle to him. I already knew where he was going with this. "I just came back from the Chambers," I went on, repeating the same steps for my beer. "It's not like it used to be. This is what they've always wanted. Sacred Sea wants Norse Woods to lose power, I can see it. Pruitt never gave a damn about our curse, balance, or our coven. They're using scare tactics to push people further away from Norse Woods. Pruitt only looks out for his own."

"Yeah, but your mother is a member of the Order," Beck pointed out. "Goody, too. There's gotta be something no one's tried before in those books. We have to steal them. We have to end this cycle."

I shook my head with the bottle in my mouth and pointed to the back door, signaling to take this conversation outside. If Jolie happened to wake, she didn't need to hear anything that would cause her more grief or worry. And Jolie would worry because that was who my little sister was. She had always cared more about the coven and Heathens than herself. She defended us, stood up for us, fought for us, even when we begged her to stop. It had only made it worse for her.

With a snap of my finger, the fire pit rekindled, and the two of us sat in the large chairs Phoenix and I had built from the wood of fallen birch trees. Beck stretched out his legs and dropped his head back. The bandana covered his nose and mouth, and his blue eyes looked up at the cloud-filled sky.

The curse affected us as well, never being allowed to see each other or our own faces.

"Why were you called into the Chamber? Did it have to do with Jury?"

Beck finally asked, keeping his gaze above.

"No. They wouldn't have proof it was me either way." But if I told him it was about Fallon, he'd see right through me and know of these ... feelings that were violating me. Feelings that were strange and intruding and unlawful and could pull my attention from our priorities. But he'd never use it against me.

Beck was loyal, compassionate, and understanding, but also a maelstrom of emotions. The sensitive one, and when prodded or backed into a wall, he'd either unleash an emotional storm from hell or withdraw into himself.

From day one, Beck had taken on everyone's pain and suffering as if it were his own. But next to his ability to feel so deeply, he was also psychic, which was both a blessing and a curse of his own, like the rest of us. Being born with magic in our bones had come with a price. A downside. And each one of us had one. Mine was my shadow-blood. Beck's was his psychic abilities. Our downside was a curse that could never be broken.

And Beck had spoken of Fallon's existence long before she arrived.

It had been a late-night drunken conversation years ago when he'd lost himself in a trance. He'd talked about a girl with white hair and the moons in her eyes, and how she'd one day fall from the night sky and bring me down with her.

I knew she was coming. We both had been expecting the moon girl, but Beck had never mentioned this feeling I'd been feeling since first seeing Fallon standing on the cliffs above the sea, as if she summoned the waves.

If Beck knew what Fallon's return meant for us, he didn't voice it. He only told me what I needed to hear.

"The Order wanted to hear my side of the story of what happened at Voodoos," I replied, tapping the talisman on my finger against the glass bottle. "I got them off my back, but she now belongs to Kane. Augustine didn't have to say the word *compel*, but everyone in the Chamber knew what he meant by it," I gritted out, annoyed with myself for wanting to talk about her. "Basically, do whatever it takes, and my mother sat there and did nothing. I don't understand why she needs protection." I would never intentionally hurt her.

"Stop bullshitting me, man," Beck dropped his chin to his fingers, studying me. "This is bothering you, just admit the real reason why."

"You already know why." He wanted to hear me say it, to admit she meant something to me. It would be the only rational explanation as to why I, Julian Blackwell, had jumped across the bar to catch her in front of everyone.

I looked into the woods instead and drank from my beer. I trusted Beck, but the feelings were hard enough to confront within the safety of my skull. I couldn't imagine saying them aloud and giving them to the world, to the ever-listening woods.

"*E pur si muove,*" Beck uttered, then drank from his bottle beneath the flap of his bandana.

I looked at him. "Excuse me?"

"It still moves," he said after swallowing, grazing his palm over his head. "Galileo was forced by torture to take back his theory that the earth orbited the sun. Do you know what he stated afterward? After all the ridicule and abuse, everyone telling him he was wrong?"

I arched a brow, and he continued, "*E pur si muove.* It still moves." Beck leaned forward and dropped his elbows onto his knees, locking his blue eyes with mine. "No amount of beating, bashing, or threats can take away the truth that the earth still is the one to orbit the sun and not the other way around. Despite what you were taught to believe your entire life, this tame person you've tried so hard to become, your virtues, your morals, the Order, or our pact, you can't ignore or run away from *your* truth, Julian. The ravens will *still* haunt you, death will *still* come, and you will *still* have feelings for this girl, and these feelings aren't going to just go away because you demand it." He sat back and dragged in a long and depressing breath. "Regardless, it still fucking moves, and there's not a damn thing you can do about it."

AFTER BECK LEFT, I STOOD BEFORE THE MIRROR.

I slid the mask off my face. I took a deep breath. I lifted my head and stared into my face.

In an instant, I was standing atop the Ferris Wheel of the grounds, looking down. Winds yanked my coat, punched my skin, wanting to take me down. Bile rose in my throat. My hands slammed on the edge of the sink.

"Fight through it!" I shouted, sweat dripping down my spine. But I became dizzy. Nauseous. "I'm not afraid," I chanted, over and over.

The wheel car rocked back and forth. I was too high. Too far off the ground. Too out of control with nowhere to run. I forced my eyes to stay open, to fight through the heights.

Until fighting became unbearable.

Vomit burned in my throat, and I lurched forward and heaved into the sink. Tears stung the corners of my eyes and ran down the face I could never look into. My knuckles on the sink's edge turned white, and I screamed, throwing my fist into the reflection that held my fears.

Blood spilled from my knuckles as I tried to catch an honest breath. One that could hold me. One that was gentle and quiet. One that tasted like revival and felt like Fallon.

I had to see her again—

just ONE MORE *TIME.*

JULIAN BLACKWELL'S CABIN   NORSE WOODS, WEEPING HOLLOW

FALLON
chapter fifteen

F ABLE LICKED THE FOAM FROM THE RIM OF HER STYROFOAM COFFEE cup as we sat in the corner table at The Bean, waiting for the rest of them to arrive: Monday, the other two Sullivan sisters, Kane, and his friends.

The sun descended, gradually burying the little light remaining over Town Square. Defy Day had arrived, and I watched from inside the coffee shop as venders set out booths around the gazebo, decorating the town for the night ahead.

Three weeks had passed without talking to Julian. Our last night together was the one under the stars at the basketball court. I couldn't stop thinking about him—couldn't stop my eyes from searching up and down the streets for him.

Fable repeated my name, and I returned my gaze to her, sipping from my pumpkin spiced latte.

"Milo told me Jury died of a heart attack, but I don't believe it," she went on. "It has to be Beck or Drunk Earl's fault. It's a conspiracy. Officer Stoker's probably in on it. He won't even bother investigating."

The truth was, Jury Smith had gone into the Parish home with a knife, and he had no idea why, or at least that was what Jury had told me. Jury had difficulty remembering anything aside from being ambushed from behind. After seeing Pennywise, his heart had burst inside his chest. It could have been Beck. It could have been Drunk Earl. It could have been Julian.

But if it was Julian, something else had to be controlling him, something dark—something sinister. That or he had done it to protect Beck and Earl. Jury had been the one to show up with a knife, after all. Julian would never go out of his way to purposely hurt someone. I refused to believe it.

"Poor Mr. Jury," Fable added when I didn't comment. "You know he was just initiated into Sacred Sea, too. What the heck was he even doing over there?"

"He was a witch?"

"No, Jury and his girlfriend were both flatlanders. Not born with magic like the founding families, but anyone can be a witch if they practice Wiccan beliefs. Years ago, he showed up when his car broke down on Archer Avenue, walked into Weeping Hollow on foot with nothing and has been here ever since. For a long time, Pruitt called him the Colorado kid and said he was born and raised in the mountains. Could you imagine?"

"Are you friends with his girlfriend?"

"Carrie Driscoll? God, no," Fable said adamantly. "Barely talk to her. That girl creeps me out, dude. But Mr. Pruitt eats out of the palm of her hand, and she's our age. I don't get it."

"But Jury was fifty-three." The age difference was a bit much—almost a thirty-year gap.

Fable shrugged and pursed her dark purple lips under her costume mask that matched my own. "They were total opposites, too. Carrie and Jury, I never understood it. Oh, look, there's Monday."

I turned to see Monday waving at us from the other side of the window. The rest of them were huddled together on the street corner.

When we exited the coffee shop, the scent of corndogs, powdered funnel cakes, and caramel apples drifted up and down Town Square. Ladders hung from storefront eaves, and pennies littered the paved walkways and streets, flickering under the yellow lamp lights like copper diamonds. Black and white striped tents were set up everywhere. Each tent offered services, such as palm readings and prophecies, merchants selling crystal balls, tarot cards, crystals and stones, censers to dispense incense, and so on.

Men walked on stilts around the gazebo, passing out pinstriped balloons to kids as the adults carried frosted chalices. Half the town was in costume masks, the other half not willing to tempt their fate.

"After about an hour or so, the kids will return home, and the real fun begins," Monday pointed out, noticing me watching the kids as we approached. By this time, the sun had died, bringing in a chilling cold front. I wrapped my jean jacket tighter around my new black leather dress.

"Fallon," Kane commanded my attention. Maverick and Cyrus, the two other guys I'd briefly met at Voodoos, were at his side. "You look amazing."

"Thank you." Another breeze swept past us, taking my hair with it in a ferocious swirl.

Kane closer, pushed my hair from my face, and took my coffee from my hand. By the time I'd lifted my hand to take it back, he'd already tossed it into the trash. "Let me get you a real drink."

I didn't let it show how much it angered me because his actions were already said and done, my sweet pumpkin spiced coffee already licking the bottom of the barrel. Boys should know never to take a coffee from the hands of a female … unless they were warming it up. However, I had no interest in wasting my energy on correcting Kane when I had profane thoughts for another; one who I was okay with never having to see his face if it meant I could be around him again.

We walked to a booth where a large cauldron sat on a tray of dry ice, mist rising from the bottom. Red and gold swirled in the liquid.

"It's my Poisoned Apple Cider," Mina Mae wiggled her brows as she filled a bronze chalice with a ladle.

"It's so good! She makes it for every gathering," Monday added, taking a chalice from the table.

For about an hour, we continued to walk the streets, looked into tents, drank poison from our cups, and goofed off with the superstitions.

When we reached the palm reader's purple tent, I'd stopped and admired the three drawings hanging from the rods. The artwork was different from anything I'd seen before, with diligent pencil lines and dark colored paint. One was labeled *Rose Madder*. Another *Wizard and Glass*.

"Did you draw these?" I asked aloud.

The girl turned around, and her smooth hair like black ribbons cascaded around her shoulders. She had flawless skin, the color of syrup with a golden tint, and her honey-colored eyes embraced mine.

"Yes, I only draw what comes to me." Her voice was like velvet. She possessed the perfect complexion and had the face of a porcelain doll.

I walked deeper into the tent. "What's your name?"

"Kioni."

"The one who sees and finds needful things," I said with a smile, and Kioni's eyes looked at me quizzically. "My nanny was Kenyan," I explained further. "Would you read my palm for me?" I'd never had my palm read, but I was desperate to get away from Kane's strange behavior, if only for a moment. He'd said he wasn't interested in me, but he hadn't left my side all night.

Kioni's face transformed, somewhat saddened. "I would love to, but I am hardly qualified. You see, I am watching the tent for my grandmother, Eleanor. You could always come back when she returns?"

"To be honest, I just need a breather. You don't have to read my palm, just pretend?" I hooked my thumb behind me and added in a whisper, "Some of the people in this town are suffocating … or maybe I'm just not used to the attention."

Kioni's laugh was breathy and sincere. She nodded, walking to the entrance and released the tent flap from its tie. The festivities from outside turned into a distant chatter. The only light now had come from the glowing crystals and battery-operated candles that mimicked a flicker.

She pulled a chair out from under a small table. "Come, sit. Hide." She smiled and slid her gaze to my cup. "Is that Mina's Poisoned Apple Cider?" I nodded, and Kioni leaned forward, setting her arms on the table. "Be careful. Mina Mae puts something in that drink. Some sort of truth potion she learned from an old witch called the Lone Luna. It's supposed to enhance parts of your subconscious. Every event we have always ends in either a fight in front of the gazebo or an orgy at Crescent Beach, or both.

Mina is known to stir the pot, as if Weeping Hollow needs any more stirring."

"Sweet old Mina from the diner?"

Kioni's eyes narrowed. "Oh, that woman may be sweet, but she's smart as a whip. She'll play both sides to whichever side suits her best at the time."

"She's not from here?"

"No, ma'am. And Mina doesn't belong to a coven either. She's the town's bibi...or grandmother if you will. But I admire her. She loathes secrets, believes in letting our truths and madness air out every once in a while, too. Says it's healthy."

"And everyone knows this, what she does to the cider?"

Kioni shrugged, leaned back in her chair, and crossed her legs. "I don't know. No one really talks about it. Since you came from away, thought I'd clue you in."

I twirled the chalice between my fingers and watched the last sip of my second cup of golden-red liquid swirl. "Well, I'm royally screwed."

Kioni laughed again, and seconds later, the flap from the tent was pushed aside with a confused Monday staring at the two of our smiling faces. Her side-swept bangs framed her small face. "I've been looking all over for you!"

I stood and held my palm out in front of me. "Just getting my palm read," I blurted as if I'd been caught with a blunt between my fingers, like I was doing something wrong. Monday made me feel like that at times.

Monday's gaze slid to Kioni, then back to me. "We're all heading to the Devil's Playground. Come on, Kane's waiting for you."

"Groan," Kioni muttered, then shot her gaze to me. "Don't forget what I told you."

The poisoned cider. "Thanks."

There was a group of us who entered through the large double doors of Town Hall. I'd only been in the west wing for the Town Hall meeting, but the grand room had been transformed into a maze of mirrors covering the ceiling and walls. My reflection bounced off every angle. The floor was glossy and the color of black licorice. Fog machines blew inside, blanketing the floor in thick brushstrokes of crawling smoke.

Adora, with her sultry lips laced with a conniving smile, grabbed Maverick's hand. She slid her gaze to Kane with a lifted chin, meeting his eyes for a fraction of a second before her and Maverick disappeared inside the maze. Ivy and Monday ran in the opposite direction. Fable and Cyrus, through another. Everyone broke apart, leaving Kane and me standing at the entrance.

"You want to check it out?" he asked, unfazed by Adora taking off with Maverick. Laughter bounced from inside the maze of mirrors against the bass of the haunting music. From here, reflections swiftly moved as if bodies were passing through glass. "Go on, I'll give you a head start." He smiled a boyish smile, but Kane didn't wear his chaste smile well. It remained crooked, whispering lewdness.

My eyes darted back to the dizzying maze, already feeling my throat constricting. I shook my head, taking a step back. *Trapped, trapped, trapped...*

Kane spoke words, insisting I join him and took both of my hands into his as a ringing grew louder in my ears. He ignored my murmurs, walking backward as he dragged me deeper into the maze. I tried to keep my eyes on his, my mask like a weight on my face. My steps, my breaths, my shuddering pulse, it all seemed heavier in here.

When we turned a corner, I was face to face with myself. Black leather dress, white hair dangling over my hips, frightened pale blue eyes screaming at me to turn and run. I turned back to Kane, and his laughter rebounded off the glass like elasticity. Why couldn't he see how scared I was?

"Come find me," he called out with his arms up at his sides and a brazen smile, then took off through the maze, leaving me here alone.

I ran after him with my arms out in front of me. I only saw myself in front of me—to my left, to my right, behind me. I was all around. My steps hurried, frantically searching for an exit.

"Kane!" I shouted. More laughter came, more mockery. But the song playing in the Devil's Playground drowned it out for it to only return between beats of the bass.

My body slammed into a mirror. I turned, dropped back against it, and closed my eyes, trying to control my quivering breath.

When I opened my eyes, a flicker of *him* stood in the mirror.

Only a flicker, yet enough to dismember my racing heart. All my worries turned to dust.

Julian, Julian, Julian … Inside the reflection, he ebbed and flowed like a shadow of death, the cycle of life.

"Julian …" I walked to him with my palms out in front of me as he drifted through the mirrors.

My hands slid across fogged glass as my steps and pulse quickened, chasing the silhouette of the guy with the silver eyes and black mask. He was *here*, and I felt myself being pulled to him like an invisible chord connecting us.

I hit another dead end and turned, seeing glimpses of his black coat, black pants, black boots, and wild black hair. *Black, black, black,* but nothing could convince me of such wickedness.

"Fallon." Kane's voices slithered throughout the maze. "Where are you?" he sang.

I pressed my back against the glass, eyes darting, hoping he wouldn't find me. There were at least three of me staring back with icy blue eyes. The reflections swirled like a drop of black paint into water, the side effects of Mina's cider. The bass from the music boomed in my ears, Julian was gone, and the fog was suffocating me, making it harder to breathe. My muscles turned stiff, and I couldn't move, couldn't turn my neck. *Trapped, trapped, trapped* … The only thing I could do was close my eyes and wait for this night to be over, to wait for the sun to rise and for someone to find me in the maze in the morning.

And that was when I felt a hand brush mine.

The cold and gentle touch slid over my skin to the tips of my beating fingers. My lashes fluttered, my knees wobbled, and a breath freed from my lungs.

"Fallon," Kane called out again, appearing in the mirrors just as I was whisked away from the wall and into another room. "You still hiding from me?" Kane's voice drifted with humor.

Julian held a pointed finger to his mask as he walked backward, taking me with him until he turned us. My back rested against another mirrored wall. A blast of cold air pierced my skin and entered my bloodstream.

Julian moved closer, and in his eyes, I saw the same stripped and vulnerable man from the woods. His gaze fluttered over my face like Morse code, taking me in. His trembling fingers drifted down the length of my arm.

"Julian, you're shaking," I choked out, doubting he could hear me above the music as my chest heaved. Despite the unsettling nerves, I'd noticed his, and it happened to calm mine.

JULIAN

FALLON WAS RIGHT. MY HANDS WERE SHAKING. I COULDN'T STOP THIS chain reaction whenever she was and wasn't near. Either way, it no longer mattered. And to be honest, I had no idea what I was doing. I shouldn't have come to Defy night pretending to help Agatha but only itching to see her after so long. I needed to find her, to search Town Square for white hair and glassy blue eyes. The eyes who saw me as more man than mask— more human than Heathen. And my heart ran freely, reminding me that there was still space in my chest for something other than darkness.

We didn't make sense, but as I stood before her, she saw all the things in me that felt too messed up. She pulled me back into the person I'd abandoned a long time ago. Fallon looked past the curse, and therefore, I couldn't look past her.

The shape of her smile colored the nightmares in the sky, and I couldn't bear to touch her without shaking, without seeing her as anything other than a rare girl who had a celestial stamp in all her details.

Tonight, I was defying everything and everyone.

Because when she looked up at me like she was doing now, lips parted in awe of me, a curiosity dancing in her irises, I didn't care anymore about the Order or to whom she belonged. All I cared about, as the music fell into the background of my deprivation, was trying to be here with her.

"I'm not very good at this," I confessed. My knuckles grazed Fallon's blushing cheek, uncaring of the consequences. I drank the poison and became mindless.

Fallon's delicate fingers reached for my mask. I snatched her wrist and shook my head before she could.

Her lips moved. *Trust me*, she'd said, but only the music pounded in my ears. I unlinked my fingers from around her wrist, trusting her. Because in the midst of wrongs, I wanted to get this one thing right. She rolled up my mask from the bottom, revealing only my mouth. The pad of her thumb stroked my bottom lip. The touch flared a wave of heat inside me.

My heartbeat thundered.

Fallon lifted onto her toes. And her lips were on mine.

Soft, gentle, fragile, and shock and horror coursed through me because I'd never kissed anyone, never wanted to before and didn't know if I could, and the reality of killing her was petrifying. When she pulled away, I blinked. My brows snapped together, studying her reaction. Fallon's dusty pink lips turned into an off-kilter smile.

I hadn't killed her. I hadn't pulled her into her fear. She'd kissed me, and if tonight was all we had, I wasn't going to waste it. I grabbed her elbow with one hand, the back of her head with the other. I pulled her in until our mouths crashed again.

Fallon's lips melted with mine. My tongue brushed across hers, and, at last, my soul breathed and my heart aired out on the line of this kiss that tasted like the real thing. And like a blanket, I felt normal fall around us.

"Fallon," Mr. Mercedes shouted again in the distance, closing in on us.

I grabbed her hand, and we took off through the maze. I looked back to see her in the leather dress clinging to her body and her hand covering her laugh, which pulled a smile upon my own. And my smile felt awkward and rusty, muscles unused in quite some time.

When we reached another dead end, my back hit another mirror. Fallon fell into me. My hands were already in her hair, her lips were already on mine. With our bodies pressed together, eyes squeezed shut, the taste of apples kindled our tongues as we kissed, drunk from the same poison, under the same maddening spell.

We kissed like we'd been doing it and denied of it our entire lives. Mouths hungry, hands grabbing, bodies grinding, my dick throbbing ... My fingers dug into her waist to pull her flush against me as all the darkened blood in my veins rushed to the surface. I grabbed the back of her head, a fist full of white hair. On my tongue, I tasted a full moon. One half innocence, the other half destruction. A snowflake lost in a nightmare.

Kane's voice drifted with the murky fog.

Fallon looked up at me, our breathing shredded. "Take me away from here," she begged against my mouth.

I pulled Fallon once more through the maze. My heart punched through my chest, needing to get her alone, yet knowing how dangerous it could be for us to be caught together.

What was I thinking? It was *already* dangerous.

Kane was right on our tail.

I paused in the middle of the maze, smoking mirrors circling us.

"Fallon, where'd you go?" Kane called out.

I had to let her go, and the mere thought caused a jolt of electricity to shoot up my spine to the tips of my fingers. The scream in my chest ached to be released.

I couldn't hold on. I couldn't let go.

The mirrors made a cracking sound, my shadow-blood causing spider-like veins to crawl across the glass. Panicked, I grabbed her face once more, slammed my eyes shut, and crushed my mouth to hers.

"I'm sorry," I said, two words of a broken fate. Two words from my own self-hating lips that could very well destroy me. I reluctantly let go of her hand and slid between two mirrors, leaving her there for Kane Pruitt—

the man who the

ORDER *had said*

she BELONGED *to.*

the secret of
BELLAMY & SIRI

J UST LIKE ME, MARIETTA," I WHISPERED, TUGGING AT MY HAIR.
"White hair, just like you," Marietta repeated. *"The girl finally stepped
out of the woods, and they called her Sirius 'Siri' Van Doren, only sixteen and
lived on the border with her mother, Ida, her mother's dearest friend, Harriet, and
her daughter, Annitah...*

*"The four of them had fled to the town before it had a name and made a home
there, long before the others. And when the two covens arrived, Ida and Harriet
taught their daughters to walk in secrecy. To walk the woods quieter than a
whisper and never even so much as cast a shadow, in fear of what kind of dark
magic the covens could be practicing.*

*"But Siri Van Doren had a taste for adventure. So, yes! After her sixteenth
year, she stepped out of one of many secret places she hid in the woods. All because
of wonder for a boy and how he had transformed into a young man over time.*

*"At first, she had watched the way the muscles in his body grew and the way
his brown hair only darkened as the days passed. She memorized every line, every
movement, the curve of his smile. Siri knew everything there was to know about
Bellamy Blackwell, except who he was inside.*

*"It was a spring month when it was warmer during the day and colder at
night—a time when Sweet White Violets and Purple Trilliums popped up wildly
like oil over a hot flame. Bellamy was alone at night, walking barefoot through*

the woods under the Full Pink Moon.

"Bellamy was rarely alone, and Siri knew this was her chance. She could meet the boy she had a deep fascination for. Much to Annitah's dismay, Siri was sure he was kind and not what their mothers had said of them.

"'And you better not say a word,' Siri warned in a hushed tone with her hands on her hips, looking up to Annitah, who was much taller than she.

"Harriet and her daughter, Annitah, were known as the protectors of the Van Doren lineage, protectors of the moon children. Annitah understood nothing good could come from talking to anyone from either coven, but she loved her friend deeply and agreed to stay quiet.

"Siri's feet maneuvered the woods effortlessly, and when she reached Bellamy, her nerves materialized because she had been waiting on this moment for more than ten years.

"She slid behind a tree and waited for her heart to calm.

"'Who's there?' called out Bellamy, peering through the dense woods with narrowed eyes. The fateful spring winds tangled her white hair with the sweeping breeze, giving her away. 'You can come out,' insisted Bellamy, noticing it was a girl. A girl who had colors he had never seen before. 'I am not going to hurt you.'

"Siri peeked around the tree at first, and the two locked eyes before she reared back.

"She smiled to herself.

"He smiled to himself.

"'My name is Bellamy,' said the young man, walking closer as if he had stumbled upon the world's greatest treasure. 'Are you lost?'

"Siri could not speak at first. Her eyes darted up to the sky, where stars sprinkled around the pinkish moon. She held her breath until it burned and she was forced to let it go, but it came out in sporadic spurts.

"Bellamy dragged his fingers around the tree, rounding it until he was face-to-face with her.

"Then he froze, for he could not imagine her kind of beauty being from this world, and his lips fell open in awe as the two studied one another. 'What do they call you?' asked he.

"'Sirius,' said she, and the sound was of unparalleled eloquence to his ears, strong enough to bury its way inside of him.

"Bellamy, with a shaken finger, reached out and touched his fingertips to her supple pink lips. Perhaps to make sure she was real, that she was warm and not something of the supernatural.

"And Siri let him, lifting her head and closing her eyes as his fingers moved gently across the most sensitive part of her face.

"'The only beauty I have seen as close to this was the rare blue moon in a midnight sky during the first fall of snow,' said Bellamy so low, she hardly heard it over her fluttering heart. He tucked a stray hair behind her ear and allowed his fingertips to wander as if she were art, tracing the sharp edge of her face. 'It is as if you were born from the moon's glow.'

"And the two spent the entire night together.

"And the night after that, and the night after that…

"Nights turned into weeks, weeks turned into months, Bellamy and young Siri keeping one another as their best-kept secret over the years in the deep dark forest while the rest of the world slept.

"At the start of spring, for her, Bellamy would pluck the first flower popping up through the blankets of snow from the forest floor, then howl with the full moon, maddened with emotion he would later realize was love. While Siri would dance with the seasons as acorns bounced in her dress pockets, hoping they would keep her young and live forever with him.

"They kissed passionately at sunrise, knowing each time the sun came up from over the cliffs, they may never get this night again.

"'Meet me at the upside-down half-heart tree,' begged Siri, reluctantly pulling away from his mouth, but needing to say it, and needing to hear the words he would repeat every waking hour.

"He pulled her in again, heart helpless.

"'Bellamy, say it,' said Siri into his mouth. 'Say you will meet me.'

"'I will meet you,' replied he, oh, so painfully, knowing another day would pass without her before he would see her again.

"Siri kissed him one last time before she took off into the woods.

"'SIRIUS VAN DOREN!' shouted Bellamy, his fists clenched at his sides in protest of her departure, to keep her a little longer and see her face once more.

"Siri twirled around, and her white hair fanned out about her. Her bright eyes met his, and his existence shattered and rebuilt stronger from it. 'I WILL LOVE

YOU UNTIL THE DAY I DIE!' shouted Bellamy into the night sky.

"Siri smiled, causing Bellamy to take a step back as if it were a force. And to him, it was.

"'And I will love you until the moon dies!" Siri sang, tears pricking her eyes.

FALLON
chapter sixteen

I WAITED UNTIL THE TOWN WENT TO SLEEP BEFORE SLIPPING out of Gramps' house and headed for the woods. It was full dark, no stars, and the shadowy streets flowed throughout the town like satanic veins in the quiet night. Once I reached the graveyard, I parked the scooter and walked between a labyrinth of gravestones, past the pet sematary, until I approached the woods.

Julian once said this town had a way of causing the mind to bend, to mix what was real and what wasn't. Had it been real? Had we kissed in the Devil's Playground only hours before?

For close to an hour, I walked along the forest floor in my pajamas with my beating heart in my stomach, a tingle still on my lips, reminding me it had to be real. But I had to see him—*needed* to see him.

Under the moonlight, the sullen breezes had morphed into a bully, yanking leaves off the branches, spreading horror throughout the woods. Branches ripped at my clothes as my feet shuffled throughout the forest for a sign of Julian.

An eerie call of an owl echoed above, and my eyes darted up, seeing the way white tree trunks slashed through darkness into the sky.

I stumbled back when my foot caught under a fallen log, and my back hit a bare chest. I looked back, my heart like a drum when I faced the person who always seemed to be there.

"You're here," Julian said, his words dancing in my hair. He lifted me upright, and when I turned, his brows jumped in a panic. "What are you doing here, Fallon? You can't be here."

I tucked my hair nervously behind my ears, remembering why I was here but too embarrassed to say.

"I wanted to see you," I admitted, my heart going a million miles per second. A shiver spread through me from being within his reach, and I took a step closer to erase it. "I needed to see you again. We kissed, and it was …" I shook my head, words escaping me. I'd seen the way regret moped inside the oldest spirits—a ghost within a ghost. Death didn't end the suffering; ghosts were haunted too. And if I didn't say these words, I knew this would be a moment I'd suffer from. I had to get it out. I had to tell him. "I want to kiss you again. I want it all," I confessed, then paused so suddenly, chin high and shoulders back as if I embodied a world of confidence. I sucked in a breath. "Do you want me the same way I want you?"

With a pained expression, Julian's gaze ran across my face as he took a step back.

I took a step forward. "Julian?"

"How do you do that?" he asked. "How do you just say whatever you want? You can't. You can't just kiss me like you did. You can't just do and say whatever it is you want. It's stupid and reckless and …" He shook his head and tore his eyes away, turning his ear to the trees as if he could hear the whispers of the answers he was seeking. His eyes squinted as if in deep thought before they slammed back into my own. "What am I supposed to do?"

"It's said and done, and I don't take anything back."

Julian's features softened. He took a step closer and laid his hands on my shoulders. Then up the length of my neck. And through my hair. He opened his mouth to speak, but something in the distance caught his attention. My gaze followed his before our eyes returned to each other. "It's too dangerous out in the open like this. Come with me."

Julian grabbed my hand, and together we walked deeper into the woods.

His steps were quick and quiet and secretive, effortlessly weaving between trees as if the map of the forest was imprinted on his soles. Anticipation hummed along my skin, having no idea where he was taking me.

Every so often, Julian looked back as if his stare could hold and protect me. It catapulted an icy wave of nostalgia into my bones.

Train tracks crossed our path, and we followed them to an abandoned train car when he let go of my hand and hopped up on the wobbly platform. Julian held out his hand, and I hesitated at first, gazing at the small, dark space, and the door that could trap us in. It was nothing but a hollow, metal bin on wheels with four walls. All darkness.

He moved his fingers, his hand stretched out for me to take. "I'll be in here with you the whole time."

My eyes dropped to his hand.

I'd come to the woods to find him, and here he was, standing over an unsteady train car platform with a steady hand and defiance in his eyes. He looked down at me, pleading for me to join him.

My hand linked to his, and he pulled me up.

Julian anchored his gaze to mine, and the platform teetered to a standstill. "There aren't many places I can take off my mask and be myself," he explained, his shoulders tensing under his black coat as if he were nervous. He unlinked my folded arms from my chest and held my hands in his. "I want this too, but I want it to be with me and not some wretched Heathen."

My heart ruptured. Those words crawled and wrapped their arms around my heart. Until a few hours ago, a boy named Roger was the only boy I'd ever kissed, and it was only because of a dare at a party. The senior class had only invited me for their entertainment, calling me a *circus act* because I was a freak.

I licked my lips and swallowed. "Okay," I said with a nod, my skin heated.

Julian pulled the train car door, and it rolled shut. The sound bounced off the steel walls. It was pitch dark, and I froze in place.

"Julian?" I whispered. My eyes bounced around, seeing nothing but black.

Trapped, trapped, trapped.

"I'm right here," he said, and I felt his fingers on my cheeks.

Julian, Julian, Julian.

I bit my lip. "Okay."

He walked me backward against a wall, and I felt his cold breath first. It tingled on my lips like a warning. He remained there, hovering, testing the waters. My mouth drew over his, and our noses brushed.

I brought my fingers to his face, noticing his mask was gone.

Julian was without his mask and exposed. I squeezed my eyes shut, holding back the blend of intensity and emotions filling the room, filling us, wondering how someone could only be free in the dark. I fanned my finger across his long lashes, the slight curve of his nose, his high cheekbones, his bottom lip, along his jaw, picturing his face in my mind. And Julian let me, sinking his face into my hands, seeking more as if it were the first time anyone had ever touched him like this.

The tips of my fingers touched every inch of his face. And touching Julian was like touching neon, invigorating yet forbidden. He leaned his hips into me, and I moved my hand to the back of his neck, threading my fingers through his soft, thick hair, seeing nothing but darkness but feeling him all around me. They were not the same.

His nose brushed mine again, then again. Then his mouth coasted over my lips. Our breaths quickened, and I couldn't take it anymore.

"Julian ..." his name hummed inside me like a chorus, and he pressed his cheek to my own, his breath on my neck, in my ear, he surrounded me like the abyss of a shadow—everywhere and nowhere enough. Inside every corner of my soul even I was too scared to venture. A deep moan rattled in his chest when he dropped his palms to the wall. The vibrations plunged inside me.

He was so loud and bold and free now.

He grabbed my jaw and slid his palm down my throat, his mouth guiding mine to open.

Then he thrust his tongue into my opened mouth with sweet and slow agony.

And I sank, sank, sank, and faded into his kiss. His taste was nocturnal. His touch, an eclipse. Every sweep of Julian's tongue, every desperate and eager touch, coursed an electric and addicting feeling, one I wanted to chain-smoke. I had no idea if I was doing this right, but I submitted, letting go and letting him have me. He pulled my top lip between his, sucking when he growled, his chest echoing against mine as we sank together. He kissed me as if he had been searching, as if he found a piece of himself again within me. A thing he'd lost somewhere along his way.

"I know…" he tried to get out, grabbing my neck and pushing his hands to the back of my head until they gripped my hair. "I know what's"—he crushed his mouth to mine once more before letting off—"happened to me, why it's like this with only you." His voice was as coarse and raw as the very moment.

"What?" I breathed out, and his mouth slid across my jaw and neck as his hands slid down the length of my arms. Our tongues collided again, and I'd forgotten what it was he was trying to tell me as he kissed me madly, unraveling me, serenading me, tasting me, dizzying me.

"*Lunaticus,*" he panted into my mouth. "When the moon has struck you, it's called lunaticus … and you struck me. Hard." He kissed me even harder, threading his fingers with mine as the taste of poisoned apple still ghosted over his tongue. When he pulled away, he dropped his forehead to mine. "Something's come over me, and I need to have you."

Lunaticus.

I pushed off his coat, and he helped me. He lifted my tank over my head, and then his own. One by one, the clothes came off, and I didn't think. I couldn't. I was utterly lost to him and this need rushing inside me down to the space between my legs. His thumbs grazed my nipples, and I should have been embarrassed, but I wasn't. My back arched into his touch, and his mouth was everywhere, kissing across my collarbone and my breast before finding my mouth again. My fingers landed over the button on his slacks when I fumbled, having no idea what I was doing but knowing I needed him too. Julian's mouth never separated from mine as he took over, working the button and zipper and sliding his pants down his thighs.

And he melted against me, his manhood pressing into my stomach. I withered away as he pinned me against the steel wall, half-naked in the dark, my body trembling.

Julian clasped my pajama shorts and slid them down along with my panties until they hit the floor, and he rolled them off the heels of my feet.

I felt his lips on the crescent of my hip bone. He moved against me, around me, with me as if he could see all of me in the dark.

"What's this?" he asked, feeling the patch on my skin.

"I'm a virgin," I blurted, then bit my lip, punishing myself for letting it slip because it made me sound so inexperienced. *Not only was she a freak, but she was also a virgin.* "It's a birth control patch to help with my anemia and … mood swings."

His fingers froze on my skin. "You're a virgin?"

My mouth went dry, and I swallowed. "Yeah."

"Okay," he simply said, and his mouth moved across my hip, to the center of my stomach, to the tenderness between my thighs. My eyes bulged and heat rocketed up my flesh. I gripped his hair until he stood and loomed over me. "For now, you'll stay a virgin," he added, his heavy breathing hitting the top of my head. Julian grabbed the back of my neck before he dipped his mouth to mine, making me dizzy all over again.

"Have you ever been touched before?" he asked, his lips and words and breath bouncing off me as his hand slid up between my jittery thighs.

I didn't know how I was standing as my legs were like water and my insides like fire. I bit the inside of my cheek and shook my head, the anticipation as deafening as his presence. "No."

Then his two long fingers swiped through my center as he sucked my top lip. A gasp spilled from my mouth onto his. My eyes squeezed closed. My body tingled, weakened, and awakened. I needed more, and I gripped his sides, pulling Julian closer, wanting him to explore me, consume me, and pull me to the brink.

He pushed his tongue inside my mouth, swallowing my whimpers as the pad of his fingers stroked the sensitive places only I'd touched. "Do you like what I'm doing, Fallon?"

"Yesss…" I shuddered as his hard-on pressed into my belly.

I wrapped my fingers around his member, and he was warm and hard in my hand … and something else. Something pulsing, like a heartbeat. My hand traveled up and down his length, moving the tips of my fingers across his thick head. A shredded sound left him, and he kissed me deeper as he slipped a finger lower, drawing heavy circles on my entrance. I stroked him, allowing instinct to take control. It felt so natural, being here with him. To be doing this at all.

I was touching him as he was touching me. Together, we explored each other in the darkness, falling into a desperate rhythm of rhapsody. Our kisses turned to oxygen, overrun by the high we were building up for and with each other. My knees were shaking, and I slipped, slipped, slipped under his touch, crumbling.

Julian growled, grabbed my thighs, and lifted me, folding me into him and slamming my back against the wall. His shaft slid across my wetness, and I broke apart into tiny pieces, seeing stars in this dark place with him. The friction of us lit a passionate fire, every nerve-ending exposed and reaching new heights. The tips of his fingers stroked me, driving me wild. My head rolled back as he moved me, grinding my wet center against his length, his moans deep and thick.

We lost ourselves in the craze. My legs, that were clenched around his waist, started to shake. Julian's fingers dug into my bottom, having complete control over me and guiding my sex to drag across his but never entering. His other hand grazed and pressed and kneaded my entrance, and I couldn't come down from this climb. And he let go of my ass to tug on my bottom lip.

"Come with me," he spurred as if he were saying, *"Come with me, and I'll show you everything no one else will. Come with me, and I will tell you things no one else will tell you. I'll give you everything, feed all your forbidden thoughts, things you never knew you wanted."*

A whirlwind of sensations exploded within me. My nails pierced his scalp as he exhumed my orgasm from me as if it were my soul. His grind turned precise and deep, my sex sliding up and down his length. He slammed his palm on the steel wall beside my head, sending a vibration inside the train car. Warmth seeped over my skin as he came, his finger dragging up inside me, petting the places no one has been before him.

My head threw back—my body in spasms. I was overrun and flying, gripped and freed, possessed and pardoned, all in a single breath that I could hardly take. Julian kissed my throat as I pulsed around his finger.

Afterward, I dropped my head into the curve of his neck and tasted nature and woods and twilight on his skin. Our chests heaved together, and Julian held me for a moment until our breathing slowed, and his palm drifted up and down my back as he buried his face in my neck too.

"You're so quiet when you come. You're like a whisper," he said into my hair. "I've tried to ignore it, but I can't. No matter what they say, you were always mine, and you always will be."

I didn't understand the words he was saying, and the tap of his pulse in his neck hit my lips, running rabid with his words. And I closed my eyes, reminding myself it had to be the poison. The poison was making him say all the things, do all the things, and eventually, this night would pass, and he would disappear again.

"I CAN'T BELIEVE WE DID THAT. I'VE NEVER DONE ANYTHING LIKE THAT before."

We were both sitting on the edge of the train car. My head was in his lap, and his hands were in my hair. Julian's mask was back on, as were our clothes, and the September winds felt like ice against my heated skin.

"Me either," he said through an exhale, then looked down at me and shook his head as if in amazement.

"You don't do that stuff often?" I didn't know why I asked but wished I hadn't. Did I want to know?

His gaze lifted to the woods as he skipped his fingertips down my collarbone in deep thought. "Never. What we did was different. I've been involved in intercourse for rituals, yes, but that was all it was. The Heathens are the only ones born with magic from my coven. But I'd never done anything without my mask before. Never gave more than my body, until now." Julian was calm, sedated, his words lazy and patient as if he were drugged. Yet, he'd said it without emotion and more of a simple fact, a duty, and my heart felt his. "They can take parts of me, but I refused to let them have all of me."

"Then, why me?" I asked, his words not making sense based on what we had just done. Even though we didn't have sex, it still was something. Or had that only been a small piece of him too? And if so, would he ever be willing to give me everything?

Julian's chest caved. He hung his head and looked down at me, resting his palm on my stomach under my tank. The stars cast little light over his flushed skin. His wild black hair was damp from the heat firing between us earlier, a glow gleaming off the tips down to his hairline. I waited for him to tell me that what he did with me was a mistake because he was intoxicated from Mina's drink, and I was only a strange girl he'd found in the woods at the right time.

"Because when you look at me, you see *me*. It's different with you. You make me forget the mask is even there," Julian said, telling me, instead, *he* was the strange thing in the woods. *He* was the freak, not me. "I'm going to break this curse," he added in a whisper. "I have to."

For a long time, we sat in the train car listening to the night. I'd always imagined being with someone as strange and weird as me, and yet how beautifully bizarre the story would be, falling for Julian Blackwell—one of the monstrous things who made the woods their hiding-place, yet looked at me as if I were a mosaic masterpiece. There was no doubt I was equally terrified and intrigued by him, one of the cursed Hollow Heathens.

Terrified … because he could very well destroy me.

But I was sure to be destined for a grotesque love my grandchildren could tell their grandchildren about, and their grandchildren's grandchildren, wasn't I? The kinds of stories written about creatures everyone feared the most, yet loved painfully without limitations. Because freaks like us deserved the strange and the weird. And a love so severe.

"I want to show you something," Julian said.

I sat up before he popped onto his feet. The train car moved when he jumped down with a loud *thump!* on the earth, then turned to grab my waist. Once my feet hit the ground, Julian was off, running through the woods. My eyes fixed on his magnificent form, the stars outlining his silhouette as it passed under the cascade of moonlight. I took off after the Heathen who wore his soul, chasing him wherever it was he wanted to go. Julian's hands slid across the skin of the trees as he glided through the naked forest, allowing it to soothe him, guide him, nurture him.

We chased each other in the deep dark woods until he led me to a tree he called "the upside-down, half-heart tree," where he lifted me and sat me in the bend. I clung on to the white bark as he gazed up at me, wonder passing through his silver irises as I smiled down at him. Julian tilted his head to the side, then looked up at me again through thick and heavy lashes.

Afterward, we balanced on fallen logs. Julian walked backward with such stealth, his hands behind his back, eyes on me.

His eyes were always on me.

"Do you like fixing cars?" I asked him, carefully putting one foot in front of the other.

"Yes," his answer laconic.

I jumped off once my feet reached the end of the log. "Why?"

He thought for a moment, looking up at the canopies. When his eyes settled back on mine, he said, "I don't really know why. I just do, I suppose."

Then we laid under the moon where he showed me constellations. He pointed out Orion's belt, the dippers, and told me the story of Sirius, the brightest star in the sky. We did all these things before we stumbled upon a hidden greenhouse. Glass windows of all sorts, shapes, and sizes made up the walls, and behind the glass, vibrant rich colors reflected off the night. White flowers bloomed from vines that wrapped around the pillars, and I followed Julian around the structure.

"What's this?"

Julian rubbed a petal between his fingers. "When I was a boy, Phoenix and I built this for my mother. It's her night garden. She owns the apothecary in Town Square, and this is where she grows her medicine," he explained, but I already knew of his mother, Agatha. I'd met her on my first day.

"Ipomoea alba," he said and plucked a white flower from the vine and turned to face me. He swiped my hair from my face and tucked the flower behind my ear, his eyes sticking to mine. "There's an entire world that wakes after nightfall. The moonflower only opens up under the light of the moon." My breath held in my chest as his fingers lingered on my cheek, as if he were telling me so much more. As if there were multiple meanings planted between his words.

Together, we spent our time in a way the rest of the world had forgotten. Unhurriedly, slow. Free to be ourselves. Free to roam. Free to wander. We kissed in the tree's shade until the sun rose, and he kissed me once more after, neither one of us wanting our night to end.

On our walk back to the funeral home, where my scooter was parked, the threatening sun spilled into the pre-morning darkness. The funeral home was in our line of sight, and Julian grabbed my hand and turned me to face him.

"Hey." He squeezed my hand with the same look he'd given me plenty of times before he was about to rip my heart from my chest. I turned my gaze away, unable to look him in the eyes. The poison had left his system, and he was about to take it all back. "Fallon, I'm a private person. What happens when we're together, I don't want anyone else to know. Even if things were different, if I weren't cursed, and you weren't … friends with Sacred Sea. What happens between us, I never want to share it with anyone else."

"I don't wanna share it with anyone else either," I agreed. "So, what do we do from here?"

"WE KEEP IT *in the* DARK."

FALLON
chapter seventeen

ONDAY GROANED IN HER CHAIR THE NEXT MORNING, FACE DOWN on her desk and arms sprawled out. "I feel like a failure today. I have no motivation to do anything," she groaned. "And I think I made a few mistakes last night." I looked over, and she turned her head to the side and opened one eye, squinting. "Why are *you* smiling?" I lifted my shoulder. Her head popped up from the desk, papers sticking to her wet cheek from the drool. "Oh, you're bad. Kane? Did he slip you the tongue last night?"

I almost said *no* but swallowed down the word. Monday would only probe until she got all the dirt, and I couldn't give her any ideas that it was someone other than Kane. Even if Julian hadn't said not to tell anyone, I wouldn't. What happened the night before was ours—only ours—and I wanted to keep it that way too.

I shrugged, giving her no explanation or reasoning.

Monday peeled the papers from her cheek and raised a brow. "Fine, I see how it is. I have a body to embalm, anyway."

Another body had turned up. This one was from a boating accident. The fisherman's spirit was still attached to his body upstairs in the morgue. Circling and lost and confused, he was most likely replaying the last moments of his death over and over as if it would have changed the outcome of his status. Once his body was six feet under, he would most likely go back home to look out for his family. He would hang around until hanging around became unbearable, or he found peace. It was hard and too soon to say.

The following day, I spent my morning occupying my rattling mind with work, then returned to sleep into the afternoon. That evening I spent time with Gramps. After dinner, we read in the living room. I snuggled in the corner of his couch with *Gwendy's Button Box* in my lap. Gramps sat in the recliner, buried in King's book, *Doctor Sleep*. Every so often, we would pass a few sentences here and there, but the night was, for the most part, silent and calm.

Once Gramps retired to his room, I lay awake for hours in my bedroom on the second floor, French doors wide open, waiting for Julian to appear. He never showed.

Instead, on the banister of the balcony, laid a white flower in his place— the moonflower. And the same happened the following two nights. After night three, I couldn't take it anymore and slipped out of the house to search for him in the bitter and selfish woods, where we once ran wild.

Julian was nowhere.

Day after day, he wasn't at the auto body garage, and he wasn't in Town Square. By Thursday, bags, the shape of two half-moons, draped under my eyes. All I was left with were these moonflowers.

For the first time, Julian made me unafraid and unashamed to be myself. He didn't make me feel like I had to hide behind anything or that he was judging me when we were together. *For the first time*, Julian didn't make me feel like the freak. And I wanted that feeling again.

I replayed our night endlessly in my mind with one of the flowers between my fingers, feeling the silky petals and remembering his words. Where was he? Why didn't he want to see me?

Kane, Monday, and Fable stopped by Gramps' house after work many times to invite me places. To walk Crescent Beach, to a bonfire, to family dinners. But I couldn't stop thinking about Julian, the only person who I wanted to spend my time with.

I'd thought about Kioni's words, the girl from the palm reading tent.

Maybe she had been right. Maybe Mina's poisoned apple cider made everyone drunk with madness, and Julian was only looking for rebellion and mischief, to let loose like the rest of the town during Defy Day. But Kioni had also said the cider would let the truths out. A part of me wanted to believe that theory more. I wanted to believe what had happened that night was our truth.

"It's been almost a week, and I'm still recovering from Defy day," Freddy said with a laugh through the radio speaker. *"Mabon is around the corner, October's first full moon is near, and then, my witches, is Samhain. So many celebrations in our future, but let's kick Friday morning off right with an eerie twist on a classic—"* the music started, and Freddy howled *"—this is Freddy in the Mournin' with your Thursday morning Hollow Headlines, and remember, no one is safe after three a.m."*

A cover of Britney Spears' *Toxic* played on the radio in Gramps' bedroom. I'd moved the old thing in here since it was harder for him to get to the kitchen in the mornings. It was my day off, no recent deaths since the boating accident, and the two of us sat against his headboard in his room, both with a copy of the daily paper in our laps.

"Hey, Gramps?" I asked with the eraser of the pencil between my teeth. "Why does he always say,"—and I cleared my throat to give my best deep and depressing Freddy impression— *"'No one is safe after three a.m.?'"*

"It's the witching hour," Gramps muttered, not bothering to look up from his paper. He was already ahead of me, half the boxes filled out. I'd told him it wasn't a race, but we both knew it was. This was our routine in the mornings, competing to finish the puzzle first, drinking coffee in his dimly lit bedroom, and listening to Freddy in the Mournin'.

"What does that mean?"

Gramps gripped his pencil and looked up from his glasses to the wall where his dresser sat, his collection of hats hanging above. I waited patiently, knowing when not to push him.

"It means how I said it, moonshine. No one is safe durin' the witching hour, especially the flatlandahs. Supernatural and dark magic and all is powahful and strongah. Yah work at the funeral home, when do yah get busy?"

"After three a.m."

"Bingo," he grumbled. "It means as yah hear it, as yah see it." And as the last word fell from his cracked lips, the doorbell rang, echoing throughout the old house. "Those whooperups. No one bothered me 'til yah got heyah. I've heard that damn bell more times this week than in the last twenty years ... And what do they want this early in the mornin', anyway?"

I got up from the bed. "It's almost noon."

"Noon?! Yah meaning to tell me we've been stuck on this puzzle all mornin'?"

A laugh bounced out of my mouth as I left the room to answer the door.

Kane stood on the other side, wearing a simple white polo under a windbreaker, khaki chinos rolled tight at his ankles, and clean white shoes. He dropped his arm, let it hang at his side.

"So, funny story. We were all up at The Bean earlier and got to talking. Monday said you have quite a sense of humor, and I thought, no way. I've hardly even seen the girl smile. She couldn't possibly be as funny as Monday made her out to be. Then I thought ... Well, hell, I need to see this for myself," he rambled on, "I need to get her out of the house, hear her jokes, make her laugh, see her smile. I need to do all these things, and I'm not gonna stop until you say yes." He paused to catch his breath and placed a palm on the side of the door. "We got off to a bad start, and I think it's only fair I get to know you better, Fallon."

"Just friends?"

Kane shrugged. "Sure, if that's what you want."

I leaned against the door, my brow in the air. "It is, and where do you propose you make me laugh at? And when?"

"Tonight. Everyone's going to Voodoos tonight, but we could branch off, do our own thing. Up to you. I'll take you wherever you want to go."

Julian had been at Voodoos the last few times, and the chance of seeing him again revived my deadened hope.

"Voodoos it is," I agreed with deceit in my heart, using Kane's kind gesture for my own selfish motives.

Kane's smile was surprised, and he lifted his chin. "Alright, should I come to get you at ten? Or ..."

"How about I meet you there?"

"Right, of course. I'll meet you there," Kane repeated, not pushing his luck. He turned and walked backward to his car, pointing at me. "Don't forget. Voodoos. Ten tonight. If you don't show up, I'm coming to kidnap you!" he called out with a playful and perfectly white smile.

Laughing, I nodded. "I won't forget."

After closing the door, I turned, and Gramps stood behind me with his long curling brows pushed down, his lips smashed together. I jumped, not expecting him to be up and about or listening in on our conversation.

"Nope. No. No. No. No," he mumbled with a shaking head, walking back to his room. I followed after him. "No granddaughtah of mine will be associated with a Pruitt! Stupid wandoughts with the ..." he grumbled before slamming the door in my face.

I dropped my head and sucked in a breath, then opened his bedroom door. "How mature of you," I said as he crawled back into his bed, coughing, his elbows and knees shaking. "I don't get it. You hate the Heathens. You obviously hate Kane Pruitt, who is only a friend, not that it's any of your business. So please, tell me Gramps, who is deserving of your beloved granddaughter's friendship?"

"A nice and well-behaved Texas boy," he stated, and I barked out a laugh. "Pruitts are good for nuthin' rantallions—"

"*Rantallions*? What. Are. You. Even. Saying?"

"Look it up, why don't yah, with yah fancy technology!" Gramps narrowed his eyes. "I don't care who in tarnation yah choose, as long as yah don't bedswerve...and no one from this town ...What ar-ya still doin' heyah, anyhow? It's been weeks, moonshine. Go *home!* Go back to the life yah made for yaself."

There wasn't a life back in Texas. I'd never made a life there for myself. With Dad and Marietta gone, I'd only felt misplaced.

But I didn't say any of this. "You basically threw me a pity party and begged me to come. You sent me the letter, gave me the directions to your house, left me a key, and got me a job. Deep down, Gramps, you want me here, but you're just too stubborn to admit it. Hell, you're too stubborn to admit to yourself that you need help."

He shook his finger in the air, and his jowls shook along with it. "I got yah the damn job, but I never sent yah no letter askin' yah. I wouldah nevah asked yah to come back heyah."

Defeated, I whipped around and rushed out of his room and ran up the stairs. When I entered my room, I snatched my purse from the floor and emptied the contents onto the bed. Proving to him that he was losing his short-term memory could crumble him and possibly cause another heart attack like the last time.

As I descended the stairs with the letter clutched in my fist, I decided to do this gently. Gramps had to see that he did need me, and it was okay. I would be here for him.

I entered his bedroom, and Gramps already had the newspaper back in front of him, working diligently on the crossword puzzle. He didn't bother looking up when I'd entered.

I sat beside him on the edge of the mattress and unfolded the letter with nervous fingers.

"When you first sent me a letter about a year ago, and you called me *moonshine*, it was the first time I was happy since Marietta died. I wrote you back, Gramps, and for a year, I looked forward to seeing your letter in my mailbox every day. It's okay if you don't need me, but I'm not too stubborn to say that I need you. I want to be here, not because you're sick, but because I want to get to know my grandfather."

I handed him the letter, yet he still wouldn't look at me. It seemed as if a lifetime passed as he read it, and I waited with a held breath for him to finish and say something. I didn't care what he said as long as he didn't get upset or angry or worse.

"Moonshine," he said roughly. "Yah wrote me sixty-five lettahs ovah the last twelve months, and I wrote yah sixty-six." He paused and looked up at me in deep thought. I could see it in his expression, the way his eyes morphed into a war. Something was bothering him, and I wished he would spit it out already. "This lettah? I didn't send this. These aren't my words. This"—he gripped the letter in his hand, shaking it—"This isn't my handwriting. I woulda nevah asked yah to come. I only wanted to love yah at a distance. Yah already experienced enough death. It would be no good to have to meet me only ta lose me too."

My shoulders went slack under the weight of his words. He'd said he wanted to love me, and that washed over everything else he'd said. His confession caused tears to brim my eyes because I knew how hard it was for him to admit. However, Gramps' expression was the opposite. His eyes filled with comprehension and a bit of horror, which pulled me back to the same question he was faced with.

"then who sent me

THIS *LETTER?"*

FALLON
chapter eighteen

CASPER FOLLOWED ME FROM THE BEDROOM AND INTO MY bathroom. He weaved between my legs as I stood before the mirror to get ready for the night. I loaded thick layers of mascara and painted wings on my eyelids as he meowed at my feet. It was as if Casper knew where I was going and didn't like it one bit.

Earlier, Gramps refused to talk about the letter and only mentioned he was tired. Both of us had remained silent throughout dinner, our thoughts straying to the letter, wondering who wrote it, and what it meant for us. Gramps didn't have the answers, and I'd never seen him more flabbergasted and panicked, which only worried me more.

I arrived at Voodoos late, half-past ten, and the place was packed. My gaze latched onto Monday's bright red hair, and I squeezed through the crowd, failing miserably at avoiding bumping shoulders with anyone. The majority of the crowd was bunched together at the dartboards in the corner, adjacent to a large chalkboard hanging on the brick wall.

Adora was seated in the corner of the room on a high-top stool with chalk between her fingers. Her long legs were crossed, and her eyes were on Kane. Despite what happened in the dressing room, I still wanted to give her the benefit of the doubt. She'd only mentioned she didn't want to see Kane and me together, and I'd shown up without thinking twice if she'd be here or how my presence would make her feel, even though I only saw Kane as a friend.

I paused in the middle of the floor, scanning the crowd, mostly made up of Sacred Sea. I felt out of place as people shoved past me, and my nerves bubbled to the surface.

"Fallon!" Fable called out when her gaze found mine from across the room. Her long and spiraling brown hair swayed above her hips as she walked to me with her palms up at her sides. "Maverick is kicking Kane's ass, and Kane is losing it," she filled me in as she walked me to where a group of people were crowded around. "Kane always wins. Every tournament, never fails," she went on, and I couldn't help but look for the Heathens—to look for Julian.

If it were at all possible, I could physically feel my heart sinking with every face my eyes crossed. It turned cold inside my chest. He wasn't here, and I returned my gaze to Fable and forced a smile.

The others greeted me while Kane threw his arm around my shoulder and pulled me into his chest. "Oh, you're in trouble now, Mav. My good luck charm has arrived," he called out to Maverick, and his hot and booze-filled breath blew into my face. I let my arms hang awkwardly at my sides, waiting for him to let me go, and eventually, he did.

"Kane, just throw the dart already," Adora said with a wave of her hand.

The rest agreed, shouting over the music and loud conversations. I sat beside Monday and Fable at the bar, watching as Kane straightened his form, pinched the dart between his two fingers with a squinted eye, and lifted his chin. Serious mode activated.

"Want a drink?" Monday asked, her attention on Kane.

I looked back. Phoenix was staring at me from the corner of his eye. He had the bar's phone wedged between his shoulder and head as he poured beer into a frosty mug.

"Bartender looks busy," I pointed out, afraid. It wasn't that I didn't want to drink, but I'd never had to order one before. I didn't know how. Like pumping gas for the first time, or summoning a taxi. *Do I wave my hand like in the movies?*

"Oh, nonsense." Monday turned and leaned over, planting her elbows on the bar. "Barkeep, ya busy or what? Get my girl a drink."

Phoenix dropped the mug on the bar in front of a customer, collected cash, and hung the phone back on the receiver before he spun to face me. His fingers gripped the edge of the bar when he leaned over. "What can I get ya?"

"A beer?"

"You're sure?" His yellow eyes crinkled above his black mask. "What kind?"

I shrugged and pointed to the place where they were poured. "One of those."

He twisted his head back for a moment, and when he looked back up, humor swam in his eyes. "You want a machine pouring beer?"

"Stop messing with her and just get her a Gin and Tonic," Fable intervened, then turned to me with her eyes skyward. "Ignore him. It's like they don't know how to talk to people," she said, loud enough for him to hear, and he slid his gaze back to her.

The group went up in a roar, and I craned my neck around Fable to see that Kane had hit a bullseye, pulling in the lead over Maverick.

My drink arrived, and I sat silently in the corner as they all mingled. Kane, the dart champion, moved on to his next opponent, sliding winks and smiles my way every now and then. Even though I'd come under false pretenses, I didn't think it would be like this, spending the night in the corner, watching him play as the girls drank and laughed freely. The rest of the guys threw banter back and forth, and I stuck out like a sore thumb, not belonging and feeling so out of place.

The music went from classic rock to party music. A DJ replaced the band, turning the space in front of the stage into a heated and sweaty dance floor. There was a shift from the dartboards to the dance floor, but Kane was still high on his winning streak, and only his friends were left to watch.

"I'll beat any of you *motherfuckers!*" he shouted, smashed by this time. His fingers moved around the bar. "I already beat your ass, and your ass, and your ass..." he rambled, pointing at each person he'd won against, but then his finger paused, and his smile turned from sloppy to devious.

I looked to where his finger landed, and in front of the entrance, the crowd parted to show three Heathens who'd just walked in. Julian, Beck, and Zephyr.

The top half of Julian's face was covered in a mask, his beautiful mouth on display. The same mouth I'd kissed. His gaze picked me out amongst the crowd, and everything inside me lit and lifted, laced in a crazed high. But the look on his was the complete opposite.

Julian's eyes were cold, detached, empty.

Kane continued, "And, Julian Blackwell"—the chatter faded, and everyone's heads turned to the Heathens who stood with their masks, dark coats, and impervious exterior—"Let's face it. You already lost."

Sacred Sea members snapped their mouths closed, the patrons of the bar waited on the edge of a breath.

Julian smiled, tilting his head to the side to hide it, but I still caught it. It was so quick and easy, it jumped like a living thing. He wordlessly took a seat at the bar with the other two as if Kane Pruitt wasn't worth a syllable. Phoenix slid Julian a drink across the bar top, and he caught it before he tore his eyes from mine.

If Julian was bothered by Kane, he didn't show it, and the night we shared hadn't affected him either. He hadn't said hello to me, not even a wave or acknowledgment in my direction.

The rest of the bar fell back into their mingling and dancing, and Kane seemed disappointed, frustrated even by Julian's reaction, or lack thereof. Which made two of us. Kane snatched his glass from the bar beside me and chugged it all in one gulp, then slammed it back down and snapped his finger in the air, ordering another.

"Fallon, it's your turn," Kane said, pulling me up from the barstool with darts piled in one sweaty palm.

I shook my head. "I've never played before."

"No, I'm playing against myself." He positioned me in front of the wall under the dartboard with his hands on my shoulders. "You just stand there and look pretty."

At first, I didn't understand. Not until Kane started walking backward and everyone was staring at me. Some with worried glances, others with humor.

"No way," I said, taking a step out of the zone and walking back to my chair.

Kane dropped his head to the side and lifted his dart-holding hand. "Oh, c'mon. Don't you trust me? Adora, you trust me, right?" And Adora shook her head with a verbal *hell no*. Kane appeared annoyed, and his entire body leaned to one side. The invisible force of alcohol. "Adora, get under the dartboard," he ordered.

Adora shot me a worried expression. Her gaze turned to Kane, a knowing glance passing between them. Adora sank from the chair to her feet, the bottom hem of her bohemian-style dress dropped to the floor as she walked nervously to the wall with terror in her eyes. It was as if Kane had complete control over her and she had no choice.

"Fine, I'll do it," I jumped in, unsure why. For some reason, I wanted Adora to trust me. I wanted her to know I wasn't the girl she thought I was. I wasn't here to make her life miserable or take anything away from her—that I could be a friend, or at least try. "I'll do it," I said again, walking in front of the board. Relief washed over her expression as she moved back to her barstool.

"That's my girl," Kane praised, then licked the tip of the dart.

With my heels on, my head reached about four inches below the bullseye, which he'd been nailing all night. Chances were, he wouldn't hit me, but it still didn't stop my anxiety from creeping in and my palms from sweating.

Then I felt the weight of something heavy sitting on my chest. I wanted to run my palm down the front of my pleated shorts, but I couldn't move. I attempted to turn my head to the side, unable to watch, but I was stuck in place. I had no control over my limbs, my movements, almost as if a force of magic bound me to the wall, keeping me here. Kane flashed me a wicked smile.

My anxiety spiraled, my breathing turned shallow, and my gaze hit Julian, who was sweeping across the bar swifter than a vulture. Before Kane had a chance to throw the dart, Julian appeared behind him and plucked it from his hand.

"Playing against yourself proves nothing. Play me." His voice commanded the attention of all.

Chatter ceased and everyone watched, gripping anything closest to them.

And I still couldn't move. I was fucking trapped. All I could manage was to blink, swallow, and focus on my breathing to make sure I still was.

Kane turned, almost as tall as Julian, and stared at him for a moment with widened eyes. "You afraid for her, Blackwell?"

Julian's mouth twitched. "The girl barely reaches the board. It doesn't take much talent to avoid hitting her unless you're aiming for her." He looked at me, and the dart squeezed inside his fist. "Release her," he ordered with a nudge of his head.

Kane pointed at me and lowered his eyes. "No, she's staying," he cocked his head to Julian, his finger turning into an up-right flattened palm, "Go for it, Heathen," he challenged. "You make that shot, I'll free her from my hold."

Silence passed between the two of them. Julian clenched his jaw, and the veins in his neck popped. He was considering Kane's words, and my eyes bounced from Julian to Kane, back to Julian, having no idea what was happening or what Kane's words meant as my heart pounded hard against my chest.

"I do this, and you'll let her go?" Julian confirmed. "You'll free her from your hold?"

"Ab-so-lute-ly," Kane sang and took a step back, hooking his thumb behind him. "But you have to do it from back there."

By this time, more people had gathered as I stood under the dartboard, my stomach feeling like it had floated into my throat. A fat bead of sweat slithered down the nape of my neck. How did it go from everyone ignoring me to everyone staring at me? It was so hot, I wanted to shed my jacket, but couldn't unglue myself from this position.

Zephyr took a step between the parting crowd. He stood taller than the rest, at least six foot four, and lowered his head to whisper something to Julian. Zephyr's dirty-blond hair fell from its slicked place and over his white mask as he looked up at me with bright lime-green eyes. Julian nodded.

Kane looked around the crowd, chuckling nervously. "Are you guys done kissing yet or what?"

The three of them broke apart when Julian took many steps back, keeping his eyes on mine. And the way he looked at me peeled away all my nerves. My panic dissolved, only hearing one distinct sound. The sound of a heartbeat. It beat so loud in my ears. Soothing. Steady. Stable. I focused on that. It granted me permission to relax and trust him.

Julian paused, at least twenty feet away, if not more, and I wanted to close my eyes, but couldn't.

Then he rolled the dart between his two fingers, and all that consumed my senses were the colors of silver and green as Julian and Zephyr zeroed in on me, feeling me, breathing me, touching me. They were everywhere as if they were standing only centimeters away.

Without warning, Julian flicked his wrist, and the dart pierced the air between us. The room was so quiet that I heard the dart's whistle before it disappeared with a quick *thump!* against the wall. I stood frozen, unblinking eyes still linked to Julian's, and waited for something to tell me to breathe because my mind could no longer put together a single command. Julian's chest caved, and his eyes briefly closed before they blinked open to mine.

Relief. We breathed in at the same time but with twenty feet between us. Everyone else remained silent. A few had their jaw dropped, eyes wide, and brows in the air.

"Congrats, Julian," Kane said with a slow clap of his hands. "You see where you're standing? That's the closest you'll ever be allowed to Fallon Morgan."

Julian's eyes narrowed with Kane's words, his chest rising and falling rapidly. I was still standing under the weight of the dart, no doubt in the bullseye but too paralyzed to check. Julian secured his gaze to mine, and I felt him calming himself down through me.

Kane laughed as my gaze dragged between the two worlds, the heartbeat still pounding in my ears. Time moved slow. And once Kane snapped his fingers, it sped and the bar fell back in tune. The weight slid off me. My muscles melted with the freedom, and my body felt as if it had run miles upon miles.

Julian gave me the same apologetic look he'd given me in the Devil's Playground. The same one he'd given me when we'd said our goodbyes in the woods. His look told me he was about to disappear again, and I shook my head, but it did no good. He still turned away, and I was too weak to use anything to stop him—not my voice, my arms, my feet.

Julian threw his hand up to Phoenix, and Phoenix nodded from behind the bar.

Then the Heathens were gone.

Kane looked back at me with the devil in his smile.

"That was freaking amazing," Adora said, coming before me, breaking my narrowed gaze on Kane and peeling me from the spot under the dartboard. She led me to the bar as Kane talked to his friends, all their eyes on the path Julian just took when he'd left. "I can't believe you did that for me," she went on, but a solemn void took over the high Julian once gave. I wanted to run after him, to thank him and slap him and kiss him all at the same time. But Adora clung to me with a smile on her pouty lips.

"It was nothing," I said with a vacancy, my eyes locked on the door Julian had just walked through. I couldn't just let him leave again. I had to talk to him. I had to know where his head was at after the night we shared.

Then my feet started moving in that same direction.

"Where are you going?" I heard Adora call out from behind me.

I didn't know, but I couldn't just let him leave like this.

My shoulders shoved through the crowd of people, and I swallowed down the anxiety threatening to come up. I had to get to him before he left. I had to know what the hell just happened, what was happening to us, and why he was avoiding me.

"Fallon!" Kane called out after me, but I kept moving.

I pushed open the double doors and stumbled out of the bar as the fresh cold air slapped my face. Julian spun around. Beck and Zephyr followed. All three stood, silver chains swinging around their necks.

"So that's it now? No hello? No goodbye? You just come here to show off, and that's it?" I called out, storming toward him with so much pent up adrenaline pumping through me. I could keep what happened between us in the dark, but refusing to talk to me or acknowledge me or pretending we were strangers was too far. Julian looked to Zephyr then back at me.

"What was the point?!" I shouted, feeling used.

Zephyr yanked on Julian's shoulder, pulling him back. "What's the freak talking about, Julian?"

Julian shook his head with shock and a million lies in his eyes.

"Fallon!" Kane called out from behind me, and the music from inside Voodoos spilled out into the parking lot with him. "Are they messing with you?"

Julian's dark gaze locked on mine, his chest heaved violently, his fist clenching. Words sprinted across his irises. Inside them, all the things he wanted to scream were there, radiating off him like an angry song. THEN HE TURNED AND WALKED *AWAY,* *leaving me in his* COLD SPOTS.

FALLON
chapter nineteen

A YOUNG WOMAN, A FLATLANDER, HAD BEEN transported to the funeral home. Jonah had taken it upon himself to pick up the body without notifying me, saying he didn't want to interrupt my morning with Gramps, knowing he was getting worse. And after what had happened the night before with Julian, I needed the extra hours of sleep.

I had been up all night replaying his departure. Julian, a man who everyone believed to be indestructible, was on the verge of breaking before an audience, but he couldn't have let that happen. The more I thought about him, the more it drove me crazy.

And I used the most recent death to distract my mind.

The body had been identified as Beth Clayton, eighteen-year-old daughter to Jeremy and Christine Clayton, who owned the hardware store on the west side. The only homeless man of Weeping Hollow, who went by the name of Ocean, had found her body.

Ocean had a tent set up in the alleyways behind the strip mall. Since Ocean had proof of his whereabouts around the time Beth was murdered,

Officer Stoker hadn't taken him in for further questioning. Even though no defensive wounds were present to indicate a struggle, Beth's lips were stitched shut by black thread post-mortem. Milo had been the first to appear at the morgue, demanding answers to the cause of death of the town's sweet and innocent Beth Clayton.

I hadn't told Milo this, but after Jonah, Dr. Morley, and I examined her body, we found absolutely no indications as to the cause of her heart failure. All the signs pointed to the Hollow Heathens—to Julian. She was young, healthy, no reason for her heart to fail her. All the proof I needed was laid out before me, but my heart couldn't accept it. Perhaps my heart was failing me too.

There were similarities between us. The long white hair, pale skin, same height, same build. Only she was six years younger than me. Jonah hadn't mentioned anything, neither did Dr. Morley, and if they had noticed, they didn't say anything. But there was no denying the obvious.

Beth Clayton and I could have passed as sisters.

I kept these concerns to myself in case it was a state of paranoia. But after the letter I'd received from someone other than Gramps to get me to return to Weeping Hollow, I couldn't help but think someone was after me.

Or maybe I was finding reasons to place the blame on someone other than Julian.

Ocean had also stopped by to pay his respects to the girl he'd found.

Ocean was a thin and hairy man who sat on the corner of Bram Boulevard and Joyland Lane, playing his harmonica. I'd never talked to him before now and only knew about him through Gramps' letters. Ocean was a knower of things. He saw things when no one knew he was watching, heard things when no one thought he was listening. Mina Mae kept him fed as long as he kept an eye on Town Square at night, her living and breathing security camera.

But in the early hours, between three and four, he'd failed sweet Beth Clayton.

Ocean didn't talk much, but the one thing he'd said that never left my mind was the way he found her. *"She was so peaceful, at first I thought she was sleeping ... until I saw her mouth stitched shut. She was just lying there on a blanket of purple flowers with her arms folded across her chest beside the dump. Sweet, sweet, Beth,"* he'd said. *"The scene was beautifully tragic."*

They were purple Hyacinths. I'd plucked a few from her white hair and checked online back in my office to make sure. Purple Hyacinths were a symbol of sorrow. Sometimes a plea for forgiveness. Were they sorry because they got the wrong girl? Had they come from Agatha's night garden? Had it meant Julian was sorry because he couldn't control himself?

When I walked out of the funeral home, Kane Pruitt was leaning against the trunk of his car with both hands shoved into his khaki Chinos.

"Hey, Fallon," he immediately greeted, his voice filled with an apology, and his expression displaying a whole mess of embarrassment. I paused for a moment to study his features, then walked up to him with my arms crossed over my chest. "Monday said you'd be off by lunch." He paused and looked around, as if he was nervous. "I was an ass last night," he finally said.

I shifted my bag on my shoulder. "Go on, I'm listening."

Kane grinned. "Well, I wanted to make it up to you."

"Are you typically the *act-first-and-ask-for-forgiveness-later* guy?"

"Honestly, yes. But I'm moving toward the *I-like-this-girl-but-I'm-so-in-over-my-head* guy."

"That's no excuse," I pointed out.

"I know, but it's the only one I've got. Well, that and my immaturity." He shrugged, looking down at me with faux innocence.

I bit my lip, shaking my head. "I guess I can forgive *that* guy then. You know, for his honesty."

Kane released a relieved breath with his hand on his chest. It wasn't like we were on a date anyway. We were just friends, and perhaps I'd overacted, being the *expecting-more-when-I-shouldn't* girl.

"Good because ..." he popped the trunk to reveal a cooler, then lifted the lid, "I got us sandwiches and drinks and thought we could eat lunch on the pier. You in?"

After the night I had last night, and the wild morning, I agreed. Kane was trying, and as long as he wasn't drinking, he was bearable. Pleasant, even.

I followed him on my scooter to the pier, which was located near Gramps' house. At the front end of Weeping Hollow, the Pruitts owned a small seafood restaurant and bait shop on the coast. Kane led me down steep wooden steps to the dock, where boats lined both sides. The cooler hung from one hand as he walked in front of me, leading the way down the stretched length of the pier. Shorebirds scurried along the dock as gulls circled above. Fishermen unloaded their boats from their morning excursions. And salt stuck to the crisp September air as waves slapped against the dock.

When we reached the end, Kane took a seat along the edge and set the cooler beside him. "Hope you like Italian." He tossed the sub up to me.

"Love Italian." I caught it mid-air and took a seat beside him, both of us looking out to the choppy waters.

I'd seen the ocean in so many different ways since arriving: smooth as a love song, restless as my nights, impatient as my mind, alive as my heart whenever Julian was in the same room. But at this very moment, the ocean was as adamant and confused as my soul, the greatest distraction and buffer for Kane, me, and my troubled mind as we ate in comfortable silence.

Sitting beside me was a different man than the one from the bar the night before. Kane was relaxed, tired, almost as if keeping up with the charade was exhausting.

"You see that, the lighthouse a few miles out?" Kane pointed off to the left. In the distance, a black and white spiral lighthouse sat in the middle of the Atlantic.

I wiped the corner of my mouth with my thumb. "Yeah."

"That's Bone Island. It's been abandoned for twenty years now. The lighthouse keeper who used to live out there died when I was five. Body washed up on the rocks. One time, my father said he sent three men to go and check out the island, but they never returned. He hasn't sent another man since, and that was, I think," he squinted one eye, "eighteen years ago. Want to know the creepiest part about it all?"

"What?"

"The lighthouse still fucking works."

"How?"

"No one knows, but some say the island is haunted."

"What do you think?"

He shrugged, then his throat bobbed as he swallowed his food. "I think we should check it out sometime. You scared of ghosts, Fallon Morgan?" I laughed. If only he knew. Kane raised a brow, and my eyes narrowed to slits. He grinned and said, "Come on, I want to introduce you to someone." He jumped to his feet, swiped the back of his pants, then held his hand out to me, offering to help me up.

The sky was sunless, a subdued pastel gray stretching above our heads. Kane nodded to a few men as they unloaded their anchored boats, one hosing down the slight fishy smell from the pier. White birds hopped down the dock, scavenging for leftovers, and water sprayed our ankles as we walked around them.

"When you comin' out with us, Kos?" a fisherman asked Kane. He had crystal blue eyes, a scruffy beard, wearing overalls and black rubber boots. He was carrying large buckets filled with something that looked like fish guts.

"When the boss gives me a morning off," Kane joked with a crooked smile. "You're getting in pretty late there, Chap. If you leave earlier, you'll have better luck."

Smiling, the older man nodded and dropped the pails onto the dock. The water splashed over and seeped through the cracks of the planks. "That's why we need yah!"

"Did he call you Kos?" I asked as we reached the staircase leading up to the restaurant.

Kane took my hand and pulled me in front, making me go ahead of him. "Yeah, it's my middle name."

"Where did it come from?"

"Glaûkos. Long story, one for another day ..."

A sea of fishermen crowded the vast white deck of Portside Pearl. Beer bottles sprouted out of buckets of ice on every table like bouquet centerpieces. Kane took my hand and led me inside the cerulean blue building where bus-boys and waitresses rushed around the emptied dining area to clean up the aftermath from the lunch rush. And inside, the Portside Pearl was fancy, grasping Maine's coastal charm in all its details.

We walked past the bar area, through a stainless-steel kitchen, and reached offices in the back. He knocked three times, and I ran my palms up my arm, looking around as workers watched us between their duties.

"Come in," a man said, and Kane turned the knob.

The office was large and had a view of the Atlantic Ocean, the long dock we'd just walked from, and the lighthouse. Bright and airy, Augustine Pruitt smiled pleasantly from behind his desk as a woman stood at his side.

"Fallon, this is my father, Augustine Pruitt," Kane introduced, but his demeanor had changed from excited to disappointed as his gaze fell on the woman beside his father. "I wasn't expecting Miss Driscoll to be here," he bit out through his teeth as Mr. Pruitt stood to shake my hand.

"Please, call me Carrie," she insisted, shaking my hand next.

Carrie Driscoll. I remembered the name. Fable had talked about her, saying she was Jury Smith's girlfriend, but Fable never mentioned how beautiful she was, with honey-dipped hair that dripped over her shoulders and foamed along her waist. And upturned eyes that held chips of a glacier.

"Carrie resides off Seaside," Mr. Pruitt informed, smiling proudly at the young female. Fable had been right; Carrie had to be around the same age as us, twenty-four but no more than twenty-six. "She was just informing me of her plans with the greenhouse behind the old black mansion off Seaside. She's interested in obtaining ownership."

Kane frowned. "No one has cared for that property since Lance died. I wished you'd speak with me before making plans. You know I have an interest as well. I'm the only one who cares about that house, and the lighthouse."

Mr. Pruitt leaned back in his seat, crossed his legs, and propped his chin on his fingers. "That's what we were discussing. She knows her way around a garden and a boat, and based on our plan, we need our own greenhouse. You hardly have the time to learn and tend to the garden, let alone the lighthouse. I thought you wanted to take over Portside Pearl?"

Kane clenched his jaw. "I want the house."

"You want the world." Mr. Pruitt chuckled, and his quick-witted gaze moved across the room. Carrie smiled when Mr. Pruitt's eyes landed on her, but it quickly faded when he turned back to Kane. "We'll discuss this later, Carrie."

An awkwardness, so thick and stuffy, squeezed the space, and I dropped my gaze to my feet as Carrie left the office. The door clicked shut behind her, and Mr. Pruitt spoke upon her exit with disapproval in his eyes. "I apologize for my son, Fallon. He must have left his manners on the pier."

At the corner of my eye, Kane shifted, steeling his spine and clasping his hands in front of him. He turned his gaze to the ceiling.

"You raised a good man," I lied, *I think*. I didn't know Kane well, but I couldn't imagine living with one of the town's leaders was easy for him.

Kane's hazel eyes swung to mine and blinked owlishly. He seemed just as surprised as I was for saying that, especially after the way he'd acted at the bar. Kane didn't have the best reputation at Voodoos, but a part of me felt sorry for him.

Mr. Pruitt cleared his throat. "Will you be joining us for dinner this evening?"

"No, I can't leave Benny all alone. Not tonight. Maybe some other time?"

"Very well, I'll be looking forward to it."

Kane grabbed my hand and pulled me from the room. Just before the door closed, Mr. Pruitt's voice boomed at our backs. "I'm glad to see you two together."

Kane turned, nodded once, and moved his hand to the small of my back before guiding me out.

"I thought you said men died out there at the lighthouse," I whispered as we walked back through the kitchen. "Why would you want to be the keeper?"

"It's not the lighthouse I care about, it's the mansion. That house means something to me, and unfortunately, the two go hand in hand," he spoke into my ear with a simmering rage. "Carrie Driscoll isn't getting my fucking house."

GRAMPS REFUSED TO EAT DINNER, CLAIMING HE WASN'T HUNGRY. I OFFERED to move him into the living room where he could read, but he shook his head vehemently, his coughing fits only worsening. Blood appeared in the white napkin. He tried to hide it, but I'd already seen it.

His health was only declining, and the only advice Dr. Morley could give was to make him comfortable. Gramps was pushing seventy-eight, but he should have had another ten years left in him, at least. Before these past few months, he'd always been healthy. There had to be a reason for his rapid decline, the fevers, the wheezing inside his chest.

Evening passed, and I collapsed onto the chaise on the balcony with my Mac in my lap, staring at the freshly laid moonflower resting on the banister. I stood and swiped it off, watching it float and rock to the ground below before sitting back down. Clouds peeled apart above, illuminating the freckled star-filled night as I clicked into the laptop's pad desperately, refreshing the internet to find a connection.

Milo was right when he had said Dr. Morley was dumb for a doctor. I wasn't going to hang back and watch Gramps deteriorate to nothing.

Eventually, I gave up on the computer and set it aside. I pulled the thick quilt up to my neck and stared above as the wind sang me a sweet and calming song. The cold kissed my cheeks, soothed me, comforted me into a sleep.

I didn't know how long I'd been sleeping for, but it was still dark when my eyes blinked open to the sound of a pained and gurgling groan. Small bumps flared across my skin as my eyes darted to where the sound had come. *It's a ghost,* I told myself. *Just a ghost.* If I ignored them, sometimes they would go away.

But the groaning only grew louder with every slam of my pulse against my tingling skin.

Reluctantly, I lifted my head …

Down below, beside the edge of the cliff, a woman stood with her back facing me. Hair hung like a white river and flowed down her back. With a blink of my eyes, she fizzled out only to reappear in the middle of the lawn facing me. Her head was down so I couldn't see the ghost's face. I blinked again, and she was standing just below the balcony, the crown of her platinum blonde head staring up at me.

I jumped to my feet. The quilt fell to the balcony floor. My trembling hands gripped the railing as I peered over, my blood pulsing through my veins like a stampede.

Blink. She disappeared.

At the corner of my eye, the ghost popped up at the top step of the balcony, snatching my attention. I turned my head until she consumed my gaze. My back slammed against the opposite railing as she walked closer, lifting her head.

The view caused me to lose my balance, but my hand gripped the railing, catching me.

Her blue lips were sewn shut, and I recognized her face immediately.

"Beth? Beth Clayton?"

She tried to talk, groaning again, but no words would come out.

"What happened to you?" my voice shook. I couldn't believe she was here. It had only been this morning she was murdered, and she'd already sought me out, not staying long with her body. "Who did this to you?"

A white film covered her big eyes, and she clawed at her sewn lips. Blood seeped from the holes where the thread wove tight together, and her nails dug into her flesh, ripping her mouth apart. Scratching and desperate, she crawled closer and closer to me with tears running from her white eyes, one hand reaching out, the other tearing out the thread.

She groaned from her throat. A scream escaped from my lungs just as the grandfather clock chimed from inside the house, the loud bells bouncing out into the night.

A warm hand smoothed over my forehead, and my eyes sprang open to see silver eyes traveling across my face.

I flinched in the chaise. My breathing couldn't slow. My nerves couldn't calm. My eyes darted around for the ghost.

Julian was sitting beside me, his hand cupping the base of my head. "Hey, hey, hey," he chanted, redirecting my attention back to him as his eyes retraced their path to mine. "It's okay, it was just a nightmare," he said in a rush behind his black mask. "Only a nightmare."

I fell back into the chaise and bit my lip, sucking in the panic. "No, I saw her," I insisted. "She was right there." Beth had to have been here, trying to tell me something.

Julian's shoulders relaxed, and my hand moved over his on my cheek to make sure he wasn't a dream either. His hand was real inside mine. I released a long breath and closed my eyes for a moment as his thumb brushed my jawline.

And then I remembered the way he'd left at Voodoos. I remembered how he treated me in front of everyone, and I blinked my eyes open. "Julian ..." I sat up taller, the blanket fell from around my shoulders, and his hand slipped from my face. I narrowed my eyes. "What are you doing here?"

He pulled his hand into his lap and turned at the edge of the chaise, glancing down at his boots. "I was with Phoenix tonight. We overheard someone talking about a girl who was murdered. All I heard was 'the girl with the white hair,' and I came straight here," he said as if he couldn't believe his actions. "I had to make sure you were okay."

"Now you talk to me?" I asked, shaking my head.

He cocked his head, and his brows snapped together. "What?"

"You only talk to me when it's convenient for you. You only see me when it's convenient for you. Last night, you couldn't even acknowledge me—" I shook my head, catching my voice shaking too. I was too far gone to stop myself, and I didn't realize how hurt I was until I'd let it out. "You need to leave."

"What? No, you have it all wrong." Julian's lost and confused eyes flicked rapidly over my face. His brows bunched together. "Look, I'm sorry about what happened at Voodoos—"

"Go, Julian," I gritted out through a whisper, my mind telling me this was for the best, but my heart knew it wasn't. "Keep pretending this thing between us never happened."

"*I CAN'T, THAT'S THE PROBLEM!*" he thundered. "You think this is easy for me? That I *want* to have these feelings for you?!" Julian seethed, slamming his fist down on his knee. My eyes widened, and he shook his head before dropping it into his palms and fisting his hair. "I didn't mean it like that. It's complicated, alright?"

I stood, and Julian's gaze followed my every move. I grabbed the blanket from the chaise and wrapped it around my shoulders as I walked to my room.

"Fallon," he said desperately, standing to his feet. "Wait, slow down and just give me a damn second."

Casper ran after me.

"Goodbye, Julian," I said, closing the doors, leaving him outside on my balcony. *and the deadbolt slid in place with a*

CLICK.

JULIAN
chapter twenty

I DIDN'T KNOW HOW LONG I STOOD THERE IN THE COLD ON FALLON'S BALCONY, staring at the doors separating me from her. The late-night wind moaned and whistled. My eyes traced the black outline of my silhouette reflecting off her balcony door because they couldn't trace hers.

She'd denied me. Yet, I deserved it after the way I'd treated her outside of Voodoos. My back had been against the wall. What else was I supposed to do?

I didn't want to leave her balcony and return to the woods. Fallon Grimaldi had shut the door in my face, and because of it, my feelings for her only intensified. She was much stronger than I'd given her credit for, and I was a stupid and sick man who'd risk everything to be around her, even if it were for five more minutes. Because, somehow, she calmed the dark half of me. And if I wanted a chance to be with her, to make this right, I had no choice but to use this pent-up frustration on breaking the curse so the Order wouldn't see me as a threat any longer.

"WE'RE TALKING ABOUT THE SAME FALLON MORGAN, RIGHT? KANE'S GIRL. The one who couldn't order a beer?" Phoenix asked, humor spiking his tone as we walked through the woods bordering the town, near the break of dawn.

He'd said *Kane's girl,* and I wanted to tear off my own ears as the rest of them laughed a handful of laughs, as if they'd held them in fists and thrown them up into the trees' canopies to only duplicate and bounce off and fill my cursed ears all over again. A constant reminder that she was *Kane's girl,* not mine. That she belonged to Kane Pruitt, not me.

I should've never confessed to them the reason I'd bolted from them after overhearing Crazy Abbott. Or the fact she'd slammed the door in my face.

"Alright, she's not so bad after all," Phoenix went on, "Has a bite back? I like it. Maybe she does have a little Grimaldi in her after all."

"Or Pruitt," Zeph added, another callous laugh to follow. Another blow to my already rejected soul. I stayed quiet, and Zeph fell back and elbowed me in the arm. "It was idiotic to go to her at all. The Morgan girl isn't a part of the plan, and she isn't our responsibility," he said low to me, his tone grim.

I may have been shadow-blooded who cast no shadow, but Zephyr Goody *was* the shadow. Our ancestors had given him all the features to persuade one otherwise—dirty-blond hair and airy green eyes. However, Zephyr, the air element, was a darkened whisper more dangerous than an omen. Devoid of all emotion. A mysterious force more dreadful than all other beings that went bump in the night.

"If the freak ends up deceased in the middle of Town Square, so be it," he continued. "One less member for them, only a favor to us."

The dark woods thundered beneath my boots as I snapped, yanking him backward through trees before slamming him into one. "Don't talk about her like that." The words exploded out of me before I could take them back, and his two green orbs glowed back with a smirk in them. I grabbed his jacket. "Remember the code we live by," I added.

Zephyr Goody may be the shadow, but I could see in the dark.

His chest puffed. The woods silenced. The Heathens silenced. My icy shadow rushed through my blood.

"He's only joking," I heard Phoenix say behind me, laying a palm on my shoulder. "Right, Zeph? It was a joke."

"Don't test my patience," Zeph warned, pushing me off him.

I let off and straightened my coat, darting my gaze around the Heathens until it landed on Phoenix, who squinted his questionable eyes. "Let's just get this over and done with."

The plan was simple yet bold: steal the books of the first families from the Chambers to break our curse.

As we stood over the trap door about a half mile behind Town Hall, which led to an underground passageway to the Chambers, the woods groaned, already punishing us for our future betrayal to the town. The leaves rustled in the wind, warning us, but this was the only way. I tried to block out the sounds, but the raven in the distance squawked, reminding me death was all around, and Fallon could be next.

The underground tunnels spread out below Weeping Hollow like a spider web in the shape of the Norse Woods pentagram. There were five points of entry. This was one, directly north of Town Hall. The second one was at the Pruitt Mansion. The third at the South-East cave under the Morgan property. The fourth, at the cemetery. And the last point of entry was at Goody Plantation. A full circle, all leading to the middle under the gazebo where the original Chambers were located.

"You sure you want to do this?" Beck asked as Phoenix tied his hair back. "Because once we do this, there is no going back." I expected this of him, to convince me to back out now because what we were doing was wrong and something I'd typically never agree to. Beck could feel my hesitation diffusing from my skin. And if I said no, he'd stand beside me because that was who Beck was.

Phoenix crouched and swiped the leaves from the wooden trapdoor before looking back up at us. "I'm going in and walking the green mile with or without you all." We called it that because prisoners had to walk the mile-long trek through the tunnel before they were sacrificed, as my father did.

Since Zephyr's father was the only one who was left standing from that generation, aside from Drunk Earl, Zephyr was next in line for the Order. It was supposed to be me before my father died, but I never wanted the weight of the Order on my shoulders.

Zephyr could execute with quick intellectual agility, and without his emotions getting in the way, whereas I couldn't. I only wanted to see that

221

it stayed fair, balanced. But breaking this curse would never cure Zeph's ghoulish heart. The only way to fix Zephyr Goody was if he found someone he loved more than himself.

Leaves and dirt slid down the wooden door as it creaked open. Once the door collapsed against the earth, a cyclone of bats blasted through the opening, throwing Phoenix backward with a high-pitched scream. I pressed my lips together, holding in my amusement.

All our eyes fixed on Phoenix as he calmed himself down with a chuckle. "Come on, none of us were expecting that."

"Whatever you say." I stepped down first.

"You know who screams like that? Girls," Beck stated, following behind me. "Girls scream like that, Nix."

"And those douchebags from the Eastside," I pointed out.

"Which are the same," Zeph added.

We all filed in and down the narrow staircase leading underground. Phoenix's torch lit from behind, and a soft yellow glow cascaded down the stone walls in front of me as I led the way. Water dripped from cracked stone and slid down the rough edges of the tunnel our ancestors had carved out. Underground, it stayed at fifty-eight degrees Fahrenheit year-round, no matter the weather conditions on the surface.

Different passageways branched out, leading to separate caverns, one where an underground spring laid. Tonight, there was no time for swimming. We needed to get to the chamber's bibliotheca—a book repository that held the journals from the original families.

We walked for over half a mile, listening to the *drip, drip, drip* of the water seeping through the cracks of the cold, wet stone and landing in small puddles lining the tunnel. Metal bars blocked our entrance once we were about three-quarters of the way in, and I clutched the iron bars in my fists and rocked them back and forth. They weren't budging—no locks to break through either.

"I knew it wouldn't be easy," Beck mumbled beside me.

Phoenix cursed under his breath and shouldered his way between Beck and me, then kicked the metal gate. A loud *zang!* rang out through the tunnel.

"Control yourself," I gritted out, laying a hand on his shoulder to pull him back. "You think you can get through it?"

"I'll need your help to control it," Phoenix admitted, dropping the torch against the wall.

We both stood in front of the bars. Phoenix reached out for the fire from the torch. Flames spread over his hand and danced on his fingertips. Beck and Zeph stepped back as Phoenix brought his hand out in front of him, and the other snatched my wrist for my energy. He chanted a verse. I followed suit, tranced by the fire in his hand, and submitting to the heat as it fanned across our skin.

Then the fire was swallowed up as Phoenix's fingers curled into a fist. The jolt of a searing hot flame rocketed through his arm to where we were linked, down to my fingertips. I felt the fire inside me, and together, we swiped a finger across the bars, slicing the iron as if by a sweltering blade.

The iron bars fell to the ground with a loud *bang!*

"Well, hot damn, boys," Beck clapped, pushing past us and rubbing his hands together, "that was adorable."

I stepped over the bars after him. "Let's just get the books and get out."

After another quarter of the way down, past the cell of the Wiccan prison, we reached the wooden door to the Chamber. I popped open the lock, no time to waste.

"Just the journals," I instructed. "We're only taking what we need." I didn't tell them I wanted the Cantini book too. The Cantini's held the secrets of Weeping Hollow. It had the answers as to why Fallon's father would force her to join Sacred Sea if she returned, and for some masochistic reason, I wanted to see his request with my own eyes. I wanted confirmation it was because Tobias didn't want Fallon anywhere near us because of the curse. That there was no other reason. I turned and found Beck's blue eyes. "You watch the exit. I'll grab the Book of Parish."

He nodded and fell back against the stone wall.

The door opened, and we walked under the curved frame into the Chamber from the back. I'd been here more times than the rest of them, and I pointed down the hall and to the left where the library was.

"This place always gives me the creeps," Phoenix whispered as shadows moved across the walls that were not our own. The watchful eyes of our ancestors.

In dusty glass cases, skulls, a bag of bones, stones, and artifacts from the past made up the shelves. I gravitated to the wall of books and blew against the spines. Clouds of dust parted, and foiled letters appeared, gleaming against the blaze of Phoenix's torch. Zephyr was busy flipping through pictures from an old box and Phoenix stood by the doorway, watching the halls. My eyes roamed over the Book of Parish, Goody, and Wildes. Only three of what we needed were here. The Book of Danvers was missing, along with the Book of Cantini and … mine—the Book of Blackwell. *Where was the Book of Blackwell?*

I swiped my hand across spines as my eyes read greedily.

Blackwell, Blackwell, Blackwell.

All my eyes crossed were dates, names, 11/22/63, and so on. I walked over to Phoenix, snatched the torch, and returned to the wall of books, holding the torch high, silently begging for our family's silver foil to bounce off the fire. "Where are you?" My eyes darted across spines, rows, and columns. It wasn't here.

"Zeph," I called out in a loud whisper, grabbing the three available books. Phoenix cocked his head at us, and my eyes slid to Zephyr, who dropped the photos and walked to me. "Danvers and Blackwell aren't here." I didn't tell him that I was also looking for the Book of Cantini. It was only a few weeks ago I'd seen the missing books during the meeting with the Order. "It has to still be at the altar."

"We have enough," Zeph stated, reminding me of his opinion: *The Blackwells are stained with dark spots and insanity.* Meaning, the Book of Blackwell was useless. "We don't need Danvers either. They've been dead for over a century." But the answers to the curse could be in either of these books. In all five of these books. And the confirmation I needed about Fallon would be in the Book of Cantini, the ones who held the secrets. These books were the reason I risked everything to come here.

"The Danvers were here when the curse began," I pointed out, impatient.

Zeph cocked his head. "The fifth family was weak and worthless."

I leveled my glowering gaze. "I'm not leaving without all the books."

I dropped the three books in his arms and walked down the hall to the same place I'd stood before the Order, to the same place Augustine Pruitt had given Kane everything. This wasn't only a mission to find the answers we needed to break the Curse of the Hollow Heathens. I was determined to know why Fallon's father would force her to a coven, to understand why, for the first time, the Order forbade me to be near someone. *"It's only one girl,"* Agatha had stated, but it wasn't only *one* girl, it was *the* girl, and I couldn't let this go.

I needed all the books. I needed all the answers. I needed her.

My boots clambered up the steps to the long table, and my eyes roamed the surface desperately.

The table was empty. I twisted around, scanning the entire room.

The books were gone.

someone else, someone other than us,

HAD STOLEN FROM THE CHAMBER.

FALLON
chapter twenty one

G OOD MORNING AND HAPPY SEPTEMBER NINETEENTH. WE HAVE A *special guest here to kick off our Saturday morning. Milo Andrews, everyone.*"—enter pre-recorded applause— "*Milo, can you give us any insight as to what the heck is going on? First Mr. Gordon, then Jury Smith, and now our sweet, sweet, Beth Clayton ...*"

"*I know, Freddy, it's horrible. And with Mabon only two days away ...*"

"*Is what you said true? All three died from heart attacks?*"

"*That's what the reports say,*" Milo confirmed.

"*There has to be more to it, and I know a group of men who are capable of something like this.*"

"*Yeah, well, my job isn't to spread rumors, Freddy. I came here to reiterate how important it is to stick to curfew, especially after our annual Weeping Hollow Movie Night tonight. The Rocky Horror Picture Show will start an hour earlier this year at eleven. Let's have a good time tonight, witches.*"

"*There you have it, your Hollow Headlines, and remember,*" Freddy started, then Milo joined in, "*No one is safe after three AM.*"

Fable's arm swung beside mine as we walked Town Square.

A large screen stood on the greens near the gazebo. The residents were starting to roll in, carrying blankets and picnic baskets. *The Rocky Horror Picture Show* would begin in about an hour, and Fable and I took off to get drinks and popcorn.

"What … the …" Fable's voice drifted with the September night. The line for the pop-up concession stand had wrapped around the street. She paused her steps and sighed beside me.

Buttery popcorn, chocolate covered candies, and beer ciders juggled in people's hands and arms as they exited the concession.

Fable stepped out in front of two boys who were passing by. They were younger than us, seventeen or eighteen.

"I'll give you a twenty for those Angry Orchards." Fable nudged her head, and the boy looked at me, considering her proposal. "I'm giving you double what you paid for, and we both know you have a kegger over there, little Wildes. Don't be stupid, just take it."

Little Wildes. Golden-flecks glittered his narrowed eyes under his wild, side-swept brown hair. He was tall, wearing a long white tee, a jean jacket, and ripped black jeans. Handsome. He smiled as if he held all the cards—*always.* "Forty, and they're yours."

"Forget it." The two words had spilled out of my mouth, combined with an incredulous laugh. "It's not worth it, Fable. He's playin' you."

Fable rolled her eyes and looked back at the line once more, almost jumping in her sneakers. "Asshole."

"Should have come prepared, sweetheart." He shoved his hand inside the tub of popcorn resting against his chest and popped the handful into his mouth as he walked off. A small group followed behind him.

"Who was that?"

"Annoying piece of shit. That was Wren Wildes, Phoenix's little brother."

Complaints and groans went off like a domino effect within the line waiting for the concession. I craned my neck, noticing Mina Mae inside the tent, gray hair falling from her braid and framing her face. She was pacing the stand and juggling the popcorn and drinks and exchanging money. Only one helper was keeping the popcorn flowing and filling drinks. Mina patted her forehead with a hand towel, looking as if she was going to pass out at any moment.

An idea popped into my head, and I took off for the tent.

"Where are you going?" Fable called out, then caught up to me as I entered the concession stand and stood behind the counter. "Fallon," she whispered, but I proceeded to pull an apron over my clothes, tying it behind my back. The sheer black sweater I wore was from The Row, and I didn't want it stained. "You're crazy, you know that?"

Mina Mae, in a black and white pinstripe apron, rushed past me. "Fallon, yah a *darling*. It's about time someone helped out. Everyone wants to enjoy the events, but no one wants to do the dirty work."

"Ten minutes," I told Fable, waving over the next customer. "Let me get this line down,"—I leaned in to catch a customer's order before sliding to the popcorn machine— "It's better than waiting in line, and Mina will reward us. Won't ya, Mina?"

"I'll throw in a few hotcakes too, dear." She winked.

Fable jumped over the threshold and grabbed an apron off the hook.

It only took the four of us, including the employee, and twenty minutes to get the line caught up. Between customers, my eyes bounced up and caught on to silver ones.

My pulse quickened. My breath caught. My insides felt like fire against the autumn breeze.

Julian was standing against the apothecary storefront with one leg propped, watching me from under a dark shade.

"You girls did good!" Mina released an exhausted sigh, and I handed a bucket of popcorn to the last customer. "Take what you want and enjoy the movie," she continued, and when I looked back at Julian, he was gone.

We hung our aprons, took two beers each, a bucket of popcorn, Twizzlers, and chocolate-covered Mashuga Nuts. My hair smacked me in the face, smelling like a blend of sugar and butter.

"Totally worth it," Fable said upon an exhale after her first sip of an Angry Orchard. "And we did a good deed." She turned to face me once we reached the lawn. "You're making me a better person, Fallon Morgan. Don't ever leave Weeping Hollow."

Smiling, I popped a Twizzler in my mouth and tore off the end.

Sacred Sea members sat at the back, and we arrived as the movie was starting. We scattered across a large blanket on the grass, and Kane pulled me down to sit beside him.

Every so often, I looked back at BLACKWELL APOTHECARY for a certain Heathen who made me feel so out of control.

Kane dropped his mouth to my ear. "Mabon is two days away," he whispered. I nodded, searching for Julian. "There will be a bonfire at Crescent Beach after the feast. It's the perfect time to officially become one of—Ow!" He whipped around, rubbing the back of his head. "Shit, Monday. Why'd ya hit me?"

"Well, stop talking then!" she whisper-shouted.

Kane wrapped his arm around me and pulled me closer, his nose in my hair. "Become one of us."

"I don't really know what *one of you* is," I whispered back, pulling away from him. Kane smelled like an ocean of liquor during a storm whereas Julian smelled of nature, of woods and fresh air. Julian smelled of a crisp winter night.

My eyes closed briefly to take me back to our nights together. When I opened them again, he was there, standing with the other Heathens under a large beech tree beside the outdoor TV screen. His silver eyes bound to mine as he leaned against the thick trunk in his black coat.

Kane's hand drifted across my cheek to redirect my attention, then he wrapped a stray tendril behind my ear. "A sweet mix of pleasure and power. That's who we are." Then he chanted in my ear, a low hum I couldn't understand, and my head dropped to the side. At the corner of my eye, Julian lifted off the tree and zoned in on us. I felt Kane's mouth on my neck, his hand skimming up my thigh near the hem of my shorts. "What do you say?"

I became dizzy, confused, buzzing with need, either from Kane's spell-binding voice or Julian's pull with a sharpness in his eyes. He was forcing himself to stay in place with his fists clenched at his sides.

"Kane, stop," I was able to get out. But Kane's hand gripped my hip, trying to pull me under and forcing his mouth on mine. I pushed him off me. "What the hell, Kane?"

"What?" He looked around, confused. "You were into it."

"No." I stood and fixed my sweater. My eyes found Julian, and he looked just as shocked as Kane from a few yards away. "Don't ever try that again on me," I said, looking at the rest of their dumbfounded expressions. "I'll see you guys later." And I took off across the greens toward my scooter, unsure of what just happened.

"Come back, I'm sorry!" Kane called out, and the townies collectively told him to shut up behind me.

My feet stayed ahead of me as I ran through the empty and dimly lit streets. The lamplight buzzed above in front of Mina's diner, and I snatched my helmet from the scooter's handlebar and shoved it over my head.

"What was that? What did he do to you?" Julian asked, appearing from the shadows between buildings.

Shaking my head, I swung a leg over the scooter. "Go away, Julian."

"Talk to me, what happened?" he insisted, leaning his palm against the brick wall.

"He was just being a jerk."

"So, it didn't work," he said more to himself than to me, running his hand through his hair. His gaze found me again, and he leaned forward. "Fallon, you didn't fall for it."

Fall for it? I raised my brows and sat back on the scooter. "Of course not, you stupid Heathen. For some reason, I can't stop thinking about you."

"Yeah?" Julian's eyes lit up as he stepped forward from the alley, then glanced around before pulling himself back under the shade. "Will you come here?"

"No, I'm still mad at you," I said, gripping the handlebar.

"You want to come here and kiss me, or are we going to argue? Because you're giving me real mixed signals here, and I don't know what to do with this. It's all very new to me, Fallon."

"Well, it's all new for me too," I started to say, finding the words. "But I still told you things, things I never told anyone. I let you in more than anyone. I *undressed* for you—" I paused when my throat burned, warning me. I looked around, seeing as we were the only two people on this side of Town Square, with a single streetlight still buzzing above my head. I was under a spotlight while Julian stayed in the shadows. "You know, just because I'm inexperienced or look like this doesn't mean I lack self-respect. You're definitely not the first guy who thought I'd be easy. But guess what, Julian? I'm *not* fucking desperate! I gave *you* a shot because I thought you were different. I'm such an idiot, thinking you out of all people would understand. I was okay with keeping things in the dark between us. I would never tell anyone what we did, but I never signed up to be complete strangers in public, pretending we're not even friends. *That* I can't do." I shook my head. "Be honest with me, is it because you don't want to be seen with me? Are you embarrassed of me? Because I'm such a *freakshow?*"

"A *freakshow?* Fallon, you've got to be kidding me. I thought we were past that."

"Then tell me something real. Tell me something that would make sense of all this. Tell me anything!" I begged.

Julian froze as silence spread between us. The air changed, the mood changed, and we both realized only two things could happen from this point. Either I was jumping off this scooter and going to him, or I was leaving. And from the looks of it, Julian wasn't taking any drastic measures to come out of his hiding place.

He would never come out of his hiding place.

I leaned forward, gripped the handlebars, and revved the engine.

"I'm afraid of heights," he blurted from the shadows, and I snapped my gaze to him. "Every day, I take off my mask and stand in the mirror, and in an instant,"—he slapped his palm against the wall— "I'm standing either at the top of a Ferris wheel or on the edge of a cliff looking down. I get sick to my stomach, dizzy, everything's swaying. I feel like I'm going to either throw up or lose my balance and fall. I know it's irrational. But I keep staring at myself in the mirror, thinking I can get over it. Hoping that I can confront my fears so I can one day get past it and see the man behind the fear. So, I can see my own face. That maybe I'm the key to breaking my curse. But just before I pass out, I turn away." He paused and shook his head as if to shake away the feeling. "Sometimes, I forget what I'm more afraid of, heights or myself." He laughed, but it was empty. "There's something real for you. I'm afraid of heights."

The scooter sputtered beneath me. Our eyes locked, Julian's holding hallows of desperation. Julian Blackwell was afraid of heights. A fear so normal—so trivial coming from a man who had half the town in fear of him.

Heights, and this feeling came over me with his sudden confession.

I hopped off the scooter and sprinted to Julian, who was straightening his posture. He didn't wait until I was in the shadows before he reached out into the light and grabbed my hand to pull me under with him.

"I'm sorry," he said, his hands already on my face, my back already against the wall. "You have to know that it's not what it seems."

He flipped up his mask and nudged his lips against mine once before he was kissing me. It pulled me into a whirlwind, like a snap of an elastic band. Time bounced with it, bringing me back to when we explored each other in the train car.

"They're all liars, but we're not. This isn't a lie," he groveled with a thickness in his throat. His tongue tasted mine, kissing me hard and deep as if I was going to disappear or turn to dust inside his arms.

With one hand clasped firmly on his neck, and the other flattened against his chest, I forced my head away. Even my mind and heart were at war. "Julian," I said, and he dropped his head and settled it onto my shoulder. A groan vibrated from his chest down to the hips that were pinned to mine.

"I'm trying, Fallon," he said, pushing *"Fallon"* into my ear.

"All I wanted was to be real with each other. Real with me, real with yourself. I *need* real," I paused and pressed my face into his thick hair. I inhaled his scent, the smell of winter and woods, forcing myself to come out and say it. "Maybe it's not heights you're afraid of. Maybe you're just afraid of falling."

Julian lifted his head and stared into my eyes.

I waited for him to say something, but he never did.

I slipped out from under him and ran back to the scooter, knowing he wouldn't run after me.

"Fallon, you don't even know what you're talking about," Julian shouted, smacking his palm against the brick wall as I pushed down my helmet and swung my leg over the scooter. "Don't do this."

I did, *AND BOTH OF US LOST* THAT NIGHT.

FALLON
chapter twenty two

I 'VE ALWAYS WONDERED about the fascination around horror.
Not just horror, but thrillers too. The suspense and gory bits ...
The very books that make me cringe, jump, hide, scream, and sleep with the lights on. The books that make my muscles tense, heart race, and bats flap in the pit of my stomach. The same books that make my entire body react, fight-or-flight.

The same books that lined the shelves in Gramps' study.

I've wondered about the fascination behind the love of horror, and now I understand.

Maybe it's a way to distract or fill our heartbreak, our grief, our loneliness. To know there's something more than this. To remind ourselves we aren't *really* alone in all the times we are. Though most can't see the things that walk beside us or hide before us daily, maybe the unseeable love exists all the same. Maybe if love had a face, it would look like an evil and addicting thing—an emotional monster with an unfathomable hunger.

Yes, maybe that's why I love horror, because it makes my muscles tense and my heart race and butterflies—*er bats*—flap in the pit of my stomach. It makes my entire body react, flight-or-fight—like the way he does. For a fleeting moment, horror satisfies whatever it is inside me that starves to be filled, faced, or forgotten.

THERE WAS SOMETHING ABOUT FREDDY AT FIVE IN THE MORNING AT THE funeral home. The whispers of electric strums spilled into the preparation room, playing my hollowed heart like an air guitar.

Darkness hugged all around me, aside from the single lamp over Beth Clayton's stiff body on the cold metal table, but she wasn't here. It was only me and an empty vessel. I clutched tweezers between my fingers, pulling thread from her stubborn lips. I'd been eager to do this, hoping she'd come back to me and spill the secrets trapped inside her soul. Maybe that was why her killer had sewn her lips shut … so that she couldn't speak to me. But since her killer had done that, it meant they knew I could talk to the dead. They, whoever it was, knew Beth Clayton would end up on my table, and her spirit would end up before my eyes.

No one could have known that.

My thoughts instantly went to Jury Smith and the people who had been there when I'd kicked everyone out of the room to talk to him. Monday, Officer Stoker, Earl Parish, Beck Parish, Jonah St. Christopher, Milo Andrews, Julian…Julian Blackwell.

Julian, Julian, Julian. "Could they hear me talking to the dead?" I shuddered at the thought.

I filled in her brows, painted light shadow on her lids, and rubbed the pads of my fingers across her cheekbones, applying thick layers to give her color. Beth Clayton was beautiful, sweet, sweet, beautiful, with her whole life in front of her. "What happened to you?"

Being a mortician wasn't easy.

Seeing kids' bodies pass over my tables was hard.

Young girls like Beth Clayton were harder, I thought.

I pressed my thumb to my lips, then to her forehead as I always did to each body I'd come across. "You're free, sweet girl, nothing can hold you down now."

A single tear warmed the corner of my eye. Just one, like every other time, and I swiped it dry.

"That was nice," a voice said. I turned, and Jonah was leaning in the doorway, his hair disheveled, but his wardrobe impeccable as always, with two coffees in his hands. He pushed off the wall and walked closer. "You always do that?" he asked, handing me a cup.

"Yeah."

His brow lifted as he held the mug at his lips. "A prayer for them?"

"Just a wish from the living to the dead, I suppose. Nothing special."

"Sounded and looked pretty special to me."

Smiling, I tapped the end of the table beside Beth's body. "She's ready to go for the funeral tomorrow."

"You out of here already?" He flicked his wrist, and his watch shifted. "It's six in the morning."

"Five forty-five," I corrected, standing and walking to the sink to flip the water on. "I've been here for about an hour now. I want to get back to Gramps and be there when he wakes." I shook out my hands and grabbed paper towels from the dispenser. "I'll be back later to clean the display and prep room. The Clayton's should be here around ten."

Jonah nodded, his gaze following me as I pulled a sheet over Beth's body.

By six, I was at Mina's diner as soon as it opened, grabbing my well-deserved hotcakes and two issues of The Daily Hollow. And by six-thirty, I was back at Gramps', standing on the cliff with a fresh cup of coffee in hand, watching the sunrise and waiting for him to wake.

This was my daily routine now, and I didn't mind it. For the first time, in a long time, I wasn't alone anymore. Gramps and I were getting along. Together, we found a rhythm. Though he never sent the letter to get me here, I couldn't be more grateful to have this time with him. And the pang in my heart only grew larger each day knowing his were numbered.

My eyes fell to the spot where I'd first met Julian.

I'd wanted to give in to him in the alleyway. It took everything not to. Everyone tells you how to live your life, but no one tells you how to walk away from the life you love when it starts to hurt. *Yes*, with Julian, I loved life because he made me feel undead. The girl who looked like a ghost, talked to ghosts, raised by ghosts, he made this girl feel like something worth looking at, someone who was wanted. But he could easily take that away from me too. If I gave into him, he'd think treating me like this was okay, and it was not okay.

When Gramps woke, we spent the next few hours eating the hotcakes and working on our crossword puzzles in his bed, listening to Freddy in the Mournin'. He was much quieter this morning, and each time my pencil hit the newspaper, he glanced over to catch my progress.

THAT EVENING, I WALKED INTO THE BEAN AFTER HEARING IT WAS THE ONLY place in Weeping Hollow to have a hope for an internet connection. Gramps had hardly eaten anything during dinner. I needed to research his symptoms, see if I could find answers to this virus.

The coffee house was on the corner of Town Square, with windows in a diamond-paned pattern. Inside, a faded brick wall took up half the store behind a long black counter, where charcoal black pendant lights hung in a row. Along the adjacent wall, rectangular chalkboards displayed a curated menu.

The little place was packed yet quiet, the young adults working behind laptop screens or indulged inside a book. I noticed Milo sitting on the opposite end next to a window with Monday and Kane.

I hadn't spoken to Kane since *The Rocky Horror Picture Show* movie night.

Kane called me over as soon as he noticed me too, waving his hand casually as if the other night had never happened. I took a quick look around, scanning for an empty table, but there wasn't one. After a short debate with myself, I walked over with my black and white striped Kate Spade laptop satchel hanging off my shoulder.

"Small world," I said, bouncing my gaze back and forth between them.

Monday wore a black velvet bow in her half-updo and a frown. "You left us last night and missed the real show," she said. "One of the Hollow Heathens went crazy and could've eaten me alive."

"Better off. Fallon could finally make you look pretty back at the morgue," Kane joked through a laugh.

"Asshole," Monday scoffed, kicking him under the table. "Mark my words," Monday held up a finger, "The only option for this smoking hot body is cremation. No one's touching me."

I chuckled, noticing Kane made no moves to make direct eye contact.

He pulled his hat further down his face, but I still saw the bruise on his eye.

"What happened to you?" I asked him. "Is that a bruise?"

"That's what I was trying to tell ya," Monday exclaimed. "Out of nowhere, that Heathen, Blackwell, went ballistic and punched him for no reason. I've never seen a Heathen lose control like that in public."

"It was a sucker punch too," Kane gritted out, dropping his fist on the table. "Didn't stay around long enough for me to get right, either."

"Because you were out for a good minute," Milo pointed out, then hid his smile behind his tight lips.

"He punched you?" A little uncomfortable, I adjusted the strap on my shoulder. "Why would he punch you?" I couldn't say he didn't deserve it because he did.

Kane narrowed his eyes and dropped his chin. "Why do you think?"

"Because we're boys." Milo threw his back against the booth. "We fight, lie, and steal."

Monday's face twisted. "Why?"

"Because. That's how we get what we want." Milo slid down the bench to make room for me. "Mabon's tomorrow. Are you finally coming with us to Crescent Beach?"

I took a seat next to him and pulled my laptop bag in front of me, thinking about my answer. I didn't want a repeat of last night, and with Gramps, I already had enough on my plate than to worry about Kane's erratic behavior. "I don't know."

"Oh, you have to," Monday said into her coffee, took a small sip, then set it down. "There'll be a bonfire at the beach, some music, dancing ..." she bounced in place, remembering something, "Oh, and at midnight, whoever is brave enough to jump into the ocean is said to have a year of good fortune."

"Like off the cliff?"

"Maverick is the only one crazy enough to do it," Kane said. He leaned back and dropped one arm on the table to cup his mug. He lifted a brow with a small smile. I didn't know what it meant. A *let's-talk?* *I'm-sorry?* Whatever it was, it wasn't going to work this time.

And the conversation rolled on. I knew they were laughing and talking back and forth, but their voices fell into the background as I fixed my gaze outside the shop window. Half of me was fully aware, looking for Julian, the other half was lost inside this body, stuck inside this coffee shop, trapped with these people. It was an odd and unique feeling. A feeling of time slipping and the world moving on without needing me—that the world would be okay, regardless if I was here or not. Being around Julian didn't make me feel like that, the reason I caught myself looking for him— either out there or in the corners of my mind.

"Yoo-hoo, Fallon." Monday snapped her fingers in the air, and I darted my gaze to her. "We were about to head out. We're going to Eleanor's across the street. She does a little bit of this, a little bit of that."

"She's a psychic," Milo answered. "Just say she's a psychic."

I immediately thought of Kioni, the girl I'd met from the palm reading tent on Defy night. Maybe she would be there and introduce me to her grandmother. It was possible I would have better luck with a reading from a psychic than results from Google regarding Gramps' health.

"Ya right out straight or what?" Kane asked.

"Okay, yeah. I'll go."

Monday and Milo walked before Kane and me. The fading sun lowered over the forest behind us, painting the sky in brushstrokes of marigold, carnation pink, and lavender.

Kane elbowed me in the arm. I looked up at him when he lowered his head. "Hey, I really am sorry about last night. I honestly meant no harm. I don't know what came over me."

All I could do was nod. I wished I could have said it was okay and pretend that it never happened, but it wasn't okay. I wished I could forget about it, but forgetting would be stupid on my part. Instead, I folded the situation up and filed it in a cabinet stored in the back of my mind marked *never again*.

"I don't know what's going on between you and Blackwell," Kane continued, "But if he knows what's good for him, he'll back off."

"What's good for him?" I asked, offended as if it were me Kane was threatening.

"Let's just say you're under Sacred Sea protection. Blackwell can't so much as be within twenty feet of you without our permission. If he goes near you, the Order will punish him and throw him in the tunnels. So, if you care about him, you should stay away too." He shoved his hands into his pockets, walking at my side. "It's what's best for everyone."

"Wait." I stopped walking, staring up at Kane. "Why can't he be around me?" Was this why Julian was acting strange? Was it the reason he was hiding us? This answered everything, but why didn't Julian just tell me?

"Do you have any idea what Blackwell is capable of? One slip up, and you're dead. Is that what you want?" His brows pressed together, and he leaned in. "You think Benny wants to bury his only granddaughter? Because I don't."

"That's low, Kane. Using Benny like that." I shook my head. "And for the record, I don't think protection means groping me, either. When I say stop, I mean it. When I say just friends, I mean it. There's no hidden line or underlying meaning. If you ever touch me like that again—"

"I said I was sorry. That was just me being a drunk and horny dick, Fallon. I got it, okay?" He stood with his brows in the air, arms at his sides. "Moment passed. *Trust me*, it won't happen again." He'd said it with such disgust, almost as if the mere thought of looking at me put a sour taste in his mouth.

Silent seconds passed between us, and the strap from my laptop bag dug into my shoulder, keeping me unbearably present in every single one. My eyes slid back and forth between his as I thought about what he'd said, that I was under Sacred Sea protection.

"Why is Sacred Sea protecting me? There's a whole town here, why me?"

Kane's eyes grew, and he shook his head. "Probably those Hollow Heathens," he breathed out, and I rolled my eyes, shifting in place when he pulled back on my shoulder. "Look, all I know is your dad asked for his coven to protect you if you returned. You came back, Fallon. This is the situation you got yourself into. My advice is to stay away from Blackwell. I've no doubt he's killed people before, and he *will* kill you. No one is immune. Do you have any idea who his father was?" I shook my head, and Kane sucked in a breath. "Javino Blackwell. Murdered half a dozen people before he was burned on the cliffs. It's in the Blackwell blood, and you can't fix something that's in your blood."

The rest of the way was quiet, and I no longer wanted to be here.

I wanted to find Julian. I wanted to tell him the same words he'd told me.

I wanted to tell him that *they're all liars, but we're not.* I wanted to tell him that I didn't believe any of them, that they didn't know him as I knew him.

But I kept my emotions bottled as the four of us stood in front of a tiny storefront wedged between a tattoo shop and a parlor. A neon-blue flashing sign ran up the side, reading, PSYCHIC.

"I warned you about them, didn't I?" Monday whispered, talking about the Hollow Heathens as she opened the door before we all filed inside.

"I just don't think they're as bad as everyone makes them out to be," I whispered back, feeling the need to defend Julian.

Kane groaned.

Monday chuckled. "Says the girl who took off and almost left Weeping Hollow because of them."

Milo, who'd already stepped off to the side, kept quiet and wandered to a wall where books crammed the shelves, stacking from floor to ceiling. Spines were worn and cracked and peeling away, evidence of being read time and time again. The font lettering had faded, and I ran my finger across the bumpy ridges, collecting dust, then blew the fuzz from the tip of my finger.

Monday dropped her palm down on the countertop bell repeatedly. "Hello? Ms. Eleanor!"

"Chill out. She's coming," Milo hissed.

Then the curtain of beads parted down the middle, and a tall woman appeared, with a shaved head and golden hoops piercing the rims of her ears. She wore a black paneled blouse over black slacks with the seams in gold detail and sequins. Eyes as black as night found mine across the room when a familiar and knowing tight grin stretched across her wide lips.

A breath left me, and my chest tightened. "You look just like—"

"Marietta," she finished my sentence and dropped her head in a single nod. "She was my twin sister." Her Kenyan accent was just as smooth and strong and stubborn as Marietta's, untarnished by the Mainers. It was like seeing Marietta all over again, and emotions pooled from my chest, up my throat, and pricked behind my eyes. I wanted to rush over and wrap my arms around her, to breathe in the distinct scent of rosemary and sage. "And you must be our moonshine."

"I'm sorry," I shook my head, trying to drag in a steady breath. "This is hard for me. You look just like her."

"Me, I miss her too, child. Come, let us talk."

Eleanor led me through the curtain of beads to the back. Violet and green velvet canvases hung on the walls, and incense burned in a corner of the narrow hallway stacked with boxes and inventory. She opened the door to a small room, and we both entered.

A purple silk tablecloth draped over a round table positioned in the center of the room, with two tufted chairs facing each other. A deck of tarot cards was fanned out across the center of the table. Candles of all different heights lined the walls on vintage sideboards, casting dancing shadows across the dark wallpaper.

For some reason, I had the need to apologize for what happened to Marietta, as if it were my fault. As if I'd taken Marietta away from Eleanor myself and forced her to raise me. I wanted to apologize for all the years stolen and for her not being there for Marietta when she got sick. But I couldn't say anything as the grief held my tongue in a firm grip.

"It is alright, child," Eleanor said, reading my mind. "We knew this day would reach."

Eleanor pulled out the large chair and offered me to sit. And I did, slowly shaking my head. "I don't understand."

Eleanor took a seat across from me. "You will." She offered a small smile, and her gold bracelets jingled as she folded the cards into a clean stack and placed them off to the side between two other decks. "Have you ever had a reading done before?"

"No." My voice was shallow as I said it. "I was never really introduced to this sort of stuff until now. I mean, I've heard of magic and witches and the supernatural, I've never doubted it. But since returning to Weeping Hollow, it's as if I was thrown into an alternate universe where normal doesn't exist. Half the time, I don't even know what's real."

"Me, I see," Eleanor said in a disapproving tone, then she nodded as something seemed to click in her skull. "It seems as if Marietta was the right choice, after all." She laughed lightly. "Tarot cards are a mirror to your soul. The biggest misconception is that they hold the key to your future, but what they truly unlock is one's inner intuition and wisdom as a guide to navigate life." Her eyes veered to the three decks resting beside us. "Go on. Choose a deck."

I examined the three decks that were all bent and out of shape and frayed at the edges, no longer sitting cleanly on top of one another. The first deck was golden, the second was black, and the third was silver, but all three had journeyed through many readings. The silver deck had a picture of a bird's claws swooping down, and it captured my attention. "The silver."

Eleanor's expression remained stoic, and she asked me to shuffle.

I did, and the cards were frail against my skilled fingers as I slid them and wove them back into place before handing them to her outstretched palm. Eleanor placed the shuffled deck between us on the table. "Sawa, make three piles, dear."

I separated the deck, as she requested. And Eleanor took the top card of one pile and laid the card face up on the table in front of that pile. Then she slipped the last card from the bottom of the same stack and laid it face up on top of the pile. She repeated these steps for all three piles.

"Your past, present, and future," she explained. Six cards, face-up, stared back at me. I leaned closer, sitting on the edge of the seat with perked ears, anxious to hear more. "Feeling tense?" she chuckled. "Little psychic joke."

Eleanor's long nail scraped along the rim of the pile that marked the past. "The hermit card. This tells me you have mainly kept to yourself in younger years and ... it is paired with the Devil reversed. Entrapment. It signifies a past of no escape, and a road leading to one. You are held captive, or a situation that happened to you. Perhaps something more literal—trapped." Her eyes bounced up to mine, and I quickly looked away. "Are you getting me, moonshine?"

A lump formed in my throat. "I ... I don't know," I lied, flashes of the horrifying night in the well replayed inside my head—the walls closing in, the whispers in the cold, wet night, my throat so raw from screaming ...

Her hand darted out for mine, but stopped halfway, changing her mind.

"Your present." Her hand slid to the next deck. "*Ah!* The trickster."

Eleanor tapped the card with a faded picture of a man or woman—it was too far gone to tell at this point—carrying a sword over a flowing river. "The card is reversed. In this case, it represents the illusion of the world around you. Do not believe everything or everyone you see or hear," she advised. Her finger moved to the paired card that read DEATH. I felt my jaw slipping open at the immediate thought of Gramps, and Eleanor clicked her tongue. "A severance is coming, and it will be painful. I know what you are thinking, but it could be in any aspect of your life. It will almost certainly be significant and absolute."

My eyes lifted from the Death card to her black ones as my heart shook in my chest. "Almost? So, this could change?"

"It is doubtful. Death is a natural process in life. When it comes, use your inner strength to embrace it. Though, your future is most peculiar." The disappointment in her tone didn't go unnoticed. The expression crossing her features revealed nothing short of pity and sorrow, not what she presumably had expected from the cards. "Here, you have the wheel of fortune, but it is reversed. You have lost control of the inevitable fate you were destined for. There is misfortune to come." My eyes steered to the card pairing with the wheel of fortune, and I saw a man and woman under two birds.

"Mhmm … It is paired with the Lovers card." Her voice changed as she spoke, shock and anger rising. "This can't be," her gaze jumped to mine, struggling to finish, "You will have to make a choice or a sacrifice. But do not make this choice lightly, as the ramifications will be lasting!"

"I don't understand any of this. What does it even mean?" Questions oozed out of me, the cards hardly revealing anything with much substance, and my heart was on standby with tears in my eyes. *Misfortune? Death? Loss of control?*

Eleanor pulled the future pile of cards toward her and quickly folded them back semi-neatly, her face stern. "Be gone. You are going down the wrong path. I'm too close. I can't help you." Her entire demeanor had changed, and if I wasn't mistaken, she seemed mad. She jumped from her chair and skated to the door. "It is time for you people to leave."

"But you have to help me. You can't tell me all this and force me out. Please," I shoved my hand into my bag and withdrew a wad of cash. A few bills slipped through my fingers and fell to the floor. I was desperate, needing to hear something hopeful. Worried for Gramps' sake, I needed to know my bad fortune wouldn't rest upon his soul. "Give me something here," I begged, needing more.

Eleanor snatched my arm in a firm grasp and set her beady eyes on mine. "Do not fall into the trickery that surrounds you. Only you have the power to determine your fate, my moonchild," Eleanor quickly said, then shooed me out of the room before slamming the door behind me.

A strong wind carried my hair, and the dropping temperatures gripped the back of my neck in a tense chill. I stood outside Eleanor's shop, dazed and confused, lost in her words, as Milo, Monday, and Kane surrounded me. Their chatter was distant against Eleanor's last words. *"Only you have the power to determine your fate."*

The mantra repeated inside my head.

Gramps was the only tie I had left to the mother I'd never known. Yet, it seemed as if his fate had been flipped over and printed upon a card—our future told within a matter of fifteen minutes. The unnerving quiver shuddering up my bones beneath my flesh made me believe it was real.

It was happening. Gramps was going to die.

"If it helps, she once told me I'd dig my own grave. You have to take what she says with a grain of salt," Monday insisted.

"Yeah, and I would get lost in time," Milo added.

"No, mine's better," Kane pumped his chest, "Under a midnight sun, I'll lose my power in the fall of a roamer, whatever the hell that's supposed to mean."

"See," Monday laughed, "It's all *just for* FUN."

JULIAN
chapter twenty three

FALLON HADN'T SEEN ME EARLIER, SITTING THERE IN the corner of The Bean with Beck as we nursed our coffees, going over our theories as to the identity of the thief who stole the books. Fallon hadn't seen me, but I had been watching her from the dark corner behind my dark mask to hide my dark soul.

She had arrived, wearing black and white leather shoes, those little shorts I'd grown so fond of, the curves of her ass cheeks hitting right at the hem, making my every blood vessel squeeze. Her white hair was unbound and left to tumble down her back like snowfall. I'd closed my eyes, inhaling the dark thoughts that stroked my shadow-blooded soul, welcoming it like a cold night.

Was this what Dad had warned me about? How could a female, a stubborn one at that, unlock these feelings? These ... these cravings? How could she be the only one who could quiet this dark thing inside me?

I had watched her sit across from the douchebag my fist met the night before, zoned out and lost in her head like she always seemed to be whenever she was around people she didn't belong with. I'd never lost control like that, but I was losing her before I ever had her. *Good god*, what was she doing to me?

But the real question was, who was Fallon Grimaldi?

Kane's witchery hadn't worked on Fallon as it did at Voodoos. I had watched from across the lawn during the movie as he felt her up, and if the devil was real, his finger had been tapping on my black lava-filled pulse, ready to pull the trigger.

But it hadn't worked on her. She'd said she couldn't stop thinking about me, and perhaps that was the key.

Beck snapped his finger between us and my eyes tore from the empty booth she was sitting at just an hour earlier. "You sure you're okay, man? You're good?"

"Yeah, what about you? How's Josephine?" I asked, changing the subject.

Josephine was his Keeper's daughter, who would eventually become his keeper once her parents passed on. She was only fourteen and had been battling the flu, and it was only getting worse.

Beck's eyes steered past me. "It's not looking good. It won't be long 'til they need us to step in."

I leaned over and squeezed his shoulder until his gaze met mine again. "Just like riding a bike, baby Beck. We've done this many times, it'll be fine. If she needs us, we'll be there. We won't let anything happen to her."

"Yeah." He nodded and blinked worry from his eyes. "Let's go hit the grounds."

The grounds were the old carnival grounds built in the early 1900s by a neighboring town, situated on the border of Weeping Hollow—taking up half our woods, the other half in the rest of the world. It had been abandoned after the townies ran the carnies out during a time when the shield was weak, but the grounds were still there, and once a year, the carnival came to life. Moving rides, bright lights, the sounds of children laughing, screaming, singing, and creepy carnival music. Every other night of the year, the grounds were dark and chilling. A quiet place harnessing enough celestial energy to tap into the darkest of magic.

My coven had said the last time dark magic was used was over a century ago. My brothers and I had never dabbled with dark magic before, and we weren't planning to tonight. As desperate as we were to break the curse, I refused to fall into the rabbit hole.

We only retreated to the grounds when we needed privacy and a location for sex magic because sex was the most potent energy source. Sex with the Norse Woods girls, a haunted carnival, and four Hollow Heathens, you'd think the grounds would sell like hotcakes. But no one aside from our coven knew of its existence. We kept the grounds masked. Sacred Sea nor the flatlanders could see it with a sober eye.

Beck and I walked out of The Bean and trashed our paper cups as soon as Fallon walked across Town Square with the reporter, the little redhead, and Kane on the other side of the gazebo. The view was like a bullet to the lungs, merciless and killing me slowly.

As much as everyone advised me to stay away, I couldn't. I wanted to stay inside her head. I wanted her to keep thinking about me if it meant Kane couldn't get to her.

Life was easier before she'd returned to town, with the cold winds blowing through the cracked casements of my soul. I didn't mind the cold or the shade I hid under, or being alone with my thoughts, but not when every thought now led to her. It was only torture. I knew she knew it too. There was no denying this thing we had. This thing I had no name for. It felt like magic and read like taboo.

What would it take for me to convince her to live in this secret with me, hide in the alleyways, make out inside the shadows, and make love in the wicked Norse woods after nightfall? Because that was the only life I could give her until I could break this curse.

Fallon didn't understand. I wasn't hiding because I was ashamed of her. I could never be ashamed of her. Fallon and me, we were the same.

But there were other ways I could prove myself …

"*PUBLIC ANNOUNCEMENT!*" I called out across Town Square, too late to stop myself now.

Beck elbowed me at my side. "What the hell are you doing?"

I had no clue, and Fallon's white hair whipped when she turned her head, the rest of them too. I was still far enough away from her per the orders, and I wasn't talking directly to her. I didn't care anymore. I had to make sure she knew how far I was willing to push my limits.

"*I WANT TO LET EVERYONE KNOW THAT I CAN'T STOP THINKING*

ABOUT FALLON!" I shouted, cupping my mouth with my hands and repeating the same words she spoke to me the night before.

Beck shook his head next to me. It was going to take more than this, I knew. But it was a start. *Because I've never been embarrassed by you, Fallon.*

Fallon tried to force her smile away, but her smile won. I was more than fifty feet away, farther than I had to be and farther than I wanted to be, and that smile still had the power to hit me in the chest, causing me to step back as if it were a force. *And to me, it was.*

"*YOU'RE STUPID!*" she called back, and I tilted my head to the side as a laugh pushed through my lips.

The little redhead took her hand, pulling her forward, and my smile faded as she rounded the corner out of view. Beck mumbled under his breath, rocky waters in his blue eyes. But he knew it was coming.

"It still fucking moves," I whispered into the night breeze.

"That woman's changing you," Beck muttered. "Haven't seen you like this since—"

Johnny. "I know."

ZEPHYR AND PHOENIX WERE ALREADY AT THE ENTRANCE OF THE GROUNDS. Four blindfolded girls from Norse Woods Coven lined up against the iron gate. The blindfolds were necessary. The girls understood the conditions. This wasn't their first time with a Heathen. We had to take measures to keep them safe. Zeph walked past Francesca, the girl he'd been paired with, and slipped through the gate's bars.

To us, sex with them wasn't for fun and games. All we needed was energy drawn from an orgasm. Plain and simple, this was a means to an end, not the final goal tonight. A business transaction. We were four Hollow Heathens trying to break a curse—only sex. Fallon was the first girl I'd ever kissed because I'd never thought it was possible. Now, she was the only girl I thought about giving myself to in a way that was more than my body. The kind of way that wasn't for magic or a ritual.

Tabitha stood blindfolded with a mop of black hair that sat on her head like a clown wig, a plastic onyx shine. She turned her head, probably listening for me, and the straight edge of her hair grazed her shoulders. She'd dressed for the occasion too, wearing a black lacy bra under her little top and a mini jean skirt for easy access as if it would have mattered.

How desperate was I to break this curse? Desperate enough to engage in sex magic when my cock only ached to be in a particular white-haired stupid freak like me? As I looked Tabitha up and down, even though it meant nothing, it all looked, seemed, felt … wrong.

Before Fallon, I'd never doubted my obligation.

She was already in my head.

Phoenix carried a backpack of books, and the rest of us slipped through the bars and took off to the old Ferris wheelhouse. I lurked in the background of the group like an evil spirit, despair and remorse pressing on my heart. I didn't like this one bit, but I was determined to bear on.

The girls grouped under the shack, gabbing back and forth, waiting for us as we stood off by the Ferris wheel. Phoenix sprawled out in the rickety and faded passenger cabin of the Ferris wheel, flipping through one of the books stacked on his lap. The rest of us passed around a bottle as the night carried on with the girls laughing in the distance. We detached ourselves as much as possible from them. No reason for foreplay.

"Julian, race me to the top?" Zeph was looking up at the large wheel we were standing under.

I couldn't look up without a sudden sickness pulling in my stomach. The thought of being that high up caused my mind to shut down, body to shake, and vision to weaken. "Oh, you'd like that, wouldn't you, bitch?"

A callous grin appeared in Zeph's eyes.

"I'd seen it in here last night," Phoenix mumbled, scouring pages of the Book of Wildes. "A passage written by Kyden Wildes from over a hundred years ago. Yeah, here it is,"—he cleared his throat— "*It was past midnight and long after the gathering of the Order when I heard the forbidden girl in the caverns. She sang, her voice flowed in a thick melody, swelling and dying away, calling out to me, or leading me, I could not be sure. But her song took me to the celestial waters where it was there I witnessed a sight I could never have imagined. The wife of Foster Danvers, Clarice, shuddered beneath Matteo Cantini with the whisperings of the Norse Woods in his ear. She made promises of pleasure in return for help to break the curse of the Hollow Heathens. Yet, what would make the Danver wife believe a Cantini would have the answers? We were told the curse could not be broken! I kept this from my fellow brothers, from my dear friend, Foster. For this news of his beloved indulging in sexual acts with a foe would be the very news that could destroy him. A risk I wasn't willing to take."*

A silence passed between us as the four of us exchanged glances.

Phoenix broke the silence first. "So, what the hell does that mean?"

"It means that your ancestor walked in on a Danver's wife and a Cantini bangin' it out in the tunnels," Beck concluded before taking a swig of the bottle.

Zeph pushed off the Ferris wheel cabin and dropped both palms on his head, perhaps needing air, space to think. Phoenix swayed in the faded car, watching him as he said, "You're telling me the answers we need to break the curse rests in the hands of Danvers's wife, who hasn't been around since … *oh*, I don't know, a century? Then, of course, let's not forget a Cantini."

"I had a feeling Sacred Sea was behind this," Zeph gritted out.

It didn't make sense. Cantinis were good people, the keepers of secrets. They'd always been the one family from the Eastside to uphold the laws of balance and respect our coven. Sure, I'd expect this from a Pruitt, but not Cyrus's family.

"This isn't making any sense, Phoenix. Go back and read it again." There had to be more of the story.

Phoenix read again, and afterward, he paused and looked up at me, his gold eyes blazing. "That's it. That's the end of it. Do you think that's why the Danvers line is gone? Someone else found out about the infidelity between covens and her attempt to break the curse?"

Danvers. The fifth founding family of the Norse Woods Coven. The element of Earth. Was Phoenix correct? Had Sacred Sea murdered them? Was that why the Danvers line was severed? "It doesn't make sense that a Cantini would be involved in this," I said, my head already throbbing.

Phoenix reached over, grabbing the bottle from Beck. "Well, tonight, we could either call upon this backstabbing wife, Clarice Danvers, or Matteo Cantini." He closed the book and sat upright.

Zeph's gaze jumped to Phoenix. "If this woman betrayed her husband, what makes you think she would be honest with us?"

"Well, we sure as shit can't call on Cantini*fuck*." Beck shook his head. "What if he goes back to Sacred Sea? Samhain is right around the corner. He could drop hints we're digging into this."

"You're right." I pushed my hand up my forehead, through my hair, and gripped the back of my neck. "We need to call on the Danvers girl, see what she knows. We need to find out if she ever got the answers on how to break the curse. Matteo Cantini won't help us." Not after hearing he was sleeping around with one of our own. I was beginning to believe the Order was as corrupt as my soul.

Zeph rubbed his palms together, dragging his hawkish gaze to the girls. "Now, choose a body."

"Tabitha," I quickly stated.

"You going solo?" Phoenix gripped my shoulder.

I felt Beck's knowing glare strum through my veins. "Something like that."

"It will still take all of us," he pointed out as if I didn't know it already.

TABITHA STOOD NAKED IN THE MIDDLE OF THE CIRCLE BECK HAD FINISHED off drawing in the dirt with a stick. She was blindfolded and shivering from both the cold and what she'd expected to come here for.

But I wasn't having sex with her. Not this time.

The rest of us spread out, and I retreated to the Ferris wheel house, where it was empty and secluded, selfishly focusing on Fallon with my cock in my hand. I dropped my head back against the wall, drowning out the orchestra of moans and slaps all around me. It didn't take much for my shaft to thicken, heavy and stretched in my fist. All it took was the mere thought of her smile. The one that haunted me when she didn't even know she was doing it. The one she'd do from twenty feet away, lost in thought, eyes distant, the small curve around her turned-up lips, the top lip a little plumper than the bottom on her diamond-shaped face with the moons in her eyes.

I thought about the way it had felt with my hand between her legs, the way she tasted, and the way her body shuddered in the dark as I pulled the orgasm right out of her, coming undone so lightly and private like a whisper as she melted in my arms. She hadn't put on a show for me. She was so quiet, so honest in the way she'd let go.

And the way she'd kissed me …

Memories of that night caused the wind to rise with great violence from the circle in restless waves, slapping at my buzzing skin as I stroked my straining length. My abs tightened and my muscles jerked, remembering the way her soft skin felt under the tips of my fingers. My eyes sprang open to see the moon had reached her summit in the sky behind thick gray clouds, and a thunderous clap broke apart the sky.

"Shit," I gritted out, slamming my eyes closed once more as my cock jerked in my hand.

I wasted away in the color of her.

White hair. Milky skin. Dusty pink lips. The winter season in her eyes.

Utterly wasted, I'd almost forgotten the reason why we were here—the reason why we were doing this.

I tucked myself back inside my pants and jumped to my feet, zipping up.

Chants grew louder around me. I walked to where Tabitha was, hazy, dazed, and selfishly high on a certain moon girl, the others joining in as they finished.

Three times, we chanted the same verse around the circle, summoning Clarice Danvers. A bolt of lightning lit above, blue neon ripping across the black sky. A dry storm circled overhead, a lazy dirt cyclone below.

Then the sky went calm, the clouds dispersed, and I dropped my gaze to Tabitha.

"What's your name?" I demanded.

Tabitha smiled. *"Kyden Wildes."* She turned her head in Phoenix's direction, and Phoenix crossed his arms over his chest. *"You're a son of fire, are you not? This time, tread through water. Your heart is entering dangerous territory."*

Phoenix narrowed his eyes. "We summoned Clarice Danvers, why are you here? Where is she?"

"*All I know is that I'm here,*" Kyden said through Tabitha.

Zephyr took a step forward. "We read your journal entry about what happened between Clarice Danvers and Matteo Cantini. Is it true? Sacred Sea was always the one behind the curse of the Heathens—"

"Do you know how to break the curse?" I interrupted because it was more important, and we didn't know how much time we had.

"*No,*" Kyden stormed through Tabitha. "*I only know this. Clarice was desperate and foolish and would have done anything, including to tempt and seduce another, even one from Sacred Sea. Then, on a separate occasion, she and Matteo fought in the caverns about our ancestors' journals. There was a missing journal. The following day, Clarice disappeared and hasn't been seen since. Foster Danvers went mad and took his own life, believing his wife had abandoned him. I've never confessed to what I've seen, and for that, I'll remain a guilt-ridden spirit. But I did what I thought was best for the coven. The Danvers element may be absent from the Hollow Heathens, but you, Blackwell, are all four elements, embodying spirit, or the dark void depending on your shadow-blood. You are the key to holding this coven together. That is, if you don't succumb to the darkness. You need to wake up, Blackwell!*" the deep voice roared from the small girl, stunning us all.

"You're telling me Matteo got rid of her?" Beck threw his arms in the air, bringing the subject back to what was at stake. "Because she went to them for help? Because she may have stolen a book from them?"

Stolen a book. "Who's journal?" I asked with urgency. Three books were missing from the Chamber. One of them had to hold the answers.

Tabitha's head turned to me. "*That, I don't know for certain. The Cantini's are the keepers of secrets of Weeping Hollow. It is possible they know how the curse came to be, but if it can be broken? I'm not so sure.*"

"Congratulations, Nix. You come from a line of idiots who are of no use," Zeph stated dryly, darting a venomous green glare at Phoenix.

"I don't get it." My fingers tapped vigorously against my thigh, and I stepped forward, needing more. "Why would she go through all this trouble? She already bound herself to Foster, accepted him for what he was. Accepted the curse as my mother had and every woman before her. Why would she betray her husband and steal books from the Order? Why would she care enough to risk everything?"

Tabitha straightened her spine. *"Why would any take such extreme measures, turning into something they are not?"*

Then it hit me, remembering a past I'd tried so hard to forget.

"For the love of a child," I whispered.

And without warning, Tabitha slumped to the ground.

And the link to Kyden Wildes *SNAPPED.*

FALLON
chapter twenty four

EARLIER, I'D SKIPPED THE MABON PARADE IN TOWN SQUARE AND ALL the dinners I'd been invited to, deciding to spend my evening with Gramps.

He couldn't make it out of bed anymore. As each day passed, his body was shutting down, failing him. Weight dropped off him so fast over the last few weeks that skin hung from his bones, and his cheeks were sunken in.

If it weren't for his stubbornness, I doubt he would have been able to hold the pencil for his crossword puzzle. It was as if he'd muster a day's worth of energy for that one task, the only thing he looked forward to.

Since Gramps hadn't been able to get up to use the bathroom either, Mina Mae had been coming by every morning and night to help. Gramps argued, of course, but Mina was just as persistent. At first, I'd wondered why she was here, with Gramps and me, but then I'd noticed the look in her eyes, the same way Julian looked at me, and I knew it was because she cared deeply for him.

As I washed dishes, Mina came in from the living room and set down a basket filled with dirty clothes.

"He's lucky to have yah," she said, admiring me from the other side of the counter with her hand resting on the dirty pile. Between all the coming and going, we barely had a conversation that weighed more than Gramps' grumbles.

I didn't know how to answer. "We're both the lucky ones." I dried the last dish, set it on the yellow drying mat, and turned to face her. "And we're extremely lucky to have you too. Seriously," I sighed, "I don't know how I could ever repay you for helping me out around here."

She nodded, eyes wide. "It's a lot, couldn't let yah do this on your own."

"Yeah," I leaned back against the counter, "I'm glad I'm here, though."

"I'm glad you're here too, dear." Mina picked up the basket and rested it against her hip. "I'll wash these for yah, and don't bothah tellin' me othahwise."

I laughed. "Hey, I'm not going to fight you on it."

"Are you doing anything around town tonight?"

"I was thinking of staying in. You know, in case Gramps needs me."

"Oh, he's out. Benny won't be wakin' up for a long time." Mina patted the counter and leaned over. "Do me a favor and go have some fun. It's Mabon, and yah nevah know what could happen or luck you could turn around." And she left with a wink, disappearing behind the wall and into the living room.

HOURS LATER, FABLE SAT BESIDE ME ON A LOG IN FRONT OF A BONFIRE, THE two of us passing a jug of homemade apple pie moonshine from Cyrus' family's cellar back and forth. Monday, Ivy, and Adora danced and twirled across the waterline, soaking the bottoms of their long, frilly dresses. They kicked the waves, water spraying as a thin slice of the moon hung in the sky. Fable and I sat back, watching the other three girls dance and sing with the wind like sirens from the sea.

Hippie Sabotage spilled from an old speaker planted in the sand, and Maverick threw another log on the fire, sending sparks of burning embers flying into the black sky. He returned to his seat beside Cyrus and shook his blond hair from his eyes in one sweep.

"Where's Kane?" Maverick asked, sliding his gaze from Cyrus to me. "He should be here by now."

Cyrus dropped his elbows onto his knees and poked a log with a long stick between his stretched thighs. "His old man wanted to talk," he explained, then his light eyes glanced up and over the fire, his black brows raised. "Speak of the devil."

Kane walked closer along the beach in drawstring linen pants and a partially unbuttoned white shirt, his bronzed skin shimmering like stars on the ocean's surface. His soft brown hair was wild tonight, thick and blowing with the night air. He carried another bottle in one hand and lowered his hazel eyes to mine, the bruising on one already turning colors.

"You made it," he said, his voice low, and I twisted my mood ring around my finger, wondering what mood he was in tonight. He paused behind me and dropped his head into my neck. "Thank you for coming."

I nodded, and Kane straightened his posture behind me, walked around the fire, and took a seat between Maverick and Cyrus. His two strung-out eyes glared at me from across the bonfire's waving flames, and he chugged from the bottle, the lump in his throat bobbing with every gulp.

"Tonight is the night, Fallon," he announced.

I glanced at Fable, who was drawing circles in the sand with a stick, keeping her gaze down. "The night for what?"

"The start of your initiation. It's a three-step process for Sacred Sea. I went through it. Cyrus, Mav, and Ivy went through it," he paused and narrowed his eyes, "Your dad went through it … It's important you do too. The other girls have been waiting for this, especially your girl, Monday." He moved his gaze to the girls dancing at the waterline. "But we're focused on you right now, Tobias Morgan's daughter and all."

"I'm not a witch," I said, almost laughing at the idea.

"Yes, you are. It's already inside you, and we're going to help pull that out during the initiation. By the time you're fully in, you'll see it too." All three guys glared in my direction. "We can protect you, Fallon, but you have to trust us. You have to drop those walls of yours and submit, or it won't work."

I raised a brow. "Can you help Benny?"

Kane shook his head. "Benny is a castaway, an old Norse Woods wiccan who happens to live on our soil. We can't help him."

"But he's my grandfather, my family," I insisted.

"No, Fallon, we'll be your family."

I shook my head, swiping the moonshine from the sand and standing. "Then I'm not interested," I said as I walked away, the sand flying up from my bare feet with every step.

After a few slugs of the spicy amber liquid, I found myself leaning against a cold rocky cliff, watching the girls in all their beauty, their arms moving effortlessly like a ballet over the water to a remake of *Tainted Love.* My eyes closed, thinking what my life had become. The only man I wanted wasn't allowed near me. Witches were here and real, murder was in the air, someone may be after me, and Gramps was dying.

To my left, Kane was walking my way, and I crossed my arms. "I can try," he said, dropping a palm onto the rock and leaning over me. I clutched the mason jar and looked down at our bare feet sinking into the sand, thinking *try* wasn't going to be enough. "Hey," Kane clipped out. "I'll do what I can to help Benny, okay? I'll talk to my father and figure something out."

In the distance, Adora's sing-song voice drifted. "It's almost midnight. Who's jumping into the ocean?"

My eyes darted back to Kane's, an idea sparking. "No, Kane. I'll figure this out on my own without your coven." I slipped under his arm and walked back to the group. "Me!" I shouted, trotting through the sand. "I want to jump." They all said jumping into the ocean would bring one good fortune, and after my reading with Eleanor, I was desperate. Gramps didn't have much longer, and I'd do anything, even jump into the ice-cold sea.

"No way," Fable dismissed, hopping to her feet. "No one other than Maverick has jumped, but he's a moron."

"Thanks," Maverick muttered.

Fable rolled her eyes. "It's no secret, dude. You're an idiot."

"But one lucky *sonofabitch*."

I pushed my hair from my face and hugged my body. "So, it's true? I jump, and good things will come?" An inkling of hope brewed inside my chest. I could turn Gramps' fate around.

Fable shrugged when Adora skipped across the sand. "Oh, I gotta see this," she sang, then grabbed Ivy's hand and took off to the rocks. The rest of the crowd followed, hollering into the night and leaving the blazing bonfire and alcohol behind.

We climbed up the north end of the beach, where the slope wasn't as steep. Maverick and Cyrus were the first ones up, pulling the girls up by their arms. Once we were all back on solid ground, we walked along the cliff's edge to the steep drop off where no rocks gathered at the bottom.

When we stopped, the eight of us peered over the edge as the neglected black mansion sat behind us. The bonfire mimicked a candle's flame from up here, and my nerves crawled over me like spiders. I turned to my left to look at Maverick when I noticed a large scarecrow looking statue at the cliff's highest peak. "What is that?"

Maverick turned and hooked his thumb behind him. "Oh, that? That's the Wicker Man."

I hadn't noticed it before, but I also had never been this far up the coastline. "What's it for?"

"He's our executioner." Maverick turned back to face me, and the tips of his toes met the edge at my side. "It's a straight drop down, no rocks, and the water is deep here. It's cold, are you sure you want to do this?"

I sucked in a breath, and the cold air shattered inside my lungs like broken glass. "Yeah," I nodded. "I'm doing this." I had to try at least.

"If you say so." Maverick took a step back, as did the rest of them. "Ladies first."

"She's not going to do it," Ivy whispered.

"A hundred bucks says she does," Adora shot back.

I shook my hands out to shake away the jitters as my bare feet teetered on the cliff.

This was it.

With one last look into the black canvas of constellations, I took a few steps back, then ran...

And I jumped.

What no one had told me was that when flying, time stopped. Air caught inside my lungs. I couldn't breathe, I couldn't think. Fear clutched my soul yet set me free, the unknown waiting for me at the bottom, breaking through a dimension between life and death.

Maybe this was the reason Dad had lost himself with his job and hobby. Perhaps here, in this in-between place, he felt closer to my mother. The reason he had always been so fascinated with model airplanes and looked forward to the single phone call that had taken him away from me and put him in the air.

And I wished the ocean disappeared and gravity was non-existent. For a short time, nothing mattered. Everything between the cliff and the sea seemed enchanting, like a peaceful dream, and I wished I could stay in this place forever, pin myself in the sky, make me one with the galaxy.

But then it hurt like a bitch.

My body slammed against the bitter-cold water as if it were concrete, biting and stinging my flesh just as a wave crashed over me. My arms and legs scrambled at my sides as I tried to take back control under the rocky waters, but the waves sent me flying against the cliff, and my head crashed into a rock.

I sank below the surface, face up and staring into the night sky. Deeper and deeper, I focused on the panicked group of people I'd left behind moments ago, pointing down and shoving each other, but I heard nothing inside these waters. I blinked, commanding my limbs to take me back to the surface—begging the hunger for survival to kick in—but they wouldn't give. My muscles froze as I sank deeper, my body rocking under the surface with the waves.

The Atlantic rushed its ice all around me, spilling into my mouth, up my nose, drinking me and filling me up with its lethal chill. The sea had full possession of me, and though my brain felt as if it were on fire, a frost flowed through my bloodstream.

I was out of oxygen, and fear raked my spine.

I needed to breathe.

Bubbles exploded from my mouth. My body jerked, and my cry distorted. The sea muted me. All I could do was stare above. I blinked when a figure appeared atop the cliff, diving head-first into the waters with precise and angelic form. My mind was playing tricks on me as I sank deeper and deeper, my white hair billowing around me like clouds.

Peace came as if the earth had gone quiet for a beautiful, full moment. The waters were full too. It had swallowed me, pressing on my body. Pressure collapsed my chest, and I thrashed one last time in the deep.

Tiny bubbles rose in front of me to the surface.

And I closed my eyes to sink, sink, sink.

Then I was lifted at my waist, yanked up until a mouth clutched onto mine, fierce and desperate, breathing warm life back into me and thawing my lungs. For a brief moment, I felt weightless in his arms like snow in the summer, and my entire being awoke when my mind registered—*Julian*.

I could see nothing in the somber black waters, yet the hands digging into my waist, the lips grasping mine, and long legs kicking us to the surface let me know I had nothing to fear.

We finally broke through the surface, and he reached behind my head and pulled me into his neck. He kicked out from under us as he swam with one arm to shore, the other locked around my back. His deep, muffled voice reached me, but in another world, a forgotten time. I pinned my eyes to the constellations, with tears frozen at the corners and frostbite slicing my flesh. I hadn't breathed. I couldn't breathe. I felt myself slipping but could still see the stars, and I focused on them.

I focused on Sirius, the brightest star in the sky.

JULIAN

"F-F-FALLON," MY WORDS BROKE APART AFTER WRESTLING HER TO SHORE.

Her wet limbs laid limp in my arms as I rocked her in the sand. My muscles jolted under my skin, desperate to raise my body temperature as she lay over me. I didn't know if it was the waters or if she'd seen my face. I didn't know, as my thoughts were panicked. I pressed my finger against her throat, my heart on hiatus for that single thump that could allow me to breathe again.

"P-p-please," I chanted, my other hand rubbing up and down her back at a horrible attempt to bring her warmth, pull life back into her.

"Breathe."

Then there it was—the thump. I felt it. Proof. She was okay.

Fallon lurched forward as the sea expelled from her mouth and onto the beach.

I fell on to my back in the sand, taking her with me, exhaling heavily with my hand pressed to the back of her head to keep her face in my neck, to prevent her from seeing me without my mask.

Our bodies shivered under the crescent moon when I heard a voice carry with the wind.

"There she is!" someone shouted. I turned my head to the side to see a group of them in the distance, and my heart slammed against my chest.

"I'm s-s-sorry, Fallon." I pressed my lips to her cold cheek before scurrying out from under her. I ran to the mouth of the cliff, where the tunnel entrance was hidden under Benny's house.

I watched from the shadows as the gust of wind carried a chill that trapped ice in my bones. The girls cried as Kane picked up Fallon in his arms and carried her across the beach. I stayed there within the rocks long after their shadows disappeared, shivering and wet and

hiding in the

DARKNESS.

LUNATICUS

N o one believed Bellamy when he said the woods spoke to him. The gentle midnight winds lulled in his ears in a fairytale hush. The branches twisted and reared their ends to the safest places. Black birds of the woods flapped their restless wings in a warning when danger drew near.

"But on this night, under a paper lantern sky, where stars dotted the black canvas above, the only sounds in the woods were the orchestra of breaths of Bellamy and Siri. He laid her down on the forest floor and loved her in the way the night loved the moon—eternal and in all phases—and afterward, he lay beside her a long while.

"Siri drew constellations on his skin, connecting his sparse freckles with her fingertips, as Bellamy fell into a contentment. In the heart of the Norse woods, he floated and swirled in the ardent fever as if it was all he tasted and breathed. 'I cannot continue as we are,' blurted Bellamy, turning to face Siri.

"'I may as well be a monster by day—an all-suffering monster—in constant mourning, longing for these short intervals of peace. My days are spent without a purpose, no longer having a heart when I am without you, walking without direction, lost and confused until nightfall, and you, the one who has me entirely, revives me only to repeat this agony all over again. How is it, my days are cold, my dark nights warm? Tell me, Siri, do you feel the same as I? Because, if so, let us walk under the sun together. Let us confront our families, my coven. Become mine, Siri. At all times and always.'

"Though her heart was happy, Siri frowned and brushed her knuckles across his cheek. She had seen what the other women looked like, everyone much different than she. Though Annitah, her beloved friend, was different too, Siri had yet to come across someone other than her mother of the same pale skin color, the same clarity in her eyes. 'They would not understand me.'

"'Ah, moon girl,' said Bellamy, a grin gracing his pain-stricken face. 'You are misunderstood and therefore a depth of brilliance.' He rolled on top of her until she was all he saw and kissed her raw. 'If no one can see that, we shall leave them all behind, as they have rejected us, forced our hand. I will take you far away from here, the sun and the moon, leaving their nights empty and their days cold as they made ours. What's worth fighting for if not love?'

"'You're a shameless Heathen, I could never ask you to abandon your coven,' said Siri, her smile undeniable.

"'You never did, and you would never have to. My wretched soul would choose yours in this life and each one hereafter because, without you, I am certain a monster is what would become of me.'

"Sirius leaned over and reached into her dress pocket. She pulled out a silver chain with a pendant attached. 'Until forever,' whispered she, slipping the necklace around his neck.

"Words were lost on Bellamy as he clutched the pendant in his fist, promising to treasure it and sealed her smile with a kiss. 'Until forever,' he repeated.

"A raven perched on a tree branch above, a disturbance in the wicked woods. Bellamy turned to the sounds, listening to what cautions the trees had to tell. 'They are coming,' his naked form pounced to his feet, 'all four of them!' In the distance, torches lit a path in a synchronized march toward them. 'Something isn't right, you must hurry!'

"'Who's coming?' asked Siri, pulling her dress over her shoulders.

"'The Heathens of the Norse woods. My father!"

part
TWO

JULIAN
chapter twenty five

TWO DAYS HAD PASSED. THE MORNING FOG THICKENED as I stood on my back porch, looking out into the forest in the middle of night. The fog rose to the branches, broke apart, twisting into thin gray claws, summoning me to the deep woods.

And the Norse woods was like a single, beating heart. A breathing organ that wanted me, and there was no name for what I was. A Hollow Heathen? A witch? A son of the woods? A murderer? I was all these things but never a hero.

Yet I had dived into the midnight waters from the sea cliff and yanked Fallon from the ocean's grip. I had pulled her to shore and rocked her in my arms. I had done these things without a single hesitation. My chest buckled at the memory of her drifting amongst the waves, her white hair flowing all around her as she sunk to the ocean floor. Memories of her. Memories of Johnny. I slammed my eyes closed.

"I still can't believe you did that," Beck announced. He'd come through the back door of my cabin with two open beers in one hand. He passed me one. "That couldn't be easy after what happened with Johnny. How are you holding up?"

Johnny. The sound of his name gripped my lungs.

I slammed my eyes closed, waiting for the horrible memory to pass.

"I don't want to …" *I don't want to think about it, talk about it, hear about it.*

I chugged the beer and focused on the way the liquid swirled around my tongue. Then forced it down. The leaves rustled when the wind came.

"Jonah said she'll be back at work in a few days," Beck changed the subject to Fallon. "Kane Pruitt is a hero." A bullet of anger had risen in his words, but he fell silent as the sound of the night festered between us.

"As long as she's okay."

He slid his eyes to me. "Are you going to see her?"

The breeze of the night held its breath, waiting on my answer.

"Not yet." I shifted my stance, envying the stability of the ground. "I don't know. I shouldn't. I can't," I concluded. "It would only make things worse for the both of us."

Beck nodded as we stood side by side, peering into the woods. "Maybe you should be honest with her. About the reasons why you two can't—"

"And what are the reasons, Beck? Because I made a blood-pact with you all? Because of the Order? Because of the curse? Because I have to be loyal to everyone in this fucking town *except* her? How am I supposed to be with her if I'm not allowed to? The deeper we go, the harder it will be, and where will that get us? It's already fucking hard enough. And worse, what if I kill her? I barely made it out after Johnny died, but with her? No, I wouldn't be able to come back from it." My chest shook, and I dragged in a steadier breath. "Everything's eventual—"

"And if it bleeds, it suffers," Beck finished for me, reminding me we were human.

"You know," I continued, shaking my head, "she asked me once, '*What was the point?*' And the point is, there is none. It just is, Beck. She's a part of me already, moving inside me along with my shadow-blood, and there's not a damn thing I can do about it." *But what if I didn't kill her? What if I can break the curse and put her above everyone? What if I held on to the only light in my dark and miserable life? The only real thing that's ever happened to me?* I gripped the beer, closed my eyes, and lifted my chin, listening to the tree's whispers. "I can't take it. I think I have to see her."

Beck chuckled. "You're so back and forth."

"Yeah, I have to see her," I repeated, resolved, mind made up.

"Alright, man."

"I'm going to go see her."

"You do that. I'll be here. Drinking. As always."

I STOOD OUTSIDE FALLON'S BALCONY. THE SEA WINDS SMACKED MY SKIN and raked through my hair. The night was black, and this time, it was me under the light of the stars and her sleeping soundlessly in the dark. Strong winds beat against the curtain. It jumped and turned as if it had come from the bazaar of bad dreams. A fire blazed in the fireplace of her bedroom, yet the balcony doors were wide open as if she were waiting for me.

I stood there for a long time, watching the girl who looked as if she had the moon tucked under her heart and the galaxy woven into her soul. Her white hair spilled across her pillow. We didn't make sense. We were so different, but still all the same. Nightmares and dreamscapes—the epitome of us.

My heart slammed inside my chest as I stepped closer into the dark, where she was lying on her stomach, tangled under thin sheets. The heat from the fire had thawed her icy flesh into dew drops on her skin. Her top had risen, revealing two dimples that kissed the base of her spine. There were still so many places I hadn't explored, and there would never be enough nights for us.

The bed frame creaked when I sat at the edge. Fallon's white cat stared at me from the dark corner of the room with mismatched eyes, threatening me. I narrowed my eyes. It scurried out onto the balcony.

My tightened fist reached out until my knuckles grazed the edge of her jawline. A feather-light breath escaped through her lips. She blinked up at me with eyes the palest of blue hues, and the flames' shadows did a waltz across her confused expression.

"Julian," she whispered, her head falling into my touch. The small gesture had my ribcage breaking apart, leaving my heart exposed. "It was you," she closed her eyes, "I know it was you. You jumped off the cliff and saved me. I thought you were afraid of heights?"

"I suppose I found something else I was more afraid of," I admitted, feeling nervous all of a sudden. "Fallon, I have to tell you something." *I no longer want to be apart from you, but I must because my curse may kill you. And I'm trying to undo it because I've never wanted anything more.* But all these words caught in my throat when Fallon sat up from the bed and wrapped her arms around my neck.

"You could have just told me you weren't allowed near me," she said into my ear.

My eyes widened at first. Then they closed, and I expelled a relieved breath. Fallon knew. And she buried her face into my neck. I held the back of her head, keeping her here with me. She held on to me. I held on to her.

Seconds turned to minutes, and I didn't know how long she was in my arms because it didn't matter. Fallon Grimaldi was in my arms, and it turned me into a man who wasn't cursed or damned. It just turned me into a man, the only thing I ever wanted to be. The thought had me clutching her tighter, pressing her entire body against me. I inhaled her folklore scent.

What if she had died. What if I wasn't there.

What if I had to go on living in Weeping Hollow without the only freak who happened to make my dark soul sing?

My eyes screwed shut.

Fallon had once said that perhaps I was afraid of falling, but I knew she was wrong. It was true, I had a love simmering inside me. This thing I felt for her, perhaps it was strong enough to tear apart a coven, a town. Maybe even bring a Heathen to its knees. But I had a darkness inside me too. It became a passenger inside my skin, moving leisurely within me like an evil spirit. And if I could not indulge in the one, I'd be overtaken by the other.

I took off my coat, draped it over a chair in the corner, and sat at the edge of the bed, facing her. "The audacity, jumping off the cliff. You know I'm afraid of heights."

Heat flushed her pale cheeks. She lowered her eyes. "I had to."

I brushed her hair from her face to see her better. "You thought that jumping would help Benny?" I raised a brow, and Fallon nodded. "What if I wasn't there? It didn't look like anyone from the Eastside was going in after you. Aren't they supposed to be your friends? Your coven?" I winced at the thought, hoping she'd correct me because I knew what Sacred Sea's initiation entailed. *Please, tell me I'm wrong.*

Fallon snapped her jaw shut, and her eyes bounced between mine.

Desperate, I tried again. "Do you belong to Sacred Sea, Fallon?"

"No," she said, and relief untangled from around my spine. "Why were you even there? What were you doing at the cliffs?"

I thought for a long moment, searching for the answers.

I found none which was worrying because that could only mean one thing: I'd blacked out again. "It doesn't matter."

"Did it happen again? Are you okay?" She looked up at me under long lashes and a worry expression marring her features.

She cares for me? And if I hadn't known before, I knew at that moment— I would have done anything for her. If she asked for my heart, I'd rip it out of my chest. If she wanted a choice, I'd give her the freedom, even if it meant not choosing me. I'd do anything. It was terrifying.

"I'm okay," I told her, my fingers strumming against my pant leg. "Tonight, can I just lay with you awhile?"

Fallon nodded, a little nervous. I left my pants on, kicked off my shoes, and sank in the bed beside her.

Facing one another, Fallon intertwined her hand with mine between us and our foreheads connected.

Fallon's smile tempted mine, pulling it into being. Her eyes fell to my mask, then back to my eyes. "Is this the part where we kiss?" I asked her. "Because you're looking at me like you want to kiss me, and I don't want to mess up all the hard work I put i—"

"Yes." Fallon laughed.

I covered her eyes, slid down my mask, and crushed my mouth to hers.

As soon as our tongues hit, a moan rattled in my throat, and Fallon's lashes fluttered against my palm like feathers. At first, the kiss was delicate and deadly, like a rare white moth landing on a bomb. Then it was enduring and full of grit, the kind of kiss to survive in a world like ours.

I pulled her into my chest to place my mask back on. I wished things could have been different. I wished I could give her more. I'd seen the way my father and mother had lived, and I didn't want that for us, but I also couldn't let go.

On our sides, we silently stared at each other for a long time, her gaze hushing my manic mind.

"Tell me a story," Fallon whispered. "About your coven."

"About my coven?" I asked, my brows raised, surprised she was interested. Fallon nodded, and I closed my eyes briefly. "My coven isn't what it used to be. It's changed a lot over the years. I'm starting to believe many lost their way. It's devastating."

"What did it used to be like?"

"I'll tell you the story of how it all began," I said, remembering the story Agatha had once told me. "But I'm not very good, so you have to be patient with me." Fallon nodded, and I felt the nerves pile as if I were revealing a journal entry. Something personal.

"Once upon a time, a boy fell from the sky, called Njǫrd, the air element. Njǫrd was satisfied being alone, but boredom was never his friend. He was much like Zephyr, independent yet curious. Had to know everything and fill the air with his words. And during this lonely time, Njǫrd had no one to hear him. Every morning, Njǫrd looked to the sky and pleaded for something big to happen. He was disjointed, confused, and in a way, lost. Then one day, a collision happened in the sky, and Ægir and Jörð appeared. Water and earth."

"Who are they like?"

"Beck embodies the water element, and the last earth witch who lived was Foster Danvers," I replied, loving the way she was interested in my coven, in the story of the Norse Woods. "The three of them crossed waters and land and journeyed through seasons. When winter came, they built a fire, and by morning, a boy named Loki emerged from the ashes.

"Loki was dramatic but fun, always impulsive in how he talked, how he lived, but he was quickly accepted by the others. They were brothers. All very different, but stood by one another despite their differences. The four made a pact," I said, brushing the tip of my finger across her temple. My gaze caught the scar in the palm of my hand. "No matter what happens, they'll always be there for one another. So, they cut their flesh and combined their blood in a pit they had formed in the earth.

"And from the pact, two *more* boys appeared from the pit filled with their blood. Baldr and Höðr, light and darkness. But Njǫrd refused to keep them both, saying there could only be room for one more. Ægir, the one who felt deeply, disagreed, accepting both for what they represented, and could not part with either. So, Loki and Jörð forged a plan to meld the two together into one. And from the blood of all elements, and the love from the heathens, Væettir was born. The spirit element."

"You," Fallon whispered, her eyes growing heavy, fluttering close.

"Yes, and the five honored the elements from where they came, their Mother Nature and Father Sky, but something was missing. They needed unity with female energy, so they set out to find it. And they each did, becoming the Norse Woods Coven. The coven respected the natural world, the cycle of life and death, and the freedom of choice. They put all above themselves and no one above all. They celebrated the change of seasons, performed ceremonies to honor their magic. As long as it harmed none, they did as they wished. And they were happy. Centuries passed, and they survived through the toughest of battles, judgments, and ridicule. All because they had each other … until now …" Fallon slept still, quiet, peaceful. "Now, it seems as if everyone has forgotten what it's like to be a Norse Woods Wiccan."

I STAYED UP FOR A LONG TIME, WATCHING HER.

AND I LAID WITH HER

A WHILE.

FALLON
chapter twenty six

W HAT IN TARNATION IS THAT?" GRAMPS ASKED, HIS EYES FIXED ABOVE his bifocals, fork mid-air, looking into one green eye and one blue. Casper meowed from the windowsill, staring back at him.

"That's a cat, Gramps. You've seen him before."

"I don't remember no cat ... I wouldah remembered a cat ... I don't want a cat."

"Too bad, you got one, and he's been here for two months now."

Gramps grunted. "It bettah not piss in my shoe, moonshine," he grumbled, going back to his breakfast and crossword puzzle. "Off her kadoova ... comin' home ... turnin' inta ... arfarfan'arf ..."

I smiled. "Glad to see you got your 'tude back." *And his appetite.*

For the first time in days, Gramps had the energy to make it out of his room and into the kitchen. It was late morning, but it meant progress. I'd suffered a concussion and stayed in bed for two days, but maybe jumping off the cliff had worked. Maybe I had turned our luck around, and Gramps would be okay.

Last night, I'd fallen asleep with Julian. He'd fallen asleep too. Every so often, his hand moved across my back and arm. It was nice. This morning, he was gone.

I didn't expect Julian to stay until sunrise, but I still woke with a smile.

A rap sounded at the front door. Gramps grumbled again, muttering under his breath when I pushed out my chair.

Monday stood on the front porch with a wide smile. "Hey." She peeked over my shoulder. "What arya doing?"

"Breakfast. Would you like to come in?"

She pointed behind me and whispered, "Is Benny in there?"

"Yeah, come on. I made extras."

"No, thanks. Old people freak me out, with their skin and arms and legs …" She shivered.

A laugh slipped out of me. "Then what are you doing here?"

"Checking on you," she paused and released a breath, "Okay, that's a lie. I know you're good. You *are* good, right? After the cliff and the ocean…"

I leaned into my hip, thinking about what Julian had said. I knew it was my fault, jumping into the ocean. I'd made the decision, never expecting anyone to come in after me. But it didn't deter from the truth: none of them did. Was it selfish of me to hold on to something that was my fault? That was my decision?

"I'm good," I told her, but the words didn't feel good coming out. They felt like a lie. I was good, but I didn't know if *we* were.

"Good," she said through a long breath. "Because a body was found on the cliffs yesterday, and I could really use your help at work. I know you're not supposed to come back until tomorrow, but I'm so used to having you around. I feel like a shit friend for not checking on you, but I wanted to give you space. You seem like the kinda girl who needs space, and I can be overpowering, and I'm working on—"

"I'll go in," I interrupted, seeing her face turning red from not taking a solid breath. Plus, I was ready to get back into my old routine. It had only been days, but days inside this house alone with Gramps, and the occasional drop-ins from Mina Mae, could drive the sanest person into The Institute of the Insane.

Relief flashed in Monday's eyes. "Night shift?"

"I'll be there."

THE HEAVY DOOR SLAMMED BEHIND ME, RATTLING SHELVES OF THE apothecary store. I darted my gaze around as if I'd get in trouble for not being careful, looking for Agatha Blackwell. A messy, black-haired bun attached to a girl popped up from behind the counter, and I froze in place.

"Sorry, the door—"

"It does that all the time, don't sweat it," she said with a wave of her hand. "Can I help you with something?"

My smile was easy but lopsided. "Please," I continued, approaching the counter and pulling my satchel on top, "Agatha made me this tea for Benny's cough, and I have no idea what she put in it, but it helped." I craned my neck, looking into the back room. "Is she here?"

"No, my mom won't be back until tonight."

My brows jumped. "Your mom?"

"Yes." She pulled a binder out from under the counter and set it between us. "Schools out for the week, so you're stuck with me."

If Agatha was her mom, then that made Julian her brother. I examined her features. She was young, black hair with a defined Italian nose. She was very pretty, all her features the opposite of my own.

"What's your name?"

"Jolie. And you're Fallon, right?"

"Right," my shoulders relaxed, "you know my name."

Jolie shrugged while flipping through pages, eyes scanning butchered lines. "Everyone knows your name. And you don't look like what I expected."

"How do you mean?"

Her eyes snapped up under her lashes. "The way people talk about you, it's as if you had three heads or something. Unless they pop out without warning."

"Nope. Just one head," I said.

"Call off the hellhounds," she said through a laugh and shook her head. "I'll tell ya, people are ruthless. And I doubt my mother wrote the recipe in here. She's always mixing up new concoctions, so I never know what she gives anyone. Maybe you could come back tonight," Jolie went on, her fingers flipping through pages some more.

"It's okay. I can come back."

"You sure?" She leaned back on her heels. "I feel bad. You'd think she would leave me with something to work with. I could probably mix something together, but it won't be the same. My mom won't give me all her secrets. Says no two herbalists are the same. That I have to find my own way." She rolled her eyes.

"No, it's fine. I have to work tonight, but I'll come back another time. No biggie." I slid my satchel off the counter and flung it over my shoulder. "It was nice meeting you, though. I had no idea Julian had a sister." My eyes widened once his name rolled off my tongue. "Not that we're close or anything," I corrected, remembering Julian wasn't supposed to be near me.

Jolie smiled, interested. "So, you're not close?"

"No, I mean, I've met him. We've crossed paths. I just…I didn't kn—"

"That the Heathens could have a family? A mother? A sister?" She crossed her arms and leaned into her hip. "You think the way the rest of the town does? That they were just what? *Monsters?* Born from a curse and not a family?"

"No, no, no. Like, of course Julian has a family." This conversation was turning, twisting, and I was starting not to sound like myself. Jolie wore a blank face. Her mouth closed, her eyes waiting. *How do I climb out?* "I didn't mean it like that, I just meant—"

Jolie's cackle slipped between her lips. "Fallon, I'm messing with you." She sucked in a deep breath and let it go. "I overheard Jai talk about you to Beck, so I already know about you two."

My breath caught in my chest. "Jai?"

"Yeah, it's Julian's middle name. My mom used to always pull the first and middle name combo anytime we got in trouble. *'Julian Jai get your hiney back inside!'*"—she laughed, remembering—"Anyway, our baby brother called him Jai. It was his first word. So, Mom and I got used to calling him just that too." She shrugged.

"You have a baby brother?"

Her expression fell. "Well, he passed on a long time ago. I'm surprised you don't know the story. People in this town love to hold it against the Hollow Heathens. They use the death of my brother to keep people afraid of them and away from Norse Woods. Sick if you ask me. It was an accident. My dad wasn't a bad man."

My chest shook. Julian's dad accidentally killed their brother? *Jai, Jai, Jai*, I remembered. The little boy in the red and white striped shirt—the spirit that had led me to Julian twice. I'd been so wrapped in my feelings for Julian that I was blind to the ghost crying out for help, not putting two and two together.

I began to feel light-headed, seeing the little boy's face again in my mind, and I shook my head to right myself. "I'm so sorry. I didn't know."

"It's not like Jai would've brought him up, anyway. He doesn't like to talk about himself. That's the thing you have to know about him, he's ... he pushes people away. But he's not who everyone says he is. He's not." She shook her adamant head. "He's not a monster. Jai and Beck and them, they have to act like that so people stay away. It's to protect them. It's really sad. People don't see the sacrifices they had to make, what they're *still* making, and what they had to give up." Her eyes watered, as did mine. "Sorry, I just ..."

"It's okay," I reassured. "You care about them."

A laugh bubbled from her tears. "Jai always said I never know when to shut my mouth." She nudged her head. "You have any brothers or sisters?"

"No, only child."

"Jai may as well be one. He's basically been living alone in those woods since I was five." She released a long breath and relaxed her shoulders. "Just don't give up on him, okay?"

"I won't," I promised with an honest smile.

In these five short minutes, Jolie confirmed everything I knew of Julian. It was reassuring and a breath of fresh air, hearing someone else defend him when the rest of the town looked down on the Heathens.

I wanted to hug her, but the counter between us only left us with smiles on our faces. Before exiting the shop, I flipped back around to face her. "Hey, Jolie? What was your baby brother's name?"

"Johnny." And her smile was weak. One that transported her into the memory of him. "Johnny Blackwell."

It was four past midnight, and the night shift, who we called the *skeleton crew*, had left hours ago.

I couldn't stop thinking about Jolie's words. The name *Jai* rang in my head. Johnny was the name of the ghost. Johnny was their little brother. My heart tightened with the possibility of what could have happened, what their father had done.

I promised myself I wouldn't dig or ask any more questions, but the truth was already sitting all around me in this dark and dimly lit funeral home. I pushed the chair back and walked to where Monday's desk was. She always kept an extra set of keys underneath. The bobbleheads bounced up and down, mocking me.

"You better not say a word," I whispered, eyeing one of Jordan Knight as my hand swiped back and forth across the wood. My finger landed on the skeleton key, and I peeled the tape back. "Finders keepers." I winked at Jordan.

All paperwork was locked away in Jonah's filing cabinet. I turned off the desk lamp and shut down my monitor before climbing the spiral staircase. Jonah's office was on the main floor, and guilt perched on my shoulder the entire walk there. I was digging into a little boy's death. But it was a ghost who had tried reaching out to me—twice now. Johnny needed me and was trying to tell me something. I could finally bring him peace. I had no choice but to do this.

In Jonah's office, I squatted in front of the filing cabinet and jammed the key into the lock. The yellow files rolled out, the tabs faded, their edges frayed. I filtered through them in search of *Blackwell*. Jonah didn't organize them alphabetically like the average person would. Come to think of it, he had nothing in this building organized. His mind was chaotically in place.

Jonah dressed as if he were from the Eastside, but openly had no ties to anyone. His mind was a puzzle, but every piece made sense to him. He only allowed me and everyone else to see what he wanted us to see, all his pieces purposely scattered so no one could crack his code. There was no doubt he would know I was here. Jonah always seemed to know everything. Jonah always seemed to be watching.

My eyes widened. *Blackwell*. I pulled out the thick folder.

Inside, multiple tabs dated back to the early 1900s. The most recent two files were from twelve years ago. Johnny and Javino Blackwell. Julian was only fourteen or fifteen when his father died.

Johnny and his dad, Javino, died within the same two-week span.

The elevation in the room changed, and the pressure pushed into me from all sides. I felt like my head was underwater, hearts in Atlantis. The proof was right here. Javino Blackwell killed his son.

An accident. I scanned the hardly legible handwriting. *Johnny and Javino were playing in the woods. Javino picked up Johnny, and Johnny tore off his father's mask. The curse took Johnny's life. Cause of death: asphyxiation.*

Johnny was only three years old.

Johnny would have been fourteen today.

A black and white photo of Johnny's lifeless little body on the morgue table assaulted my senses. My eyes watered, and I squeezed them shut and tried to find a stable breath. My legs gave out, and my bottom hit the concrete floor. My back fell to the cabinet, and the papers scattered around me. Words repeatedly screamed at me from the tile.

Asphyxiation. Tore off his mask. Three years old. Johnny Blackwell. Norse Woods.

A Hollow Heathen killed a three-year-old boy. Someone so helpless. The curse didn't care. It didn't care who it was or how strong the ties were. The curse could take anyone, even the people they loved the most.

My palms dug into my eyes, my tears hot and burning, my blood cold and churning. *It didn't matter because the curse didn't care,* my mind repeated. My breathing shook, and the face of Johnny painted on the black canvas behind my lids. I dropped my head back and blew out a sharp breath. *The curse didn't care.*

When I dropped my head back down, my gaze swept across the tile. At the corner of my eye, a letter with intricate handwriting peeked from under the photo. My fingers quivered as I uncovered the rest of it. It was dated six days after the incident. The letter was from Julian Jai Blackwell.

To the people of Weeping Hollow,

If you are receiving this letter, then my father has taken the blame for what happened to Johnny. Here is my official statement. Let it be known, Javino Blackwell was only trying to protect me as a father should. I beg of you, do not condemn my father. Do not take him to the Wicker Man. Javino is a good, respectable man of the Order. I cannot watch my father burn for my carelessness.

I take full responsibility for what happened to Johnny. I killed him! Take me! There is no one else to blame but me! Please, rid me of this guilt and lie and set me free, set me aflame! I cannot live like this anymore—

"What are you doing?!" Jonah snatched the letter from my hands and ripped it in half. "You have no business coming into my office!"

I jumped to my feet, tears rolling down my face, papers at my feet.

Jonah slammed his fist on the shredder's *on* button and sifted both halves of the letter through the machine, his face angry, eyes in a red rage.

"You're protecting him," I whispered, understanding. "You protect the Heathens."

"Pack all your things, Fallon," Jonah stated, the paper shredded and gone forever. "You're fired."

"I would never tell anyone," I cried. "Please, I lo—" I paused, tears frozen at the corners of my eyes. I dragged in a deep breath and straightened my spine. "I love him, Jonah. I would never say anything. You have to believe me."

"GET OUT!" HE SCREAMED.

JULIAN
chapter twenty seven

J ONAH HAD APPEARED AT THE CABIN THIS MORNING, rapping at the door before sunrise. *"She knows,"* he'd told me.

I didn't know why, but relief had swum through my soul at that moment. Someone other than Beck and Jonah knew the truth. The lie had been slowly gnawing at me.

Fallon knew, and I could finally breathe. Fallon knew, and maybe it was for the best. I didn't have to worry about the possibility of hurting her, killing her, breaking her heart. I didn't have to be the one to do anything to her. She would be the one to do that to me. And I was okay with that.

I preferred it this way. I killed a three-year-old boy, who could look past that? I deserved nothing less than the pain she would, indeed and unknowingly, inflict.

Hate me, my moon. Hate me like I hate me.

Because if you don't, you will die, and it will probably be my fault too.

We all had a story. They said our pasts didn't define us, but they did. My past molded me into this. It had been the reason I'd changed courses. At the age of fourteen, I'd begun to understand why there were rules in place. I'd begun to appreciate and follow the code and respect the Order. I didn't just play along for the sake of breaking the curse. I'd ingrained the rules into my brain because I'd seen how being myself could endanger lives. I'd become the mask I wore.

Before Johnny died, I'd pushed limits because magic and ignorance flowed in my veins. I'd once been a boy who ran naked in the woods, howled into the night, wasted time with the boys, laughed, played, and made mistakes. I had it all—before Johnny died.

Because I was once too wild and too free.

Since I was Dad's firstborn son, I was the only hope to continue the bloodline of the spirit element. Dad was of no use anymore, and the perfect Heathen to take the fall. It was up to me to continue the Blackwell bloodline by having a son, and it couldn't be severed like the Danvers bloodline had.

I was the only hope, or so Jonah had explained after I'd confessed to sending the letter to the Order to admit my guilt. Jonah had intervened and retracted my confession before it reached the wrong hands, more than willing to sacrifice Dad's life after the recent killings he committed—because of our shadow-blood. It was the perfect lie.

And I'd lived with insomnia until Fallon's return.

Now, she would be gone too. But it was for the best.

I was one of the cursed. Being a monster was my birthright.

I skipped a stone across the surface of the Atlantic. The sun peeked across the horizon, just a soft wink of pale yellow. I felt her pull like the way the moon pulled the tide. She was here.

I turned to her. She stood feet away, watching me with an admiration I could not understand. She was wearing a large sweater covering those little shorts she usually wore, her long legs taking up more than half her body. She was always one way or the other. She was either pajamas, free of make-up, hair a tangled mess, and innocence on display. Or, she was brand-named denim, expensive shoes, every strand in perfect place, and stubbornness in the way.

But I would take Fallon whichever way I could have her. It was possible she felt the same in return. Perhaps she would take me whichever way she could have me—my shadow-blood too—until she let it kill her.

Fallon walked closer, her eyes bouncing below to rocks before she stepped onto each one. Once she was at my side, she held out her hand. I dropped a few stones into her palm. We faced the sea again.

We continued to skip the rocks for a long time, allowing her quietness to shape us into one.

The moon and sun shared the same sky for a while. The same way we shared the same rock we stood on.

"I can see ghosts," she said so suddenly into the space between us. Into the air. I didn't know how she did it, how she spoke so freely. I envied that about her. "I've never told anyone before, but it's true. I can see them. Talk to them. Most times, help them. There was one I could never help, though. I never knew his name, but I don't think he did either. He had white hair and black eyes. He was always so cold. Almost like he was frozen."

Beck was right, and this didn't surprise me. Fallon was just like her mother.

Fallon could speak to the dead. I stayed quiet, nervous.

"I think a part of me never wanted to help him because I never wanted him to go away. He was my only friend for a while. But then one day, he never returned, and I never understood why. I don't know if I even gave him peace, and it makes me feel like I failed him ..."

I opened my mouth to interrupt her, knowing where this was heading, but nothing came out.

"I've seen Johnny," she stated, and my head fell back under the sky with a sudden intrusion of emotion. "He's not here when you come to the ocean, but he hears your messages."

I clenched my fist. The stones pierced my skin, drew blood. "I don't want to..." *do this,* I wanted to finish off.

"Julian, he forgives you. He knows it wasn't your fault. He loves you so much," she whispered.

I squeezed my eyes shut. My past sliced me open, my baby brother beating against my chest at the memory with the slamming of the waves.

Johnny Blackwell, my little brother who'd feared the water. My little brother, who'd feared the ocean would swallow him whole, and eventually, it did because of me.

"He's been with you this whole time, and he's so sad when you're screaming." At the corner of my eye, she turned to me. "The whole world's sad when you're screaming, Julian."

His frantic limbs had scurried in my arms as he gasped for air, choking on his nightmare, the sea of my face stealing his breath.

Why couldn't we escape it? Why couldn't I break us free?

He'd been too small, too weak, too fragile to climb out of his fear. My hands shook as I lost myself in the memory. With all the power in the world, I was utterly powerless. My throat burned, remembering the scream that had ripped through it.

"I killed him," my whisper broke as my confession slipped into the morning. *It was me. I did it. I killed my baby brother.* "I didn't mean to do it!" I turned with my arms at my sides. The stones fell from my hands. *"I'M SORRY, JOHNNY!"* I screamed, scanning the ocean, the cliffs, hoping he could hear me. Words tumbled from my lips, but my mind was in a fog. Winds thrashed against me, the sun now blinding and dangerous.

I didn't remember the rest before my knees hit rock.

"No, Julian. Your pain is enough. You loved him, and he knows, and it was enough," Fallon whispered, and my mask slid off as she pulled me into her neck. Her arms covered me like a solar eclipse. I breathed her in, I breathed her out, finding refuge. "He knows, Julian. Johnny knows, and he still loves you so much. He's always there when you're in that dark place. He's right there with you, every time. You were never alone, and he never stopped loving you."

And under the shining sun, I felt a piece of the man I used to be *settle back into* PLACE.

FALLON
chapter twenty eight

LIGHTER DAYS HAD COME AND GONE. EACH MORNING WHEN I WOKE, a white moonflower rested on the pillow. I hadn't seen Julian, though. Not in over a week. I'd told him not to come. It wasn't worth him being thrown in the tunnels, and he'd said it was the very reason he didn't want to tell me. But every morning, the white moonflower still appeared. And every morning, I smiled, knowing he'd been here.

It was October the first, and Gramps had made it to the breakfast table, Freddy in the Mournin' cranked up so he could hear. We'd finished the crossword puzzle in record time, slamming our pencils down against the table. And in the late morning, I'd dressed for the chilly temperatures to head into the square, in my skinny black jeans, favorite leather jacket, and black suede booties.

The golden and fiery leaves fell from trees and bedazzled the streets, swirling and waltzing in the air as if it weren't a death sentence. I breathed the color deep into my lungs, knowing winter would soon rob me of this hue. It smelled of a campfire, soured apples, and new beginnings. New beginnings because I was jobless, but *oh*, like the fall, how I was falling.

I parked the scooter in front of The Bean, and my reflection bounced off the diamond-paned storefront window as I switched out the helmet for a slouchy black beanie.

"Mornin', Fallon," Mr. Hobb of Hobbs Grocery mumbled as he limped across the paved pathway with a nod of the head. He was carrying a briefcase as if he were on a mission.

I turned to wave, and my eyes fell on Agatha Blackwell, who was sweeping autumn leaves from the stoop of her shop a few blocks down. Which only reminded me to stop and pick up her secret concoction for Gramps later. Agatha waved, and I returned the gesture before dipping out of the cold and into the coffee shop.

The bell chimed when I opened the door, and a line wrapped around the corner. I took my place at the end, and my hand reached for my phone to kill time, forgetting it wasn't there.

I'd been without my cellphone for months now, powered it off, and dropped it inside the top drawer of my nightstand. Hadn't needed it since. In a place cut off from the rest of the world, I'd been forced to confront both the judgmental eyes of others and my thoughts.

I mindlessly moved along with the line, lost in those very thoughts when a soft buzz hummed inside me. Chatter sounded distant within the café, a million miles away but right in the background.

"Where'd you go, Fallon?" A whisper in my ear, icy breath in my hair as if it were a cold front. I went to look behind me when he gripped the waistline of my jeans and pulled me flush against his frame. "Act casual, would you?" Julian whispered, a playfulness in his tone. I dropped my chin and smiled. "Where'd you go just a moment ago?"

"What do you mean?" My voice was low as we took a step forward, darting my eyes around. No one noticed us. No one was paying attention.

"You do that a lot. You get lost inside your head and stare into nothing. I know this sounds strange, but," he brushed his knuckles across the base of my spine, sending a surge to the rest of my body, "I want to know what you're thinking. I want to be there, wherever it is your mind takes you to."

My smile was embarrassing. "You're already there."

Julian released a sound, something like a hum mixed with a sigh in his exhale. I wished this feeling, the feeling of us, was tangible. I wished I could capture this rush and bottle it. Save it for eternity.

"I don't want to be apart from you," he said into my hair. "I'm coming to you tonight." I shook my head, and he growled. "Oh, you're cold-blooded." His fingertips traced the ridges of my spine and dropped to the hem of my jeans. "But I'm still coming. Be ready for me."

His breath was in my ear like a heartbeat. My eyes closed, feeling dizzy.

And then he was gone—just like that—leaving me in his cold spots.

The door chimed, and I glanced out the shop window just as Julian passed with a hood pulled over his head, no one realizing a Heathen was here at all.

I took another step forward; my body still buzzing.

Once I reached the counter, River Harrison greeted me with a fat smile. "Your usual Pumpkin Spice?"

"*Eh*, I need something stronger." Something to wake me up from Julian's spell. I looked over the festive coffee choices written on the chalk board behind her.

"Brave enough to try Weeping Hollow's own Wicked Death Wish?" River's brow spiked as her lips pressed together in a tight line. I shifted on my heels.

"Let's make that two on this fine day," Kioni cut in, skipping the line and slapping a ten on the counter. "Heavy on the whip and extra drizzle." River worked the register, handed her change, and Kioni and I stepped off to the side. "Did not mean to intrude, but I refuse to wait in that line, and don't bother paying me back. You can get the next one." She eyed me as I searched through my purse for my wallet.

I thanked her, and she shook her black hair, her eyes flickering cinnamon brown, like newly minted copper pennies.

"How are you? Good to see you are still here."

"I didn't think I'd last this long, to be honest."

"Where you off to now?" she asked, and the simplicity of her question reminded me how I'd lost my job.

It was bitter-sweet. I had the rest of the day, free to do whatever I wanted, yet the only thing I wanted to do was isolate myself inside the morgue and bring the little life I could back into a corpse.

Or be with Julian. Preferably, with Julian.

"I don't really know. Walk around the square, I guess."

Kioni's jaw dropped. "No," she shook her head, "You just ordered a Wicked Death Wish. You will be beside yourself. You cannot just *walk* around town—" Our drinks were up, and we both slid the paper cups off the counter. "Today, you will join me."

"Join you?" I smiled, brows raised while bringing the cup to my lips, and a waft of something that smelled like maple, cinnamon, and graham cracker exploded through the tiny opening of the coffee.

"Yes." Kioni pushed open the door, and the cold came at us from all sides. "It will be a good day."

"HAVE YOU EVER FELT LIKE EVERYTHING INSIDE YOUR BODY WANTS TO leave you. Like your heart is pumping so hard ... as if it senses danger is near, or something exciting is about to happen. But you can't move?" I asked Kioni as we laid on our backs, staring up at the back wall of the hardware store where she got lost in her art.

She'd graffitied the brick wall with paint chalk. *Lie Lie Land*, it said. A bouquet of black balloons beneath it.

"Yes. Yesterday. When I had my morning dose of Wicked Death Wish."

The black words so sharp, her lines so clean. "What does it mean?"

"My every fine day, moonchild. So, you feel the side effects?"

"*Moonchild*," I moved my head from side to side with a groan, "Yes, I feel like I'm fucking dying. Like my whole body is like ... *Boom! Boom! Boom! Boom!*" I stretched my fingers out at my sides, sweating, but my sweat ran cold. "But then my heart is like *ba-boom! Ba-boom! Ba-boom!* I want to run *so* fast, get it out of me. You drink this stuff every day?"

"Wow, you're definitely under a caffeine high." She laughed, then it faded. "Yes, every day. When you grow up in a world where life is controlled and planned, you find resilience. Mine is Wicked Death Wish and art. We're all addicts, but my addictions aren't in secret. They're for all to see." Kioni turned to me, grinning.

I envied the way she seemed so comfortable in her skin. With her thoughts, lying on a sidewalk, not needing anyone. The way she was so much on display, so confidently her own person—the kind who didn't need to be accepted by anyone.

Kioni seemed like the girl who could say no and set boundaries. The kind of girl who could say yes, too, because she wanted to. The kind of girl I strived to be. The kind of girl who could just tell Julian that yes, I wanted him to come tonight. That I never wanted him to leave. But with his arrival always came his absence.

And suddenly, a wave of resentment toward the Order and Sacred Sea flooded me. The very ones who were keeping Julian and me apart.

Julian had been right, no one from the east side dove off the cliff after me. For the past two months, they did nothing but push their coven on to me.

I closed my eyes, deciding I needed a break from them for a while, to figure things out.

After the Wicked Death Wish side effects wore off, we jumped to our feet and said our goodbyes, promising to meet each other for coffee again. Being around Kioni was easy. She made me feel as if we'd been friends our entire lives. No pressure, no rules, no ulterior motives. A feeling where I didn't have to watch my back.

I stopped at Blackwell Apothecary on the way home and picked up Gramps' tea. Mina came by for dinner, and while she kept Gramps busy, I cleaned his room and changed his bed linens. Once Gramps fell asleep, Mina Mae and I drank moonshine on the back porch, listening to the ocean. A misty rain kissed our faces, and black clouds rolled above.

Julian said he was coming tonight, to be ready, but I couldn't let him risk—what *would* he be risking exactly? What did the tunnels entail? I turned to Mina, who had her eyes closed as the rocking chair creaked. She was so relaxed, her face wrinkled with wisdom, a few generations full of knowledge. Maybe she could help me better understand.

"Do you know anything about the Order?"

Mina's eyes stayed closed when she answered, "Yes, I know about the Ordah."

"If someone doesn't follow the rules, what happens to them?"

"It depends on who doesn't follow the rules. Are we talkin' about a flatlandah or a witch?"

She'd said witch so casually as if it were so normal. As if it were a gender or a race. "For a witch."

Her eyes opened, and she looked at me. "Javino Blackwell was the last witch punished. Yah have to understand the balance of ordah is the one thing protectin' this town, keepin' it hidden. Witches of the covens are expected to keep the peace. We are fair, Fallon, but sacrifices must be made to keep the shield intact if a witch steps out of line."

"What happened to Javino? What did they do to him?"

"Yah askin' a lot of questions. Yah sure you're ready to know?"

No. "Yes."

Mina hummed in the rocking chair, bringing a mason jar of golden liquid to her lips. After she took a sip, her lips smacked together, and she closed her eyes as if to bring herself back to a distant time.

"Javino was a good man. Those Blackwells got what's called a darkness inside them, but Javino fought it. For as long as he could. Then people started goin' missin' around town. Then little Johnny died. Little Johnny, such a sweet soul. Everyone knew little Johnny. Much like when Julian was little, the kid was everywhere. Always laughin' and yellin' and in yah face. Had to be the centah of attention. So, when little Johnny died, the whole town just got quiet, yah know? No one could look past it. The town wanted answers. Then Javino stepped forward, admitting to it." She shook her head. "I'll never forget the pain in his eyes. The curse taking his son was enough punishment, in my opinion, but not for the Ordah, and not for the town."

"What did they do to him?"

"For a witch, they lock 'em away in the cell for seven days. Weaken 'em, leave 'em alone with what they've done. Killin' people, breakin' the rules, it doesn't mattah the extent of the crime. Balance and the safety of the town come first, ayuh. And on the seventh day, they walk the green mile to the Wickah Man, and the Ordah burns 'em. Offahs his soul for the wrong-doin's, askin' the natural world for forgiveness. Bring balance back to the town and shield. If they don't, the shield will fall."

My eyes widened. My chest clenched. "They burned him alive?"

"You have to remember, by this time, he was already livin' in that half-dead place. Seven days without food and watah, not much left of a man after that. And any last bit remainin' is left on the green mile as they walk it. A man would only beg for the fiah to take him."

"That's horrible. It's ... it's *wrong!*"

Did Julian have to witness this? My heart ached at the thought. I shook my head, not understanding why Julian would go out of his way to see me, to be around me, to save me. Every time we were together was a risk. A death sentence.

I was just a girl, no one special. All thoughts led me to reasons I couldn't understand. He already had to struggle with his darkness, and if anything happened to him, if the Order took him, I couldn't bear it.

He was coming tonight, and the only right thing to do was push him away.

The rain worsened, and we escaped indoors. Drunk on moonshine, Mina Mae curled up on the sofa and pulled the quilt over her. She mumbled on about the Wicker Man, the Order, slurring words, her face twisting with anguish.

Once she was fast asleep, every step I took up the stairs was breaking my heart. It physically ached. Casper followed me up, and the creak of the floor mocked me. *Please be there, Julian. Please don't be there. I'll have to make you leave. I want you to stay.* My mind swirled with a selfish indecisiveness. *What am I supposed to do? What's the right thing, Julian?*

I opened my bedroom door, and there he was.

On the other side of the French doors stood the silhouette of a mistake I was about to make.

My heart was like a somber song, clapping against my ribcage.

I closed the bedroom door behind me, keeping Casper on the other side.

The balcony doors swung open, and Julian turned in his black coat, black slacks, his white mask covering the top half of his face. Rain blew in from outside, his clothes soaked and freezing.

"Fallon," he pushed out, shaking his head and coming at me in a rush.

"Why would you ask?" He gripped the back of my head and pressed his forehead to mine, his fingers digging into my scalp. He was upset and desperate, pushing himself against me as if nothing was close enough. "Why do you always have to know everything? Why do you have to dig and dig and *dig*? I heard you down there. Knowing doesn't help. It makes it worse," he said, his tone pained and angry.

"You didn't tell me how bad it could be. You didn't tell me what they could do to you."

"Every day in this curse is a prison. I'm *already* in prison, Fallon, but not with you. You have no idea what it's like, what it's been like before you got here. With you, I'm more myself than I've ever been. And I'd forsake everything and everyone just to be near you, don't you get it?" he rushed out in a single breath. My tears raced down my face as he was kissing me. "I'm going to break this curse. I *swear* I'm going to fucking break it, but don't push me away before then."

I shook my head, his lips on mine. "And what happens when they take you?"

"Then it was all worth it," he said, walking me backward against the bed. "You wanted me to be real? Well, here you have it. I want you, and the rest doesn't matter."

My back hit the bed, and Julian slowed, unbuttoning my shirt and pushing it open. The cold floated over my skin before his palm flattened against my stomach and slid up between my breasts. My lungs stretched, filling with air.

"Remember when we were in that train car?" he asked, and I bit my lip, nodding as my back arched into his touch. "Are you ready?"

"Yes," I said, and it came out as mist.

His hand covered my throat. "Prove it."

Our eyes locked, and for a moment, we stared at one another. Insecurities passed between us, but without hesitation, I abandoned mine. Julian's hand fell from my neck as I rose from the bed and walked to the balcony doors. A full moon hung high in the sky, and I turned to face Julian.

He stood there, watching me from the darkness. His silver eyes were so bright, so loud, as my shirt dropped to the floor. Then I took off my bra, one strap slipping off my shoulder at a time, and my heart was beating so hard in my chest. My hair fell around my breast, covering me as I bent over to slip off my pants. And then my panties.

From feet away, Julian's heavy and heated gaze touched my body until I was down to nothing. Just me.

Something came over me. A rush of adrenaline, a charge of excitement. Under the full moon, I'd become someone who was understood by another. Someone who was undoubtedly accepted.

"Come here," Julian said, his voice thick, and I turned to close the balcony doors, pulled down the blackout shades. For him, I erased every bit of light in the room, so he didn't have to hide. So he could be himself with me as it was always meant to be.

Without warning, he approached me from behind. His pants grazed across my backside and the tips of his fingers brushed my neck. In the darkness, my pulse slammed when his palm smoothed over my throat and jaw.

"Are you afraid?" he asked me, and his palms moved down my arms, then up my sides. Unable to speak, I shook my head. I was never afraid.

Julian gathered my hair in his fist and bound me against him. He nipped the rim of my ear, kissed the tender spot below it, and he flattened his other hand against my stomach. I became dizzy and weak and melted in place as his lips brushed the length of my neck the same time his palm slid up to cup my breast.

Desperate for more, I turned in his arms. Julian picked me up, and I wrapped my legs around his waist. Our heads connected, and he grazed his mouth against mine. His lips spoke of many words, none of which made it to my ears but straight to my soul. With one hand clutched to the back of my head, the other squeezing my bottom, he walked me to the bed.

I took off his mask, and our mouths hovered as we tortured ourselves, hanging on to these screaming moments.

No dawn, no day, no nightfall. A space-time, where we only heard the anticipating thudding of our hearts. Like Wicked Death Wish.

Boom ... ... Boom .... Boom ... .

"Just don't let anything happen to you," I begged.

Julian shook his head. "I won't," he promised … *Boom* … … *Boom* … "I don't want to be anywhere where you're not."

This is it, my thoughts taunted me … *boom*…this is it …

Then my mouth filled with his kiss.

It felt as if I were kissing the dark woods and not a man. But then he fell back against the bed, taking me on top of him as if I had all the power, making me believe it was the other way around. I kissed his throat, grinding against his thick arousal inside his pants. Julian moaned, I whimpered, and we kissed madly as his hands were everywhere: in my hair, on my neck, my breasts, my thighs. He kissed me with intensity and hunger. He kissed me deep enough to ruin me for any other man.

Julian pressed his finger against my entrance, finding me soaked. "*Oh, fuck,*" he moaned, nudging his finger inside me, then through my slit from behind. "Oh, *fuck,* Fallon," he moaned as my hips thrust against him again, starving for friction, for release, for more praise.

I'd become someone I didn't recognize.

Maybe it was the full moon. Maybe it was us.

Julian rose from the bed with me in his lap. He sat up fully, ripping off his coat and shirt, only breaking our kiss for quick moments until our bare chests collided. He kissed my collarbone, wrapped his lips around my nipple. His finger inched deeper inside me, the other hand clutching the back of my head as I ground against his pants, wanting to feel him everywhere and begging him to take me there.

He stood, and I clung to his waist as he undid his belt and zipper, then he pushed his slacks to the floor.

Julian took us back to the edge of the bed, and my slick center slid up and down his hard and tight shaft. He lay back, allowing me to rub against him, explore him, use him, trust him as he kissed me madly. His large palm grabbed my ass, dragged up my spine. My lips found his throat again, and his moans fueled me.

"You should know I don't deserve this," he said, hooking his arm around me, throwing me on my back.

Rain pattered against the windows with the song of my desire. The cold

October air slipped through the fireplace, creating an icy draft in my bedroom as he moved over me. He kissed, licked, and touched me as if he were learning me, coloring me with his grotesque grace.

My nails raked through his hair when his mouth dragged down my stomach. He sank lower between legs, and the utter darkness pulled me in. I felt myself pulse in the expanded time he spent kissing the sensitive space around my sex. His hands smoothed over my thighs, and the sensations were explosive, convulsive. All nerve-endings alive, dipping into his black waters, and my body convulsed with the inability to handle his lips.

I dragged my hand through his hair. "Julian," I gasped, my hips rolling, my knees falling to the sides, needing more.

Then his tongue stroked me once, twice, *three times* before his mouth wrapped around me. My eyes bulged in the black room as he dragged his tongue through my slit deep and slow. I didn't know whether to slam my legs shut or spread them wider. It felt too good to be lawful, and I clutched the sheets into my fists, and my head rolled back. Julian moaned from his throat, and the vibrations hit my center as he worked his tongue. My body thrashed in a spasm, climbing higher and higher and higher.

"Julian," I warned, a surge shooting through me.

"Fallon," he argued, pressing his palm against my chest and pinning me back down. Face flush between my spread legs, his tongue lapped as I bit my lip, legs shaking with this white-hot heat searing through me.

The orgasm gripped every muscle. The orgasm turned me into white noise.

I reached heights, feeling Julian's eyes on me as he slowed his pace.

He kissed me once on the thigh. "I like the way you come, how you're so quiet." His voice was broken as he crawled back up my shuddering torso, and I grabbed his head and pulled his mouth to mine because I couldn't speak.

His tongue swept into my mouth when his lean and warm naked body covered mine, and his hard dick glided through my slick center. I knew this was it, and I was sure Julian was either torturing himself or me.

Then he held himself up on his elbow to find me and align himself. I reached up and placed my hand on his cheek, and he moved my fingers to his lips, kissed the pads of my fingers, keeping them there as the thick head of his cock kneaded my entrance.

I felt the moment halt. I felt the single slam of my heart. I felt his eyes on me. I felt all these things in a matter of a heartbeat ...

"This is going to hurt," he panted, snatching my wrist in his grip.

Then he slammed himself inside me, breaking me open in a single thrust.

Julian cursed against my fingertips in a feral growl.

A painful pinch stabbed from inside, and my body instantly tensed as it burned. Just as a cry pushed through my lips, Julian dug his teeth into the tips of my fingers. All pain shifted from my sex to my hand, and I couldn't understand why.

I tried to pull back, but his grip was tight around my wrist, his bite almost breaking the skin. My chest held, and a hot tear slipped down my cheek as we stayed connected like that.

It didn't feel good, and I shook my head.

It didn't feel good, and I didn't understand why people did this.

Then he slid my two fingers into his mouth, gently sucked them.

"Fallon," Julian said, kissing my fingers, my palm, my wrist. "Trust me."

He pulled out, and his dick inched slowly back in as he hovered closer. His nose grazed the rim of my ear, and then his mouth moved across mine. He pulled my hand between us until it reached his lower abdomen, and my fingertips grazed a light patch of his hair.

"Touch me," he told me, and his voice was rugged and shredded against my mouth like the rain pounding against the window. "Touch us. Feel how real this moment is."

He wrapped my fingers around the base of his cock, and he slowly inched back inside until he was deep and filling me and there was nothing left to hold. Again, we were connected, and the pain simmered, and Julian's mouth drifted over mine. My hand trailed across the hard lines of his torso to feel the way his body moved as he rocked inside me.

"Are you alright?" he asked, his nose brushing my skin as he ground himself in and out of me at a slow pace. I nodded because I was. "I'm trying to go slow, but I'm shaking from holding back because you're so tight, and this is so right, and, *my god*, Fallon … it's as if you were made for me. This is maddening."

"I'm okay," I promised, cupping his face, and he sank into my hand. "I trust you."

Then Julian ground into me with deep and hypnotic thrusts, his pelvis grating against my clit, causing me to see vibrant colors behind my eyes. His teeth dug into my lip, and we kissed hard until it bruised, selfishly claiming and searing an impression on one another deep enough to run below the surface. Deep enough to brand us. The friction of every grind pulled me into a dizzying spell. We fit perfectly. Our blood flowed in the same direction, hearts beating at the same pace. Bound under a sinfully black full moon. He hurt so good.

Julian crushed his mouth to mine as he came, pulsing inside me and filling me with warmth, and afterward, he moved over me like a fickle dark cloud, kissing my mouth, down the side of my throat, my collarbone until he laid his head flat upon my breast, sinking between my legs.

Our chests heaved, and I felt his heartbeat against my stomach. I felt his lungs rising and falling against my sex. "How do you feel?" he asked, a cold breath blowing on my sensitive skin.

I moved my fingers through his hair, then down his neck and back. "Like I got hit by a planet."

Julian dropped his head onto my stomach and laughed. The sound was breathy, flaring goosebumps over my skin. I'd hardly heard his laugh, and now I always wanted to make him laugh.

He lifted his head, and I felt his eyes on me. "Some theorists would call that a big bang," he said, chuckling, then kissed the curve of my hipbone and smoothed his finger across my skin. "I never noticed this before."

"What?" How could he see in the dark?

"This," he kissed my skin again, then traced my flesh with his tongue. "It's like the shape of a moon."

"Oh, my birth control patch must've come off," I swayed my hips, hating that he saw my birthmark. I'd always been self-conscious of it.

"I like it." Julian moved up the length of my body and tucked me into his naked side with his hand between my thighs.

Whispers passed between us through the night until, eventually, I fell asleep in the comfort of his arms.

WHEN I WOKE THE NEXT MORNING, THE MUSIC OF THE OCEAN DRIFTED through the opened French doors. The fresh autumn breeze swept through the room too, commanding my eyes to open, but I'd already felt the emptiness crawling around me. I squeezed my eyes shut, forcing my heart to steady because he wasn't here.

Eventually, I had to open my eyes. The sky was a swirl of pale blue, pink, and gold. The full moon was gone. Julian was gone.

AND I WAS ALL *alone.*

JULIAN
chapter twenty nine

I AVOIDED THE HEATHENS, THE TOWN. AS FRANKENSTEIN ONCE SAID, ALL noise that wasn't misery was torture to me. Solitude was a monster's only solace—*deep, dark, deathlike solitude.*

Being inside Fallon had been better than I could have imagined. Images replayed in my mind, and I closed my eyes, recalling the way she'd ground against me as the ends of her white hair brushed my face. Her light kisses that trailed down my neck.

There had been no shame in the way she moved on top of me, using me to pleasure herself. And I'd let her all day long if that was what she wanted because I knew her intentions were pure. All strength I'd embodied became water. I'd slipped through it, almost busting before I'd flipped her onto her back to taste her innocence before I took it. Then, when I finally had, I became powerless.

It should have been my first time because it damn well felt that way.

I'd laid with her awhile, naked and at peace, talking through the night hours until sleep took her. I'd stayed up for a few hours more, thinking of all the ways I could live like that forever. The things I would do, the people I would betray. My mind spiraled as she slept soundlessly, curled in my arms with her face buried in my chest.

The things I would fucking do terrified me to the point I'd gotten lost in my own head, fighting with myself. Back and forth, back and forth until I'd driven myself mad and felt the vibrations return. Darkness pulled me under right on time—at three in the morning.

A scream had lodged in my chest to break free from it to the point it pained me. I'd felt it, and I tried to ignore it for as long as possible, held her tighter to stay with her longer. I tried to force it away, but it only grew stronger. It felt like the cruel sun, blazing and stifling and burning my skin. And I hated myself for it.

I had no choice but to slip out from under her and run to it, wishing I could give Fallon more than half a man. If I hadn't, I feared my Darkness would take her too.

I opened my eyes again, and my gaze transported back to the here and now, the cabin and not the likes of Fallon's bed. It was mid-day, I believed, and I was sitting on the floor of my cabin, not even on the comfort of my broken-in leather couch. In the dark, on the floor, surrounded by broken beer bottles, glass from a shattered lantern, with a blazing fire breathing on my feet and Fallon's sweet scent still lingering on my skin. The last thing I remembered was waking up naked against the Blackwell mausoleum in the cemetery with no memory.

I didn't know how long I'd been sitting here either. I turned my head left, then right. All that surrounded me was evidence of a broken Heathen.

The rapping at my door sounded so far away as I gazed into the fire, believing I'd imagined it. Not caring if I'd imagined it.

Bang! Bang! It came again.

I drank from my bottle.

"Heathen, I know you're in there!" an agitated voice called out, and I rolled my head back. "You wretched Heathen!"

Whoever it was, wasn't leaving. I stumbled to my feet, scratched my bare chest, and stumbled to the door, righting my mask.

When the door cracked opened, Gus Hobb was on the other side, fist raised mid-air to knock again.

"What?" I asked through a tight jaw.

Gus took a step back and fanned the air between us. "Yah smell like death, Heathen." He peeked inside my cabin, and I stood in front of the small opening from the shadowy depths of my pity, narrowing my eyes. "Now, I've been waitin' outside the shop for thirty minutes. My cah supposed to be done. What yah got goin' on in theya? Don't tell me you've been workin' on my cah like that."

"Shops closed for the day," I snapped and went to close the door.

Gus' palm came up and slammed on the door, trying to push it back open. "Now hold on just a minute. I need my cah. Pruitt's already bustin' my balls about the window. If I don't get it fixed, I'll be closed down for a month. Yah gotta a month's worth rent? 'Cause I sure as shit don't."

"You're behind two months, Gus. Two months. Because I prepare for the unexpected, I can afford to close shop whenever I want. If you were smart with your money, you wouldn't be in this predicament. The car will be ready when it's ready. Today, the shop is closed. Now, get off my property."

Gus wedged his foot in the door, preventing me from closing it any further. "I need a cah, Heathen. The only way I'm gettin' outta this rut is by makin' deliveries, and yah bettah get yaself togethah, or all of Weeping Hollow will know by sundown that a Hollow Heathen has lost his damn mind."

For a mere moment, his threat reached into my dark mind and provoked disturbing thoughts. One where I snapped his neck only to watch him collapse on my wooden porch with a thud.

One where I strangled him until his face turned colors.

One where I took the bottle in my hand, smashed it against the door frame, and slit his throat with a broken, jagged piece.

For a mere moment, these evil thoughts played out. But then I thought of her.

I thought of Fallon, and I reached for a set of keys on the wall beside the door and tossed them at him. "Take the Bronco. And be easy on her."

"Now that's what I call customer service," Gus said through a smile. He turned and limped down my front porch, patting his bad leg like a giddy-up, mumbling through his whistle.

I closed the door and slid the lock in place. Both my palms fell on the door, and I released a heavy breath.

DAYS HAD COME AND GONE, THOUGH I HADN'T RISEN FROM THIS SPOT, THE safety of my cabin floor. The fire had died, and I was left here in the cold, in the dark, where I belonged. Whilst I hadn't eaten, I wasn't hungry. The sickness and hatred filled me in more ways than one, always reminding me that the darkness could take me whenever it wanted. That it had complete control over me.

Every second on this earth wasn't a gift. For a shadow-blooded Blackwell, it was a punishment. I didn't deserve to be happy. Therefore, I deserved to live like this. That was what the Darkness had told me. *Scream as loud and as passionately as you desire. No one hears you.*

And yet, Fallon heard my screams. She didn't just hear them.

Her soul screamed back.

"Julian." My name flowed around me, surrounded me. It sounded detached, not really here. "Julian!" It swirled again.

I lifted my head and was looking into golden eyes that seemed so alive, so intense. Phoenix Wildes. And his arms crossed over his chest, looking down at me as if he were studying a corpse, searching for cause of death. *Self-destruction, Nix.*

"It's time we call Clarence," he said, his voice flooding my ears.

Clarence Goody. My gaze drifted lazily around the room when the other Heathens came into view. A wave of worry in Beck's neon blue eyes, his tattooed fingers curled around his mouth. A chilling and knowing gaze from Zephyr, which only spoke a language he understood. They were all here, staring down with scrutiny.

"Fuck off." I turned my head, dragging my gaze back to the fireplace where the ghost of the fire swayed. But it had been days since it died.

I blinked, seeing nothing but ash and diminished colors. I drank from an empty bottle. It angered me that they were seeing me like this. The only Heathen who held the four of us together was falling apart.

The only one they could count on was ending up like his father.

Ice-cold water engulfed me at that moment. Every muscle awakened, and I jumped to my feet. My hair, chest, pants soaked, and I snapped my gaze to Phoenix, who stood with a large pot hanging at his side.

"Wake up, Blackwell!" he shouted, throwing the pot into the fireplace. Ash exploded from the brick hole. "Do you have any idea what you've done?!"

Water dripped from my hair and down my back as I stood frozen.

Phoenix's eyes were hard, swirling pits of embers. "River Harrison was found this morning."

"I didn't know she'd gone missing," I said through clenched teeth, body shaking from the shock.

"River Harrison was found this morning," Zeph repeated, voice more adamant, "Strangled and neck broken at Whister Park. You *killed* her."

Beck stayed quiet in the back when Phoenix spoke up again. "You're lucky Jonah found her body on the way to work, but it's River Harrison." His chest was heaving, eyes blazing. "What's going on with you? Why can't you get a handle on this, Julian?"

"Don't call me that. Don't humanize me," I lashed out, no longer deserving a name. Monstrous things didn't deserve names.

And I was frustrated with myself for the things I'd done but had no memory of, frustrated I wasn't strong enough to fight my shadow-blood. Frustrated that I'd left her after I fucked her. My god, had I completely lost myself?

"Clean yourself up and get to work. At least act the part and pretend you didn't kill a girl." Zephyr shook his head and walked to the door, hanging back to wait for the others.

Beck's face softened, and his eyes filled with something that looked like pity. "Don't forget the pact. If you can hold on to anything, hold on to that. We're so close, and we can't do this without you."

The door shut with their departure. The walls of the cabin rattled.

And I sank to the floors in a puddle of where I'd wasted away.

The only thing I could hold on to, the only thing my chest had room for, was her.

I spent the rest of the afternoon cleaning the cabin, throwing empty and broken bottles into trash bags, chugging water bottles, and eating leftover Italian shrimp n' pasta and blueberry lattice bars Agatha had left at my front door. I had no doubt Beck visited her after witnessing my condition.

After showering, I stood before my broken mirror in only my boxer briefs, keeping my eyes on my feet and determination running through me. The idea couldn't be as irrational as I thought. I'd jumped from the sea cliff for Fallon, but could I face the man in the mirror?

I pinched my eyes closed and filled my lungs. I could do this. I was no longer afraid of heights, but I was afraid of myself and the unknown awaiting me.

I slapped my face to pull myself together, bent over, and clutched the sink's edge.

When I lifted my eyes, a black hole sucked me in.

In an instant, it felt as if someone had punched through my gut and ripped my lungs from my body. Fallon lay limp in my arms. Her long white hair tangled in my fingers—my hands … They were shaking and out of control.

I couldn't breathe. I couldn't fucking breathe!

In a desperate frenzy, I pressed two fingers to her neck to find no pulse because my hands were shaking and wouldn't stop. I couldn't grasp on to anything. *My chest*, it felt like it was on fire. My eyes burned. My gaze darted over her blue and cold face.

This isn't real. This can't be real, but it feels so fucking real!

"No …" My heart buckled. I lowered my ear to her mouth and heard nothing. "No!" I shook her, begging her to wake. I grabbed her jaw and blew life between her cold lips. "Fallon," I cried out. Her lifeless body wouldn't wake. "FALLON!" I pulled her close to my chest and held the back of her head, rocking her and calling out to any god that would hear me as a scream ripped through my chest and up my throat, piercing the night sky.

When the nightmare spat me out, I collapsed to the floor. My back hit the wall. Panic climbed into me, shared my body. I gasped for a solid breath, but all oxygen was sucked from the room.

I'd had a panic attack before, when my entire body had filled with my heartbeat, and I wanted to flee from my own skin. This was different.

This felt like panic attacking a panic attack.

And I never wanted to see my *reflection* AGAIN.

FALLON
chapter thirty

I WAS VERY MUCH IN LOVE.
And it was nothing as the famous poets had said.
It was a *strange love* ... the kind that didn't feel good
all the time ... the kind where my greatest fears crawled, but an undying
acceptance too. The kind where I had to stand in front of a mirror, forced
to see me for what I was. What this was. The kind to question myself and
everything I knew. I was certain this was like no other ... though I had
nothing to compare it to. Maybe no one could ever. And perhaps that was
the point we could not see. No two were the same ... or would ever be.
And there would never be an answer for what it was, but I was in love ...
the kind where King had said; how, *"Blood called to blood."*

Because I was so much in love. And, *maybe* ... he was too.

"OH, LOOK—ANOTHER GLORIOUS MORNING. THE FULL HARVEST MOON IS IN
*our midst, and what better way to celebrate our small business owners of
Weeping Hollow than during today's Hollow Fall Festival? Show your
support and dance on over to town square with your wallets. This is Freddy
in the Mournin', have a wicked Sunday, witches, and remember, no one is*

safe after three a.m." Freddy's howl from the gazebo speakers faded into Michael Jackson's *Thriller*, and I closed my eyes as my head fell back, the Sunday morning sun heating my face. Pumpkin, apple, and cinnamon from Mina Mae's pies weaved into the crisp fall air that brushed my skin, and Monday bumped my side.

My eyes snapped open, and her red locks grazed my arm when she whispered, "This sucks."

A laugh sputtered through my pressed lips. I turned my attention to the handful of residents forming lines on the grass surrounding the gazebo.

"What's happening?" I asked, scanning the crowd. Then, all at once, townies broke out into the Thriller dance in perfect synchrony. "No." I laughed, my palms hitting the table under our tent. "This is great."

Monday rolled her head back with a groan. "Oh, that's nothing. Just wait."

At my side, Monday crossed her arms over her matching red shirt Jonah made us wear. The shirts read MY DAY STARTS WHEN YOURS ENDS, with the funeral home logo on the back.

It was just this morning when Jonah had shown up at Gramps' house and offered me my job back. I couldn't help but think Julian had something to do with it. Our sales goals at the fall festival was to get three people to put a deposit down on a pine overcoat—what Gramps liked to call a coffin—and to reserve a grave.

It was ten in the morning, and I hadn't gotten one yet.

"And here we go," Monday whispered, her finger pointing at Milo, who moon-walked across the grass to the center just when the chorus rang through the speakers. Milo broke out into dance in his suspenders and newsboy hat.

"No way," the words sailed out of me. "Milo!" My palm hit my chest. "Monday, this does not happen. This isn't normal."

"Unfortunately, it's our normal." She released a sigh, and my smile burned as I watched everyone dance, Michael Jackson's voice slithering through the square. Some people were in costumes, some in their everyday clothes, some old, some young. "This happens every year. Milo says he does it for the kids, but c'mon, look at him," she tsked, her flat palm in his direction, "he loves it."

I shook my head, disbelief carving into me, and my eyes continued to roam the square for Julian, hoping I would see him here.

The memory of us from only a few days ago slammed inside me as if my lover were visiting—the heat spiraling between us, the ice swirling around us, ripples of pleasure and pain. Why was it that I felt so happy, yet so miserable? That to be able to think and go about my day after the night we'd shared, and the way he'd left, *oh!* it felt like walking on an ivory moon with a dark cloud looming close behind.

Somehow, Julian felt undeniably close to me, in my blood now. I suppose it was Love's weakness that turned our eyes from what stood in the way, allowing our hearts to wander in this feeling. Or could it be Love's strength? And I knew where my thoughts were ... If Julian only knew ...

Julian had once said he would never give himself entirely to anyone, but that night, he'd given me everything, as I to him. Could I look past his continuous absence? The ghost of him after the sun had fully risen, the moments just after his departure. He'd always left me, but not ever really *leaving* me. He said he never wanted to leave me, and perhaps he meant it in some other way. Like this way—inside of me, all around me, in my heart, in my head, so loud and enduring and *permanent* now.

I'd woken alone, and the worry of something happening to him kept him in my mind. The thought of him kept my eyes everywhere, looking for him. Kept a knot in my stomach, an ache in my chest.

But how could I know if he wasn't okay if I couldn't go to him?

"Incoming," Monday whispered, straightening her spine and painting on a fake smile, the kind of smile I knew so well.

Jonah appeared from behind, carrying a box. "Anything?"

"Nope," I said, eyeing Monday. "I don't think anyone's rushing to pick out linens for their coffin."

"They'll come," Jonah insisted, his eyes scanning the crowd. "No one wants to be buried next to Jasper—" his voice dropped suddenly when a customer approached the booth. "*Miss Driscoll*, good morning!" Jonah's octave changed. "Thank you again for the shirts."

"Jonah, we talked about this," she smiled, blinking her long, heavy lashes, "Call me Carrie. You make me feel like an old woman." When her glare hit me, her eyes were like blue lightning—sharp and quick and sliced through me. She returned her gaze to Jonah, and her features softened as conversation carried on.

I froze, admiring her posture, her golden tendrils, her flawless skin.

"She's so perfect, it's sickening," Monday whispered as Jonah and Carrie walked away from the booth, side by side in light-hearted banter. "If she takes my spot in this October's initiation into Sacred Sea, I'll be pissed," Monday went on. "They don't just let anyone in, and I've been workin' on it for three years now."

"Why do you want to be in their coven so bad?" I asked, turning my attention to unloading the box filled with pens, clipboards, and sign up forms Jonah had dropped off.

It was hard to keep my distance from her when forced to work with her. It was hard to keep any of those from Sacred Sea at arm's length when this town was impossibly small.

At the corner of my eye, Monday turned and leaned into the table, her bright red hair falling down her back. "You don't get it. It's like being a part of a family. Somewhere to belong and people to fight for you."

"What about your parents?" My eyes drifted from her to the cup I was filling with blue pens.

"They never gave a damn about me." Monday turned, eyes narrowing across the square. I turned too, following her gaze. On the other side of the gazebo, three bodies stood under a tent. *Wicked Soul Cakes* was printed on the banner running across the top. "I was always the different one," she whispered. "The milkman's baby."

The edge to her voice, the hurt in her eyes, the longing in her expression, it was all too familiar. She had a family, a home inside this town, and she still felt rejected by them. For a brief moment, I felt for her. I could relate to her.

"Is that your brother?" I asked and threw my hand over my eyes to see better. Under the tent, a blond-haired boy stood with the blonde-haired parents.

"Yup, the one who can do no wrong."

"Their loss," I said, an attempt to put her at ease. Although, I knew there was nothing I could say to help.

She smiled, but it was empty.

As the day went on, I talked the legendary Jasper Abbott, the town's blabbering crazy man, into securing two graves. One for him, one for his dog, Cujo. Jonah hadn't mentioned it had to be for a human. I only needed one more when Monday and I finished our coffee.

"I'll head to The Bean, get us two more. Watch the booth," I told her.

Monday nodded when Kane and Maverick approached our table just as I was leaving. "I see how it is," Kane called out, and I turned and held up my palms at my sides with a shrug, the timing perfect.

Jolie waved at me from under her mom's tent in front of the apothecary store as I passed, hay bales decorating both sides. My gaze roamed their booth and inside the store, hoping to get a glimpse of Julian, but knowing it was a lost cause.

My fingers touched the cold metal of the knob when "Fallon" carried on the wind. At first, I thought it was all in my head. Until I heard it again.

I whipped my head to the side and squinted, seeing him standing there, leaning against the corner of The Bean, his passionate eyes touching me in a way that was a fluent language only we spoke. The sun hung directly behind him, drawing his outline in silver. He looked haloed in the light as he moved closer. I raised my hand to my forehead to shield my eyes as he peered down at me.

"Come with me," Julian whispered, then took a quick glance at our surroundings.

I couldn't believe he was out here so exposed at this hour in Town Square. The wildness in his eyes was a telling of a secret, and it made me smile. "I can't, I have one more grave to fill," I explained, trying to play off the effect his presence had on me. "You interested?"

"Fallon Grimaldi," Julian clicked his tongue, "I knew you only wanted me for my body."

A laugh left me, and I scanned the square to see if anyone was watching us, and there wasn't. No one was watching the freak. No one cared about me or what I did. We stared at each other in an odd way, as if it were a silent argument. Our gaze battled each other until my voice arose. "Julian..."

"Fallon," he insisted, a nudge of his head. "Come with me. I only need a moment of your time."

I glanced around once more before sliding around the corner of The Bean after him.

I followed Julian down Seaside Street and into an alley, and my chest fluttered like there was a heart racing inside my heart. Once shadows swallowed us, Julian turned and caught my hips. My breath suspended for the briefest moment, anticipating him.

His fingers locked onto my sides, walking me backward. A spiral of heat climbed inside me, poured into my blood. And his scream-filled eyes latched to mine when my back hit the brick wall.

"Once upon a time," he said in a rush, leaning into me. "There was a Heathen so lost, he screamed so loud …" He lifted my hands high on the wall and interlaced his fingers with mine. "He followed the rules, followed the code, but never followed the useless thing inside his chest." His hands traced along my outstretched arms, and his palms smoothed over me like sleet against my heated skin.

My body sank against the wall, and I cleared my dry throat, keeping my eyes on him. "Until now. You're supposed to say … until now."

Julian pressed his hips into mine and dipped his mouth to my ear. "Until now."

My mouth parted, and I closed my eyes. My breath seized as he cupped the warmth of my neck, replaced it with his chill. His breath was like cinnamon, biting as he seduced my senses.

His voice dropped into a whisper, "Until you." And I heard the crack in it, the chasm of hurt that crept around the curves of his syllables.

Until you. Two words that connected us.

"I'm sorry," he continued in my ear. "For not being there in the morning after."

"It's okay," I cut him off, shaking my head. "You're okay." I bit my lip, laid my hand on his chest. He was here now. "That's all that matters."

Then he kissed me. Oh, *god!* and he was kissing me. I couldn't hang on to a solid breath as his tongue moved against mine like an obsidian vortex, a desperate force demanding to accept him for all that he was, to accept this position we were in. I kissed him back, a push and pull and a fight and a scream.

I hear you, Julian. I already have.

Secrets and promises exchanged between us like a pact. He cupped my face and pulled me onto my toes, and I was a wave carried on his current, on his lips.

He was kissing me, and I was flying …

"AHHHHHHH!" a scream erupted and pierced my eardrums.

Like a reflex, Julian's palm covered my eyes the same time his head turned to the side. His chest was heaving against mine, his muscles twitching under his skin, ready to bolt—to run.

"SOMEONE, HELP!"

"I'm so sorry." Pain etched in his words.

Then his hand fell from my face, and a rush of cold wind smacked my skin.

I didn't have to open my eyes to know Julian was gone.

I was shocked by how the cold pierced his absence.

"Fallon, oh my god, Fallon!"

My skin, my lips, everywhere he'd been felt strange from the rest of my body now. Not fully mine anymore.

"Are you hurt?!" Carrie Driscoll appeared before me with a gaze scanning my features. "Don't worry, help is coming," she told me, and I wanted to say something. I wanted to tell her I didn't need help, that he did nothing wrong. "Thank goodness I came just in time."

Just in time, her words echoed.

JULIAN

I WAS RUNNING FASTER, HARDER, MY LEGS THREATENING TO BUCKLE. I was running until my sight became hazy. My breathing echoed in my head, jolted my chest. Inhaling, exhaling, I was running, past the pain, to the Norse woods, where I was loved and not feared.

And I didn't stop there. I was running, my chest burning. I'd felt the betrayal of my witchery begging to be released—the jerk of my hands, the vibration in my veins. It pulled me, and it wasn't even nightfall. I couldn't understand it. My mask was gone, lost somewhere along the way. The temperatures were biting my face, sinking its nails into my eyes. I forced them open, dry and burning and running.

Then I collapsed somewhere in the heart of the Norse woods.

The canopy allowed little light to filter through. There was no sound aside from my starving lungs. My arms spread out at my sides, and I curled my hands into fists under the dark tresses of the trees, grasping to the velvet flesh of the forest ground, desperate to release this build-up.

I couldn't feel my legs, yet I felt every morsel of inescapable torment. When I opened my eyes, the sun's rays glittered off the reds and golds of the fall leaves—October's kaleidoscope. One mad burst of flames around me, inside me. *I'm on fire!*

I squeezed my eyes shut and let go.

My scream reverberated, unleashing me. It burned in my chest, tore through my throat, and filled the woods. I screamed, expelling the fire until I could no more. I screamed until darkness engulfed me, silenced me. All that lighted my way was the will to lay here because I couldn't lay with her. And the trees answered as they always did, the whispers of the woods telling me it would all be okay. The Norse woods hadn't left me, though my heart had left the Norse woods.

And nothing would ever be the same.

FALLON

TOWNSPEOPLE CROWDED AROUND, THEIR FACES BLURRED. CARRIE Driscoll had pulled me to a bench outside of The Bean and had her hand on my shoulder as Monday, Kane, and strangers talked all around me, cursing the Heathen. Outrage multiplied, and I was coming down from shock as it turned to a boiling turmoil.

"No," I kept repeating, "It wasn't like that, it wasn't. You have it all wrong."

I didn't know if they could hear me, as they twisted my words, filled the spaces between. My head shook, clouded, and I couldn't breathe.

I stood, looking for air. "I need space," I chanted as pressure piled on top of me, their chatter not ceasing. "Why won't anyone listen to me?"

"Fallon," Jolie said, coming through the crowd of people. "Fallon, come with me. Let's get you some water."

She grabbed my hand and led me to the apothecary, and with every step, the flustering heat lifted. My mind was lost. My eyes darted for Julian, but all I saw were people and tents and worried, watchful eyes of Weeping Hollow.

The bell rang as we entered the store, and Jolie guided me to the back and through a swinging door.

"Sit down," she insisted, then turned to the sink to fill a cup. "What happened in the alley? What happened to my brother?"

My fingers gripped the edge of the plastic chair, and I looked up at her. "I don't know. He just took off." I thought of Julian and all the things they could do to him. "*Oh, my god,* this is all my fault, isn't it? What are they going to do to him?"

Jolie turned to me with a paper cup of water. She offered it to me then leaned against the counter. "It won't get that far. Nothing happened. It's all speculation unless something happened, and there is no proof. If anything, the Order will question you, but that's it. I have no doubt Jai is in the woods. He's safe there, and they'll make this go away."

They'll make this go away. She meant Norse Woods, Jonah even. Or both, if Jonah was a part of Norse Woods.

But hearing Jolie's steady voice brought me comfort.

"This can't happen again," she continued, laying her hand on mine. "I'm happy he has you, Fallon. Really, I am, but I can't lose him. You two have to be more careful. No one can see him with you again. Once, maybe it was a fluke, but twice?" she shook her head, "It just can't happen again."

"It won't," I promised.

"Fallon?" a voice called out, and both of our heads turned to the doorway to see Agatha Blackwell. "Is everything okay?"

"Yes," I quickly said, rising to my feet. Jolie straightened her spine, and I felt her eyes on me as I brushed my hair from my face and stood tall. "Everything's okay. I just got a little light-headed."

Agatha squinted her eyes, studying the two of us. "What is going on outside, this talk about a Hollow Heathen?"

"It was nothing," I assured her. "I was walking in the alleyway alone, and I'd crossed paths with one. Someone thought they lured me into the dark, but it was all just a misunderstanding. He hardly said anything to me, let alone touched me." Lies. *They're all liars*, even me. "Carrie screamed, and he took off, but he didn't do anything wrong," I reiterated. Agatha Blackwell was part of the Order. She had to know her son didn't hurt me. *Truth.*

"Oh, good," she nodded, "People like to get carried away. It's not like this hasn't happened before." Her eyes lingered a moment longer, and Jolie stood silent, but I felt every fragment of energy radiating off of her as if it were a struggle to keep her thoughts at bay. "I'm sorry for all the drama."

"It's okay." I waved off the incident as everyone else should have. "I have to get back to the booth. I doubt Monday returned, and someone should be there in case someone is dying to pick out a coffin. Or a grave. You know, the things that put the fun in funeral," I rambled, then stopped before rambling myself into more trouble.

I thanked Jolie and Agatha, rushed out of the apothecary, and back to the fall festival, forcing myself not to run to Norse woods to find Julian. It would only make things worse.

THIS WAS THE WAY IT HAD TO BE.

JULIAN
chapter thirty one

I BURNED THE BODY LAST NIGHT," JONAH SAID, LEANING IN THE doorway separating the garage from my office. "That was your responsibility. Where were you?"

Sitting on the blue crate in front of Phoenix's motorcycle, I turned the key to see if the engine would start. The engine sputtered, a horrible coughing sound, and a cloud of smoke blasted through the exhaust pipe. Sweat dripped from my brow into my eye, and the fumes mixed in the air caused my eyes to burn. I squeezed my eyes shut.

When I went to lift my hand, my arm grazed the pipe, and the hot steel seared my skin. "Ah, fuck," I hissed, yanking my arm back.

"Julian?" Jonah barked.

I jumped to my feet and drove my boot into the wheel, kicking the bike out from underneath itself until it laid on its side. Plastic crunched, and parts flew upon impact. *"What?"*

"Where have you been? You missed the monthly Town Hall meeting on Monday. People were outraged with the stunt you pulled during the Fall Festival, and it could've helped if you were there. You could have explained yourself. Then you leave me with a dead girl at the morgue, which, by the way, I can't account for. I'm not your damn clean-up crew, Blackwell."

I took off my hat and dug the heel of my palm into my eye.

"I need air," I muttered, exiting the garage and walking into the parking lot.

Black clouds moved furiously overhead, blanketing the town in a démodé grayscale—muted of life. As of late, my days had been blurred. No dawn, no nightfall. An endless span of twilight. I pulled my shirt up and over my eyes when Jonah's hand gripped my shoulder.

"You love her, Blackwell?"

The question struck a chord, and my being froze in its afterword. I'd come from a breed notorious for being hollow, but the four-letter word was a poignant shot to swallow. After everything I'd done, I couldn't possibly be capable of such a thing.

Perhaps I was in love with the feeling.

"*Love?*" Air blew from my nose, and I shook my head, remembering my father's words. "Love doesn't live here, only fear grows in Weeping Hollow. Love is a fool's fantasy and a monster's nightmare."

For a Heathen, love was a curse all in its own. If I admitted to myself that I loved her, I would have no choice but to leave her. With love came freedom, and the Hollow Heathens didn't have either luxury.

I turned my gaze down Seaside, watching as dead leaves tumbled down the empty street of the late afternoon, wondering what would become of me if I kept my distance from Fallon.

"Something's got a hold on me," I confessed. "It's only getting worse."

"You're being pushed and pulled and ripped apart from multiple directions," Jonah said, and there was so much truth in his words. "The Heathens, the coven, the town, the Order, the darkness ..." he took a breath, "And then there's Fallon."

And then there's Fallon. "What do I do?"

"I can't tell you what to do. You have to decide for yourself, but what I can say is that from experience, the fastest way to kill an addiction is by another. If you want to rid yourself of the darkness, you will have to hold on to the very thing that is more powerful than it, and let it take possession of you. Your soul has been dying to live, but fear is holding you back. It's the most tragic thing I've witnessed, and that's coming from a guy who owns a funeral home." Jonah's laugh was light and hardly made it to my ears before it died away. He shoved his hands into his pockets and rocked on his feet. "It's not fair to anyone going on like this. You'll have to choose. Her, or everything else."

An exhale slipped from my split lips, and I pinched the bridge of my nose, nodding.

Jonah squeezed my shoulder. "And your silence tells me you've always known your answer."

ON THURSDAY MORNING, I LEANED AGAINST THE BRICK BETWEEN BUILDINGS, drinking coffee and watching Fallon through the window of The Bean as she smiled across from the Kenyan girl. Her smile painted my morning in colors I didn't deserve, made them bright after the dreadful week without her. I liked her new company. I'd taken notice in the way she put more distance between herself and Sacred Sea, as well as fall into a routine here in her hometown. Fallon Grimaldi had always belonged here, the same way she belonged with me.

The past few weeks with her had taken my mind away from my responsibilities. Phoenix was right, but Jonah was right too. I'd chosen Fallon, but the only way to be with her in the way she deserved was to break the curse so the Order no longer saw me as a threat.

Fallon smiled on the other side of the window. Her hand covered her mouth, and I straightened my spine, stretching my fingers at my side. Heat waved inside me the same time the breeze *whooshed* through the alley, and the thing inside my chest wept.

I'd never told her how beautiful I thought she was.

I'd never told her all the things I should've said because I thought if I didn't tell her, it would give me more time. And I was scared. I'd never been good at getting close with someone, and despite it, she always returned to me. Somehow, I was good at all things Fallon.

My gaze slid around Town Square, wondering if anyone noticed her the way I did. Kane and Maverick were walking on the other side of the gazebo toward Town Hall. Adora Sullivan stood outside the boutique's door, waving at them. Jasper Abbott was sprawled out on the lawn, looking up into the morning sky and speaking of banshees and sirens and old tales. The three old ladies sat on the bench in front of the gazebo, surely gossiping about Fallon still, or noticing River's disappearance and forming rumors.

My eyes darted to Town Hall, where Mr. Pruitt chatted to an irate Irene on the steps, facing The Bean. In his shadow, Carrie Driscoll stood in a floppy woven sun hat, her eyes hidden behind large sunglasses. A selfish rage simmered just looking at her, the way she caught me with Fallon, the way she tore us apart.

Then her face turned to me, and I slipped under the shadows.

FALLON

"IT'S OUR FAVORITE MONTH OF THE YEAR, AND SO THE COUNTDOWN begins. Twenty-two days until Samhain. This is Freddy in the Mournin' with your Friday morning Hollow Headlines. And remember: dear monsters, you are insignificant, only one in the infinite number of creatures. Hear me when I say, no one is safe after 3 a.m....Owooooo!" Freddy howled, and I wanted to take my pen and shove it in my ear.

"Do you get trick-or-treaters?" I asked Gramps, sitting across from him at the breakfast table.

Gramps cackled, and my eyes bounced up to him. It was a strange laugh, one I'd never heard before. One I'd never expected to hear. One I'd probably never hear again. I smiled a real smile, the kind to burn my cheeks.

"Swipe that gigglemug off yah face ... lookin' like yah nevah heardah laugh b'for in yah life."

I laughed harder and grabbed my mug that read, GOT THE MORBS, and brought it to my lips to hush it.

"No, they be maffickin' in the streets, though." He chomped on his dentures, then slammed his pen down before he rose to his feet. "I take the egg, moonshine. C'mon Caspah, the old man needs a cat nap."

My eyes bulged as I watched Casper follow Gramps out of the kitchen to his bedroom.

Alone again, I looked out the bay windows and into the backyard where the bony trees lost all their leaves, leaving them piled in the garage's gutters and covering the back porch. Since I had no reason to go into work today, I spent some time cleaning up the kitchen, hand washing dishes. Doing anything to keep my mind occupied and off Julian.

It didn't matter whether I was alone or surrounded by people, thoughts of him always open fired. I hadn't seen him since the alleyway during the Fall Festival. He hadn't shown up for the Town Hall meeting either.

I'd asked Jonah about him the other day. The only thing he could tell me was that Julian was okay. That had been it. *Julian is okay.* But I wasn't okay, and it wasn't fair.

My thoughts catapulted as I walked to the living room, wiped down bookshelves, the side table, and coffee table. I rearranged books on the shelf because I couldn't rearrange my thoughts.

Taking a moment, I sat at the edge of Gramps' recliner and picked up King's copy of *Song of Susannah* when his bookmark teetered to the floor. An old photograph, a little distorted with the corners faded, touched my feet. I bent down to pick it up, and my heart jumped in my chest.

It was me, but it wasn't.

It was my mother, and she looked just like me, but didn't.

Her long hair stuck to her face as she laid with a baby in her arms. With *me* in her arms. My breath held, and my fingers trembled. I'd never seen a picture of her before, and it was too much. This was too much. A tear escaped, and I dropped my head back for strength. Composure.

I'd never known her, but the absence of a mother, wondering all that I'd missed, filled me like a landslide of grief and all the things I never had. When I looked back down, my vision blurred, and I pulled my tee over my eyes. *Why did she have to die?*

I sucked in a breath, let it go, and looked down at the picture again.

I looked down at the way she was looking down at me. *Did she know those were her last moments?*

In the corner of the picture, Agatha Blackwell stood at her side with her hand on my mother's shoulder. She had her other hand bracing my little head as if my mother wasn't strong enough to hold me.

She was dying, and I was living, and it didn't seem right.

I shoved the picture inside the book, slammed it shut, and returned it to the side table. I wasn't ready. I wanted to know my mother, but I wasn't ready. Would I ever be?

A knock sounded at the door, and I sucked in a breath to stand.

The grandfather clock said it was only an hour before noon.

I opened the door.

"Fallon, hi, dear," Carrie Driscoll greeted. She was wearing a yellow dress laced at the top and the fabrics ruffled down to her hidden feet. I stood taller, fixed my hair that laid messy on my head, and straightened my long tee, feeling uncomfortable even though it was her that had come to my house.

My house, my mind repeated. Yes, this was my home.

"Hi," I replied, but it came out child-like. I cleared my throat and tried again, "Hi, Carrie." Her golden locks rippled over her shoulders and fanned around her breasts. A plastic container carrying a pie with Mina Mae's logo cradled in her hands. She looked as if she stepped out of a storybook, so perfect and here, and… "Why are you here?"

"I've been thinking about you. I've been trying to find the time to come and check on you and see how you were doing after the close encounter you had with a Heathen," she insisted, a beautiful smile gracing her features. She lifted the pie higher as an offering. "It's Mina's Autumn harvest cobbler. The apples are home-grown from Goody Farms."

"You really didn't have to," I said, awkwardly taking the cobbler and holding it out in front of me. "Just like I said in the meeting, it was a misunderstanding. It was my fault. I shouldn't have been there. I thought I could take a short-cut through the alley. Wrong place and time I guess."

"I couldn't imagine what could've happened if I wasn't there. I know you haven't been here long, but you can never be too careful, Fallon. I'm just so happy you're okay," she continued, and as she went on, the more her dramatics on the situation were pissing me off. It may have been irrational of me, but all I could think about was how it was her fault I hadn't seen Julian in almost a week. It was people like her who spread fear across the town, never getting to know him. They were only making it worse. I held my tongue and nodded, forcing a smile as my thrashing emotion slid down the back of my throat. "The Pruitt's are hosting their annual Samhain ball, will you be attending?"

"I haven't heard anything about it," I answered honestly. "But even if they sent me an invite, I couldn't leave Benny here all alone."

"Nonsense, you must go. You would be doing the Pruitts a disservice if Tobias Morgan's daughter didn't, at the very least, make an appearance."

"Maybe." I'd managed to steer clear of Kane and the rest of Sacred Sea. The only people I'd seen were Jonah, Monday, and Kioni. I didn't know if Kane was still eager to reel me into his coven. If he was, my dodging methods to avoid him when in Town Square were obvious enough to let him know I'd had enough. It was crazy to think about how I'd always wanted to have friends and fit in, and now I was pushing people away. "We'll have to see."

"Very well, give Benny my best, Fallon. You take care of yourself."

Once she left, a blast of air released from my lungs as I fell against the closed door.

"Who was that?" Gramps call out from his bedroom.

"Carrie Driscoll," I replied, scanning the pie to see if there was any evidence of the container being tampered with, finding some kind of proof of her poisoning it.

There was none.

"I don't like her," he mumbled from his cracked door.

I sighed. "You don't like *anyone.*"

FALLON
chapter thirty two

THE WOODEN FLOORS CREAKED, THE NIGHT AIR RASPED, AND THE COLD darkness licked its lips before lapping my skin, a forewarning pulling me from my sleep.

I tossed and turned onto my back and faced the opened balcony doors where the topaz moon hovered the Atlantic in the matte-black sky. The house whispered another faint *creeaaak*, and I darted my gaze to the sound, seeing nothing in the dark corners of my bedroom. Not even Casper, who was probably sleeping with Gramps.

I kicked the rest of the blankets off my slick body and trained my heart to calm.

Then a shadow emerged from the dark corner and lunged at me.

The weight of him bound me to the bed.

My eyes went wide with fear and confusion as I swung my arms out in front of me, pushing against him.

Against Julian. It was *Julian*.

"Julian!" I cried, but with all his strength, he gripped my throat and choked me, digging my neck into the mattress.

In an instant, oxygen vanished. I clawed at his chest, his shoulders. I couldn't breathe. *Julian, I can't breathe! JULIAN, IT'S ME!* I wanted to scream, but my words and voice were all trapped in my frantic mind.

The blue vein in his neck popped, and Julian's silver eyes, empty and hollow, stared blankly down at me with every intention to kill me. Inside them, all the lights were out. The dead zone, empty rooms, uninhabited planets. The same look I'd seen before.

I clawed at his shoulders and dug my nails into his straining neck. I pierced his skin. Blood seeped down his throat as his grip tightened around my throat.

Julian, please! My wide eyes burned, and my tears froze, blurring my vision as he held me there in a locked grip, blacked out and cold. My body thrashed against his, but it was no use, for his legs had straddled me, pinning me in place.

JULIAN, STOP! My mind became hazy, my limbs going numb. I didn't know what to do. *What do I do?*

All I saw were two silver slits above his black mask as my lungs ached for air.

I stopped fighting, for it was useless. He was killing me. He was trapped. I couldn't make sense of it.

He wasn't here. In Julian's mind, he was lost and somewhere else while I was dying beneath him. I felt every last second tick by, and I cradled his head in my hands, placed my fingers against his slamming pulse.

He was killing me, and I loved him.

Then Julian blinked. Once, twice, three times.

He'd blinked, and his confused gaze ran across my face, then his hand around my neck, and then the body it was attached to. Recognition kicked in. I noticed the change in his eyes and how they shifted from cold to something of twisted injury.

"Fallon," he gasped and released his grip. His chest started to heave, his body started to shake. "No ... Fallon ... no, *fuck!*"

I choked on the abundance of air, feeling it slide down my throat and fill my lungs. I couldn't catch a solid breath as tears rushed from my eyes, my chest wheezing for oxygen. Julian lifted his shaky hands from the mattress, yanked at his hair as he pulled away from me.

I felt his distance, his pain. I felt it as real as I felt his hand around my throat. Under his tight skin, his muscles flinched as if it were a command to bolt from me. My head shook as the tears finally were able to fall.

"Julian, don't," I pleaded, gripping the collar of his shirt, tearing it as I tried pulling him back to me. Every muscle in his neck flexed when I grabbed his mask-covered jaw so he would look at me. "Julian!"

He pinched his eyes closed, then opened them, and his eyes were strung out, confused, seeming as if he were bouncing between what was real and what wasn't.

"What is wrong with me?" he shouted in anguish. Sweat covered his forehead and hairline. His pupils were dilated, only a silver outline around them now.

He scanned the room, drifting and shaking his head. I went to grab his face again, but Julian's hand shot up, blocking my every attempt before he jumped to his feet.

Desperate, I grabbed his coat, and he doubled backward. "Julian, I know it wasn't you. I know you, and that wasn't you. It's okay, let me help you."

"No, Fallon, you don't know. You have no idea. Don't say that. Don't pretend you know me when you have no idea. You don't know me. *Please*, just let me go!"

"*No*," I cried, sounding senseless and pathetic. He yanked from my grasp. Panic cut every dreadful second in two with each step he took to the balcony. I followed after him. The cold wind rushed around me from all angles, freezing the tears against my cheeks. "Julian, stop!"

But he wouldn't stop. He wouldn't even turn around. All I saw was the back of his head as he slipped onto the balcony and disappeared into the night.

My heart slammed as I pulled open a drawer and shoved on a pair of shorts. I swiped the keys off my dresser and didn't bother with shoes. Disoriented, the only thing consuming my mind was going after him. I couldn't let him go like that. I couldn't let him do this alone.

As I rode down the streets, the cold was like ice against my skin. My hair smacked against my face. I accelerated the speed, trembling and white-knuckling the handlebars on my way to the woods. Time was lost on me, somewhere between dusk and dawn—a time when the night crawled cold and strange creatures came out. But also, a time when Julian and I were able to burn so bright.

Street signs, buildings, and trees passed by me, and before I knew it, I'd reached the start of the woods. I slid off the scooter, dropped it to the ground, and took off running to the tunnel of complete darkness.

My breathing was in my ears as my feet moved faster. The woods robbed me of one sense and heightened the others. Everywhere I turned was black. All I could hear was a mixture of my breathing, flapping wings, and ravens crowing into the night.

"Julian," I called out as the wind hissed through the tree's naked limbs. The forest was a backdrop of nothing, and I whipped my head and turned my body at every sound of the woods. My imagination began to run wild with horrors to fill the void, so I ran faster to push it away.

After a while, I slowed my pace and stood defeated, clutching my aching side for a solid breath. But every attempt pulled in a chill that only dried my lungs.

My palms hit my knees as I heaved, my muscles sore, my feet raw. It felt as if I could pass out at any moment, but I still managed to pull myself together and straighten my back.

"I'm not leaving, you coward," I called out to the woods, frustrated. "You're always running and hiding. For once, could you man the fuck up and face me?" I dragged in another breath and removed strands of hair sticking to my tears. "This darkness controls you, I know that. I *do* know you, Julian. For a long time, you were always a mystery to me, but I know you better than I know myself. We're no different." I paused, my throat still raw and my voice harsh, but I wasn't giving up. After a few coughs, I cleared my throat, and continued, "You know why you love working on cars so much? Because it feels good to bring something to life when you're surrounded by death, and if anyone could understand that, it's me."

A breathy laugh left me, and I held back my tears. "You've got this song in your soul, and it's so loud, I can hear it. And I know when you smile. You wear a mask, and you still tilt your head to the side when you smile because you don't feel like you deserve to have it. But you do, Julian.

"I know when you're anxious about something because you tap those stupid rings you wear against your thigh. And the way you hold all your thoughts in for so long and then blurt everything all at once in one breath with so much passion. I love when you do that. I know that you never know how to say the right thing, but you still say it because you believe it and stand by it, and you don't care who it offends. Then other times, you say nothing because you want to say everything. I know that you are always trying to do the right thing even when it doesn't feel right. And because we feel right when everyone says it's wrong, it has you questioning everything.

"I know the way your body moves now, too. Your muscles twitch under your skin to run and *run* and *run* because it's the only time you feel like you have control again. And I know you scream because it's the only thing that helps you break free from what's going on inside you that no one else can see. You're loyal to everyone else but yourself. But you're a leader, Julian. You can do anything you want … save your coven, break this curse, *anything!* if you would just stop listening to them!

"And I know that wasn't you back there, and I also know how scary that is when something's got a hold on you because that's what you have on me," I screamed into the darkness, my voice slowly failing me. "I know you can hear me right now. After everything, I'm still here because I love you, you stupid jerk, and I'm not going anywhere," the sudden confession struck me. "Why can't you see that by now?"

A cold front knocked the air from my lungs when I felt him behind me. His footfalls had fallen on deaf ears, but his presence was so loud and surrounding me now. I froze in place. My chest held, and I curled my fists at my sides to keep myself from falling apart at the sound of his breathing.

"Julian, I—"

"You were wrong about one thing," he said, his voice thick and his breath hitting the back of my head. "Screaming isn't the only thing that makes me feel free."

Emotion barreled through me. I squeezed my eyes shut.

Julian exhaled, and his frame pressed against me from behind. His chest was bare and brushing my back now as he moved my hair to the side.

"I'm so sorry," he told me, fingering the strap of my tank and sliding it off my shoulder. His knuckles grazed my arm. "You love me?"

Nodding, I said, "Yes." And he sighed.

Sighed. Like it was something tragic yet inevitable.

He kissed my shoulder, and his lips moved up the length of my sore neck where his hand once choked me, and I sank into him.

Then Julian slipped something over my eyes.

It was his mask.

He replaced the darkness with his own kind. I stilled, utterly dependent on him, yet trusting him. He was everywhere, a severe and passionate force of a shadow.

Julian's finger traced my jawline as he tilted my chin to the side, guiding my mouth to his, my entire body turning with it to face him. And through the opening of my split lips, his tongue slipped and filled me with his taste as he steered me backward.

My back slammed against a tree, and he yanked my shorts and panties down. I kicked them to the side, and a blast of cold hair rippled over my buzzing skin. Julian picked me up at the backs of my legs, and they clenched around his waist when he gave me his mouth again. A moan came from somewhere deep inside him and vibrated against my tongue. He was so intense and breaking apart, as if he were made of stardust in my arms. As if he were a product of the night sky, infinite and significant. *Oh*, how he was beautiful like that.

So, I kissed the night, got lost in his sky and suspended in his time. I kissed the darkness too, as if it was all I knew because it was a part of him.

My back slid against the rough bark as he ground my bare and slick core against the sliver of his tight stomach. "Julian," I shuddered, my body pulsing with the foretaste of him.

"I know," he panted.

All I could see behind this mask over my eyes were black shadows of him. I grabbed the back of his neck, dragged my nails through his thick hair, and a moan spurred from his chest. He kissed my throat, and the soundtrack of him undoing his pants counted the seconds. When he released his cock, he wasted no time plunging himself inside me.

He was breathless and in my ear, sinking his hands between my ass and the tree, grabbing hold, and thrusting himself deeper. A wave of tingles and heat charged from my core. It rushed up to my belly and made every blood cell come alive.

"You're right, we feel so right," he said with a shredded breath, and I threw my head back against the tree when he slammed into me again, burying himself.

Our noses brushed when his mouth found mine, and he pinned our hips together and ground against me with him deep, driving me insane.

the real of us,
ALL IN THE AIR NOW.

JULIAN
chapter thirty three

FROM A BUICK 8, MY FEET LANDED ON THE GROUND OF Goody Farms, located on the northwest end of the border. The white plantation home nestled between cornfields. Rows of apple trees, wild blueberries, cranberries, and strawberries blanketed the acreage. Most of the town's food source came from Goody Farms, making Norse Wood's own Goody family one of the wealthiest of Weeping Hollow.

Goody Farms and the Hollow Heathens were the solid two reasons why Sacred Sea hadn't successfully taken over the town, despite what the law of balance stated.

The night was full, and iridescent gray clouds slid lazily across the phasing moon. A crow squawked in the distance, and Phoenix tossed a knowing glare at me from over the hood of my classic car.

It was me the black birds followed. Crows, ravens, it hardly mattered anymore. It was never-ending because Death wasn't finished with its massacre. Their sounds always followed, always reminded. Always kept me on edge and aware. Darkness could take me at any moment.

Winnifred, Zephyr's sister, played a depressing tune on the piano, and the notes echoed in the hollowed home, carrying through the already opened front doors. The two of us passed by her, a nod our only greeting. Winnifred was a promiscuous creature, with wheat-blonde hair and upturned eyes. Her fingers never left the piano's keys as one side of her mouth lifted, her plump breasts pressed together and up by a corset. Moonlight streamed in from the floor to ceiling window, casting a beam of white light over the grand piano.

My eyes landed on Phoenix's back as he led the way through the living room toward the back of the house. Nerves bounced in every step we took until we reached the carved wooden doors of the room I hadn't entered since I lost both my brother and father.

When we entered, Zeph and Beck were already present, as well as Clarence Goody and Drunk Earl. The last of the Hollow Heathens filled this very room. My glare slid from Beck to Zephyr to Phoenix, searching for answers but finding none.

"Take a seat," Clarence Goody announced, gesturing to the three empty chairs surrounding the sacred Heathen table.

Each chair was hand-crafted by the Wildes with our family name carved into the wood, the matching element symbol etched below it. Two of the five candles flickered from the center table, a matchbook at their side.

Phoenix ran his hand across his candle, and a flame ignited. Before taking a seat, I did the same, my gaze lingering on the Danvers chair with the earth element symbol underneath. The upside-down triangle, a line straight across. The only unlit candle spread an emptiness which lasted for over a century.

Phoenix's hawkish gaze darted around the room as he followed suit, sinking into the chair his father once sat, the same chair a distant relative of his once built.

He broke the silence. "What is Drunk Earl doing here?"

A stained bandana covered Earl's face, his gray hair sticking in all directions. Off the arm of the wooden chair, Earl's wrist hung loosely, grasping a lowball glass of expensive brandy. A smug smile coated his face.

Beck's elbows dug into his knees with his thumbs under his chin, his impatient knee bouncing beside his father's. Zeph seemed relaxed, right at home in the discomfort of it all.

"Earl is a Hollow Heathen, he deserves to be treated as such," Clarence

Goody answered, his straight white hair curtaining his mask.

"Earl is a waste of magic," Phoenix hissed.

Drunk Earl waved his hand out in front of him. "Go on and pretend I'm not here."

"What do you think I've been doing for twenty years?" Phoenix Wildes. Always the protector of baby Beck.

Beck shoved a cigarette into his mouth, leaned forward, and snatched the matchbook from the table.

"What are we doing here?" I asked, wanting to get back to Fallon, the shop, anywhere else but this place.

This small, insufferable room was my martyrdom—a reminder of when I'd been forced to listen to Jonah, Clarence, and Agatha conspire to give up Dad instead of me for the *greater good*. It was a time just before they took Dad to the cliffs and shoved him inside The Wicker Man. A time before they set his body aflame. *Anywhere but here...*

Bright green orbs beamed from behind Clarence's white mime mask. "Are you any closer?" he asked, his voice like a bass filling even the cracks of the room, the nooks and the crannies.

Beck began to speak, but I intervened, "What are you referring to?"

"Breaking the curse," he answered, and I darted a glare at Zeph and back to his father. "When the books went missing in the chamber, I was questioned. Don't take me for a fool. You think you're the first Heathen to break into the chamber for answers?"

"No, we're not close," I gritted through a clenched jaw, hating that he knew. Hating that someone within the Order could threaten us with this. Even if it meant risking Zephyr, his own son.

Clarence nodded. "I didn't see it until they called you in, ordering you to stay away from Tobias Morgan's daughter. I don't know what they are up to, but I'm not going to stay two steps behind. It's time we put the coven before the town, same as Sacred Sea has been doing."

"I agree," Phoenix said, and I sensed relief in his voice. Perhaps he was relieved Clarence could be in on this too, with breaking the curse. He could be on our side, but I still couldn't trust him.

"Oh, good. The son of fire," Clarence crossed his legs and leaned back. "You're the oldest, Phoenix, and you still haven't chosen a mate from the coven. Shall we discuss the reason why?"

"Found no one worth choosing," he snapped. Phoenix's eyes glowed with a neon-yellow hue, and I knew right then he was lying before the table. A sacred space where treachery and betrayal weren't welcome.

Phoenix lowered his eyes, and Goody set his glass down on the side table. "Twenty-seven years ago, I sat at this very table when your grandfather spilled the importance of continuing each bloodline. I was sixteen, Phoenix. You're almost twenty-eight. Julian and Zephyr, you two are not far behind him. Before you know it, I will retire, but I cannot rest easy knowing this coven is without solid plans for continuance. This is the *worst* we've been in almost two hundred years. What are you waiting for? Why hasn't either one of you had a son yet?"

Zeph sat up. "Being forced—"

"Relax. I'm not forcing you, Zephyr. Not right now," Clarence interrupted, then returned his attention to Phoenix. "And don't tell me you're waiting to break the curse, because every Heathen before you tried, and every Heathen failed. The only certainty we have is making sure you pass along your magical element." He slid his eyes to Drunk Earl when he added, "And preferably not with a flatlander. You four are what binds the coven. You have many people depending on your magic."

"We have until we're thirty," I announced.

"My daughter understands what it's like to be a Heathen," Clarence offered.

Phoenix winced at the insinuation. "Winnifred? You must be joking."

"Careful," Zeph warned.

Phoenix inhaled deeply. "Listen, Mr. Goody, beauty has never been the issue when it comes to Winnifred. Anyone can see the good genes your wife passed along to your daughter. But I have two years. If I can't break this curse in two years, I'll pass along my fire sperm. But until then, and with all due respect, I don't want to hear another word about it."

"They see us as weak," Clarence replied dryly. "Change needs to be made now."

Phoenix cocked his head to me with disbelief in his eyes, and his brown hair fell from its hold, the ends hitting his jawline. He returned his wide eyes to Clarence. "I have until I'm thirty. I'm taking the time I'm owed."

"Then you give me your word?" Clarence countered. "Two years, and you'll choose my daughter, Winnifred?"

Phoenix's muscles tensed. His fiery eyes narrowed. My eyes dragged across the room. Everyone was waiting the same as me, yet no one knew what he'd say.

Phoenix Wildes was the wild card, unpredictable and expressive. *Think about what you're about to say before you say it,* I thought.

"Yes," he agreed, but his words were etched with insecurity and doubt. I closed my eyes. Phoenix always kept his word once stated. "For the sake of the coven, I give you my word."

"See, now we're getting somewhere. Now, Julian," he called upon me. *Please do not ask me about Fallon.* I couldn't lie if he did. Not here. "Your shadow-blood has taken six lives, Blackwell. Six!"

"It wasn't six." The truth was, I couldn't remember for certain. "Five, tops."

I hadn't realized until Jonah found River how out of my mind I'd become. Then what happened with Fallon had pushed me over the line. Their blood was on my hands, each death devouring my conscience. It was a vicious circle, and only Fallon could pull me back out of it, but I couldn't become dependent on her alone.

Clarence Goody raised a brow. "Beth Clayton?"

"Beth Clayton's lips were stitched with a needle and thread. Have you ever seen me blackout and walking around with a sewing kit?" I leaned back in my chair, gripped the arms at each side. "It couldn't have been me," I said angrily. And then, a long, silent moment later, "Could it?"

"The coven has received confirmation it was you," he stated. "Regardless of proof, they'll blame the rapidly decreasing numbers of these residents on you because of your shadow-blood and what happened with Javino. If this continues, the Order will have no choice but to burn you in The Wicker Man, and you have yet to have a son." Panic enveloped me whole. "Your shadow-blood has gotten out of hand, and that's why I've come to the conclusion that by the Full Cold Moon, if things haven't changed, I'm attempting an expulsion."

It felt as if all the oxygen had been sucked from the room.

I'd become paralyzed as Beck and Phoenix jumped to their feet at my defense.

Their words flew around the room as Drunk Earl fell into a laughing fit from the safety of his seat.

"You can't do that," Phoenix's voice fired off at my side. "He would become catatonic. He'll be nothing."

"That's if he doesn't die," Zeph muttered, then drank from his glass.

"He won't *die*," Clarence tore his eyes from mine, breaking our stare-off. "He may become catatonic, but he'll still embody the element of spirit. We'll put him into comatose lucidity. It will be the only way to control him during the expulsion as well as contain his sperm."

"You sick son-of-a-bitch!" I slammed my fist on the sacred table. "For twenty-six years, I've bowed down to this coven. I've given up my life, relationships, my morality, my freedom, my manhood. And now you're taking my soul? Are you fucking kidding me, Clarence?" I blew out an incredulous breath, unable to believe the absurdity of this. "You have lost your damn mind. It's not supposed to be this way."

"I am your high priest, remember where you are and who you are speaking to. You are nothing but a tool for the sake of the coven, or have you forgotten that?" Clarence's voice shook. "You murdered six people. I should have taken you to the Norse chambers myself after Jury Smith. The natural world has been looking out for you, but not for long. I'm giving you advanced notice, Blackwell. You take one more life, and the coven will take action."

"I won't let this happen," Phoenix assured, then turned to Clarence. "The coven will never agree to this. Agatha will never agree. We should be helping him, not *imprisoning* him. Think about how many lives he's saved."

"This meeting is over," Zephyr stated, and a gust of his wind rushed through the room. The candles flickered.

"I'm not finished," Clarence's voice vibrated the walls. The four of us stood, towering over the round table, eyes glaring down at Clarence. "The Pruitts are hosting their annual ball during Samhain, and I have a feeling he is hiding the missing books. I've spoken with Pruitt myself. He has agreed to let the four of you bartend the event. You have your way in. But it is up to all of you to take back the missing books."

When I didn't think this meeting could get any worse, it did. I'd lost all trust and respect for Clarence a long time ago, and yet, he continued to surprise me. Augustine Pruitt may be a smug prick, but he and Viola Cantini were only following Fallon's father's wishes. I knew where this was going, and it would take more than a *feeling* to convince me to walk into the Pruitt home to snoop around for the missing books. This plan—if one would call it that—was different than breaking into the Chambers. This was someone's home.

"How are you so certain Pruitt has the missing books?"

"You forget I am a Heathen as well. A very old Heathen. My magic may have faded over time, but I still hear the whispers in the wind." He slid his gaze to Zephyr then back at me, almost as if Clarence couldn't stand to look at his son. There was no doubt in my mind Clarence would never have passed along his air element if he weren't forced to do so, selfishly keeping it until the day he died. "The books are in the Sacred Sea chamber under the house."

"Let me rephrase and try to understand this. You want us to break into Sacred Sea's chamber? All four of us could be executed," I reiterated, shocked he was ordering this of us.

I wasn't surprised Clarence was just as desperate as we were to break the curse, but risking the Heathens? The only ones who held the coven together? Had he lost his mind?

"I told you, change needs to happen for this coven. Breaking this curse *needs* to happen, so don't get caught," he said and drank from his glass. "Start preparing. I will see you four at the Samhain ritual. *Now*, you are dismissed."

The candles flickered until the flames were engulfed by the Goody wind. AND DARKNESS *befell us.*

341

IPOMOEA ALBA. MOONFLOWER; blooms under the moon's light, pollinated by creatures of the night.

JULIAN
chapter thirty four

ONCE, I'D READ THAT WOMEN HAD SOMETHING WOVEN INTO THEIR genes that allowed a man to break down and expose his feelings without it compromising his manhood. I suppose that was why I'd ended up on Fallon's balcony, distraught and out of my mind, needing the same comfort and peace she'd always been able to satisfy. For Fallon Grimaldi had become my safe place.

The meeting with Clarence and the Heathens reminded me I was nothing more than an object or a weapon, whichever way they required me to be and saw fit at the time. A host for magic.

I'd been loyal to my coven. I couldn't recall at what point things had turned, for it seemed as if the corruption itself had become corrupt. Perhaps it had always been this way, and I'd been a blind fool, or it could have been the moment Dad had walked the Green Mile in my name.

I didn't know, and for a mere moment, I thought it would do the town and the Heathens a favor if the coven did fall. But only for a moment. Because in spite of everything, they were my family.

"Something's bothering you," Fallon pointed out. I was lying back on her bed as she was straddling my waist. Her white hair was curtaining my face and in my eyes, but I didn't mind it.

"Nothing for you to worry about." She didn't need to know that

Clarence had threatened me. And if he found out about River Harrison, it could be over for me. My days could be numbered, and I'd rather spend them with Fallon, not talking about it. I only needed to be around her. For her to fill me with her peace.

"Were you close with Tobias?" I asked, changing the subject. "Did he ever warn you about anything? Talk to you about the town, us, or anything strange?" The more information I had, the better.

Her father had taken away her choice, and I had to know why. Was it solely to protect her from the monsters of Weeping Hollow, or did he know something I didn't?

"No, we hardly talked. He rarely talked about my mom, let alone the town," Fallon said, pulling back from me and sitting upright. "Why are you asking me about my dad?"

I unlinked my hands from behind my head and wrapped my fingers around her wrist, pulling her back over me. "Your father asked for Sacred Sea's protection. I want to know why," I told her, her hair falling back over my face again. I liked her on top of me, her lightness touching me as if it could fix me.

"Well, I got this letter sent to me back in Texas. It's why I came in the first place, but Gramps said he never sent it," she explained, her finger drawing lazy circles on my temple. Her expression turned distant as she recalled. "We passed letters back and forth for about a year, you know. Then I got the last one, and I should have known it wasn't his. But when I read how sick he was, I just packed my bags and jumped in the car. I didn't even think twice about it."

"How do you know it wasn't from him?"

"He told me himself. You should have seen the look on his face. It scared me. And you know I don't get scared easily, but, Julian, he looked like … I don't know, but it was like everything he was so afraid of was staring back at him. He wouldn't talk to me for days. Come to think of it, his health really took a turn after I showed him the letter. And I know this sounds crazy, but my thoughts go and go then spiral, always assuming the worst. Still, I can't help but think Gramps was giving up, so his body was giving up too." She paused and moved her eyes downward. "Like he knew something bad was going to happen to me, that there was nothing he could do to stop it, and he wanted to die before I did. Or maybe it's all in my head."

My chest tightened. "Let me see it."

Fallon's clear eyes jumped to mine. "See what?"

"This letter. Show it to me."

My hand fell from her thigh as she turned and hung off the edge of the bed, her bottom in the air as she searched through something. My gaze flicked over her little round bottom, the small space between her thighs.

I'd never experienced the same form of intimacy with anyone else as I did with Fallon. Before Fallon, it had always felt forced and unnatural, and I'd been ashamed of doing it because it felt as if I were forcing myself on a female even though *I* was the one being forced.

But with Fallon, it was freeing, the reason I could never pull away from her at the last second as I had with everyone else before her. Fallon willingly gave herself to me. Fallon trusted me. Fallon moved with me. She never cared about my magic, never asked a thing of me other than to be myself.

"Here it is." Her hand raised from the edge of the bed with the letter between her fingers. I sat up against the headboard, and she crawled next to me, handing me the letter before crossing her legs at my side.

Moments passed in utter silence as I scanned over the letter, feeling the weight of her stare with her nail between her teeth. "Has Benny always written with a quill pen and ink?"

"A what?" she asked, her finger still between her teeth.

"This letter," I flipped it over, "It was written with a quill." I looked up, and Fallon lifted her shoulders in a shrug. Any time I'd received any correspondence from the Order, it had always been with a quill pen and ink. But I didn't recognize the handwriting. "Do you have the envelope?"

"No," her shoulders sank, "No, I don't."

"I want you to think hard, Fallon. Did it have any seal on the envelope? Like a wax seal with the Norse Woods symbol? The star inside the circle?"

"No, I know the symbol you're talking about. I would've remembered that."

I folded the letter into a perfect square. "I'm keeping this," I told her, leaning to the side to tuck it into my back pocket.

I knew no one else in Weeping Hollow who wrote with a quill pen and ink. It had to be from the Order, and if it were, I had every right to question Augustine Pruitt as to why someone lured Fallon back home, knowing her father never wanted her to return.

However, confronting them without solid proof could backfire or draw attention to Fallon. For now, the only option was to move forward with the plan to steal the books back from Sacred Sea and see if the answers I needed were there. It was a major risk ... but I was going down anyway, may as well bring the Order down with me.

"You already have so much going on. This is my problem, not yours," Fallon insisted.

I placed my hand on her bruised and purple throat, not thinking. But Fallon didn't flinch. She tilted her head to the side, stretching her neck and offering herself to me, and I watched her as she closed her eyes in my touch as my palm slid up the length of her neck.

The small reaction from her made my mouth part behind my mask, words sprinting from my chest but never making it into the air between us. I'd choked her only nights before, and her trust in me was unconditional. At that moment, I almost told her I loved her, and the sudden thought caused my heart to splinter.

Instead, I pressed my lips together, traced her sharp jawline with my thumb. "Please, it's a distraction from my tragic life."

"There's something else..."

I raised a brow. "What is it?"

"I'm gonna sound crazy," she started, shaking her head with her eyes downward.

I lifted her chin. "Tell me."

"Remember Beth Clayton?"

I swallowed. "Yeah," I said, and my voice shook. I cleared my throat. "Yes, what about her?"

"I can't help but think someone thought she was me. Like they got the wrong girl. She's the only girl I know in all of Weeping Hollow who almost has the same hair color as me. Same height as me. Same build, everything. What if whoever killed her thought she was me?"

My hand dropped from her. The possibility of my shadow-blood attempting to kill Fallon again fogged my head and fisted my heart. Would I ever have it under control? Was this all a crazy coincidence?

My eyes bounced between hers, wanting to believe I could never hurt her, but I already did once. What's not to say I wouldn't try again, and worse, succeed?

Fallon had this plea in her eyes, asking for me to believe her thoughts and that she wasn't alone in them. She had these eyes that trusted I had nothing to do with it, and it made me feel like a traitor somehow.

"I believe you," I told her, then tore my gaze away for a moment before hitting hers again, unable to lie to her. "But, what if I killed Beth Clayton? The possibility isn't too far-fetched, considering ..."

"No," Fallon shook her head, leaning closer and grabbing my hand. "I know what you're thinking, don't go there. You didn't send me a letter, so it couldn't have been you. That's ridiculous—" she paused, then, "Someone else was trying to get me here. Someone else did this."

Clarence confirmed it was me who killed Beth Clayton, but I had a feeling there was nothing I could say to convince Fallon otherwise. "You have too much faith in me when you shouldn't."

We stared at each other for a long moment, then, "She came to me, you know," she drew closer to me and rested her knee against my side, "Her spirit did. She was trying to tell me something, but she couldn't because her lips were sewn shut."

"Whoever killed her knows you can see spirits," I concluded, trying to rack my brain for a memory of the incident for answers. Why couldn't I remember?

"That's what I was thinking too," she whispered, looking at me but not *really* looking at me. Behind those eyes, her mind was somewhere else.

"Don't act like you're scared now, Fallon Grimaldi," I told her. "You're not afraid of anything, remember?"

"You know that's not true."

"And you know I'm not going to let anything happen to you, right?" The words came out so quick and easy, but I meant them.

"It's all too much. Are you sure this is something you're up for?"

My brows pinched together. "I jumped off a cliff. I'm pretty much down for anything at this point," I said with a chuckle, then sank into her bed on my side, pulling her down with me, determined to change the subject. "Now, tell me something about life on the outside." This had become a game of ours.

The tip of her finger drew imaginary lines on my chest and stomach, connecting the dots of my three freckles. My abs clenched. "No, it's your turn to tell me a story," she whispered.

"A story." I laughed. And from me, she always wanted to hear stories, ones that were real. And ones that weren't. Legends and tales and ones about my childhood. "Okay," I said, closing my eyes, one coming to mind that may put her at ease. "When I was a boy, before Johnny and Jolie were born and it was just me, Agatha used to make me moon milk every night. I wasn't a very good sleeper either, never slept like everyone else in the way I should. And even after I fell asleep, I would wake after the witching hour and sleepwalk through the woods as if I were on the hunt for something, always searching and searching. Agatha always made a joke about me being born from the womb of the forest with only half a soul. I didn't understand it really, but nights she made the moon milk were the quietest ones. The ones I slept without waking. She would make me moon milk with chamomile, fresh strawberries and sprinkled red flower petals, lavender cacao, and some with graham cracker and marshmallow. But my favorite was the Blue Majik moon milk. Cinnamon, maple syrup, and vanilla—" I paused, pushed my hand through her hair. "I'll have to make it for you one day."

Fallon nodded, smiling. "I'd like that."

I didn't tilt my head to the side when my own smile appeared behind my mask this time. Perhaps I deserved this one. "So, after Jolie was born, I was about nine or ten at the time, she had a hard time sleeping, crying all hours of the night. I remember waking up to make her the moon milk so my mother could rest, but the drink never worked on Jolie. Then with Johnny, I did the same thing, and still, it did nothing for them. I'd asked Agatha about it one day, why it was only me who found so much reprieve with the midnight drink. She'd said the moon milk recipes had come from the Lone Luna of Weeping Hollow, meant for only the first-born son of a Blackwell to offer him peace during restless nights. And I never understood it, not until a few months ago, I suppose."

"Why's that? Why only a few months ago?"

"Because the Lone Luna was Freya Grimaldi. Your mother."

FALLON

"THE HARRISON'S ARE LOOKING FOR ANY INFORMATION THAT COULD HELP in locating missing eighteen-year-old River Harrison. If you know anything, head down to see Officer Stoker," he paused, gathered a breath, *"In other news, there are two weeks until Samhain, witches. I hope you're stocking up on candy for the little flatlanders and finalizing plans on where you'll be celebrating. Who knows, I could be right next to you and you wouldn't even realize it. Spoooooky, right? This is Freddy in the Mournin' with your Saturday morning Hollow Headlines. Keep safe out there, and remember, no one is safe after 3 am. Owooooo,"* Freddy howled.

The flyer pinned to the Beech tree in town square flapped with the mid-morning winds, a *"Have you seen me?"* tag line printed on a black and white photo of River Harrison.

Kioni and I walked through the pumpkin patch as pies and crumbles swelled in the air, everyone in wool coats and snug hats to cover their ears. Leaves tumbled from stubborn branches. Each one fell as if plucked by an invisible hand, Fall's version of a snow globe.

"This one," Kioni stated, standing in front of the largest pumpkin with her arms crossed, a cup filled with Wicked Death Wish hanging from her fingers. I pulled the wagon closer to her and dragged my gaze from the pumpkin to her maple eyes to the wagon, then back to her. She shrugged, studying the pumpkin. "We'll need a bigger wagon."

"We need a smaller pumpkin. Or a forklift." I squinted an eye. "Maybe a crane."

"No," she shook her head and set her coffee down, "I refuse to leave this for the Goodys. Winnifred always wins. This year, I'm winning. Come on, help me." Kioni parted her legs, squatted in knee-length boots to secure hold at the pumpkin's base. When I hadn't moved, her desperate eyes bounced up to mine. "Please, Fallon."

"What's the prize?" I asked, dropping the wagon's handle and walking to the opposite side.

"A year ... supply ... of—" she released a heavy breath as we tried to lift it off the palette "—Mina's hotcakes." She groaned before the pumpkin slipped, and we both fell back on our asses. "What could possibly be in this thing, a dead body?"

"Could very well be River's," a voice stated, coming up behind us. I looked up, and Kane held out a hand to help me up. I didn't take it. "Would you look at that, Fallon has a new *friend* and suddenly she's too good for us." He withdrew his offer, fastening his hands together behind his back and looking down at me as Maverick and Cyrus appeared at his side. "Has she been filling your head with nonsense about us?"

Leaves crunched and shuffled under my boots as I got to my feet, tucking my hair behind my ears.

Kioni took a seat atop the giant pumpkin. "Yes, Kane, because the three of you are so interesting. Please, go on." She waved her hand in a *get-on-with-it* gesture. "I need more material for the afternoon."

Kane smiled with tight lips. "I see living on Goody Farms has soured your mood. Why don't you and your mother stay with me a while? I have room for the both of you," he said, lifting his arms out at each side. "I'll even make sure you're ripe before I drop you back off at the farm." Maverick laughed, and Cyrus stood silent with foolproof posture.

"You're disgust—" Kioni started, when Kane's voice swallowed hers, "Oh, calm down. I only want my girl back." He looked at me. "This is your last chance, Fallon. Come to Crescent Beach tonight. Your coven will be there waiting for you." I couldn't come up with something brilliant to say in time before they walked away without a trace other than my angered heart.

A tension-filled silence moved in the air as we watched their backs.

"Asshole," I whispered.

Kioni side-eyed me.

THE WAGON'S WHEELS SHOOK FROM BEHIND KIONI'S BICYCLE AS WE RODE the beaten path up the willow-lined dirt road to her cabin, her fat pumpkin slowing her down. I was less awed by the tunnel of autumn colors and more concerned for Kioni as her breathing became harsh and as rugged as the rocky path.

"Goody Farms?" I asked, riding next to her in my scooter as she struggled up the hill. "Did he say you live on Goody Farms? Like Clarence and Zephyr Goody Farms?"

"Well … there's … no … other … Goody … here," she huffed out through strenuous breaths.

"Let's switch," I suggested, feeling terrible even though she was the one determined to have this specific pumpkin because it was *the one.*

Kioni shook her head, my offer to help only giving her momentum to push through with determination. "I've got it."

"Do you talk to them?"

We'd reached a plateau, and Kioni's shoulders sank with relief. "Not really, no." She blew a wayward black curl from her face. "Winnifred talks to me the most, or really, talks to herself. *'Kioni, isn't this dress beautiful? It is, yes.' 'Oh, Kioni, fetch me a carafe of water.' 'Kioni, the ivory silk or lace? Ah, the lace, will do,'*" Kioni mocked in a light and bubbly voice undoubtedly foreign to her lips. "They leave the daily schedule posted in the breezeway, so I don't have to speak with them. For anyone else, I'm sure it seems like an awkward situation, but it has always been this way."

Rolling hills stretched out around us. We meandered through cornfields, passing a scarecrow tied to planks of wood. A crow perched on the straw hat, flapping its wings and crowing into the somber afternoon skies. To our right, rows of apple trees led the way to the white plantation home in the distance, and we followed the property line until we arrived at a small cottage hidden inside a hill.

My scooter rolled to a stop just as Kioni swung her leg off her bicycle's banana seat. She pushed through a gate no higher than three feet that was attached to a wooden fence enclosure. Green moss covered the front of the cottage and outlined two small windows and a curved, wooden door. The cottage was something enchanting you'd only find in a storybook. As I stood beside the scooter, my mouth fell open in awe.

"I'll be out in a second," Kioni called out, walking past the black pot hanging over an unlit fire pit.

Minutes passed in eerie silence as I waited, and when Kioni returned, she had a cotton tote hanging from her arm and a tumbler cupped in each hand.

"My bibi says hello." She smiled, walking the stone path to me. "She whipped up spiced mulled apple cider. Says you can't carve a pumpkin without it."

"I think your grandmother hates me," I admitted, thinking about the time she had forced me out of her shop after the very vague yet brutal psychic reading. The same reading that had led me to jump off the sea cliff.

Kioni laughed. "She's very passionate about her work and gets intense when emotional. If she was dramatic, it only means she cares." She passed the gate and asked for me to take the blanket from her bag and lay it out. "We'll carve it right on the wagon. I have a feeling if we manage to get the beast off, we won't be able to get it back on."

I agreed, opening the blanket in front of the wagon before taking a tumbler from her hand. "Is it just you and your grandmother?"

"No, my mother's here too. Not right now, but most likely still working at the estate."

"So, you both work for them?" My face pinched, finding myself being nosy, but questions had always flown from my lips without thinking first. "Sorry, I don't mean to be so intrusive."

"Fallon, it's fine," she insisted. "I know it seems weird, living all the way out here alone with the Goody family, but really, they live with us. My ancestors were here first before they took the land right out from under us. To *settle the inconvenience they'd caused,* the Goodys made a deal with my great, great grandmother. We can stay in our cabin as long as we tend to the farm and living quarters." She shook her head and released a breath. "It's not ideal, but Bibi was able to open her business." She plucked the carving tools from the tote bag and spread them out around us as she continued, "My family has been in this cottage for over two hundred years, maybe even longer. It's our home. We pick and choose our battles but stand our ground because our home is our home, as a home should be," she explained as if rehearsed or had been told the same thing her entire life.

Kioni cut a circle around the pumpkin's stem, and together, we scraped out the pumpkin. We sifted the sticky and stringy guts and seeds into a plastic bag for later to make pies and pumpkin dishes. Once Kioni's pumpkin was finished, we moved on to my smaller sized pumpkin, repeating the same steps.

We spent the rest of the afternoon carving, drinking our refilled hot cider, and talking about everything from Gramps' health, me jumping off the cliff, to a missing River Harrison.

"It's not everyday people just go missing. I mean, the town is like four miles wide. Where could she possibly go?" Kioni asked, bewildered. "Her parents showed up at my bibi's shop, trying to find answers."

"Did she find anything?"

"No," Kioni answered, and her voice sounded more like a question, as if she couldn't believe it herself.

If River Harrison was dead, she would have come to me. But she hadn't. Maybe she wasn't dead. Maybe she left town.

But when I asked Kioni about it, she said, "It's possible. After all, she was a flatlander and could leave whenever she wanted. But she loved it here. I don't see any reason why she would want to leave."

Her comment tangled my thoughts, spinning and spinning them together in a chaotic mess. I lay back on the blanket and looked up into the gray clouds as the fall winds bit my cheeks. "I don't ever want to leave this place," I whispered, surprising myself.

Kioni lay on her back beside me. "Then don't."

At that moment, I wanted to tell Kioni about Julian. I wanted to be the girl who could talk freely about the man I was in love with, confirm that everything I felt was perfectly normal. I'd never had a mother or a girlfriend. I'd only had Marietta, who told me bedtime stories about the kind of love that only came out at night. The kind Julian and I shared, and the place where it all needed to stay. In the dark.

So, I kept my mouth shut. *Maybe one day*, I thought.

"Lie Lie Land," Kioni whispered at my side. "The place we go when the world gets too loud. A quiet place inside our minds. A wild imagination filled with what-ifs and what-could-be." I turned to face her, and Kioni's eyes were closed as her silky locks blew across her cheeks. She must have felt my gaze because she turned her head to face me and opened her eyes.

"Don't go to Crescent Beach, Fallon." She'd said it with worry as if it were a warning or a plea. Or something in between.

"I wasn't planning on it." In fact, I'd forgotten about it until she'd brought it up. "I get a strange feeling when I'm around Sacred Sea. Not *good* strange, either. I guess I was so desperate to have friends or feel closer to my dad, you know, because he was a part of Sacred Sea. I thought being around them would help me understand, but it only confused me more. I thought I knew my dad, but I can't see him being anything like them."

"Because he was not," Eleanor stated, and I pushed myself onto my elbows to see her standing behind the closed gate. "Tobias was a good man, moonshine. One of the only things good in Sacred Sea. Hold on to the memory you have of him. It is the right one."

She reminded me so much of Marietta, and emotion tugged at my heart. I nodded.

"I am off to work now," she said as she passed by us. "Fallon, you should sleep here tonight."

"Thank you for offering, but I should be getting home to Benny."

Eleanor's face turned grim but nodded before taking off.

As I tied my pumpkin to the back of my scooter, my gaze found a figure standing in the upstairs window of the Goody home. From here, I couldn't know for sure, but the silhouette seemed to belong to Zephyr Goody, *and the blood in my veins* RAN COLD.

FALLON
chapter thirty five

JULIAN STOPPED BY BRIEFLY ONLY TO KISS ME, AND HIS KISS WAS HUNGRY and urgent out on the balcony under a milky half-moon.

"Go," I insisted with a light laugh, his lips on my neck, his mouth in my ear. I kept my eyes closed as he adored me. Whispers and moans had flowed between us just before his mouth covered mine once more, sweeping his tongue and tasting like a rush of heat in December. My entire body had heated, from my head to my heels—a warmth spreading in my lower belly.

"I'll come back," he promised, landing a kiss on my forehead. "Let me get Beck off my back, and I'll return to you. Now, sleep until I wake you."

He was gone before I opened my eyes, so swiftly and without a trace, only the warmth still lingering and the goosebumps on every surface of my skin.

I waited up, staring out the opened French doors. Sitting in the corner, the candle burning inside my pumpkin lit an evil smile with slanted eyes. It was the last thing I saw before surrendering to sleep ...

12:33 a.m.

I was startled from sleep when hands grabbed my ankles and bound my wrists behind my back. There were so many of them. They pulled a gag into my mouth. A sack was shoved over my head. All that moved on the other side were shadows.

A scream burned in my throat and tore through the air. I kicked my legs, my body sweating as panic possessed me and turned me manic. Their hold was slipping as they tried to get a grip on me, then I was yanked from the bed and dropped to the cold hard floor. I was scooped up. Manhandled. Long arms wrapped around me, pinning me to their chest.

"Stop fighting," he said into my ear.

"*GRAA—*" I tried through the gag before a hand suffocated my cries and wrapped me tighter against them.

My heart pounded in my ears, and my skin felt as if it were on fire, anger rising from the marrow of my soul. Fingers gripped my skin, twisting my flesh until it burned.

"Moonshine?" Gramps called out from the bottom of the stairs.

"Everyone, shut up," the man said.

"*Moonshine? What's happening?*" A terror laced Gramps words, and I heard the hollowed bluster as he stumbled up the wooden steps. He wouldn't be able to get to me. I didn't want him to get to me. I had to get to him.

I kicked my foot forward when it hit a body. Something crashed to the floor. Gramps called out, screaming from the steps. "*LET HER GO! PLEASE, LET MY MOONSHINE GO!*"

I shook my head, trying to free the hand from my mouth. Casper hissed and released a desperate cry. I whipped my head, but darkness was everywhere.

"*Ah*, the fucking cat!" someone shrieked, and after a *thud!* Casper made a second sound, one I didn't recognize but like a plush dog toy being squeezed.

Every sound in my ears was like a slit to the wrist because I couldn't break free. I couldn't do anything. I was trapped, pinned down, muted, restrained no matter how hard my limbs fought.

"*I beg you, please. Moonshine! Don't...hurt my...grandbaby...*" Gramps cried in a desperate struggle from the stairs just outside the door, and my chest felt as if someone drove a stake into it. I stopped struggling, not wanting

Gramps to fear. Then a loud clatter bounced off the stairs and a *thump!* echoed throughout the home, throughout my head, throughout my heart.

Then the world went silent.

Still.

"*No! Gramps! No,*" I tried to scream out against the gag. I cried into the hand that was held over my mouth and shaking my head with a fierce force, imagining Gramps lying at the bottom of the stairs, so helpless. "Please, stop," my words were muffled and strained. "Please, my Gramps. You can take me, do whatever you want to me, just please, let me help him first."

They were silent for a moment, and then, "Keep going," one instructed. "Grab her legs."

I heard the ocean breaking against the cliff. I felt the icy sea breeze slap my sweaty and burning skin as they carried me down the balcony steps. They tossed me into the back of a truck of some sort. An SUV. The scratchy flooring was hot against my already irritated flesh. Low beams of light passed as if I were going through a tunnel, but I knew it was the corner street lamps of Town Square as my body rolled in the back when we circled the gazebo.

The car was silent, but not my racing heart. I felt the pulse everywhere—in every cell—as my thoughts ran wild for Gramps. *The thump.*

I squeezed my eyes closed, knowing the worst had happened. *The thump,* it matched the pounding of my heart. Like someone was knocking, delivering me a message. But I pushed it away, living in an alternate universe where Gramps was the strongest person I knew.

He could get through anything, and my head shook as tears pushed out with a painful force, my entire being bleeding. *Be okay, you asshole. Get up for me, and be okay!* Because I jumped off the cliff, and I was supposed to have luck, and he was supposed to be okay.

Be okay, my soul screamed, and it ripped through me as his stubborn face flashed in my mind.

Then the car rolled to a silent stop.

1:06 a.m.

When the trunk door opened, the night called. I tried to cough out the

357

burn that settled in my throat behind the gag in my mouth. My gaze tried to pierce through the cloth over my eyes, and the air around me smelled of death holding its breath. Trees rustled, and a raven *cawed!* in the distance when I was picked up and carried. They tossed me onto the earth. I shuffled backward until I slammed into something hard.

When they tore off the sack from over my head, it wasn't what I'd expected to see.

Monday was wearing the black track-suit, a shovel in her hand. Half her body was inside a hole, her red hair tossed and forehead sweaty. Khaki pants walked past my line of vision before they squatted before me. Kane's pained expression stared back at me, his somber eyes as hurt as mine.

"It wasn't supposed to happen like that," he said to me in a low whisper. "Why couldn't you just roll with it? Why did you make it so difficult?"

My eyes pinched closed, and I shook my head, my cries muffled through the gag.

"Fucking cat got me good," Maverick hissed, sucking blood off his forearm.

Kane cocked his head behind him. "Stop being an infant. Get the coffins ready." He turned back to face me and plucked my strands of hair sticking to my cheek and forehead. "This is the start of your initiation, Fallon. I gave you the same option as Monday, and you never showed. I don't have a choice. This is the way it has to be. You'll have five hours underground in that coffin. There are three ways this could go," Kane propped his elbow on his bent knee, raising a finger, counting out my options. "Slow down your heart rate and spare your oxygen to survive the full five hours, use your magic to save you, or die. It's your choice."

Magic? I darted my gaze to the coffins, to Monday, to the graves, to Kane. I couldn't do it. I *couldn't.*

I shook my head, scurrying away from him and wanting to become one with the tombstone behind me. I couldn't go back to the trapped place—the place where I was surrounded and suffocated. I *couldn't.*

The panic stirring in my bloodstream rose to unbearable levels, and I threw myself to my right, desperate to flee from them. The side of my face met the ground, and dirt clouded my eyes and seeped into my mouth. An animal-like sound pushed up my throat.

Kane groaned and stood. Leisurely, he walked behind me, hooked his hands under my armpits, and pulled me into a standing position.

My body was tired of fighting. Energy had drained from my bound feet as he supported my weight.

"Your father did it," he cooed in my ear, pulling my hair off my shoulder. "You're a Morgan. Sacred Sea has always been a part of the plan. I know you're scared, but if you don't calm down, your magic is the only thing that can save you."

"I'll be in the ground right next to you," Monday said, looking up at me from the hole with an apologetic look in her eyes. "Look on the bright side, Fallon. We'll be sisters." She shrugged as if it were no big deal. As if Gramps wasn't lying at the bottom of the steps, helpless.

Kane hooked his finger in my gag, yanked it down before he grabbed my jaw and twisted my neck to the side. "Stay alive."

My eyes widened, and I bucked my hips back and lurched forward, spitting dirt and tears from my mouth.

"*Please*, Kane," I cried, bent over. "Check on Benny, *please*. I beg you. He could be hurt. He could be ..." I couldn't say it. *I couldn't.*

Kane threw his hand against my mouth, crossed his arm over my chest, and held me to him.

"What happened?" Monday asked, looking confused. Maverick's eyes drifted to Kane behind me. "Did something happen?"

"He's fine," Kane stated. "Open the coffin." Kane leaned to the side and scooped up my legs, cradling me in his arms as he walked to the grave.

"Please, check on Benny," I begged again, yet Kane ignored me, his expression sober and unreachable.

He pulled me into the hole, laid me in the coffin, and the two stood over me as I heard Monday climb willingly into hers when a thought occurred to me.

"Guess Eleanor was right, Monday. You dug your own grave," I called out. Oxygen blew from my nose, and a new wave of anger raged inside me. "You know what that means, Kane? You'll lose all your power one day from the fall of a roamer. Just like she said you would. And, hey, maybe *I'm* the roamer, but you have the choice right here and now to do the right thing. To change your future around. Help my Gramps, Kane. Don't let him suffer there alone, please."

Kane stood with one hand on the coffin's lid, his face blank with the moon behind him. For a moment, I thought he'd changed his mind, but then he said, "I'll see you in five hours."

The coffin door closed, and darkness consumed me.

JULIAN

4:36 a.m.

The four o'clock hour had passed. Phoenix and Zephyr had left about an hour ago. The plan was set and ready to go for the night of the Pruitt Ball in less than two weeks' time. Baby Beck sat on the other side of the swaying fire as it roasted us from the front, October temperatures freezing our backs.

There was something about the flames that rendered us without smiles yet kept us content. Echoes of the fireside perhaps. And the fire bowed and swayed between us as Beck mumbled as if hypnotized by the flames.

I'd tuned him out a while ago, leaning back in the wooden chair, waiting for him to pass out or leave so I could run back to the girl. *My girl.* The girl who held more possibilities than a midnight sky.

Branches swayed overhead as the wind hissed, an angry breeze sweeping through the forest.

To my right, a raven's grave caw cut through winds, and my head turned to the sound. With ink-stained wings, the bird drifted over me. It landed on the low hanging branch at the start of where the forest ran deep, and cawed once again. It pulled me from my chair, and I walked to it, unable to ignore its tell.

I could feel it boring its eyes straight through me and tap along my spine as if it knew I was listening. Then another raven came. Then another.

An orchestra of wings flapped around me and surrounded me. A flock of them. The skeleton-like branches were weighed down with birds so black they looked more like shadows cut from something more sinister.

My breath turned shallow, and I stumbled backward when a hand landed on my shoulder. I twisted in place, and Beck's glazed and blank expression shoved into me.

"Go to her," he stated, his usually luminous arctic-blue eyes swirling with life now dim and dazed. "Fallon, it's Fallon."

My chest caved. I gripped his shoulders, shaking him awake. "Beck, what is it? What's wrong?"

Beck's expression did not change as he stood vacant. Empty. There was only one other time I'd seen him this inscrutable, this beyond reach, for he was far away, nobody home. My heart pounded in my ears as the ravens screamed around me.

Desperate and out of my mind, I pulled him close to my chest and pulled back my arm, punching a right-handed hook into his gut.

Beck doubled back, but I kept him close, grabbed his masked face, and trained his eyes on mine. "What did you see? Beck, tell me what you saw." Beck looked around in a daze in my firm grip. I patted his cheek. "Right here, Beck. What is it? Where's Fallon?"

He pinched his eyes closed and opened them big, coming to.

My heart slammed in every wasted second.

"In the ground," he mumbled and shook his head as if it wasn't making sense to him. "She's in the ground. Trapped." His eyes dragged to mine, and he clutched his side and gasped for air. "She can't breathe.

TIME'S *RUNNING* OUT!"

the consequence of
BETRAYAL

The rainy night had brought in a misty morning as Bellamy sat opposite his father inside the cabin. 'We are to be together, whether it be here or somewhere else, it all depends on the coven and your ability to accept that I have chosen her. You cannot keep her locked away,' said Bellamy. The faint dawn of his father's smile crawled over his flesh with caution. The warring of his gaze turned to despair. 'What will you do to her?' asked he, pounding his fist on the wooden table before the fire. 'If you hurt her—'

"'Oh, it must be a dark, carnal creature. You cannot see what the thing has done to you! It has seduced you in more ways than one, and how long has this been going on for? How long has it tampered with your creed? We must cleanse your soul at once!' Horace held Bellamy's arm in a tight grip and dragged him from the table. The chair tumbled backward with the commotion as he brought him out into the morning.

"Once outside the cabin, Horace shoved his arm into the back of Bellamy's neck and against a tree.

"'Do what you must to me but not to her,' pleaded Bellamy, his cheek pressed against the trunk of a birch tree.

"'The creature of the night will get what is coming to it,' Horace seethed into his son's ear. 'Goody will strip the thing of all its lewdness to make sure it can never seduce another again. Could you love her then?'

"For hours, Bellamy was beaten by his father. He endured the pain with a held tongue and gritted teeth, grasping the pendent in his fist until it broke the skin of *his palm, knowing whatever punishment he was receiving could not be worse than what would come upon Sirius.*

"And the days following, Bellamy searched the Norse Woods for his love, Siri. No weather held him back. The nights were so cold, as cold as ice! but he refused to give up, clutching on to the silver chain. The promise of forever. The woods had become his bed where he slept, and depression had taken him until he was physically sick with suffering and misery.

"Still, Bellamy waited for her.

"Weeks had come and gone by this time. It was a bone-chilling night when Sirius escaped the cottage and made it to Bellamy, who was found shivering under the tree they had spent so many nights. Bellamy kissed her with blue lips and his words lost on him. He touched every inch of her body as if he could not breathe without knowing she had not been harmed. His fingers ran across a deep scar on her hip, and tears pushed out with striking force from his eyes.

"'I am all okay,' assured Siri, cradling his head in her hands. 'It is healed, see?' Vehemently, Bellamy shook his head before throwing his face into her chest, gripped her upper arms as she stroked his unruly, dark hair. 'I am to have a baby,' she whispered as she continued to comfort him with a gentle touch.

"Bellamy looked up at Siri and examined her expression. 'We are to have a baby,' Bellamy corrected her.

"Siri's face fell under his hopeful eyes.

"'It is not yours,' she whispered again until she found herself crying too.

"Bellamy held her cheeks and rubbed his thumb across her tears to wipe them away. 'What did they do to you?' He paused after seeing the frightened look in her eyes, and he dragged his palm over her white hair, trying to find the right words because it was then he knew. In his gut and his heart, Bellamy knew of the things they had done. He pulled her into his neck as the two cried. 'If it is yours, it is mine. I will love the child as I love you, and my father and Goody will pay for what they did to you!'

"'Bellamy, no. You will only make it worse!' All her words muffled as she clung to him as he stood, his body visibly shaking with the utmost rage.

"'I must! I will murder him,' he spat. 'I will murder the both of them, and after I do, I will come back for you.'"

JULIAN
chapter thirty six

S ACRED SEA'S INITIATION PROCESS WAS NO SECRET TO NORSE WOODS. We understood what it entailed. The burial and drawing of fear to pull magic was first. If no magic, they must simply survive. After they were reborn, then came the bond with the sea—days left out in the open, surrounded by water. The last one was the bond with the coven. Stripped and united with the members through a Great Rite ritual. They'd all pass her around and fuck her, but she wouldn't do that willingly. Not to me, not to herself. Not to us. Would they have forced her? My stomach turned...

It was foolish for me to believe they'd give up after hearing how determined Augustine Pruitt had been in the Chambers. I'd told myself lies, self-soothing and blinding lies, that her simple refusal would be enough, yet Sacred Sea must be as desperate to have Fallon as me. Both for different reasons.

4:49 a.m.

And yet, still, Sacred Sea's initiation had started, and the bastards ... they took the girl. My girl! The girl who held my soul in every subtle breath. The single thought of her terrified, and me not being there when I should have, pulled something new from within me. It wasn't darkness this time, as it was as scorching as the sun bursting from my chest. I stepped on the gas as the rumble of the car burned my rage, set it on fire.

I drove through the graveyard, eyes narrowed on two figures in my line of sight. The Bronco ran down tombstones, disrupting sacred ground and heading straight for them. I didn't stop, as something had possessed me. The thought was maddening; my girl six feet under instead of on top of me. It all pushed me forward in a love-sick haze. I white-knuckled the wheel, seethed death in the night's breath.

The speed hit sixty when my eyes settled on two mounds of freshly disturbed dirt in my path. *Fallon.* I whipped the wheel when the Bronco slid to the side until it came to a full stop in front of Kane and Maverick. I jumped out of the SUV, not bothering to close the door. My chest heaved so hard, every cold breath burned in my lungs as I charged for them.

"It's already begun," Kane stated. "There's nothing you can do."

Adrenaline pumped in my veins, and the night sky dropped so low my heart was claustrophobic. Clouds hovered and intensifying winds swirled, and I hadn't noticed the coming of blinding rage. I hadn't noticed, for I was so far gone.

I grabbed Kane by the shirt collar, held him high in the air as lightning ripped apart the surrounding black clouds. "Which one is she in?" An oppressive boom clipped my gritted words. Sweat pricked his forehead, and his fingers dug into my forearm. He choked on my tight hold, refusing to tell me. "*WHICH ONE?*" I screamed, and the malevolently charged winds threatened to rip him from my grip.

"Julian," Cyrus's bark came from behind. "Think about this before you do something stupid. The Order will come for you. It's just one girl, and you need to think about what is right for your coven," he added, using the same words Agatha had used in the chambers. Cyrus Cantini, the man of reason, yet there was no reasoning when it came to Fallon.

Screaming, I threw Kane through the air, and he slammed against a mausoleum. The stone cracked upon impact, and I turned with something black strumming through my system.

Maverick and Cyrus backed away with eyes wide opened, bewildered expressions marring their faces. Clenching my fists, I dropped to my knees and pressed my ear to the earth. I laid my palms on the graves and closed my eyes to feel the familiar pulse of her heart. Then I picked hers out and latched on to it. She was alive and breathing.

Her heart, it pumped in my ears now. So loud and filling me down to the tips of my fingers. My palms slammed against the damp earth as a new scream ripped from my chest, burning up the ground as if it could burn up my rage.

Dirt came off the ground and slipped into the high winds. It felt like a heat was drying up my insides and skin. It burned, but the agony of not seeing Fallon yet pushed me forward, motivated me.

The wind's howl didn't reach my ears as the only thing I heard was the sound of her beating heart. I fisted dirt and raised my clenched hands when soil lifted from the ground and swirled with the cyclone. The earth submitted to my ardor and defied gravity until the rest of the grave lifted, and the wooden coffin appeared.

Inside the hole, I pressed myself to the edge of the grave and pulled open the lid. "Fallon," I gasped.

Fallon squeezed her eyes shut and opened them again. Her face was red, stained streaks ran down her cheeks. Her eyes were bloodshot and dilated. Dirt muddied her long white and tangled hair. Raw and bloodied fingers trembled as she reached out for me, her lips shaking.

I grabbed her arms and dragged her barely naked body from the coffin.

"I'm here," I told her, falling against the side of the grave, taking her with me. Fallon buried her face in my chest, every muscle of hers tense. I stroked her hair, held her together. "I have you."

The storm faded into a calming night, and dirt snowed over the two of us like black confetti.

"You're going to regret this," Kane cautioned, hunched over and gripping his side as I pulled Fallon from the grave. "I'm going to the Order at first light. You will burn for this, Blackwell." Ignoring him, I scooped Fallon into my arms and carried her to the Bronco. I laid her inside the passenger seat and rounded the SUV. "You just sealed your death!"

5:23 a.m.

Fallon sat in a shock-filled silence the entire way to my cabin. Her slender and nervous fingers twisted in her lap as she kept her gaze forward, her long-suffering body still trembling and detached and far away in the passenger seat.

I'd witnessed her fears before. I'd been there with her in her childhood trauma. I'd watched her from the outside in as if I were a phantom half of a soul that had separated from hers, but I'd felt her suffering as if it were my own. I wanted to soothe her the same way she had always been able to soothe me. There were many things I wanted to say, but none of which I found would be good enough nor a language that had been spoken to express myself in the way she deserved.

I reached out my hand to take hers. And while doing so, I feared, so much, that it wouldn't be enough. I wanted Fallon to know that it was never a choice.

Whether in this life or our reincarnated one, it would always be her. As it always had been. The nature of our danger would be overbearing, but as her fingers slipped through mine, it felt like life and not death—so strong, so inseparable, so everlasting. And, I thought, perhaps the brave hand of a crippled monster could speak for itself. That it wouldn't need words to hear its devotion.

Her eyes closed for a brief moment. Then they opened and her breathing shuddered. She gripped my hand tightly, and we continued our drive through the night.

When we reached the cabin, I pulled the Bronco into the graveyard of vehicles I'd collected and jumped out to round the truck to her. After opening the passenger door, Fallon turned in the seat and clutched both of my hands.

"Gramps," she whispered, new tears shaking in the corners of her eyes. "You have to take me back home. Gramps … he's dying, I can feel it. Something happened, Julian. *Please.*"

I didn't know how to answer. I couldn't bring her back there.

The front door to my cabin creaked open, and Beck emerged from the porch. On impulse, I turned, keeping Fallon behind me.

"Are you out of your mind? You brought her back *here?*" Beck asked, craning his neck to take a look at her. "Jules, she can't be—" he lowered his voice "—she can't be here. Once the others find out, they won't be ... as accepting."

I clenched my jaw. "The sun will be up soon, and I need you to do something for me."

Beck crossed his arms over his chest and dropped his head. He dragged in a breath before peering up at me through loyal eyes. "What is it?"

I tossed him the keys to the Bronco, and he caught them mid-air with one hand. "Go to the Morgan property and check on Benny."

"You honestly think that asshole will let me near him?"

"I can't—" I started to say, then grit my teeth. I turned back to see Fallon sitting with a distraught stare, gazing into nothing. I took a step forward, clutched Beck's arm, and led him off to the side so she wouldn't hear. "I can't bring her back there, Beck. I can't do it. And I can't leave her alone, either. Please, I need you to do this one thing for me."

His brows twisted as he took a step back. "One thing? I've supported you through all of this, as a brother should. Without question. But this is a lot, man, and you know it. You know I would follow you anywhere. No hesitation, I'd die beside you in The Wicker Man. But what about Jolie? Your mother? Have you thought about them? The coven? Think about the people who are counting on you, Jules."

I pushed my fingers through my hair, drenched in guilt and desperation. "Yes, I thought about Jolie. I thought about what was right and what she'd want me to do. I'm finally doing something with my fucking life rather than running away and hiding like we've been doing. Beck, the decision has been made and now we don't have much time. If ..." I glanced back, seeing Fallon looking out at the cabin in a daze. "If Benny's still alive, he could confess in front of the Order that this was all forced, and I had no choice but to pull her from the grave. It would be both Benny and Fallon's word against theirs. The more witnesses, the better, and I need it to buy me some more time."

"Still alive? And what if he's *dead?*"

A silence settled over us.

369

"I can't think about that right now. Just go, time is running out. You should be able to enter the house from behind. Take the stairs to the balcony."

5:46 a.m.

Lanterns tucked in various spots beamed a soft glow throughout the small cabin. Daylight crept in during the early hours, eating pre-morning darkness. For a while, Fallon walked about the planked flooring as I watched her from a dark corner of the room. I'd told her Beck would take care of Benny to calm her nerves, yet her restless mind and heart couldn't stay in one place. And I didn't think she would be able to after the night she had.

Many times, I opened and closed my mouth, wanting to say something. Until Fallon's whispered, "Maybe I shouldn't have screamed. Maybe if I just stayed quiet and let them take me … If I never fought back, he wouldn't have tried so hard to help me." Her finger dropped from the mantle she'd traced, and she turned to look at me.

"Don't do that," I told her, shaking my head. I couldn't stand to see her like this, and I knew it was ripping me apart because I felt it at the back of my throat. "I've been there, in that place filled with all the things you could have done differently. It wasn't your fault, Fallon. You were home. You were supposed to feel safe there. They should have never broke into your house like that and take you from your sleep. This is their fault, not yours."

"You should have heard him," her voice shook. She sucked in a breath, and her chest expanded. "I've never heard Gramps like that before."

I could have said something to ease her troubled mind. Maybe something like, *"Let's not jump to conclusions,"* or, *"It will be okay,"* but I couldn't know or say it. I didn't know if Benny was okay or if it would all be okay. I didn't know, so instead, I led her to the back of the house, grabbed fresh clothes, and started her a shower.

While Fallon was cleaning up, I paced the cabin, waiting for Beck to return with news. I started a fire in the fireplace, warmed milk in a saucepan on the gas stove, and stared out the fogged window at the back of the cabin in a daze. The magic I'd used had weakened me, and the only thing keeping me from passing out was Fallon being here. In my cabin.

Fallon Grimaldi was in my home, and it should have been a heated moment and not a time to mourn. Yet every second she was in my shower, I couldn't help but fear the worst.

When Fallon emerged from the hall, I looked to her and straightened my spine. She was in one of my shirts. The bottom hem hit her mid-thigh and a pair of plaid pajama pants I'd never worn bunched around her ankles. Exhaustion set in her swollen, light eyes, and I didn't know how much time had passed before I realized I'd been staring.

I cleared my throat and turned back to the stove. "I grabbed blankets and a pillow from my bedroom." I tapped the spatula against the stainless-steel pot filled with the Cyan blue hue. "I thought you would be more comfortable on the couch."

Fallon nodded and circled the living room. "I won't be able to sleep."

"I know, but you have to try." I turned off the gas and grabbed cinnamon from a wooden shelf above the stove. "You need rest, and I promise to wake you once Beck returns with an update."

If I were her, I wouldn't be able to sleep either, but I'd noticed how she was struggling to keep her swollen eyes open. Fallon took a seat on the couch. She looked so tiny in the deep leather.

I poured Blue Majik Moon Milk into a mug and brought it to her. "Drink this. It will help, or, at least, I think it will. Maybe a little." Fallon sipped from the mug and her eyes drooped closed. I raised my brows. "Do you like it?"

She nodded and took another sip. My shoulders relaxed. "I'm going to take a quick shower. Drink up and lay down. Beck should be back soon."

I went to kiss her forehead and paused midway, remembering I wasn't normal. That I couldn't just do whatever I wanted or kiss her whenever I wanted. I was a cursed Hollow Heathen, forced to wear the mask of docility. An exhale drifted from my nose, and my forehead connected with hers instead.

I rushed through the shower and pulled on cotton pants, then my mask.

On my way out of the bathroom, I stole a glance at the broken mirror, deformed with cracks and missing pieces. A negative reflection of my soul. My chest tightened, realizing Fallon had seen proof of my self-destruction.

When I returned to the living area, Fallon was fast asleep with the empty mug sitting on the coffee table. Perhaps it wasn't only me who fell to the drink's natural spell. The recipe had come from her mother, and it was then I remembered the story I'd told her. Maybe she remembered too, and her knowing that small piece of information comforted her in a way— made her feel her mother's love during a time she needed it most.

The fire simmered to a low burning flame, and I grabbed the mug from the table when there was a soft knock at the door. I glanced back at Fallon, who was curled into the crack of the couch, and I walked quietly to answer.

Beck stood on the other side, his expression indecipherable.

"Talk to me, is Benny all right?"

Beck shook his head and took a step back. I followed him out on to the porch, closing the door softly behind me but leaving it ajar. Early morning temperatures swept across my bare chest and back. My patience was growing thin as I watched him in distraught thought.

"Is Fallon—"

"She's sleeping," I interrupted and nudged my chin for him to continue.

"Benny's dead," he whispered in a rush, taking a step forward. "He must have tried to climb the steps to get to Fallon, but when he fell …" He shook his head. "I touched him, Julian. I saw those last moments and heard Fallon's screams. H-he," Beck choked, almost breaking down, nothing like the monster everyone claimed him to be, "He tried, man. He really tried, but he was so terrified, and his heart couldn't hang on." Beck ran his palms over his shaved head.

"This cannot be happening." I turned, rubbed my temples. *"This cannot be fucking happening,"* I growled, dropping both hands on to the cabin, hitting my palm against the siding. *"Fuck!"*

"Fallon is with you," he whisper-shouted, matter-of-factly and appearing at my side. "She's with you, and Benny is back there at the Morgan property, lying dead at the bottom of the stairs from a *heart attack.* Kane and them, they'll spin this whole thing on you. You have to take her back."

"No," I said, shaking my head. There was no way I'd force Fallon to see Benny like that for my sake.

"Yes, Jules," he seethed.

"No!" I snapped, and my eyes grew *when I heard her soft cries*

BEHIND ME.

JULIAN
chapter thirty seven

I PEEKED THROUGH THE DOORWAY TO SEE FALLON WITH HER HEAD IN HER hands as she wept for Benny. She heard, and I stood torn between two worlds. Between Beck and Fallon.

I closed my eyes. "Go to Jonah. He'll take care of Benny," I advised Beck. "As for the rest of them, let them come."

"You're making a mistake," Beck said, his eyes judging me, punishing me. When I didn't answer, he shook his head and took off down the steps.

I slipped past the door and closed and locked it behind me. "Fallon, I'm so sorry," was all I could say as I walked closer to her, knowing what she needed but still unsure if I could deliver it in a way that would bring her comfort. My words seemed pointless; deep, scratched things.

With a flick of my wrist, the blinds drew close, hugging darkness all around us. The couch dipped as I sat beside Fallon and pulled her close to my chest. For a long time, we stayed that way. And as time passed, we found ourselves lying on the couch, limbs tangled and mended together. Fallon sucked in a shaky breath and shoved her face into my neck. Her body trembled in my arms, and tears felt like icicles against my skin.

The only tears Agatha had cried were that of confusion and rage. I'd witnessed Jolie's cries on numerous occasions, and Jolie cried as if she put her entire body into it: sloppy and wet with a reddened face, hands wailing and shoulders shaking, making sure the whole town knew Jolie Blackwell was upset. I'd learned how to help them, I'd evolved with Jolie and Agatha, but this … this was different. I heard Fallon's heartache escape in every broken breath.

Fallon's cries were quiet and soft and gentle like unsound raindrops sliding down a fogged window. Each tear slipped over my skin, each one a tiny drop of water, so small compared to the ocean. Almost insignificant. But not. Certainly not. She cried for no audience but used me as a shield. She wanted to be alone in her tears and needed me here also. I kept quiet and gave her time until her soft cries rocked her to sleep. Then, at last, sleep took me too.

EVENFALL WAS UPON US. WHEN YOU WERE A SON OF THE WOODS, YOU happened to know things like that, which only meant we'd been sleeping for at least ten hours. The longest I was sure either one of us had ever slept.

Fallon stirred, and a feather-light breath left her lips and touched my neck. We were on our sides, and my hand had slipped under her shirt, holding her to my chest. She had curled into my body, belonging there and filling all my hollow places. I buried my face between her and the pillow, wanting to live right next to her forever.

The threat of what was to come was always one, vindictive step behind us. Going after Fallon and disrupting Sacred Sea initiation had shown a sign of defiance against the Order, on two separate counts. I not only interrupted a ritual, but I'd taken a girl I was told was never mine to take.

But she was, and as I thought back, I would have done it again and again and again.

By now, Jonah would have gone to the Morgan property and transported Benny's body back to the morgue. He probably had cleaned up too because he grew a liking to Fallon and wouldn't want her to be faced with the aftermath. Yet, the town hadn't come to raise hell. The Order hadn't sent someone for me. Something had to have happened during these past ten hours to buy me more time. Perhaps my coven intervened.

While lying here with her, I thought about running and confronting my coven to ask for help, to get Fallon and myself far away from here. Not once had I ever thought about leaving Weeping Hollow until this moment. We could be together. But the coven would never agree to part with me, and as long as I was cursed, every day in the outside world would be a risk to Fallon. Plus, Norse Woods Coven was my family, corrupted and led down the wrong path, but still my family.

These were my decisions, my doings, and for that, I would have to face them. Running away was the reaction of someone afraid. I'd rather die an honest man than live this life a coward.

There was a rap at the door. I slipped out from under Fallon, stood tall, and adjusted my waistline. The knock came again, and I moved across the cabin in complete darkness, habitually making sure my mask was secured. My breath stuck at a standstill in my chest. My thoughts ran rabid.

They're here, I thought. *This is it.*

Before opening the door, I looked back once more at the girl. *My girl.*

I turned the knob on the lantern until a flame ignited, then lifted it off the hook. The door opened a sliver. A chilling breeze slipped through the crack, and Agatha stood on my front porch, huddled inside a thick coat. Gray strands of her hair fell from their tie and were now strung out and framing her face.

"Is it true? You intervened in Sacred Sea's ritual?" Agatha quickly asked. I stepped out onto the porch and closed the door softly behind me. Agatha looked into my eyes when hers transformed all-knowingly, equal parts confused and distraught. Her hand shook as she laid it upon the base of her neck. "*My god*, Jai, is she in there now?"

I could barely look at her. "Yes."

Her firm hand struck my face, and my head whipped to the side. "I can't believe you. Why would you do that to me?" I closed my eyes, hearing the tears brimming hers. "No … *no, Jai.* Why couldn't you just stay out of it? Why couldn't you keep your distance? *Why?*" she shouted through a whisper, failing at holding her emotions in her throat. "*Oh, god*, they'll sacrifice you. They'll burn you in The Wicker Man, *Julian Jai. Oh, god!*" she cried, "Why? Why would you do this to me?"

Shaking my head, I lifted my shoulders, trying to find the words to explain I couldn't be apart from Fallon. Doing so was damaging to my soul. I couldn't ever rip the Darkness out or scrub it clean. But with her, around her, I was different. I was *me* again, and not something cursed or diseased. With her, I was myself as much as I was hers.

So, when my eyes settled on Agatha's hurt and fearful ones, I could only speak of the truth. "I love—"

"Don't you dare," she shouted, shaking her head. "Don't you dare say those words, you have no right!" My mother slapped me against my chest, again and again, she continued to beat me, and I let her. The lantern knocked from my hand and crashed to the floor. "You're a monster," she cried out. "Only a monster would give me the same grief you've given me. You took away my baby Johnny. You took away my Javino, all so you could die too? You *are* nothing but a monster, Jai! I can't believe you put me in this position ... I did everything to protect you, and this is how you repay me?" I stood frozen as she beat me, pain and betrayal bleeding from her heart.

Eventually, her limbs gave out, and I wrapped my arms around her and held her tight against my chest. There was nothing more I could say that would make her see. Agatha's evanescent cries were swallowed by the deep and dimming woods around us as I held her close.

She gathered herself and pulled away. "You think she could honestly love you? A Hollow Heathen?" she scoffed. "She's never even seen your face." My jaw tightened as she continued, "She's not one of us. Do you think she would be willing to watch the coven use you, *beat you! violate you! abuse you!* all to pull magic from you in the way you were born to be used? Do you think she would stand for it? Do you honestly believe she would always agree to come second to your coven? Does she have any idea what she is in for?" She dragged in a full breath, both of us knowing these were the very reasons she'd never allowed for me to call her Mom. It was all a way to distance herself as much as possible because she couldn't endure it herself. It was the only way for her to live with a Hollow Heathen as a son. "Not to mention what will happen to you once the Order finds out you've been sneaking around with one of theirs. You are a Heathen, not a man, Jai. You are living in a fairytale."

"She *loves* me. The rest is nonsense," I said through gritted teeth. "It isn't logistics or a matter of checking off a list, Agatha. She's not *just* a girl, and I'm not *just* a Heathen. I'm done answering to you, the coven, and the Order."

"Then you're an abomination, falling for it all. You need to bring the girl back," Agatha said, more composed than before. "These were your decisions, and now you must face the consequences because if you don't, you'll only be making it worse for her too," she lifted her chin, two iron fists in her eyes, "You need to let the Order decide your fate. Get rid of Freya's girl before you pull her into your miserable life."

After Agatha left, I walked back inside to find Fallon sitting up on the couch with a blank face in the dark. "You heard," I concluded, walking closer to her. Fallon didn't say a word, and the silence was deafening. "I hate to say it, but she's right. I'm only making things worse for you. *Life* would be worse with me. And Agatha would know, Fallon. She's been through a lot, and she's just trying to do what's best for everyone. After everything I've done, the death I brought upon this town ... These past months with you were the best months of my life, and I can die knowing I was capable of being something more. That I *can* be me again."

"That's not fair," Fallon whispered. "Did you ever think about me through your experiment?"

"Oh, come on, Fallon, this was hardly an experiment. I didn't expect this to happen to us, it just did, and you know it. I don't regret it. I don't, and I wouldn't change anything ... but I always knew it would come to this."

"Oh, my god, she got into your head that fast? So, they are going to take you, and you're going to let them. You're going to leave me here all alone, without once thinking about what this would do to me?"

"Regardless, I'm a dead man, Fallon. Stop kidding yourself. You knew it was me who killed everyone. Johnny, Tom, Jury, *for fucks sake*, River Harrison. I probably killed the town's precious Beth Clayton too, and the list goes on, a long string of deaths before you even arrived. But deep down, you have always known it was me. You knew, and you were still the one who—" I paused, shaking my head, standing over her now, pressing my finger into my chest, "*You* were the one who found *me*. *You* talked to me. *You* kissed me. *You*. Fucked. Me, Fallon! This is your fault as much as it is mine. What was it exactly you were expecting? That my coven wouldn't punish me? That the town would just pretend nothing happened to these people? No, Fallon, it doesn't work like that. Either way, the Order will eventually find out what I did. It was never going to end well for me."

Fallon looked up at me with striking, glassy eyes bouncing between mine. Her brows bunched together. I sucked in a breath and tried to calm my slamming heart before I continued, "The town thrives on balance. I've always known the day would come after the shit I did. I never deserved to live another second past the day I killed Johnny, but something beyond magic let me keep living them. Perhaps it was to meet you. Perhaps to at least break the curse for the Heathens to redeem my soul before the earth takes it. I don't fucking know, but it was always a matter of time, and ... fuck! *Damn* Julian Blackwell for just wanting to be with you a little while longer."

"Your mother got into your head." She pushed her fingers through her hair. "You let her get into your head like they've all been doing your whole life," she whispered, looking up at me as she stood from the couch with disgust. "No, I know you, Julian. I know you, and I know if you had a choice, you wouldn't have done any of those things. You're good, Julian. You're so good. That's not you. That's not you. How could she? Your own mother called you a monster!"

"BECAUSE I AM!"

Fallon continually shook her head, not seeing things for what they were.

"No, you're not. Have you ever once stopped to think that you're not the darkness and everyone else is? Julian, over and over and over, they repeatedly broke you down with these words, for I don't know how long, to keep you exactly where they wanted you. To keep you tamed. To steal your voice. Your confidence. You taught me that." She looked up at me, her eyes wild and alive. "Monster. Heathen. Murderer. A hollow fucking thing, look at you!"

"Fallon, stop," I gritted, and she shoved her palms against my chest.

"No," she tilted her head, "That's what, Julian? Twenty-something years of you letting them define you?" she mocked, using my words against me and pissing me off. "You became everything they said you were, but thanks to you, at least I fought back. When will you stand up for yourself instead of letting your little sister do it for you?"

I grabbed her delicate neck and yanked her into my heaving chest, my blood boiling. "I don't have that luxury."

Fallon's jaw clenched. She grabbed my forearm. "Says who?" she whispered against my hold. My eyes bounced between her fierce ones, and she laid her hand on my wounded chest. "How did *this* happen, Julian? Does your *coven* do this to you?"

My jaw tightened, muscles tensed. "You wouldn't understand."

"Of course, you won't tell me." Fallon laughed, but it was as hollow as me. "It's clear, from the moment you were born, the whole town cast you aside. They did this to you. And you weren't made for this, Julian, you weren't. You have so much love and passion for your coven, you were born to lead it and bring it back to how it used to be. Not become *this* and hide in these woods. You are better than them!"

My heart clenched in my chest. My vision blurred.

I couldn't blink, afraid of what may come out if I did.

Still, the threatening tears shook in the corners of my eyes as I spoke, "Where were you twelve years ago when I needed you? Where were you before I killed Johnny? Where were you before the hollow took me? You have no right to do that to me. You have no right to come here now and feed me bullshit when I can't go back and change anything. The facts are still the same. What's done is done. I can't go back and undo it. That was a very nice speech, Fallon, but you're twelve years too late!" I shouted, shoving her away before I did or said something more I would regret. I clenched my fists and turned my head. "Get in the car. I have to take you home."

"Coward!" she spat.

"Monster," I corrected, taking off to my room for a shirt.

Fallon followed behind me. "Hypocrite."

"Guilty." I snatched a shirt from my bed, slipped it over my head.

When I turned to face her, tears were rolling down her heated face. "Don't do this to me," she whispered desperately. "Please, Julian, don't let them take you."

"I don't have a choice."

Brave headlights shone out in front of us only to be swallowed by the night. An anxious silence filled the inside of the cabin as I drove to the Morgan Property. If Fallon could become the car door she was pressed against, she would have. She kept her eyes looking out of the fogged window, her gaze connecting stars.

I wondered what was going through her mind. I wondered why she was shivering though I had the heat blasting. I wondered if she would one day forgive me for this.

And when I pulled into the driveway, I almost changed my mind.

"I love you, Julian Blackwell," she whispered, her gaze locked on the house before us. "Nothing's changed. It's always been you. Every time."

Fallon pulled the lever on the car door, and my chest clenched. The car door opened, and a pain throbbed in my heart. She planted one foot on the ground, and I couldn't bear it.

"Fallon, wait," I blurted, grabbing her arm.

The car door hung open, and I grabbed the back of her head, looked in her eyes. All the things I wanted to say were burning in my windpipe. I closed my eyes. Opened them. I swallowed, feeling the tightness in my throat. The words wouldn't come out, and Fallon shook her head and yanked herself from my grasp.

I slammed my palms against the steering wheel before dropping my head in my hands, unable to watch her *walk* AWAY.

FALLON
chapter thirty eight

THE PAIN I'D BEEN HOLDING INSIDE ME WAS COLD AND HEAVY, LIKE cement drying in my chest.

I didn't want to enter the house. I was stuck between Julian in the car behind me and the eerie emptiness of Gramps in front of me. Misery in the shape of a needle injected my chest, and heartbreak sliced my back like a whip. I couldn't escape this pain coming at me from both sides.

As soon as the front door closed behind me, a foreign wail pushed up my throat. I fell back against the door, slid down to the wooden floors. And when I thought there were no more tears left, there were.

An endless sea of them. And each one as hot as a blue flame.

The house was cold and heavy, too, like everyone had packed up and left. Gramps' body wasn't here. Gramps' spirit wasn't here, and I'd been lying here, curled at the bottom of the stairs in front of the grandfather clock. It chimed every three hours, reminding me time was passing. Without Gramps. Without Julian.

When Dad died, I thought there was no greater pain. At that point, nothing else mattered. The things people said about me, the way people treated me, nothing. Nothing hurt as badly as realizing I'd never see Dad again, even more so because his spirit never came to visit me.

Then Marietta died, and I thought I was prepared, since I had already experienced the greatest loss. But I was wrong. There was an entirely new level of pain. Like when a mother would say she didn't realize how much love she had in her until she had a second baby. I didn't know how much pain I was capable of feeling until I lost again. And again. And again. When did it ever stop?

The house was so quiet that I fell asleep here, on the ground, but only because I couldn't bear to stay awake any longer, waiting for his spirit to come. Hours passed. A *thump!* at the door woke me when I forced myself onto my feet, still wearing Julian's shirt and his pajama pants that hung from my hip bones and covered my feet.

I opened the door, and the morning newspaper was laying ironically on the leaf-covered doormat.

I stood there, staring at it.

It was ironic because the mail kid had finally learned to get the news to the front door, but only after Gramps couldn't be here to see it.

Fucker. Or as Gramps would have said, *dunderhead.*

I suppose it was true. *It's not until after you die when people start to listen.*

As if I'd done it a thousand times, and with the newspaper clutched in my hand, I made it to the coffee pot, started it. Freddy in the Mournin' played in the background, talking about Halloween, the Samhain festival, some other things too, I was sure. None of it mattered.

I finished the crossword puzzle for Gramps because he couldn't, arrested to this routine as if it were a sick twist of Gerald's Game—a book written by King about a girl who was handcuffed to a bed in a secluded lakehouse by her husband just before he died of a heart attack. Just like her, no matter which way I looked at it, I was still here. I was stuck. I was alone because Gramps' spirit still hadn't visited me.

It had taken me two days to shower.

Three to clean the house.

Four to leave it, realizing Gramps wasn't coming.

I'd have to go to him.

With every passing street sign to the funeral home, I noticed every breath I took. White clouds of moisture expelled in every exhale. The cold bit my skin, an icy kiss of a winter's warning. A promise the new season would still come. Time still moved on and wasn't controlled by the loss of the world's oldest asshole or the abandonment of a lover. All around me, skies were a harsh gray, the passé town locked in the colors of somber ash. I could smell nothing as my face was numb.

I pulled into the parking lot. In the graveyard, to the left of the Blackwell mausoleum, Beck was picking up pieces of broken tombstones and tossing them into a wheel barrel. Tarnished leaves crumbled under my boots as I walked toward him, ready to confront him and ask him questions. I'd never talked to Beck before, but out of the three other Hollow Heathens, Beck Parish seemed the least intimidating.

Maybe it was something about his eyes …

"Do you need help?" I asked, my gaze darting back and forth to his bent back and the clutter of stone around us.

"Nope," he said, cradling the rock in his hands before tossing it into the wheelbarrow with a *thump!*

He brushed his hands together and hung them off his hips under his jacket, looking at me as if he was giving me permission to speak or leave. The blue in his eyes was fathoms deep, from the ocean's surface to the floor of the sea—a thousand hues of blue running on a current of emotion. Lost in them, before I could breathe, I drowned. Every time. Unlike Julian's, whose eyes were shields and swords, Beck's showed me everything, telling me everything. All things except the things I wanted to know.

"How's Julian? Did they take him? Is he okay?"

Beck shook his head, darted his gaze around us, then leaned over to pick up another stone. "I shouldn't be talking to you—"

"I know," I rushed out. "But, please, it's been days, and I don't know anything. It's killing me. Just let me know he's okay."

"Julian's okay."

"Are you just saying that because I told you to say that, or is he really okay?"

Beck stood tall and squared his shoulders. "The Order showed mercy, considering the circumstances with what happened to Benny, thanks to Agatha and Goody. I was there, able to recount Benny's last moments." He paused to wipe his brow. "And, no, Julian's not okay. Julian's a fucking wreck." He tore his eyes from me, bent down, grabbed another stone, and tossed it into the wheelbarrow. "He's just trying to do right by everyone."

But he was okay. They didn't take him. I dragged in a full breath and closed my eyes, letting it go slowly.

JONAH WASN'T AT HIS DESK WHEN I ENTERED THE FUNERAL HOME. THE closer I walked to the morgue, the colder the air turned. Julian had mentioned that Gramps was here, and that Jonah would take good care of him.

A chilling breath traveled to the base of my neck, sending my pulse racing when my hand pushed open the cold silver door to the morgue. The steady *tick-tock-tick* sound of the chrome clock hanging on the white cement walls slapped the floor and ceiling.

Tick-tock. Tick-tock. Back and forth. An unnerving timepiece.

I rubbed at my neck, trying to quiet my anxiety. There was more than air in this room with me. Here lay all my sleeping beauties. My Gramps, too. Nerves thundered, questioning if I was ready.

Questioning if anyone would ever be ready.

Rows of holding lockers lined the far wall. I stood before it, scanning for Gramps' name yet unsure if Jonah would have marked it. I took a step back, then my eyes drifted to the right, feeling a pull toward the locker at the far end. I closed my eyes, and a new gust of nerves raked through my spine, settling as if it belonged there. As if I were used to losing people. But I wasn't.

Before I could bolt, I wrapped my fingers on the lever and pulled back the door. Freezing temperatures from inside brushed my face. The cot easily rolled out, and a thin white sheet laid over his body. No one should have to do this alone. No one should have to do this at all.

I filled my lungs and pulled back the sheet, and as soon as my gaze settled over his frail, pale face, my senses became useless. My fingers shook, finding the edge of the cot to steady my legs. I found myself nodding, trying to force myself to accept he was gone, but I couldn't, then my head was shaking.

"I'm sorry," I cried, leaning over. My tears fell and landed on the sheet.

My nose dripped, but I couldn't remove my grasp from the cot to wipe it. "Give me one more day, *god*, please, give me one more day with him. I need more time," I sputtered through it, tears and snot mixing and my eyes blurring. "You can't leave me, Gramps. You can't leave me. Why did you have to fucking leave me? Why won't you come see me?"

I threw my head back, looked to the fluorescent lights. I wanted to hear his voice, but I would never hear it again. And I couldn't feel him. He wasn't here. I couldn't say goodbye, and it hurt *so* bad.

"Come back to me, Gramps. I fucking need you, you asshole! You never told me about my mother. You never told me a damn thing, and you were wrong. You said knowing the truth was crippling. But not knowing who I am is crippling."

Hyperventilating, I released the rod to grip my side to find a solid breath. "I'm so sorry. I don't know why I'm like this," I could barely get out, talking nonsense but couldn't form thoughts the way they should form. Someone forgot some parts when they put me together. "I don't want to say goodbye …"

I was afraid to open my mouth again. I didn't know what would bubble up. Blaming him when I didn't mean it. Cursing him. Another heart-aching cry. A scream. Or some monstrous combination of both. My legs gave out, and before I collapsed to the floor, a pair of familiar arms caught me, pulled me up into his chest.

"He's not coming back," I cried into his shirt, gripping the cotton in my fists. "Why won't he come back?"

"*Shhh …*" Julian rubbed behind my head and my back. He took us to the floor against the lockers, held me together in his arms. "Death isn't the end. What was, will be again."

I didn't know why he was here after the things he'd said.

I was just glad he was, and I clutched his shirt tighter.

"THIS CAN'T BE RIGHT," I SAID, SNATCHING GRAMPS' LETTER FROM JONAH'S hands. "Gramps hated both covens."

"Once you're a member of Norse Woods Coven, you're family, Fallon. Always. It wasn't Benny's choice or Norse Woods' choice for him to leave, it was the union of Tobias and Freya. That letter was written just last year. He still wanted to be cremated in the same place where his wife was cremated. Unfortunately, Javino is no longer with us to perform the ceremony, so Goody will have to do."

I shook my head. "No. If this was what Gramps wanted, I'll give him his ceremony *and* with Norse Woods, but Clarence Goody will not perform it. You will."

"I'm not the high priest."

"I don't care. That man, Clarence Goody, gives me a bad vibe. You have to do this for me. I can't even think about Clarence heading Gramps' funeral. No, I won't let that happen."

"Since you are his next of kin, I'll grant your wishes. We will perform the ceremony this evening. Is there anyone you would like for me to invite outside of the Norse Woods Coven?"

"I don't know. Mina Mae?"

"Okay, I'll contact Mina." Jonah tapped a stack of papers on his desk, and they settled back in place before he turned in his chair, filed them in the same filing cabinet I'd once broken into.

"Hey, Jonah?"

"Mhm?" he huffed, a pen in his mouth.

"Will Julian be there?"

Julian had stayed with me in the mortuary for as long as an hour before Jonah arrived and brought me into this room. Then he'd left. It was all so brief.

"Yes, Julian is part of the ceremony," he answered matter-of-factly. "If you are worried about the two of you being close and everyone watching, they won't be. Sacred Sea nor the Order can interfere with our custom beliefs or rituals. They cannot discipline him for being around you during a funeral."

Later that evening, I stood in front of my full-length mirror, smoothing down the white cotton dress I'd unearthed from the back of the closet. The top section of my hair was loosely French braided, the tips touching my ribcage. I looked to the floor, expecting to see Casper, but he wasn't there. Casper hadn't returned since that cruel night.

Mina Mae picked me up from the house in a Chevy Woody Wagon from the eighties, and together, we rode in silence to Norse Woods with my stomach knotted. Mina sniffled before she leaned over, patting my twisted fingers in my lap, letting me know she was there, that she was close. Maybe the gesture was more for her than me.

The car passed through a tunnel of trees, its boughs twisting and bending overhead. Once we reached the end of the road, she drove upon the leaf-covered ground and parked the car.

"That door doesn't open from the inside, dear. I'll have to come around the front and get yah," she said. I nodded even though she'd already exited the cabin.

The sun slowly dipped into the forest, splashing sepia colors across the sky, and after a long walk through the quiet and dimming woods, we arrived. I froze in place, seeing at least twenty to thirty people who had formed a circle around an altar, all holding hands.

There were some I knew in passing, and some I'd never seen before. Jolie and Agatha. Wren Wildes. Mr. Hyland and his daughter, who owned the tattoo parlor. Ocean, the homeless man. A few others, but I couldn't process any more names.

The women wore dresses and flower crowns on their heads. The men wore forest green robes, with bones and chains with pendants, the same ones the Heathens wore, hanging from their necks. It was quiet and peaceful here. My heart pounded, unsure of where to go, or what to do. Mina stood next to me, an outsider as well.

The circle broke when Julian walked through, wearing only slacks and an animal skull attached to his face. Barefooted, he walked closer with a flower crown hanging from his fingers. His steps made no sound against the earth, and he stopped at my feet.

"Are you okay?" he whispered, placing the crown on my head, his silver eyes darting back and forth from mine to the top of my head. I nodded, staring at his sharp lips, and the way they were equally proportioned. The dip of his cupid's bow, his chin, the angle of his jawline, searing it all into my memory, unsure of when I'd see him like this again.

He held out his hand. "Come with me."

I placed my hand in his before he led me back through the circle. I felt everyone's gaze on us, but it wasn't a gaze of judgment or scrutiny. It almost felt as if he were a thing to be admired and nothing as I expected.

Julian lowered his head. "This is a safe place," he assured me through a whisper. "Do you feel comfortable?"

"Yes," I said, my voice low, and looked around to see Jonah standing behind the altar, the other Heathens standing beside Jonah. Clarence Goody was joining hands with others in the circle around me, and my gaze followed the circle when it landed on Mina, who'd made a place for herself.

Julian stayed beside me, clutching my hand in his when Jonah cleared his throat to speak. He introduced himself and his position, the owner of the funeral home, and what has brought us here. He said my name, Gramps' name, and thanked the coven for their support. Julian moved his hand across the top of my hand and wove our fingers together. Then he gave my hand a gentle squeeze as if he were pushing love through me.

"Mother of us all gather us in your arms. You, who know the grief of losing a loved one, send us comfort. Father and protector stand by our side. You, who know life and death, send us guidance ..." Jonah continued, and I couldn't keep my gaze off Gramps' body lying before me. I hadn't noticed when Jonah stopped speaking.

"Fallon?" I turned my head to the sound, and Julian was looking down at me. "Would you like to say a few words before we set the fire?"

My throat clogged up, and my mouth went dry. "The fire?"

"Phoenix and I will guide his soul to The Summerland, where he will be at peace and awaiting his return. You will see him again. I promise," he reassured.

I looked back to Gramps, wondering about my ability to slip between worlds—between life and death—and how my curse to see the dead couldn't always be dependable. As I stood with my hand clutched in Julian's, and Gramps and I existing on opposite sides of the divide, I wanted to believe Julian. I did believe Julian. I believed in his belief as he spoke about it with immeasurable credence.

I walked closer to Gramps and leaned over his body. Closing my eyes, I placed a kiss on the fabric where his forehead was, and a single tear slipped down my cheek.

"You're free, Gramps, nothing can hold you down now." The same prayer I'd said a hundred times before. "What was, will be again," I added through the whisper. The same words Julian had told me back at the mortuary.

As I took a step back, Jonah spoke of a poem. The second time it was chanted, the Heathens joined in. Then the third time it was spoken, everyone in the Norse Woods said the same words of deep peace.

Julian left my side and stood across from Phoenix with Gramps between them as they lay their palms over his body, the muscles in their arms flexing as they pressed down. The rest of the circle continued the prayer when Gramps ignited into flames, and I burst into tears.

The night played on as embers and sparks of the fire swam up toward the starry sky. I kept my eyes in the sky, watching yellows and oranges and gray smoke against the black canvas. At one point, Julian had stood behind me. Together we watched for a long time without saying anything.

During the cremation, one by one, each person bid me peace and a kiss on the cheek before they departed. Jolie and Agatha hugged me. Mina Mae, too, stating she would be back to take me home once the cremation was finished.

So, I stayed for hours.

Past midnight.

The Hollow Heathens and Jonah stayed too.

It remained quiet.

And once the flames died, Julian pulled something from his pocket. A delicate silver chain hung from his palm as he stepped up to the altar. When he returned to me, he placed the necklace around my neck. It matched the one Julian and others in the coven wore against their chests. My eyes squeezed shut, and once the necklace was on, I gripped the pendant of Gramps' ashes.

"Thank you," I cried.

Before leaving, I watched in awe as Zephyr pumped his hands at his sides, creating a reverse tornado. The rest of Gramps' ashes slipped into Zephyr's winds and spiraled up into the stars.

I love you, Gramps.

FALLON
chapter thirty nine

RAIN SLAPPED THE BALCONY WINDOWS, AND A scratching was coming from somewhere. It sounded like the pointed tips of tree branches dragging across glass, like nails. It was the sermon of the storm, all wanting to come inside. All the windows and doors were closed, doing their best to trap the whistling wind outside. Still, the tempest caused the air in the house to swell. Lights in the house flickered on and off. Outside the balcony doors, waves grew louder, churning harder, whitecaps pounding into the cliff.

The old house fell into utter darkness.

I grabbed the railing and walked carefully down the stairs. In the hall sat a vintage hutch. Inside, there were an assortment of candles. I grabbed candlestick holders in one hand and filled my arms with candles of all sizes. I opened the drawer and shuffled through clutter, feeling my way for a match book's square shape.

Each time lightning struck, navy-blue ripped across gray skies, giving me little light to navigate into the living room. Thunder clapped behind every strike, and I unloaded the items onto the coffee table, lighted each candle, and scattered them throughout the house.

The hairs on the back of my neck stood straight, the feeling as if someone were watching me, but the house was empty. The only soul inside these walls was my own, but I still couldn't shake the feeling.

I sat, curled in Gramps' recliner, listening to the scratching, the rain, the thunder, when a dark shadow moved across the living room floor. I turned to the window, catching half a silhouette on the other side of the fogged glass. It was only for a split second before it disappeared.

"There's no one there," I convinced myself. "It's not real." How was it that I was more afraid of the living than the dead at the moment?

I pulled my grandmother's thick quilt tighter around me, but the strange feeling never went away.

Then three loud and striking raps cracked against the front door. I got to my feet and grabbed a candle from the side table, my heart strumming like the door knocker's stray echo. No one would come here, especially during this storm. And it couldn't be Julian. He'd never knocked on the front door before. He'd always walked up the balcony steps and entered on his own. Who the hell was it?

When I opened the door, Kioni's smile was tucked into a straight line as she stood, shivering in her purple raincoat.

"Are you going to let me in or what?"

"Are you crazy? What are you doing here?" I stepped to the side as ferocious winds grabbed my hair and pulled on my cardigan. Kioni quickly slipped out of the storm. I fought winds to close the front door again and lock it in place.

Kioni stripped off her drenched coat. I grabbed it from her and hung it on the coat rack. When I turned back around, she was fixing her hair.

"I borrowed Bibi's car. You shouldn't be alone in this right now." She pulled off a boot, then the other. "You know how long I've been sitting in your driveway, counting how many steps it would take to get to the door before I got struck by lightning? That's a real friend."

My shoulders relaxed. "Oh, it was you in the window?"

"Me? No, why? Did you see someone in the window?" Her head cocked, gaze darting to the window.

"No, I guess not. It doesn't matter." I hugged her, just happy she was here.

Kioni squeezed me back, and when I released, she held up a finger before opening the bag in her arms. "I brought us some snacks. When was the last time you had a sleepover?"

Aside from Julian? "Um...never." I laughed, then there was another knock at the door. "Now who in the world could that be?"

Kioni stepped behind me when I opened the door. The wind howled as two bodies pushed through the doorway, and I slammed it closed behind them. The entryway was suddenly feeling too small. Monday and Fable stared back and forth at Kioni and me.

"This is going to be a strange night," Monday muttered.

"You're telling me." I pulled my cardigan around my waist. "What are you even doing here? You're not welcome in my house."

"You and me," Monday's finger waved between us, "we need to talk. You might hate me right now, but at least hear me out. Besides, you can't kick me out when there's a storm. That would be cruel."

"Oh, so you have it all planned out."

"Yeah, I kinda do," Monday said, dropping her bag onto the floor beside the iron coat tree stand. "I brought Fable as a referee, but it looks like you have your own."

"This is ridiculous. I don't want to talk to you." Thunder shook the house, and Monday lowered her eyes. Fable looked down the hall awkwardly. Kioni stood beside me with her arms crossed, eyes narrowed at the two of them. Did she not like them for a reason? I'd noticed it from day one, never thought to ask about it until now. "You can stay until the storm ends."

"But no eating my Whoopie Pies," Kioni blurted.

"No one wants your Whoopie Pies," Monday scoffed.

Kioni rolled her eyes. "*Everyone* wants a Whoopie Pie."

Fable lifted a finger. "Yeah, I might want a Whoopie Pie."

"Oh, for fucks sake, stop with the Whoopie Pies," I groaned.

THE GRANDFATHER CLOCK CHIMED, RINGING IN MIDNIGHT. THE FOUR OF us had been sitting in the living room. Not talking. We were all spread out by at least three feet. Fable and Monday on the far couch, one at each end. Kioni by herself on the longer sofa, and me back in Gramps' recliner. It had been awkward as hell, but the storm was still going strong, and no one was leaving any time soon.

"I have an idea," Fable blurted. She'd arrived in leggings and a large drawstring hoodie with a Voodoos logo. She unfolded her crossed arms. "Let's drink. I'm sure Benny has good alcohol in this house somewhere. He's a Grimaldi after all. Fallon, do you mind? Or …"

"Yeah, because alcohol solves everything," Monday said from the other side of the couch.

"It's fine." I waved her off.

Fable stood from the couch. "Alcohol *does* solve everything … temporarily," she muttered, walking around the couch, on her way to the kitchen. "At least it will get us through the night, because … awkward."

Monday's gaze followed behind Fable when Kioni jumped up from the couch and headed for the stairs.

"Where are you going?" I asked, turning in the recliner, not wanting her to leave me alone in the room with Monday.

"There has to be something here we can do. I'm going to go look in the spare room and see if I can dig something up."

The sound of pots banging against the floor echoed from the kitchen. "I'm good! Everything's good!" Fable called out.

I sucked in my lips and settled back in the recliner, refusing to look at Monday. The tension blazed as I felt Monday's solemn stare on me.

"I'm sorry about Benny," she said low from across the room. "I had no idea what happened, and if I would've known …" She shook her head. "No one meant for that to happen, Fallon."

My eyes widened. "It wouldn't have happened at all if Kane didn't break into my house," I reiterated. "You don't get it, do you? We're not talking about a ruined dress or a lost pair of earrings, Monday. My grandfather is dead. *Dead!* because of Kane's stupid prank or whatever the hell that was. My *grandfather*, Monday. Kane should rot for what he did, but he won't. Nothing will happen to him. He's an asshole. Why are you even hanging out with them?"

Monday bit her lip, eyes watering. "You know why. I told you why. Sacred Sea is my only family. I thought you understood that."

"Well, that stunt took the only family I had left, and you just expected me to forgive you?"

"No, I never expected you to forgive me, but I at least wanted you to hear me out."

Fable's voice drifted from the kitchen, interrupting us. "I found a bottle of tequila literally shaped like a heart. And not a Valentine's heart. An organ heart." When she stepped into the living room, she shook the bottle above her head with four plastic cups in her other hand. I flashed Monday a glare, not wanting to talk about it anymore. "Can I have the bottle when we're done?"

"You don't honestly expect us to finish that bottle in one night, do you?" I asked, perplexed.

It should have bothered me that they were all here, going through his house, drinking his liquor. It didn't, though. This was all stuff. Insignificant things a person couldn't take with them when they died. Not once had a spirit asked me to keep their *purse* or wrist watch safe. None of those things mattered anymore.

"Do you know who you're talking to?" Fable challenged, placing the bottle and cups on the coffee table. She began to pour when Kioni's footfalls resounded off the stairs. "One for you, and one for … you." She began passing around the plastic cups with Hobb's Grocery printed on the sides.

When Kioni plopped back on the couch, she had a box in her hands and a hat on her head, a deep purple one with a peacock feather from something of the Gatsby era. Her palm swiped dust off the top of the box. "I haven't worked with a Ouija board in a long time."

"It's like sex," Monday mumbled. "Nothing in the game has changed."

Fable took the last cup and returned to the couch. "I wouldn't call it a game."

"Are you sure a Ouija board is a good idea?" I didn't mean for my voice to come out so nervous.

Kioni smiled. "What's the worst that could happen?"

We all took our first shot of tequila, pulled pillows and blankets from the couch, and sat around the floor with the Ouija board.

Monday sat across from me, and candles flickered in the dark room, casting dancing shadows across the walls. Outside, rain still hit hard in a calming and rhythmic sequence, and the storm whistled through the crack under the door.

"Okay, so how do we do this?" My eyes bounced between all three of them.

Monday nudged her head. "Kioni's the psychic girl."

Kioni stretched out her arms and cracked her knuckles. "Just because I come from a line of psychics doesn't mean I know how."

Monday quirked her brow. "So, you don't know how to do this?"

"No, I know how to do this. I'm just saying … you shouldn't assume."

"That makes no sense." Monday smiled, incredulous. "You're psychic, and you're saying I shouldn't assume, even though I was right."

Kioni closed her eyes and placed her fingers over the planchette. "Hush, you're giving me a headache, and I need to concentrate."

Monday groaned.

"Okay, okay, okay, let's just do this," I told them, and the rest of us laid our fingers over the planchette too.

We all went silent, and the only sounds remaining were the ones coming from outside the house. For a brief moment, nothing moved when someone asked, "Shouldn't we get like paper and pen before we start?"

I peeked one eye open. "We're not calling upon a ghostwriter, expecting a novel," Kioni explained, her face deadpan, and a laugh slipped between my lips. "We'll ask simple questions, and I'm sure we can remember the letters. Now everyone take another shot and close your eyes. And don't force the planchette. The movements happen on impulse from the other side."

"Okay," we all agreed and swallowed down a shot.

I was last, making the mistake of holding the burning liquid in my mouth and drinking it down slowly, which was worse. It tasted like straight nail polish remover.

"Are we ready?" Kioni asked one last time, all of our fingertips now on the planchette.

Fable and I said "yes" in unison.

Monday stayed quiet.

Kioni's eyes closed, her expression turned calm, and her chest expanded as she inhaled deeply, then released it through slightly parted lips like she knew exactly what she was doing. The candlelight glowed over her face with a soft flicker like that of a projector.

"Are there any spirits who would like to come forth?" she asked with a serious and calm, velvety tone.

I peeked one eye open again, seeing Monday trying to contain her laughter when the planchette started to move. "Oh, shit," Fable gasped, "Okay, who is doing that? Monday, is that you?"

"No, dude."

The planchette moved over the *Yes* and we all whispered the word simultaneously.

"Okay, thank you, this is wonderful." Kioni was in her respectful mode. "Can you tell us your name?"

"W ... H ..."

"Are they trying to spell Weeping?" Fable asked. "What's W H? What does it mean?"

We all hushed her.

"O ... O ... P ... I—" Monday's laugh slipped "—Whoopie?"

Kioni dropped her hands from the planchette. "This isn't funny."

"Maybe we should've started with an offering." Monday smiled. "Where're the Whoopie Pies?"

"No one touches the Whoopie Pies." Kioni grabbed the organ bottle, drank from it, and passed it around as everyone fell into a fit of laughter, including me. "Okay, let's be serious this time."

It took a minute or two for our laughter spell to die before our fingertips returned to the planchette. "Calling out to any spirit who would like to come forth," Kioni started to say. "We are ready. Please, tell us your name."

Candlelight flickered and the room dimmed. A chill swept between us, and I darted my eyes around, not seeing any ghosts present. The planchette slid swiftly across the board. It was fast. "F," we chanted, and it slid again, "I."

Monday's eyes widened. "Okay, this is not me this time," she admitted, shocked.

"N" ... "D" ... "M" ... "E" ...

The planchette stopped, and goosebumps coated my skin, my heart in my throat.

"Find me," I whispered, my fingers falling from the planchette.

I shook my head. It couldn't be him. It couldn't be the ghost who'd left me so long ago. The one with the white hair and the galaxy in his eyes. Eyes so black. Demonic. The one who first came to me when I was only eight years old.

"I can't *find* you if I don't know your name," Monday called out with her palms face up at her sides.

"Because he doesn't remember his name," I whispered to myself.

"Fallon?" Kioni laid her hand on my thigh. "Everything okay?"

I nodded, shifting in place. I fixed my pajama shorts, my cardigan, wrapped it tighter. I couldn't sit still. "I'm fine, pass the bottle."

"Are you sure—" Fable began.

"Yes," I choked, then cleared my throat. "I just need a drink." I waved my hand in a *pass-it-over* gesture. The tequila burned going down and warmed my chest and cheeks. I exhaled in relief.

"Let's just not do this," Kioni spoke up, setting the planchette back in the box and folding the board.

Fable sighed. "I'd like to know what the hell just happened."

"And I liked to know why on earth you're wearing that stupid hoodie." Monday plucked the fabric.

"So, we can get drunk there every Friday night, but I can't sport the merch?"

Monday's brows snapped together. "And Phoenix Wildes has nothing to do with it?"

"What are you implying?"

My eyes bounced between them like a tennis match.

"I see the way you look at him every Friday night with those *fuck-me* eyes," Monday said, and the two continued back and forth. At my side, Kioni shoved an entire Whoopie Pie into her mouth. I grabbed the bottle from Fable's distracted hand and unscrewed the cap.

Kioni leaned to the side and dropped her mouth to my ear. "Are 'ey a'way' 'ike 'is?" she asked, her mouth full and eyes on the girls arguing.

I nodded. "Pretty much."

Kioni swallowed, then clapped her hands once. "Fable Sullivan, I have an idea on how to settle this," she stated. "Want to meet your husband tonight?" The two girls looked at Kioni, and Kioni's smile spiked in the corner of her mouth. I admired the way she so easily broke up tension. "Come on, it's October." She shrugged. "Or have you done it before?"

"No way." Fable shook her head. "I haven't and I won't. I'm not messing with my fate. I don't want to know."

"Afraid to see Phoenix in the mirror?" Monday asked, and turned to Kioni and me. "I'll do it."

"Do what?" I asked.

"During the month of October, they say if you go into a pitch-black room with a candle and stare into a mirror, you will see your one true love's reflection over your shoulder," Kioni explained.

"It's just a superstition," Monday added. "And Fallon doesn't believe in those sorts of things."

"So, I'm the perfect subject," I said, then looked to Kioni. "I'll do it."

"But if you see him, it'll fuck with your head, and you could subconsciously screw things up without knowing," Fable replied lazily, the effects of alcohol getting to her. "You can't have your cake *and* eat it."

I narrowed my eyes. "Yeah, I'll take my chances," I said, rising to my feet. "What do I have to do?"

"Fallon Morgan, look at you." Monday smiled a sly smile from below. She leaned over, grabbed the candlestick, and held it up for me. "Take this and go to the bathroom."

"She has to eat an apple," Fable added. "You have to eat an apple, or it won't work."

"She doesn't have to eat the apple, she just has to peel it," Kioni corrected her.

I looked between all three of them, the hot wax dripping on my fingers. "You guys are so strange."

FIVE MINUTES LATER, I WAS STANDING IN FRONT OF A MIRROR IN THE downstairs bathroom. The candle reflected a soft glow around my face in the mirror as it sat on the sink. I held the apple in one hand, a peeler in the other.

"This is probably the stupidest thing I've ever done," I told myself, then tore my eyes from the mirror and began to peel the bright red skin into one coiling spiral. The color reminded me of Julian's lips. It had been long—too long—since I'd tasted them, since I'd felt them on my mouth. The last time I'd seen Julian was at Gramps' funeral, which had been days ago.

I had never expected him to be the one to make it so memorable for me or for his coven to be supportive.

Julian hadn't returned to the balcony since then, and my chest ached, missing him. My fingers gripped the peeler tighter. A *drop! ... drop! ... drop!* ... came from the leaky faucet, and sheets of rain splashed across the bathroom window.

I kept my focus on the apple and what my hands were doing, unsure if I wanted to do this, or if I was even doing this right. But I couldn't stop either. Something took possession of me as my fingers kept moving, the apple spinning between them. The air was cold all around me, and the small hairs on my arms stood straight, a soft buzz in the room.

"Fallon." The whisper of my name weaved into the air, but I kept peeling, my body humming. "Look at me." A deep voice so soft and angelic.

I shook my head, kept peeling and peeling and peeling. Julian wasn't here, and even while I thought that, it hurt somewhere inside me. Julian wasn't here. Perhaps if I said it often enough, I would start to believe it. And it wouldn't hurt as much.

Julian wasn't here.

The peeler sliced my finger, and the apple dropped from my hands. Blood ran a river of red down the white porcelain sink to the drain. I watched as the blood dripped from my finger, and my gaze followed the crimson current. Hypnotized, my eyes grew lazy as the blood moved into a pattern, drawing a shape by an invisible finger. Crossing patterns at first, until it made up a star. A five-pointed star.

"Fallon," the voice came again, along with a drop in temperature. White mist clouded from my lips. Suddenly, it was so cold.

That was when I felt his chest press against my back.

Five beautiful fingers trailed down the length of my arm until he grasped my hand and pulled it off the sink's edge. He guided my hand higher, and I lifted my gaze to the mirror's reflection. Julian stood behind me, the impala skull attached to his face. Two ash-brown horns pointed to the ceiling. Silver chains hung from around his neck, one with the cylinder urn—ashes from someone he loved. My breath caught, and he brought my finger to his lips and dipped it inside his warm mouth. I felt his tongue slide up the length, and I couldn't move.

"Julian," came out upon a shaky exhale. He grabbed my waist with his other hand and bolted our hips together. He was so real, I could feel him all around me. Everywhere ...

I closed my eyes as Julian's palm moved across my bare stomach under my shirt, just below the waistline of my shorts. Heat exploded inside me when his fingers grazed the sensitive skin. I opened my eyes and locked them to silver ones as his tongue swirled around my finger. Then he pulled it out of his mouth and painted his bottom lip with my fingertip. Every touch of him was light but like touching a nerve-ending.

"I miss you too," he whispered into my ear, knowingly, and I wanted this to be him because these sensations were combustible ... these feelings were dangerous ... it was all too much ...

"Where were you, why haven't you come back to me?"

"They bound me to the woods as punishment. I can't leave. I've been stuck here, and I can't stop them," he said into my neck almost painfully. "Please, Fallon. Come to me. *You* have to come to *me*."

Bang! bang! bang!

And then, "Fallon, it's been a while, are you okay in there?" someone asked.

Fable?

My gaze snapped up from the sink, seeing only myself in the mirror again. I took a step back, and the blood in the sink was gone. There was no cut on my finger. When I looked down, my body shuddered.

Around my feet, the apple peel spelled out one word.

real.

JULIAN
chapter forty

I N AN INSTANT, MY EYES OPENED, WIDENED.
My consciousness plummeted back to reality—my personal
hell. I turned my head, seeing Zephyr to my right, Phoenix to my left,
and Beck across from me.

We'd been here for hours, the storm still strong just outside the barn.
A heavy mist whipped through the opened barn doors, freezing my naked
flesh as I shivered in place. My body's weak attempt to fight off the painful
jolts.

One of our hands were chained to the ceiling. Our feet were shackled
to the steel bars drilled into the ground. Zeph was lost somewhere now,
his eyes closed as Rebecca used a belt wrapped around her wrist to drive
out his element. Phoenix seethed beside me, foam spilling from the
bottom of his mask. Every agony-filled groan that came from my brothers
clutched at the thing inside my chest.

I squeezed my eyes closed, wanting to return to Fallon, pleading with
the gods to take me away from this barn and back in her presence where
it was peaceful, calm. I didn't know how I was able to do it just a moment
before because that had never happened until now. It was a brief moment
with her, and I suppose I'd somehow created it from the pain, officially
losing my mind to a transient state. *Take me back, take me back.*

Another slash, and then, "I can't anymore," Phoenix growled, his head thrown back, brown hair drenched and sticking to his forehead.

"Now, now, Heathen. Remember who you're doing this for. It will all be over soon," Clarence's voice bounced off the barn walls from behind us. Groans and cries mixed in the humidity as one of the girls in the coven slashed Beck's skin. A cold sweat split down the side of my face just when a whip cracked against my spine. The pain spread throughout my body.

"Fuck," I seethed, tensing and throwing my head back. Both of my hands were clenched into tight fists, knowing I couldn't release my element right now. *Not yet.*

"Give it up, Blackwell," Clarence barked, then another crack against my lower abdomen.

I hunched forward, and my arm yanked against the chain wrapped around my wrist. I grabbed my stomach with my free hand, my skin blistering, burning, and raw. I just wanted it to stop, but I had to hold on. My eyes squeezed closed again when fingers brushed down my chest and my tightened abs. When they opened again, I saw a head full of brown hair. Flo, Winnifred's friend, looked up at me with a fire in her eyes.

"Keep going, Florence. Don't stop now, he's almost there," Clarence ordered.

Grinding my jaw, I shook my head, using everything to hold myself together. "You can't touch me," I gritted out. My chest heaved, and I yanked against the restraint. *"You can't fucking touch me."*

She cracked the chain against me again, and I focused on the bottle in the center of the Heathen circle that was ready to trap our elements. I didn't know how much longer I could hold on, but the torture was the only way to exhume all five of our elements at once.

Zeph suddenly seized, and a green aurora radiated from his chest—the purest form of his magical air element. He dragged in a breath, still able to control it after his seizing dissipated, having done this a dozen times.

Zephyr Goody was the best out of the four at controlling his magic, and I focused on the way his free hand guided it into the bottle from his chained position until a chartreuse-green hue filled the decanter. Winnifred plugged the opening, waiting on the next element. The girl unchained Zephyr, and he collapsed to the ground.

"Julian," Flo sang, pushing her fingers through my wet hair.

My head swam in agony, my body spent. I lifted my gaze to Beck, and I could tell he was giving up. I slowly shook my head, prompting him to keep going. The only way out of it was *through* it.

Beck squeezed his eyes shut then returned his gaze to me. I lifted my chin and nodded. He wrapped his hand around the chain to pull himself up once more when another *crack!* pierced the air, and next to me, Phoenix's chest buckled, his body tensed as he tried to fight back the wail I knew was stuck inside his throat.

"Clarence, that's enough," I spat. Clarence's only reply was to force the girl to slash him again and again and again. Phoenix's body went slack, and I tore my gaze away.

"Focus, Julian," Flo said in my ear, pulling me back to what was in front of me. The room was spinning, but I had to hang on. "What do I have to do to get it out of you, Heathen?"

My head bobbed backward until my gaze settled on hers. "Be someone else."

Flo's smile fell, and she struck my face. My head whipped to the side, where Phoenix could barely hold his head up, the girl using every tool in her arsenal on him. I returned my focus to Flo, her chest rising and falling as she breathed hard.

"Hit me again," I ordered.

And she hit me harder.

I swayed to the side, feeling the energy bounce through my veins. "*Again!*"

Flo whipped the chain in the air like a lasso before it cracked against my side. The pain fired into my marrow, shot across my skeleton. I saw black for a second, and I forced my head up when Beck ascended, his blue water element swirling from his sparkling chest. He could barely keep his eyes open, and I shook my head, all my worry now on him.

Just before his color dimmed out, Beck pulled through and guided his element to the bottle, where Winnifred captured it. The girl unchained him, and he too collapsed to the floor, arms sprawled out at his sides as his breathing matched that of the pelting rain.

One more Heathen, and I could let go. I would never release my spirit element until all my brothers were finished, needing to be there in case something went wrong. Phoenix was last, and he could hardly hold himself up any longer.

"I'm done," he said low, his words running together. Blood seeped from his wounds, down his tanned skin. He dropped his head back. "I can't anymore."

"Yes, you can. It's only you and me left, Nix," I told him. It was always the two of us left because he experienced more torture than any of us. His body had the scars to prove it.

Phoenix dropped his head to the side, following my voice, his golden eyes glowing.

"If it bleeds, it suffers," I said, reminding him he wasn't an object. This pain was proof we were men, warriors, and we had the strength, heart, and will to get through anything.

Phoenix's ankle rolled over the hay as he hung from the chain. He blew out a harsh breath and pulled his other foot up until it met solid ground. At the corner of my eye, Clarence came up behind Phoenix with his belt and whipped him, slashing it across his back. Phoenix's back arched, and he lurched forward, but the chain caught at his wrist, yanking him back in place.

After a few more minutes of watching Phoenix being tortured from both sides, his fists clenched so hard, blood seeped from his palms. His magic pulled him up onto his toes as a bright yellow cloud expelled from his nose and under his mask.

"Control it," I screamed, watching him let it control him. "Nix, fucking control it!"

Phoenix was out of it, locked in a zone somewhere that wasn't here. Clarence gripped the back of Phoenix's neck, and I snapped.

My hand shot out, and a magical force expelled from my fingertips, throwing Clarence backward until he was pinned against the barn wall. Focusing, I kept Clarence there and narrowed my eyes on the fire element, guiding it with my gaze to the decanter in the middle of the barn until it blended with the others into a dark greenish color. Winnifred popped in the cork, and her eyes lifted to mine.

"Let him go," I told the girl standing in front of Phoenix, refusing to release Clarence until he was free.

Scared, she quickly unchained Phoenix's wrist, and his body slumped to the floor with a *thump!* The girl then dropped to her knees and freed his ankles.

I released Clarence and turned my attention back to Flo, who had been watching this entire time. "You'll have to beat it out of me," I growled. Flo shook her head. I'd scared her, and now she was worried about what I could do to her if she continued. *"Do it!"* I wanted this over now. Flo narrowed her eyes as she reached for the whip again.

"As you wish," she whispered, taking a few steps forward.

I was far past the point of pretending this didn't hurt. I didn't have to hold on any longer since the rest were finished.

"Come on, Clarence, what are you waiting for?" I mocked, and he laughed behind me. I heard him step closer through the hay, and I straightened my back, begging for it.

Then the slashes came from both sides, one right after the other. I squeezed my eyes shut, focusing on the pain. Vibrations jolted my veins once again, and I clenched my fists.

"Harder!"

I felt the breaking of my skin, each time worse than the last. Flo sliced my side, and after a few cracks more, my body shook. A scream ripped from my throat. A bright silvery light erupted from my chest. With it, a tainted black cloud swirled in its color.

I flexed my muscles, gaining control. Through the transparent cloud, Winnifred waited with the decanter, and I used my heavy arm to guide it to her. Two colors warred with each other, silver and black. Every vein in my arm pumped against my skin, and the swirling cloud moved toward Winnifred and into the bottle.

She plugged the hole, and my arm dropped at my side.

"Good job, Blackwell," Flo said in a sing-song voice, running her fingers across my wounds. After so long, they would heal like the rest of my scars, tarnished red and white lines, but not until they seeped into my soul first.

Internal scars never heal when they always bleed.

Using the little strength remaining, I released myself from the chains.

Zephyr had already recovered and was back in his pants and helping Beck off the ground. I slowly bent over, fighting through the pain as I snatched my pants from beside the chains I'd been locked in.

I looked one last time at Clarence Goody. "I'll be waiting at the Edwin's," I told him.

Phoenix was lying on his side, and I yanked on my pants before lifting him off the ground.

"Is it over?" Phoenix asked, unable to open his eyes.

"For tonight," I told him, clutching his waist. "Until next time."

And the four of us exited the barn into the cold storm, together.

THE EDWINS LIVED IN A SMALL CABIN ON THE OPPOSITE SIDE OF NORSE Woods between my home and the Goody estate. They were recluse members of Norse Woods Coven and keepers of the Parish bloodline. They lived in the way other people had forgotten, eating resources from the land and not from in town, no electricity, and only using water from the spring. Victor Edwin was a good man, who'd built everything around the chair I was sitting in—including the chair.

We waited in the living room. The only source of heat came from the fire burning in the fireplace. Zephyr was sleeping on the couch, Phoenix in a bedroom. Mrs. Edwin tended to our wounds. We knew better not to refuse after the first time many moons ago. She'd always been like a mother to the four of us.

"You poor boys," Mrs. Edwin cried, pressing a wet towel to Beck's side. I caught Beck's low hiss, the wince in his eyes. He hated to be touched. "I hate to see you go through this." A small tear slipped from the corner of her eye. I blinked away, pretending not to see.

"It's Josephine," I told her. "She matters to us. All of you matter to us."

"But it still doesn't make it right," she whispered, applying ointment from Agatha's shop on Beck's wound before taping it closed. "It shouldn't be like this."

"This is what we do," Beck reminded her, tilting his head to catch her eyes. "This is why we were created, for people like you. Mrs. Edwin, I'd do it a thousand times over for your family."

Josephine, Mrs. Edwin's daughter, coughed from inside the bedroom as we waited for Clarence to arrive with the decanter. I pulled myself up from the couch to my feet. "I'm going to check on her."

Mrs. Edwin nodded. Her expression held a world full of guilt.

I clutched my side as I walked through the dark hallway. Josephine's door was cracked, and I knocked twice with my knuckle before pushing it open. Josephine was lying on her back, her face glistening from sweat.

I pulled up a chair and sat beside her.

"Jojo, it's me," I said, grabbing her hand.

It seemed it took much effort for her to crack her eyes open. Her face was pale, her long black hair wet and sticking to her neck. When she smiled a small smile, another cough came up from her chest. I couldn't believe someone so small could produce a sound so painful.

I closed my eyes and squeezed her hand again. "It's coming."

"Julian?" she whispered.

"Yeah?"

"What did you have to do to get it?"

I forced a laugh, trying to play it off. "Well, that's not really any of your business, now is it?"

Josephine was fourteen, a little younger than Jolie, and Mrs. Edwin was very adamant about not telling her everything. I respected her mother's wishes. We all did.

"You don't look so good," she told me.

"I'm fine."

Her body shook, and I touched her forehead. She had to be at least a hundred and five degrees. Where the hell was Clarence? I grabbed a rag from the side table, dunked it into a small bucket beside the bed, and wrung it out.

"We have to get this fever down." If Clarence didn't show, I doubted Josephine would make it through the night.

"How is she?" Beck asked from the doorway.

Shaking my head, I folded up the towel and laid it across her forehead. She reminded me so much of Jolie, it was hard to see her like this. Beck walked in, took a seat at the edge of the bed. When he laid his palm upon her chest, his head cocked to mine.

"It needs to come down," he whispered, talking about the fever.

"What's going on?" Josephine asked, her eyes moving behind her lids

411

as if searching for something.

Beck smoothed his palm up and down the center of her chest. "Nothing. Sleep, Jojo," he hushed her, then looked at me. "We should bring her to the spring."

"We can't. We can barely walk, and it's storming outside. It may do more harm than good."

"Then I'll bring the spring to her," he said with panic laced in his voice.

"You just used magic. You have nothing right now."

"We have to do something."

"We *did* do something."

Beck leaned across the bed and cracked the window. "Where the fuck is—"

"Mr. Goody," Mrs. Edwin's voice spilled from the living room. "Hurry, she's in here."

Beck and I looked at each other, then to the door when Mrs. Edwin and Clarence walked in. In his hand, the decanter with our magic seemed to have reduced to half the size, like the few times before.

I leaned over and snatched the bottle from him. "Don't think I don't notice," I said to him, then turned back to Josephine. "Quick, someone grab me some clean water."

Mrs. Edwin hurried out of the room and returned shortly with a ceramic carafe. I got to work, popping the cork and filling the decanter with water. The liquid swirled with color as I spun it, mixing in the mist. My gaze bounced up to Josephine, who was barely holding on.

"Beck, hold the back of her head," I instructed.

Beck climbed into the bed and propped himself up beside Josephine, then lifted her head. "Jojo, you gotta wake up now," he whispered, moving her hair from her face.

"Becks?"

"Yeah, I'm here," he said and tapped under her chin. "Open up for me."

Josephine's body started to convulse, and my gaze darted over her body, dread pooling into my gut. Mrs. Edwin cried out behind us.

"Beck, she's seizing, man. Get her on her side," I said in a panic.

Beck attempted to turn her over, but it wasn't working. The magic sloshed in the glass as I jumped to my feet and shoved the decanter against

Beck's chest. Beck took it, and her shakes turned violent. Her body jerked the entire bed as if possessed. The headboard slammed against the wall, and Beck backed away until his back met the window.

I pushed until she was on her side, trying to be as careful as I could until the seizing stopped.

"My baby!" Mrs. Edwin cried out, and I swiped my arm across my forehead, sliding my eyes to Beck.

Then her seizing stopped. She wasn't breathing.

My heart pounded as I pushed her onto her back.

"No! Come on, Jojo!" I grabbed the back of her neck and tilted her head back to open her airway. Beside me, Beck took control. When he went to rip off his mask to give her CPR, I turned my head away.

"Get Mrs. Edwin out of here!" I called out to Goody, not wanting Mrs. Edwin at risk of seeing a Heathen's face, or witnessing her daughter's death.

My breath held and my heart waited as I watched tears fall from Beck's eyes as he tried bringing her back to life, his body shaking.

The cruel silence ticked by, but Beck refused to give up.

I couldn't watch anymore, and just as I turned away, Jojo gasped.

Every muscle in my body melted with relief. Beck sat back on his legs, throwing his head back and covering his unmasked face as a cry escaped from him.

"Get yourself together, we're not done," I reminded him, keeping my head down to avoid seeing his face as he secured his mask.

We still had to get the elements into her system. I tapped against Josephine's cheeks to wake her. She wasn't moving. Breathing but unconscious. She could go into another seizure if we didn't act fast.

I continued tapping Josephine's cheeks desperately, not wanting to hurt her. Her jaw had locked up, and I grabbed the back of her neck with one hand, squeezing her jaw with the other until it popped open. "Now, Beck!"

Beck unplugged the decanter and poured the magic into Josephine's mouth. The liquid turned white as it soaked her face, the pillowcase, and sheets. Gagging, Jojo tried to spit it out, and I pushed her jaw shut, forcing her to swallow. Jojo's eyes opened, and her arm swung into my side. Pain rocketed through my body, and my jaw clenched when I grabbed her arms with my free hand to keep her still.

She held the liquid in her mouth, and I put all my weight on her to keep her arms pinned, kept one hand on her jaw, and with the other, I flicked her throat repeatedly.

"Swallow, Jojo." My strength was depleted, and we were using borrowed energy.

At last, the lump in her throat bobbed, and I closed my eyes, releasing an exhale. Josephine calmed, and I let go of her, smoothing my palms down the edges of her face.

"Now you can sleep," I panted, my chest heaving. Beck fell back against the headboard and pulled his hand over his eyes as he tried to catch his breath.

I pat his leg. "You did good."

He shook his head. "That was too close," he whispered, pinching the bridge of his nose.

"Is my baby okay?" Mrs. Edwin's voice shook through her tears from the doorway.

Dropping my head, I let go of a breath before turning to face her.

I stood tall. "She's going to be fine. She just needs to get some sleep now."

Mrs. Edwin thanked me, cried, thanked me, and cried again before she ran past me to her daughter, coddling her. I left the room, but on my way out, I stopped in front of Clarence.

"One second more, and she could have died. What took you so long?" I whispered, looking back to make sure Mrs. Edwin couldn't hear.

"Now's not the time to discuss this."

"I'm going home," I told him. "But I'll be at Goody plantation at first light to get my rights back. You cannot keep me locked in these woods forever, Goody. I don't belong to you."

"There's nothing I can do. Next time, don't interrupt a Sacred Sea Ritual. You're not leaving until the night of the Pruitt Ball. Until then,

you are bound TO THESE WOODS."

414

FALLON
chapter forty one

T HE SCENT OF DAMP AND UPTURNED EARTH FILLED THE MORNING. I
took A deep breath and plucked Fable's arm off me, slipping out from
under the covers. The coffee table had been pushed to the bookcase,
and all the girls were scattered across the living room rug, sleeping with
limbs poking out from everywhere. A mountain of blankets and pillows
and bodies. Black party cups lined the bookshelf, and the organ-heart-
shaped liquor bottle sat empty on the floor next to a heap of brown hair.

I hadn't been able to sleep, tossing and turning throughout the night.

Julian had been in the mirror.

Real had been shaped from an apple peel on the floor.

The ache in my chest from missing him would never go away.

Missing him was like missing every missed chance at anything.
Standing right in front of me but so far away. I reached and reached, and
he slipped and slipped like smoke, like mist. And there used to be a garden
in my soul, filled with colors of crimson and midnight and pearl. But now
all the flowers were dying.

And I missed him. That was it. I missed him.

The sunrise came as if it had missed the sky too. It settled above the ocean, splashing colors of its own garden across the horizon, gold and rose petals stretching outward and beyond—the soul garden of the morning.

I tiptoed to the kitchen as a song of light breaths and snores filled the house, the girls sleeping so peacefully. There was a natural glow around the house as if it had been a while since it had embraced life and witnessed, for the first time, drunken laughter during a stormy night. Dust particles floated in the sun's beams through the kitchen. Everything was bright and alive but me.

I put a pot of coffee on, needing to go to Julian, planning to go to Julian.

He wanted me to go to him, and I would.

I would go wherever he wanted.

The coffee gurgled behind me, filling the air with its awakening aroma as I looked out the window where a new day laid out before me, but not another day where I wouldn't get to be with him. I was determined.

I took my coffee out back and sank in a rocking chair. Broken tree limbs and leaves and evidence of a storm covered the short distance between Gramps' house and the edge of the cliff.

Gramps' house.

But Gramps was no longer here. Did I have to leave and find a new place to go? Who would I even go to regarding these matters?

"Good morning," Monday whispered, coming through the back door and interrupting my thoughts. Black eye makeup smudged around her eyes, and her red hair was pushed and tangled to one side. She took it upon herself to sit in the chair beside me. The small creak of the chair filled the awkward silence for a moment before her eager voice returned, "When you first got here, I told Kane and Maverick that you were going to be working at the funeral home with me. I was just excited to meet you … I didn't expect them to use me to get to you."

Her words called my attention, and I turned my head to look at her. "How could they use you to get to me?"

Monday pulled her feet up on the base of the seat, pressed her knees to her chest. The air outside was brisk and comforting. I'd never noticed before how dark-green her eyes were. They weren't bright like Zephyr's or faint like Adora's, but a deep, forest-green.

416

Then I noticed the way she clutched the warm mug. I noticed the way her eyes cast downward. I noticed the short intake of breath ...

"They said if I could convince you to join Sacred Sea, it would be my ticket in, too. But then I started to like you, Fallon. Like, we could really be friends, you know?" She shook her head. "I've been holding on to this guilt since we met. Like it was always standing in the way between us."

Really be friends? Like the friends who jumped off a cliff to save one another? The kind who wouldn't force the other into a coven when they didn't want to be? The kind where we could tell each other anything, without judgment? I wonder what a real friend was like ...

But then I thought of Julian. He had done all these things. My mind spiraled, and I began to question all the people in my life. Fable and Kioni, *hell*, Adora. Were they holding on to any guilt or had ulterior motives to be my friend?

"I just wanted to join so bad," Monday continued. "To finally be a part of something and be somewhere I belonged." I remembered what she'd said about her family and how she felt so different from them. I, too, knew what rejection felt like. How it felt not to be accepted. "I just wanted to tell you the truth. I don't expect you to forgive me, but I at least wanted you to know the reasons, not that I'm justifying my actions." She inhaled deeply and dropped her head back, then looked at me. "I wish we could just start over."

I nodded, rocked in the chair, drank from the mug, then set my head back as well. "What's the status with Sacred Sea then? Are you one of them now?"

"Not yet. I'm not finished with initiation, but after it's done, I will be. But I promise, I'll never push anything on you again," she told me. "And if it makes you feel any better, I'm pretty sure Kane got punished for what happened to Benny."

"Oh yeah?" I asked, surprised.

Monday nodded. "I haven't seen Kane since that night, so who knows for sure. But every time he's gone for this long, it's always because he did something wrong. And if I'm right, it will be a while before you have to see him again. Mr. Pruitt handles family business in-house. He's not easy on Kane."

Monday and the rest of the girls gathered their things to leave after that. We all hugged and said our goodbyes. Kioni hung back for a moment to ask if I would be okay here all alone. I told her that being alone was all I'd ever known. I didn't mean to say it in a way to receive pity or attention. But it was true.

I'd known aloneness, rather than *loneliness*, and, most recently, accepted it as I accepted myself. Here, in Weeping Hollow, I learned to love myself and found a home within my own bones, no matter what would become of me. And I accepted the permanent ache too, the one that was always there and only grew. Because it reminded me of all the times I'd been swallowed by a pair of silver eyes, and it punched me with a fist full of fortitude to never let go of Julian Jai Blackwell.

Tonight, I would go into the deep, dark woods for him—the Hollow Heathen. The one who everyone called a monster yet lived with a triple existence: *the ruthless villain* he made all believe he was, and what the town made him out to be; *the gentle one* no one else could see, a delicate being who wore his soul like skin and a halo around his edges, fiercely passionate, with a severe thirst for more of everything and an appetite for audacious love; *then the miserable creature* when he was alone, retiring into himself, branded with guilt and shame and submitted to the darkness for solitude because he couldn't bear to face the mere fact of solely existing.

I would go to him, and I would love him. All of him. Over and over … on repeat. Because I was certain all these things he was made of were the very parts missing in me.

"WE MADE IT THROUGH THE STORM, WITCHES. IT'S WICKED WEDNESDAY, and only three more days until Samhain. The rumors are true! I will be at the Pruitt Ball. If you can identify me, a surprise you will receive. This is Freddy in the Mournin' with your Wednesday morning Hollow Headlines. Stay safe out there, witches, and remember, no one is safe after 3 a.m."

Freddy's announcement had come later in the morning. Almost as if there was a skip in the town's step after Gramps died. Almost as if the entire world had been affected by the loss of him. It warmed my chest knowing the world noticed.

After finishing the crossword puzzle, I called Jonah from the house phone.

"You're on bereavement," he told me. "You can return after All Souls Day if you choose to stay in town."

I did choose to stay. Weeping Hollow was where I belonged, where I'd always belonged.

The ghost of Casper's pitter-patter followed behind me as I spent the rest of the afternoon cleaning the Morgan property. Numerous times, I'd passed Gramps' closed bedroom door, unable to bring myself back to the bed where I'd sat next to him in the mornings, me laughing and him mumbling insults and things I could hardly make out half the time.

I couldn't confront the bedside where I'd spent many sleepless nights to watch him sleep, watch him catch his breath. It was the same place where I'd had to call Mina Mae or Dr. Morley because I didn't think I was doing it right, or if he would make it through the night. I couldn't confront the hats on the wall, or inhale his distinct scent that smelled like the last drop of aged-whiskey from the bottom of a barrel, or see the imprint of his head remaining on his pillow. Not yet.

I cracked his bedroom door open to see if missing Casper was trapped inside, but he wasn't. Then I spent an hour making flyers with markers from the hutch in the hallway to pin around town.

By the time the sun was setting, I'd showered, dressed in a black bra and sheer white top, leather pants, and slapped on heavy make-up to make me look normal and less like a corpse. Then I pulled on my oversized jean jacket and black boots.

I clutched the urn hanging from my neck and lifted it to my lips to kiss the cold metal. "Wish me luck, Gramps."

IN THE DETACHED GARAGE, I SAT ON MY MOTHER'S SCOOTER THAT WOULD not start. After every failed attempt, the nighttime wind howled, testing my determination. I wouldn't let it stop me. Nothing could prevent me from entering the woods.

I jumped off the scooter, closed the garage, and started the long walk.

From the sea to the forest, it was four miles under the milky moon and a dank blanket of rolling clouds. Temperatures dropped into the thirties, and my nose had gone numb about a mile back. At about the halfway mark, cutting through Whister Park and crossing Archer Avenue, I realized I'd chosen the wrong shoes. Each blistering foot forward became a prayer to make it there before my feet fell off at my ankles. Every inhale formed icicles inside my lungs.

And upon every step, another echoed behind me.

I stopped and twisted my head around.

But nothing was there.

My steps quickened, and I continued forward, my senses alive now.

The *click-clack* of the copying steps that were one key off behind me quickened too.

I turned my head back and pushed my hair from my eyes. In the night, a figure in a black robe emerged from the dark, erasing the space between us. A chilling breeze burned in my eyes, and my nerves gripped my spine. I took off in a sprint with the outline of the woods in the distance, my heart rattling in my chest.

Julian! I wanted to scream, but fear stole my voice. I weaved between headstones as I flew through the cemetery. The loud cry of a raven pierced the air before taking flight, swooping over my head and disappearing behind me. I dared not to look back, for it could slow me down. Leaves rustled with my stride, flying up and stirring boneyard dust.

They were right behind me. The black figure, the one who'd always been watching me. The real thing and not a ghost. *Not a ghost*, I thought. Whoever or whatever it was, was real, and it was chasing me.

I ran harder, my breath bottled and tossed to the side somewhere.

Faster and faster, I ran until I reached the forest.

After a sharp right, I looked back, regretting it. *Julian!* I wanted to scream so he could hear me. Why couldn't my lips move? Why wasn't anything working? My heart pounded so fast and not at all, when I tripped over a root.

I clawed the ground and tried to gain traction with my boots, but the earth slid under me.

Whoever it was, was here.

I felt it. The tingle. The cold grip at the back of my neck.

It was … right … behind me …

I flipped on to my back to face whatever it was, crawling backward to put more distance between us. Inside the robe was utter darkness. I shook my head as they moved closer.

"Julian!" I screamed, then my back hit a tree. *"JULIAN!"*

"He can't save you," a sing-song voice said. Delicate and manicured hands raised at their sides to pull off the hood. "I've been waiting a long time for this."

Her face came into view. Her face. Her beautiful, flawless face and honey-dipped hair. Her eyes were like blue lightning—sharp and quick and sliced through me.

"Carrie," I whispered, and her perfect lips smiled. "What are you doing?" I asked. "What do you want from me?"

Carrie Driscoll shook her head. "The time has finally come."

"Time? What are you talking about?"

"Do you have any idea how long I have waited for this? The measures I've taken?"

"It was you," I whispered. I cleared my voice, waiting for my thoughts to piece together. "You sent the letter to get me here. Why? Why did you want me here? What did I ever do to you?" I didn't wait for her to respond and scanned the forest. "Julian!"

"He's not coming, moon girl. The Heathen is under my control."

"Julian's under no one's control," I spat, screaming his name again until my throat turned raw.

She laughed, the kind of laugh men could fall for. The sound spiraled with the wind when Julian appeared from behind a tree, stepping forward. He was wearing jeans. His boots. His black coat. His black mask. His eyes were on her, not me.

He was looking to her, not me.

"Julian," I shouted, jumping to my feet to run to him. Then his arm snapped up, and suddenly, a force shoved me backward and pinned me to a tree, knocking the air from my lungs. My body froze against the tree, all oxygen stuck somewhere inside me and not coming out.

My eyes ping-ponged back and forth between Carrie and Julian. I swallowed and managed to whisper, "Julian, what are you doing?"

He stepped beside Carrie, and I couldn't understand it. I couldn't put the pieces together.

"Julian," I cried, feeling the heaviness weighing upon my chest, his power pressing in on me from one side, the tree from the other. It felt like I was wedged between two brick walls.

My gaze darted from Carrie to Julian, my chest suffocating with pressure. I tried to push through it, fight against his power, but he was too strong. "Julian, she can't control you."

Julian cocked his head. His gaze was nothing more than a cold current beneath long black lashes. My heart shuddered.

"Kill her," Carrie ordered, and Julian's eyes froze on me, unblinking as he drew closer and closer and closer …

The toe of his boots met mine, and I tried to shake my head, to move, to stop him, but then he gripped my throat. And it felt like a noose. She had complete control of him. It all happened so fast, but I understood.

Carrie Driscoll had been controlling him this entire time.

"Kill me," I told him, lifting my chin and looking him in the eyes. His hand tightened, and it felt like my windpipe was crushing, cutting off all air supply. Then he raised me higher, and my back grated against the tree, the bark cutting into my flesh.

My feet dangled. Adrenaline rushed in my pulse, causing it to pound against Julian's fingers desperately. Time ticked by, counting down the seconds as my body locked in his death trap, paralyzed. There was no sound here, only my heartbeat *thumping!* inside my ears. My vision grew hazy, only two silver bullets aiming at me.

And I didn't know how long we were frozen there, in our suspended time. I didn't know, but I watched the change flicker in Julian's eyes.

Two silver irises bounced between mine, confused.

His brows snapped together, and his grip loosened.

I gasped for oxygen as my toes found ground again. Something was changing inside Julian, but I grabbed his wrist to keep him here, to keep his hand on my neck, so as not to sever our connection. I didn't know if it would work, but I had to try.

"They're all liars," I whispered. "But we're not. This isn't a lie. This is real. We—" I pushed my hand through whatever magical force he had against me, grabbed the back of his neck, and pulled his forehead to mine. I looked into his eyes. "*We* are real."

JULIAN

DO NOT FALL IN LOVE WITH THE MOON, THEY SAID.

I fell in love anyway, and they would all laugh. They could not see her beauty. No one would believe me if I said the moon breathed life into me. That it was here, inside her, where I found myself again. They would not be able to understand. And no one could ever love her as deeply as I did. No ordinary being was created to fall in love with the moon, only that of the aberrant. The strange. They said you couldn't know the moon, touch it, kiss it, make love to it. You could only watch from the dark trenches of the earth, admire it from afar.

Yet, still, I fell in love with the moon.

And she, too, fell in love with me.

MY THUMB STROKED FALLON'S DELICATE NECK, FEELING THE FRANTIC tapping of her pulse as reality set in.

Guilt climbed up my spine and squeezed my ribcage. My chest heaved, my blood turning black and having no place to go anymore because Fallon was here, refusing to let go of me.

She was like a whisper who almost slipped through my fingers. My head shook, realizing what had almost happened. What could've happened. What had been happening to me.

"Kill her!" Carrie ordered behind me.

I flinched. Confused but not. My thoughts plummeted as it made sense. She'd found a way to become the master of my shadow-blood, and the rage coiled inside me. She had been manipulating me this entire time, killing all these people. And for what?

I pulled away from Fallon, my hands shaking.

It was Carrie all along.

"Why?" I shouted, and I didn't recognize my own voice. Fallon's face fell, and she reached out for me, but I turned to face Carrie. *"WHY DID YOU DO THIS TO ME?"* The burning filled my chest, which made it harder to breathe, to think. "Why did you use me? How?" The scream built up, so heavy and painful.

Carrie held up a hand, taking a step back. "This is your fault, Blackwell. I'm fixing your mistakes. None of this would have happened if it weren't for you and the *freak.*"

"Fallon," I screamed, "Her name is Fallon!" I charged forward. I felt someone yanking my coat from behind, but I didn't stop until I had Carrie Driscoll in my hands.

I heard Fallon's sweet voice, the cry as *my girl* pushed me from behind, begging for me to let go. But I couldn't stop. Something had taken over me at that moment. My darkness. One controlled by no one, only a passionate, wild thing coming from inside me.

A scream ripped through my throat, and the winds it caused carried Fallon a few yards away.

I held Carrie up under the night sky before I took off my mask. Then I was sucked into Carrie's fears, transported through decades, consumed by a different time.

They said in the moments before death, you could watch your entire life as it happened before your eyes. And I watched Carrie's.

Though it wasn't Carrie's soul I had gripped in my fist.

It was that of CLARICE DANVERS.

the curse of the
HOLLOW HEATHENS

The sky was a grave gray as the elder Heathens crossed Norse Woods, carrying lit torches. Angry and spewing threats bled into the beast of the forest. 'Sirius!' they called out, flames from torches moving swiftly like fireflies. Usually, the forest was calm, unstirred, and the place where they fed and nourished, but on this night, the dead would rise, and the Heathens of Norse Woods Coven wreaked fury, searching for the moon girl who threatened a coven. The white-haired witch with the dark soul. The one who tempted Bellamy to slaughter two of the Heathens but failed.

"Bellamy Blackwell was tied to a cot drenched in sweat.

'Let me go,' cried out Bellamy. His cries lowered to whisper, 'Please, do not hurt her!' He had never experienced this type of pain, this kind of evil surrounding him. Thoughts of his beloved Sirius stacked, building four walls around him and caging him and consuming him entirely. 'Please,' he croaked through the agony. 'Do not hurt her, let me go to her.'

"'It is for the best, Bellamy,' cooed his mother. 'You are not yourself anymore. The creature has turned you into a monster.' She dipped a cloth into a bucket and wrung it out before patting his forehead, keeping him tied to the bed. Chaos stirred just outside the small cottage doors. Shouts and chants became one with the woods, embedding themselves into the trees.

"A song that would replay for centuries.

"On the border's edge, Bellamy's father, Horace, and the other Heathens captured the witch. Horace's strong hand tangled into her wretched white hair. He dragged her through leaves, twigs, and dirt as they marched between trees.

Branches cut her flesh as she cried out. The sound of her hair ripping from her skull was inside her ears.

"Sirius' white dress, muddied and torn, turned to rags dangling from her bloodied body. After tying her to a tree, the Heathens surrounded her. Fire from torches formed a perfect lit circle as twine squeezed and pinched into her flesh. 'I love him,' cried she, helplessly. 'You are making a mistake. I would never harm him, I love him!'

"The coven worked together, gathering broken tree limbs and dropping them into a pile at her feet. Then they leaned them over her body. 'Bellamy!' she screamed out for him, begging for him to save her as terrified tears rained from her eyes, but the woods and Heathens swallowed her cries.

"'Bellamy doesn't want you,' spat Horace. 'You are nothing but a pesky wench!'

"'Lies!' cried Siri, trying to break free from the tree, seeing their glowing faces through the branches surrounding her. She'd never been so scared. 'You are all liars. You know nothing about love.'

"Horace retrieved Bellamy's necklace from his pocket, the one Siri had gifted him, and hung it in front of her on the branch so she could see. 'You do not see Bellamy here, now do you? Where is your beloved Bellamy?' He turned, calling out, 'Oh, Bellamy. Your sweet Sirius will be dead soon, where art thou Bellamy?' The Heathen's laughter bounced around the night air. 'Why, look at that. Bellamy is not here. He does not care. It seems Bellamy has come to his senses and wants the wench gone.' He walked closer, and his hot breath seeped through the cracks of the branches. 'For he was the one to arrange your death!'

"Siri shook her head and darted her scared eyes around, to the green, the blue, the gold, the black. The Heathens of Norse Woods.

"To her, she realized the truth. Bellamy would never come.

"'You kill me,' she continued, desperate, 'your coven will burn. Instead of lusting over your desirable features, women will only see their greatest fears in your faces, as you have shown me!' She looked up to the sky, lips trembling as they lay their torches at her feet. 'No one will love you, and those you love will only fear you!' She remembered the night Bellamy had spoken of becoming a monster without her, and the fire blistered her feet, the pain excruciating. 'You are all monsters, as Bellamy said he would one day become. Nothing but monsters who will live the rest of your days in the dark. I sentence your souls to an eternity *without love, without compassion, without freedom. Only then will you know such pain!'*

"'You know nothing,' Horace shouted in return, the fire crawling up her ragged gown. 'Things of the night cannot know or understand such things. You never belonged here.'

"A gut-churning cry left her lips as the fire melted her flesh, yet she continued to chant, keeping the image of her new-born daughter in her mind for something to hold on to, knowing her baby, her blood she was leaving behind, would forever be safe in the hands of her keeper. 'The curse shall crawl through the Heathens veins and into your first-born son. Misery will repeat. Over and over and over,' cried she as the fire took her. 'Love has turned us into the darkest of monsters of all...'

"And a black wave rolled through the Norse Woods and throughout the town. Something dark. Something malefic and prophetic.

"Something that would later be called The Curse of the Hollow Heathens ..."

JULIAN
chapter forty two

THERE WAS ONLY ONE BOOK I COULD EVER CONNECT WITH. ONE. I'D read it many times over. Cracked its spine. Folded corners of the pages. Blurred the ink with the only tears I'd cried; hid them inside the walls of its bindings where no one could ever see. The oil prints from my fingertips stained its curled and yellowed edges. The book had rested under my moon milk atop my nightstand during restless nights. I'd memorized every word, line, paragraph, and page. Recited it as if I'd lived the life myself—as if I'd wrote it in another life. I'd allowed no one to touch it, for it had become my most prized possession. I was both the creator and the monster in the story—the creator who shut himself out from the world due to his tortured mind, and the monster who never deserved a name.

And there was one sentence that came to mind from *Frankenstein* at this moment: "Anguish and despair had penetrated into the core of my heart; I bore a hell within me, which nothing could extinguish." *Nothing.*

Clarice Danver's life flipped through my brain like a Rolodex. The memories were so quick, but I grasped every single one. Her greatest fear was not being able to save her *son*.

Her greatest fear was not being able to break the curse of the Hollow Heathens.

All for her *son*.

My emotions spiraled from adoration, anger, hopelessness, desperation, to rage all over again as she had experienced them.

In the early eighteen-hundreds, Clarice Danvers was pregnant, desperate to find answers to break the curse.

She had stolen the books and was caught. Before being banished from Weeping Hollow, she had written the answers into the Book of Danvers before Matteo Cantini confiscated them.

The mark of the moon. The birthmark. Sever the curse by severing the life which held the birthmark of the moon. It was all right here—the truth flashing through her memories in my mind.

Months later, Clarice was forced to give birth to her cursed Heathen in the woods all alone. It was always Clarice and the cursed baby, with eyes so black and hair so white. Bottomless and Demonic. She'd named him Stone. She promised him things, like a normal life.

Through her eyes, I'd watched Stone grow up in the woods outside of town. I'd watched with a stolen breath as it all played out. They'd met a witch from whom Clarice learned dark magic. Together, they cast a spell that would freeze Stone in time and use his earth element to buy Clarice more, keeping her young until she could cure him of his curse.

Fast forward, I'd watched as she sailed through the Atlantic with Stone frozen in a casket at the orlop of a ship. Once the boat reached the outskirts of town, a man helped them to a smaller boat until they arrived at the shore of Bone Island. It was there they stayed for many decades, Clarice and Stone. But Stone was frozen, and Clarice was all alone, her harboring rage only growing over the years.

She continued to practice dark magic, learning to control the shadow-blood to do her bidding. First with my grandfather, next my father, then, after my father had passed, with me.

I'd watched as she compelled me, used me, tempted me. First with Tom Gordon. Then she'd hexed Jury Smith to test my loyalty. Beth Clayton,

River Harrison … Clarice was always in the shadows. She was the Darkness. It was always her, each trial closer to her goal: to kill the girl with the mark of the moon. The girl who had the curse running in her veins. My girl.

But what she never expected were my feelings for the moon girl.

"Do you understand now?" Clarice Danvers asked in my arms. My head spun, reeling back to the now. She'd survived seeing my face just like she'd been surviving for over a century. "She has to die," Clarice croaked in a whisper. "It's the only way to fix him."

Him. Stone.

My head shook her words away. The truth of what I'd witnessed only seconds before was suffocating me. There was this thing inside my chest. It was beating. Hard. Fast. My hands were shaking. "I won't do it."

"Why, Carrie?" Fallon cried out, clueless behind me, not witnessing Clarice's fears the way I had. My muscles tensed. "Why did you send me the letter? Why would you control him? Why did you want Julian to kill me? It doesn't make any sense!"

My jaw clenched, eyes widened. Fallon couldn't know. Knowing was dangerous. A burden. I couldn't let Fallon live with something like this. That as long as she was living, the Heathens would always live this way, too. I didn't know how she would take it. I didn't know what she would do. I didn't know if she would ever trust me again. And worse, I couldn't let anyone else know, either.

"TELL ME!" Fallon demanded, her voice piercing the night.

"Don't," I think I whispered, shaking my head and looking down at a smiling Clarice with blurry vision.

Fallon's desperate pleas amplified in my ears.

Clarice laughed, but before she could say a word, I clutched her head with both hands and *snapped* her neck.

"*NO!*" Fallon screamed from behind me. Her voice was a lifetime away. Outside of this one. "Why did you do that? We could have brought her to the Order. Her life for yours. She killed all of those people, not you! They need balance, and we needed her," Fallon cried desperately, all her words weaving into the cold air and around me. "She was the answer to everything, Julian, and you killed her!"

431

Because I love you, my brain sputtered the string of deadly words, wanting to scream them into the air in a sudden burst. The thought came out unexpectedly and so foreign from my head. I'd never thought I would believe it. And I *shouldn't* have loved her but could no longer deny the truth—this monster's greatest nightmare.

Because I loved her—the girl who had to die to break the curse—and I would take everything I now knew to the grave. Leave nothing behind. Not even a human. *I killed her. I killed her. I killed her.* Not by my cursed face or shadow-blood, but by my bare fucking hands. The hands that were shaking.

Leave nothing behind.

If Clarice knew how to break the curse, chances were, Stone, who was frozen and stranded on Bone Island, knew how to break the curse too. I couldn't bring him here. And I had to make sure no one knew about his existence. Unwilling to take the risk, I had no choice but to forget about him.

Voices sounded in the distance.

Beck, Phoenix, and Zephyr were heading this way.

I had to get Fallon out of here.

The corpse fell limp to the forest ground with a hollow *thump!* My mind turned to fog. I shuffled out from under Clarice's dead body. My fingers trembled as I reached for my face. My mask was gone. I hung my head, dropped onto all fours, and swiped my hands across the ground for the mask.

I scurried frantically on my hands and knees. *Where is it?* My fists clutched leaves. I was made to see in the dark, but my eyes were tearing up and blurring my vision.

"*Fallon,*" I shouted while searching. The rest were coming, and soon, the other Heathens would ask questions as to why Fallon was with me. I had to get her away. I needed my mask to get her out of here. "Fallon, my mask!"

Then I felt my girl.

The girl who had the birthmark of the crescent moon.

I froze and kept my head down. My muscles were twitching under my skin. The heart punching through my chest was trying to leave me. I couldn't move even though the rest of my body wanted to escape my soul. Why couldn't I breathe?

She slipped the mask over my head. Air came out in uneven spurts when her arms covered me. I turned in them. Took her in mine.

"I'm so fucking sorry," I rasped out, rising and pulling her face into my chest. "I'm sorry..." Her peace hushed me, consumed me, made me breathe a little easier. "I didn't have a choice."

"I don't understand," she cried in a whisper, footfalls coming closer. We didn't have much time.

"Come on, I have to get you out of here." I grabbed her hand and took off into a sprint. Together, we weaved between trees toward my cabin. I couldn't think about anything aside from replaying Clarice's memories, trying to find a loophole. Something that wouldn't link Fallon to my curse. Something that could have been misinterpreted, mistaken. But I'd read the pages from her eyes. I'd seen the same words she'd seen. I saw the same mark in the book as the one that marked Fallon's skin.

Fallon kept up with me, trusting me when she shouldn't.

If she knew what I knew, she wouldn't.

We came upon my cabin. "Wait here," I told her, then ran up the porch steps and entered the cabin. I fumbled, grabbing a set of keys off the wall. I flew back down the steps and pointed to the black GS-R. "Get in the car."

"Julian, you're freaking me out." Her body was shaking as she darted her gaze around in the dark at the bottom of my porch steps. "Tell me what's happening."

"I'm taking you back to—" Then I froze. A standstill. It had hit me. I couldn't leave, not until the following night. I was arrested to the woods as punishment for saving her from the coffin. *"Dammit."* I slammed my fist on the car's hood. I pinched the bridge of my nose, squeezing my eyes closed.

"What's wrong?" she asked, staring at me. She wasn't afraid of me. She was afraid for me. "Julian!"

I took a step closer, took her hands, and put the keys in them. "You have to get out of here. You have to go back to the Morgan property. I'm bound to the woods. I can't leave."

"Why not?"

"Fallon, please, listen to me. You cannot be here, you have to go back. Trust me on this. Take the car and go." I needed to tell Zeph and the others what had happened, but I had to keep Fallon out of it, or they would ask questions. I needed to convince them to help me get Clarice's body to The Wicker Man for me to restore balance for her wrong doings. For the town.

"What if something happens to you?"

"I'll be fine, but you need to go." I dragged her to the driver's side and opened the door.

Fallon got in. I leaned in between the opened door and her, drumming my fingers on the roof of the car.

"Julian, if they take you—" Black streaks stained her cheeks. The moon cried black tears. Who knew? If love cut me open, would I bleed black too? "I can't—not without you." She shook her head, sniffling. "Don't leave—" she hiccupped "—me. Don't let them take you."

My face fell, still unable to comprehend the way she felt about me after the things I'd done. She was the freak who was always alone, and she never knew that everyone died so she could live. And I was the monster who was always alone, and I wanted to die so everyone could live.

We were different, but the same, with a love so strange.

"Tomorrow night," I promised, dropping my head to hers. "After the ball, I'll find you. I need you to trust me." Fallon closed her eyes and nodded against my head. "Now go."

I closed the door and tapped the hood.

Then I watched her drive away.

The red taillights faded just as three Heathens stepped foot onto my property.

"Something you want to tell us, Blackwell?" Zephyr seethed, green eyes whirling.

Beck and Phoenix appeared from the trees behind him.

I rolled my shoulders back, dragging my gaze across all three of them.

"WE NEED TO *talk.*"

FALLON
chapter forty three

REAKING NEWS! A FIRE WAS REPORTED FROM THE WICKER MAN EARLY
*this morning at Crescent Point. We haven't seen the Wicker Man's
flames in over twelve years, and my sources say it could be an All
Hallows Eve prank. But conspiracy theories are already flying around that a
secret sacrifice has been executed. Whatever it is, the truth will come to light.
Nothing in Weeping Hollow is buried forever,"* Freddy gathered a solemn
breath, *"The Pruitt Ball is still on for tonight. Tomorrow is the start of
Samhain. This is Freddy in the Mournin', and these are your Friday morning
Hollow Headlines. I'll see you at midnight, witches. And remember, no one
is safe after three a.m."*

The headlines streamed through my blank dream, waking me. I popped
up from the kitchen chair, ran across the living room, and pushed my way
through the back door. My stride didn't stop until the tip of my toes
touched the edge of the cliff, and I leaned back for leverage.

I threw my hand over my squinted eyes to see a shade of smoke
billowed in the distance, clouding the morning sky at the far end of town
where The Wicker Man stood. My heart shuddered, but I could not bring
myself to believe something happened to Julian.

No, he said he would find me. Tonight. Maybe it was a prank like

Freddy had said. A prank … or Carrie Driscoll.

Carrie Driscoll's dead, my brain reminded me. *Yes*, it was a possibility the Heathens had helped Julian burn Carrie in The Wicker Man. For Balance. Julian had found a way for balance. *Because of what she made him do.*

My heart calmed, and I released a nervous exhale.

But it still didn't erase memories from last night.

Julian had broken her neck. For some strange reason, his face didn't kill her, and he still had broken her neck, never giving her the chance to explain anything. I couldn't blame Julian for being so angry after what she'd done to him for so long. She'd compelled him to kill all those people, but there was a reason she wanted me here, wanted me dead, and a part of me felt like now I would never know.

Carrie was dead, and my head throbbed with flashes of memories. She'd chased me in the woods. She'd wanted to kill me. *Why?* My head was reeling with all the unknown possibilities, trying to connect dots and forcing dots to connect, making straight-edged shapes that didn't have names, like constellations in my empty skull. Carrie was with Sacred Sea, and Sacred Sea had been pushing me to join them since I'd arrived.

Maybe it was them all along. And now I would never know for sure.

I wanted to be angry with Julian for never giving me the chance to find answers, I should have been mad at him, but I wasn't. I'd never seen him so … distraught, so hopeless. It was the first time I'd seen an ounce of fear in him.

He was something fragile yet still something so dark. An oxymoron of ink and ivory. A ferocious thing with a fistful of desperation, holding triumph in his throat. And, as he'd looked up at me on all fours, stuck in his war, it was the first time I'd seen it. His silver eyes had saturated with love just after holding death in his arms. And maybe that was what love did to him, a heavy thing that left him on his knees, wrapped around his spine, filled his lungs with the sea until he couldn't breathe. Maybe love to a manmade monster was weighed down by magic and mourning.

But the town did this to him.

Everyone made him into a monster but feared it when it couldn't be contained.

The sun dipped into the ocean and bled its colors across the waters.

The cold wind thrashed, and I took a step back from the edge and returned to the house. My eyes were heavy but there was no possible way I would be able to get any more sleep.

"After the ball, I'll find you," Julian had said.

The Annual Pruitt Ball? Did that mean he was going? Did he expect me to go too? Carrie had come to my house days before insisting that I go. It had to be connected somehow.

I took a quick shower and changed. I had to busy my mind. I couldn't think about things that were beyond my control at the moment. Things like Carrie Driscoll, what had happened last night, and Julian's determination to get me out of the woods. Instead, I focused on what I could control like the Morgan property. I was the last living Grimaldi and Morgan in Weeping Hollow, and it was up to me to find out what I should do with the house and all the history that lived here.

I walked to the end of the property and retrieved the mail and shoved the envelopes into my backpack.

Then I looked to my left, where the pebbled driveway was. Julian's black Integra I'd driven to get here last night was gone. How was it gone when I had the keys inside the house?

I hadn't driven the Mini Coop since I'd taken Gramps to see Dr. Morley. It felt wrong driving it around Weeping Hollow. It didn't feel like *me* anymore. And since there was something still wrong with the scooter's engine, I made the two-mile walk into town where the color of oak and fire covered the sidewalks and streets. Cobwebs decorated the corners of storefronts, and children skipped from door to door in witch costumes and pointed hats, cloth bags filled with candy swinging from their arms.

Halloween had already begun for the flatlanders, and the residents greeted one another as if it were the best month of the year, standing under the sun's smile to feel its warmth. For the first time, Weeping Hollow felt alive, no one knowing of what happened in the woods the night before.

It was October, after all. And October was poetry all in its own, where dying leaves were the flowers, and the chill nibbled your flesh like a lover's bite.

The bell chimed as I walked into Mina Mae's Diner. I spotted her in the far corner, taking orders from the three old ladies who had all the latest news and gossip in Weeping Hollow. They'd always sat on the bench in front of the gazebo with their vintage hats and Easter-egg colored dresses, pointing and laughing and reminiscing. I overheard them giving Mina a hard time about fraternizing with the enemy. Something about switching the brand of syrup.

"I've been usin' the same syrup for ovah forty years now, Gertie," she laughed, "You're off yah kadoova."

I took a seat, feeling my chest warm at the sound of something Gramps used to say as I buried my nose into the menu.

Mina made her way to me. "Oh, Fallon, dear. You're here." Mina blew a wayward gray strand from her eyes. "Did yah see the lineup out theyah for the pumpkin cahvin' contest?"

"Yeah, I saw it. It's incredible." I looked out the window, seeing if I recognized Kioni's fat pumpkin. "Who are you voting for?"

"Ah, nice try, but I can't tell yah that. The people around here take this seriously, so I wouldn't go out and put yah two cents in eithah. Theya's already gossip floatin' around that the whole thing is rigged, and we can't lose a tradition ovah soah losahs...But don't forget to drop in yah vote," she quickly added at the end, tossing me a wink. "Whataya havin', dear?"

"I actually didn't come to eat. I wanted to ask you about Benny's house. Do you know who I need to talk to about it?"

"What do yah mean?"

"I don't know what to do with it or any of the belongings."

"Do with it? It's yoahs, dear. All of it. If yah need peace of mind, you could ask Jonah. He handles most of the records in town. I thought yah knew that. He's got the wills. Yah know, the wishes. Yah fathah's, yah mothah's, and Benny's."

My chest clenched. "Really? My mother's will?" I shook my head, "I didn't know she had one."

"Everyone's gotta have one," she said, and I leaned back as my hands slid across the table. "If yah want, I can help you soaht through the house one day."

I nodded, my gaze out in front of me, wondering if seeing my mother's will was something I wanted to see. It seemed like an invasion of privacy. I didn't know her as the town did. I'd always wondered if she ever loved me. Until I'd seen that picture of her holding me in her arms when I was born. Her face said yes, but then I took her life. Was that why she'd never visited me?

"Yeah, Mina, I could really use your help." I cleared my throat and returned my gaze to her. "I don't know what's important to keep and what's not. Maybe have like a yard sale or something."

"Ayuh, a yahd sale sounds great. We'll get it taken care of, no need to worry." She patted my hand. "But I gotta ask, Fallon, yah plan on leavin'? Don't tell me yah leavin' us…"

A smile graced my cheeks, and I shook my head. "What's that saying? You can take the girl out of Weeping Hollow, but you can't take Weeping Hollow out of the girl." I laughed. "All these years, this town was always where I belonged. I can confidently say I'm home, and I'm not going anywhere."

Mina smiled, her eyes glistening. "Good, because we wouldn't let yah go even if yah wanted to."

On my way out of Town Square, I cast my vote. There were no names as to who carved the pumpkins, but all the pumpkins lined the gazebo with their unique taglines. I'd known right away which one was Kioni's since I'd helped her. The detail she'd added was impeccable. The pumpkin showed two faces, one half beautiful, the other distorted and ugly. Under it, a sign which read, *The paradox of a man/beast.*

I dropped the house key into a dish by the front door after walking through the entryway, and I stacked a pile of mail beside it when a crisp ivory envelope caught my eye. I grabbed it from the stack and looked over the front. It had come from the Pruitts. The handwriting was delicate and of a different time.

I broke the Sacred Sea seal and retrieved the invitation to the annual Pruitt Ball. The scroll detail around the edges was an oily navy that shimmered a brighter hue in the light. This year, the theme was a masquerade ball, to begin at midnight. Cocktail attire required.

Julian would be there. I had to go.

I dropped the invitation on the table, hung my purse, and walked to the living room, where I curled myself into Gramps' recliner until sleep took me.

THE HOUSE WAS DARK WHEN I AWOKE. THE GRANDFATHER CLOCK CHIMED, and someone was rapping at the door. I pulled Gramps' blanket around me, rubbing my eyes on my way to the entryway. The haunting song rang in my ears when I opened the door.

"Please tell me you're going," Monday rushed out with a gathered breath.

My gaze followed her silhouette. "Hello to you too."

She ignored me and pushed past, arms lined with bags and curlers in her hair. "I'm freaking out. This is my first time ever going to a Pruitt Ball as a Sacred Sea half-member, and I am not going without you." She spun and looked me up and down. "Don't tell me you're making me do this on my own. Fable is going with her sisters, and I have no one. Oh, my gosh, I'm going to have to talk to Augustine Pruitt. No, Fallon, you *have* to go."

"I don't understand why you're so nervous, but I'll go with you," I said, helping her with some of the bags.

I was going to go anyway and partly relieved she was here so I didn't have to go alone. I was never one to hold a grudge. Monday had been sincere, never expecting for things to go the way they did. The only thing Monday was guilty of was being persistent. I couldn't blame her for what had happened to Gramps when she wasn't even there. Since I was staying, maybe it would be good for us to start over and rebuild from the ground up. This time, on honest intentions.

"Come on, we can get ready upstairs in my room. I'll do your makeup too because that eyeshadow is terrible."

Monday threw her head back and released a groaning sound mixed with relief. "Thank you."

It was an hour before midnight. I stood in the bathroom, applying makeup while Monday talked to me from my bedroom. Heat from the hair appliances turned the bathroom into a furnace, causing my loosely curled hair to stick to the back of my neck and skin as it hung around my hips. I leaned forward and painted my lashes before capping the mascara and blotting the black smudge in the corner.

"You still have tags on half your clothes—three hundred dollars!" She exclaimed from my bedroom. "Fallon, why on earth would you buy a sweater for three hundred dollars?"

"Get out of my closet," I yelled back. She wouldn't understand.

For years, I'd thought looking the part would help me get friends. If I didn't look like a dead body, maybe people back in Texas wouldn't see me as the freak. If I'd learned makeup and wore the right things, I could make friends outside the spirits who visited me. It had never worked, and my passion for fashion only grew. Nothing could translate the way it felt when I slipped a sweater around my shoulders, and how it made me feel protected when open and vulnerable.

"You know, Adora makes all the clothes for the boutique," Monday continued, "She's really talented, and could easily make this, or anything you want, really. And for way less—oh, Fallon. Look."

When I peeked outside the bathroom doorway, Monday was standing in the middle of my bedroom, holding up a dress in front of her. "You should wear this."

I stood motionless, releasing a breath trapped in my chest.

The dress was beautiful. A mixture of white material. Lace, chiffon, and silk. The neckline was a deep V shape, hitting almost above the belly button.

I gasped. "Is that yours?"

Monday shook her head. "Can you believe I found it all the way in the back of the closet?" She turned the dress to face her, and the back was just as beautiful. "You think it was your mom's?" And the comment hit me in the chest, knocking the air from my lungs.

My mother's. And suddenly it burned behind my eyes. I'd been forcing away the idea that my mom could have stayed in this room, slept in that bed. She could have worn the dress Monday was holding.

"If you don't wear it, I will," Monday went on, filling my silence.

"No," I stepped forward, gripping the sides, and fanning it out in front of me, "I want to wear it. I just, I don't know. It's so beautiful, and I never had anything that belonged to her."

"I was hoping you'd say that … because there is no way my boobs would fit in that dress."

At midnight, Monday and I stood outside my front door. The fat white moon hung directly above, and darkness floated everywhere. My mother's dress fit seamlessly on my body like a second skin, and Monday's dress dripped of gold down to her feet. Something a Greek goddess would wear, with a matching band around her forehead.

"Okay," she said, shaking out her hands. "This is it."

"This is it," I agreed.

Silence.

An owl hooted.

"Do we just walk there? I mean ... we can't exactly ride scooters in these dresses." Monday turned to me.

"I didn't think about that." *Silence again.* "My scooter is broken. We'd have to both fit on yours."

Monday laughed. "Yeah, okay ... because that would work." As soon as she'd said that, an idea came to mind. I took off my heels and held them in my hand as I flew down the porch steps to the garage. "Where are you going?"

"We could take my Mini Coop, but there's one thing I want to check first."

In the garage, there was a car under a cover. I hadn't found the time before to see if it worked, but it was worth checking. I pulled the garage door up, and it rolled open and slammed against the top.

"That isn't what I think it is, is it?" I heard Monday ask as I uncovered the vehicle. "No way. No. I can't believe it." Under the white cover sat a black vintage car. I pulled the dusty cover into a heap in the corner and swiped my hands together. "The Mystery-mobile."

My gaze swung to hers. "The what?"

Monday laid her hand on her chest as she approached the car. "Every Winter Solstice, this car would be in the parade passing out sparklers to kids before the bonfire. No one has seen it in years. Geez, it's been like five years, maybe?" She shook her head as if in amazement. "It was Benny all along ... I can't believe it. Cranky Benny was the man in the Mystery-mobile."

I eyed the vintage Phantom. We couldn't be talking about the same man. "My grandfather?"

"See if it still works. Do you realize how amazing this is? Showing up to the Pruitt Ball in the Mystery-mobile? Iconic."

"Don't get your hopes up," I warned her, opening the car door. I sat in the driver's seat, searched around for a key. I flipped down the visor and a key fell onto my lap.

Monday got in beside me. I tossed her one last look before inserting the key into the ignition. Then I turned it.

The car rumbled at our feet.

"oh, this is all very CINDERELLA," *she squealed.*

FALLON
chapter forty four

C ARS LINED THE CIRCULAR DRIVEWAY IN FRONT OF THE PRUITT
mansion. Bystanders gawked and whispered as we pulled up.

Monday wore a proud smile as we exited the dusty Phantom, and my gaze followed the pale-yellow mansion to the black sky. The bones of the estate had white Victorian architectural elements, mixing both the coastal charm and something belonging not of this time.

A tall, thin man greeted us at the door, wearing a butler tuxedo, and checked off our names before we entered. Haunting music bounced off the pristine glossy floors. My vision flooded with cocktail dresses, black tuxedos, and masquerade masks. Monday grabbed my hand and led me between the twin grand staircases, where I looked skyward. A crystal chandelier hung in the foyer and music filled my ears. All around me, people laughed, smiled, and drank from brass and pewter goblets etched with the Sacred Sea symbol and scrolls.

"I wasn't expecting to see you here." Fable placed her hand on my arm, and I turned when she hugged me. "Fallon," she gasped. "This dress is gorgeous. Monday, too. Wow, you two look so beautiful."

I pulled away to admire her emerald green dress, her fawn hair lying lazily around her shoulders like mine. "You, too."

"Fallon," Adora shrieked, hugging me as my eyes widened. I hadn't seen her in so long. She pulled me away to look at me and wrapped one of my locks around her finger. "Dance with me." She smiled in all blue. Her glassy green eyes glistened through her embellished white mask.

"She's already drunk," Fable whispered, patting my arm to drag me away. "Soon, Adora. Let's get her a drink first." Then her voice lowered, "This is going to be a night you will *want* to forget."

As we walked between bodies, with my heart in my stomach, my eyes looked for him amongst the sea of masked faces. Ladies wearing beautiful gowns danced in the main room as men surrounded them, watching them. I looked all around, and I stood on my toes to peer across the crowd as Fable stopped in front of a waiter.

Fable nudged a drink into my hand, and I looked in front of me.

My eyes met with silver ones.

"Julian," I whispered, his name falling like mist.

Julian cleared his throat, and when I thought I could breathe again, another breath was imprisoned in my lungs. I stood motionless, listening to my heart knock inside my chest above the music as my eyes locked on his expressive ones. He was wearing a fitted black tuxedo with a crisp white shirt underneath, a white mime mask covering his face. Very few times had I seen his lips, the ones I'd kissed numerous times now. The mouth that whispered to me in the dark of sweet nothings and feelings and once-upon-a-times. Delicate lips with sharp edges and painted in the color of blood yet tasted like cinnamon and a dash of sweet wickedness.

Nerves crawled up my spine to the back of my neck, and Julian's eyes bounced from Fable to me. My mouth went dry. His eyes turned to slits.

"Excuse me," Julian gritted through a clenched jaw, then blinked once more before turning and walking away, carrying a server tray filled with drinks. I watched as he dropped the tray on a table. Drinks spilled to the ground and glassed shattered to the floor. Guests threw up their hands, tossing insulting words at his back.

I took a step to go after him when Fable caught my wrist.

"Don't," she said, and my gaze steered to her with tears burning in my eyes. Her grasp on me tightened. "If you love him, let him go."

My eyes narrowed. "I can't," I whispered, and Fable released her grip.

Her eyes drifted to the other side of the room, and I followed her gaze to where Phoenix was watching her from behind the bar, his tortured gaze in a golden blaze.

She turned her eyes back to me. "Then you're a stupid girl for falling in love with a Heathen, and now you will spend the rest of your days knowing what it's like to be hollow." My eyes dragged between Fable and Phoenix, and Fable closed her eyes. "Sorry, I need a second," she whispered and took off across the room.

"Fable, wait!" I called out, going after her, but she'd already disappeared.

I looked back to Phoenix. He was gripping the edge of the bar, seeming as if he was holding himself back from jumping over it and running after her. He dragged in a breath and looked back to me with caution in his eyes—a warning.

And in one sweep, he gathered himself, reining himself back and pretending as if nothing happened. It all had happened so fast, and I darted my gaze around the room, no one noticing. Why hadn't I noticed it before?

Alcohol slipped down my throat easily in one gulp, and I placed the chalice on a tray being carried by another server walking past. I grabbed another chalice off the same tray and left the ballroom to find air.

I needed air. I needed to find Julian. He looked so upset that I was here, and I thought this was what he wanted.

Before I could step foot into the hallway, Adora appeared and hooked her arm in mine just as the music changed. "I love this song," she sang. "Girls, let's dance."

Monday and Ivy surrounded me and dragged me back to the center of the ballroom, where the instrumental music playing picked up a much faster pace. The girls pulled me into a dizzying crowd of dancing ladies, and my world spun on its axis as we danced and danced and danced. Then my eyes fell upon him.

Julian was there, standing in the corner of the crowded ballroom with his hands clasped in front of him. With every turn, my eyes met his rigid frame. His expression neither faltered nor shifted, his gaze locked on me as if it could touch and hold me.

My heart grew tattered black wings, longing to make the flight to him.

I was breathing hard and dancing, and in his eyes, he was dancing along with me. Adora grabbed my hand and spun me again. But all I saw in a room full of people was him, as he was seeing me. The starry sky, the sea, and every wonder the moon touched after the sun died could not measure up to the look in his eyes.

"If I'm not mistaken, I think a certain Heathen has his eyes on you," Adora sang in my ear.

"You see that too?" Monday asked. The girls giggled, and I looked around the room, nervous.

Adora spun me again. "Oh, I think all of creation has witnessed that look."

"Be careful, Fallon. They may be on the prowl for a white-haired virgin to sacrifice tonight," Ivy joined in.

With brazen smiles, the three girls glanced back at Julian, and he swung his head to the side and gripped the back of his neck.

"Yeah," Ivy laughed, "because that's not any more obvious."

I didn't know how many songs had passed. With every drink, the thirst in my throat and the dryness in my mouth only craved more, needing the thick amber liquid to soothe it. Yet, after each filled chalice, the quench was only temporary.

Every so often, my eyes found Julian to stabilize me. To calm the panic rising in my chest, knowing something wasn't okay.

The moment I found an opening to leave the dance floor, music stopped, and the room went silent. Adora clutched my hand, and all masked faces turned to a gentleman who stood in the corner of the room, who wore a white Bauta mask with gold swirls around the trim. It became clear to me it was Mr. Pruitt who was speaking, thanking everyone for attending.

At his table, three men stood and walked toward us, and the crowd parted down the middle to make room for them.

"The Samhain brings new beginnings and awakenings, so drink and drink and spin and sing. The night is calm, the cups run clean. Soak the folly into thee, and rise to carnal madness ..." Mr. Pruitt's words trailed when a suitor took my hand. My head was spinning, and I couldn't lock my gaze onto any solid form.

The man was in a cat mask, the colors in gold, black, and crimson. The other two wore masks with hooked noses. One nose was longer than the other. All three wore black tuxedos, and for a moment, it all seemed like a hazy dream.

Ivy and Adora branched off with the other two, and my head swirled around the room to see pairs dancing and drinking and bodies pressing closer together. The music changed too, the sound of an old music box at first. Then it faded into a symphony of violins and keys of a piano.

"It's okay. Dance, Fallon," the suitor whispered into the air around me. He grabbed me at the elbows and pulled me forward into his broad chest.

Panic only thickened in my lungs, and I couldn't breathe. I turned to find Julian, unsure of what was happening to me. The room spun, I became dizzy. In my hand, another drink appeared. The suitor's fingers were stroking my arm.

"Drink and dance," he continued to chant in my ear as music and laughing stacked inside the room.

"I need air," I thought I said aloud, but the creepy music drowned out my voice. The suitor clutched my waist with one hand as the other helped the drink to my lips, tipping it back. My head shook, and the dance floor seemed to wave under my heels like water.

Then someone else grabbed my arm, attempting to pull me away, but I was held firmly in place and the suitor was not letting me go. The desperate fingers dug deeper into my flesh, attempting to pry me away, to redirect blood flow if need be, when he wedged himself between me and the suitor who was keeping me here.

A palm laid against my suitor's chest, and it was Julian who leaned over and whispered something into his ear. I'd recognize his shape anywhere, the vein popping in his neck, the staccato chest heave when he was upset. Julian was no longer in his jacket, and his sleeves were pushed up to his elbows.

My fingers clutched to his shirt, wanting him to take me away from here. My sights were dizzy, but when I looked up, all I saw of Julian's face was a profile of a full-face venetian style mask with black ink around the eyes and dripping like tears below them.

The suitor released me, and Julian pulled me a few feet away, darting his head all around for an escape with his fingers interlaced with mine.

Dancing couples bumped our shoulders, lost in their own worlds as if in a trance. Time seemed to pass fast and slow, but the closer we got to the hall, I felt the clean, cold air soothe my deprived lungs. Julian squeezed my hand, and just before we made it off the ballroom floor, Augustine Pruitt circled the area.

Julian reeled back, turned, and pulled me into his chest.

"Julian?" I whispered, wondering what was happening.

He grabbed the back of my head and dipped his mouth to my ear. "Don't say my name," he told me, weaving his fingers with mine. He guided my other hand around his neck before his palm slipped down my spine to the small of my back, and he pulled me closer. "Just dance with me."

The pulse in his neck was hammering against my fingers, and his hips were nailed to mine, guiding me in a soft rock. My skin hummed, hearing his breath in my ear, feeling his fingertips graze my bare skin at the base of my spine. A cover of *Eternal Flame* wrapped its musical thread around us, binding us with every heart-pounding beat.

"Fallon," he said, taking my other hand and hanging it around his neck as well. "Why did you come here?"

"I thought ..." I focused on the way his chest was moving, so much calmer now. A slow rise, a deep fall. Gone were the shallow breaths and panic.

Julian lifted my head to redirect my gaze. "You thought what?" he asked, and I shook my head, trying to put words together, but my brain was foggy and falling apart. Julian placed both hands on top of my head, pushing my hair back until my eyes met his. "Focus, Fallon. I need you to snap out of it. It's stupid magic. It's not real, all right?"

I nodded, squinting, trying to remember something. Anything. "You wanted me here, though."

"What?" Confusion was sewn into his words. "Why would I want you at Pruitt's house? That's absurd."

"You said you would come find me after the ball."

"After the—" Julian paused and looked around before lowering his voice. "*After* the ball. Not at the ball," he emphasized, moving his hands back to my waist. They slid up my sides, and he dropped his head to mine.

Julian closed his eyes, dragged in a breath before he opened them again, his gaze falling down my deep neckline. They bounced back up. "You're beautiful. Have I ever told you that?" I shook my head. Julian blinked. "Has anyone ever told you that?"

I lowered my gaze, shook my head against his, feeling the onslaught of my past pile in my chest. He laid his warm palm on my stomach, where the dip in my dress ended, then dragged up between my breasts, to my heart.

"To me, you are beautiful. And not just tonight. All the time. I should have told you that a long time ago." My chest caved, but he didn't remove his hand. His touch and words, it was all unseaming my soul. "Your heart is beating really fast," he said, and I heard the smile in his voice as we gently danced in place. Julian returned his hands to my waist, rolled his mask-covered forehead over mine. "How are you feeling now, better?"

"I must have drank too much," I admitted.

"Okay, listen to me," his eyes glanced up for a moment to look behind me, "in ten seconds, we're walking casually through that corridor behind me without looking suspicious. There's something I have to take care of, and I can't leave you now that you're here. Nod if you hear me." I nodded. Julian gripped the nape of my neck and pinned his eyes to mine. "Don't ask me any questions, I don't want to have to lie to you," he warned.

My eyes slid back and forth between his serious ones. "I trust you."

His eyes softened, then darted to the right. "Five seconds, Fallon."

I didn't know exactly what would come in five seconds, but the anticipation was—

"NOW."

JULIAN
chapter forty five

FALLON TUCKED HERSELF INSIDE MY ARM AS WE WALKED THROUGH the hall to the bathroom. I'd planned to have left the mansion twenty minutes ago, but Fallon being here threw everything off-kilter.

Maroon and gold vintage rugs lined the halls and quieted our footfalls. Partygoers paired off under Sacred Sea's heated spell, their moans and whispers echoed in the corridor. Fallon had no idea what she had walked into. She had no idea Augustine Pruitt always used a room full of carnal passion to awaken their ancestors for guidance into the new year, to harness beauty and keep his members agreeable—open to suggestion and submissive to him and his devious ventures.

Before we made a sharp right, I chanced a look back to see if we were being followed or if anyone had noticed our departure from the main room. My sight caught three familiar servers entering the corridor from the bar area. Phoenix, Beck, and Zephyr. The wall ate my line of sight when we disappeared behind it. The right-wing was empty. We needed to move fast.

I clutched Fallon's hand and sprinted down the deserted hall, having memorized the layout of the mansion. Jonah had pulled blueprints from property records, and we'd spent all afternoon burning them into my memory. My brothers were under different knowledge of how tonight would go. I assumed, rightfully so, they would continue without me once realizing I was nowhere to be found. I should have been gone from the property by now.

Fallon almost tripped on her floor-length dress, and she hung back to gather the bottom of it in her hand. I forced down my agitation. It wasn't her fault. I may have had a plan, but she hadn't planned for this at all. She should have never come, but I refused to leave her to be seduced and used by Sacred Sea.

When we reached the end of the hall, we disappeared into the bathroom.

Fallon fell back against the door, trying to catch her breath. I approached the laundry chute and retrieved the screwdriver from my pants pocket. I stripped off the mask I'd stolen from a hired server and tossed it into the trash, still wearing the one I had on beneath it.

One by one, I unscrewed the bolts, letting them fall to the floor as pressure clouded my blood. Fallon stayed silent behind me. I hoped she couldn't hear the loud beat of betrayal slamming inside my chest. It was never a choice when it came to her, only one answer. Her.

I thought and moved forward with tunnel vision.

Love could only be understood by looking at the story backward. But I no longer had a desire to understand why, only that it was, and I was never letting it go. To think a monster who could hate so passionately could love so profoundly shook my very existence. Everything I'd known I questioned, and everything I was, I was no more. It was her, always. Every time.

The Book of Cantini and the Book of Danvers both had the answers on how to break the curse, and if I couldn't get to them before the other Heathens, they would kill her, and once they had her, I couldn't stop them.

The steel chute plate hung from the last screw. I held it to the side and waved Fallon closer. "You have to jump through," I insisted. Her slender fingers twisted in front of her. Her gaze bounced from me to the dark hole. "Come on, Fallon. You can do this."

The doorknob jiggled, and Fallon jumped from her spot and backed away from the door.

"Fallon, now," I whispered-shouted in a panic, resisting the urge to pick her up and throw her in there myself. *Bang! bang! bang!* and her eyes widened with mine. "Get in the hole." I wanted to scream the words, but I was able to maintain a steady whisper.

Fallon hiked up her dress and clutched my shoulder as she pushed one leg inside. Then she paused, looking up at me with fear in her eyes.

"I'm right behind you," I promised, nudging my head. She nodded and crawled the rest of the way in before sliding and disappearing through the hole. A few more raps at the door and my head cocked from where Fallon disappeared to the doorknob. It wouldn't be long until they found another way to the cellar.

I shoved the screwdriver back into my pocket, ducked, swung my leg into the hole, then turned to push the other through.

Then I let go.

It was a straight drop down to the cellar, and I fell into a heap of dirty laundry beside Fallon. Her silence was killing me, but I couldn't think about that right now. Not when we were running out of time. I climbed out of the laundry cart and helped her to her feet.

Down here, the walls were made of stone with very little light. The temperature had dropped by at least ten degrees. Wood beams ran across low ceilings. I peered down to the right, then left. I pinched my temple with my forefinger and thumb. I was spun around. Behind us, an industrial-sized washer and dryer buzzed, flirting with my nerves.

"Which way?" Fallon asked with her arms across her chest. Her white dress and white hair were disheveled, and her eyes held a million questions, none of which I could answer.

"I'm thinking." I paced with my hands on my hips. Above me, the chute had a slight angle. I closed my eyes and imagined the faded architectural lines from the blueprints. "This way."

The underground tunnels shaped into the pentagram below Weeping Hollow kept evil spirits away, and kept those who didn't belong here lost. It was easy to get turned around, and we weren't even inside yet. Each coven had their own cavern underground, a smaller chamber only accessible from certain entry points. The only way into the Sacred Sea chamber was through the Pruitt mansion. This was my only shot.

Fallon followed a few steps behind in a light jog, her heels *clicking!* and *clacking!* against tile grated my anxiety. "How much do you love those shoes?" I asked her, keeping my attention forward. Fallon huffed out air through her nose. It was loud, then the clicking stopped. I turned to make sure she was still behind me, seeing her walking in her beautiful dress, her heels in her hands. Her mask was gone, and she forced a fake smile. "I'm sorry, but you should have never gone to that party."

She stayed silent. With every step, a soft glow of a motion-sensor light kicked on, then disappeared behind us. The silence was thick as if our heads were submerged in water. I couldn't take the pressure of betraying the Heathens as well as the tension between us.

I looked back at her once more. "Fallon, you can talk to me."

"I know," she told me. "Right now, I'm mad. I don't want to say anything I don't mean."

"I don't care if you mean it or not, I want to know what you're thinking."

Fallon laughed. "No, you don't."

"Yeah, I do."

"You wanna know what I'm thinking?" She sighed. "The truth?" And she didn't give me a chance to speak before she continued, "You fucking *killed* Carrie!" she shouted at my back. I glanced back at her, narrowed my eyes, and she lowered her voice. "She wanted me here, and now I have no idea why. And at the same time, I'm so relieved you can finally see what I've always seen. It was never you doing all those things to those people. It was always someone controlling you, but instead of letting me be there for you—because, Julian, let's face it, you were a mess—you just dragged me out of the woods and pushed me away.

"Ever since I got here, no one tells me shit. Everyone's all cryptic. You keep everything hidden from me, yet here I am, walking behind you, trusting you, and it pisses me off how much I trust you. Like I'm some weak and stupid girl or something. And you're so vague and back and forth. Like '*Fallon, there's no time, I must leave. Fallon, I can't be apart from you. We are right together. Fallon, you need to go, it's dangerous. Fallon, I can't live without you,'*" she mocked.

I was smiling, shaking my head. "I do not sound like that."

"Yeah," she laughed, "that's exactly how you sound."

"I sound like a dick."

We reached the end of the hall. Fallon stayed a few steps back as I placed my palms on the stone, where a hidden door should be, and pressed my ear to the cold wall. I closed my eyes, listening for the hollow.

"This is it," I whispered, straightening my shoulders. I pushed up my sleeves, shook out my hands, and returned my palms to the stone wall. Squeezing my eyes shut, I cleared my head to pull forward the Earth element—an element I hadn't used in quite some time.

The short chant slipped from between my lips. The muscles in my arms shook, the power transferring from somewhere within, rushing through my blood, to the tips of my fingers.

For the briefest moment, my head swam with a rush of power fortifying my being. The wall groaned as it inched back and to the left. We were in.

I dropped my forehead to the stone, feeling lightheaded all of a sudden. It had been too long. Starting a fire, creating a windstorm, moving water, it was all easy because I had the Heathens to channel through for twenty-six years. I had to learn the Earth element on my own.

Fallon's hand laid on my back. "You okay?"

I rolled my forehead over the stone, tilting my head to look into her cloudless blue eyes.

Something jump-started my being.

Her eyes. There was always something about her eyes.

"Yeah," I said through an exhale. "We're almost there."

I pried the hidden door open the rest of the way, and we took narrow stairs down until we were officially in the tunnels. Darkness fell around us, and Fallon clutched my hand. She walked closer behind me as I led the way in the damp cold. "How do you know where you're going?" she asked, her small voice sounding much bigger down here.

"I have night-vision goggles," I joked, squeezing her hand.

Fallon smacked my arm. "No, you don't." It came out like a question.

"I can see in the dark."

She was silent as we walked, her abusive hand clutching my forearm.

"So, every time we—in the dark—you—"

"Saw everything," I confirmed, looking back with a grin. Fallon dropped her head, and I knew she was blushing. I squeezed her hand again and

457

pulled her closer to pin her to my back. The tension I felt before was long gone, and now I didn't think I could have done this without her. It was almost as if it was meant to be this way, her and me against time, the town, everything, everyone.

After a short walk, we reached a barrier, and I froze.

"What is it?" Fallon asked behind me.

"This gate is steel," I felt around the edges and shook my head, "It's not supposed to be here." Manmade. Chemically processed. I needed Phoenix's heat to sear through it. It wasn't the same as lighting a fire. I needed more for this. I wasn't expecting this. I couldn't do this without him.

On the far right, there was a blue blinking light. Beside it, a card scanner.

"Shit," I groaned. I couldn't fry the electrical panel or destroy it with water. I couldn't risk an alarm going off. All we needed was two bars removed for us to slip through.

Pushing my hand through my hair, I turned to Fallon. "This is going to sound really bad, but I need you to get me off."

Her eyes widened in the pitch black. "You *what?*"

"I'm serious. I need to pull pure magic out of me to get through something like this on my own. I don't have Phoenix to burn through it, so I need pleasure or pain to exhume that level of magic."

"I'm curious. What would you have done if I weren't here?"

"Jerk off," I stated.

Fallon smiled and tapped her finger on her chin.

"That's ridiculous when I have my girl standing right in front of me, who, by the way, would do a much better and quicker job. This is serious, Fallon. A matter-of-life-and-death serious."

She rolled her eyes. "Oh, okay. If it's *life and death.*"

"Look, I would never use you the way I've been used," *no one should ever be used the way I'd been used,* "so I need *you* to use *me.* However way you want."

A breathy gasp escaped her lips. She crossed her arms. Un-crossed them. "That's a lot of pressure."

"There's literally nothing in this world you could do wrong, I promise.

See," I grabbed my aroused cock, "you're only standing there, and I'm already hard. You just have to ... back into it. Easy."

Her cheeks flushed around her incredulous smile. "Back into it?"

"I'll steer."

A laugh pushed through her lips. "Okay, no. You're making this really awkward right now. And this is my mother's dress. I'm not doing whatever it is you're thinking in my mother's dress."

Gripping the back of my neck, I looked at her for a moment. I couldn't believe what I'd just asked of her. *Back into it?* I rolled my head back.

"Fuck, I'm sorry." I massaged my temples. "You're right. I don't even know what I was thinking." I'd become desperate, but I needed to get through this gate. I needed to get to those books.

"If you only understood the lengths I'd go for you," I told her, watching her from only feet away as she was looking around the dark for something her gaze could land on. Then Fallon's head moved to the sound of my voice, and she was looking right into my eyes. I almost wondered if she could see me in the dark too.

She stayed silent, and I wanted to reach out and touch her. And then my mouth was moving. I couldn't stop it. "It happened slowly and then all at once for me, you know." My back fell against the stone wall of the tunnel. "The way I feel about you, it runs deep—an unheard of deep, blue thing. So blue, it's black like the color of a ravens wing ... In an ocean beneath an ocean on top of another ocean. Where you don't know which way is up or down. No shallows, no bottom. That's how deep, and it scares me sometimes. But then you're there too, and we're floating together in that deep place. And it's peaceful there ... quiet." I'd lost myself in her eyes, and I hadn't realized the rest of me stood paralyzed. I cleared my throat. "It's strange when we're together. Like a hurt so good type of strange."

Fallon whispered, "Isn't that the point of us?" A slow smile curved her lips, and she bit her bottom lip to stifle it. "Julian, if you keep thinking someone else needs to provoke you to trigger something, you'll never be able to do anything on your own." I opened my mouth, then closed it when she continued, "How could you need anyone else to unlock something that's already inside you? That doesn't make any sense."

"I don't know any other way," I admitted. "This is how it has always been."

"I call bullshit."

My brow spiked. "Bullshit?"

"Yeah, I've seen what you're capable of, and still, you let everyone control you." She leaned forward and slapped her palms together as she said, "Stop. Letting. Them. Control. You."

I smirked. "Did you just one-clap-syllable me?"

A door creaked closed, and both our heads turned to the sound. They were here. Time was running out.

"Julian," she whispered, finding my hand in the dark. "It's already inside you. It's you. You were the one who was able to pull yourself out. You fought against the darkness every time. You got yourself here. You climbed and clawed and are so much stronger than you give yourself credit for. You don't need anyone. It's always been you. Only you. You can do this."

Me? I thought of all her words. *Me.*

I nodded. I kicked off the wall. I dragged in a breath. I wrapped both hands around the steel bars. I felt Fallon beside me. I heard the march of footsteps in the distance. Both our heartbeats pulsed in my ears. Fallon's words echoed in my mind. And something didn't feel right.

Then it made sense.

It wasn't me.

She was wrong. I wasn't the one who pulled me out, she was. I'd only fought against the darkness because of her. She got me here. She climbed and clawed her way inside me, making me stronger than I ever thought to believe. I did need someone. I needed her. It had always been her. Only her.

We could do this. Together.

I grabbed her arm and pulled her in front of me to cage her between my arms. Her shoes dropped to the ground, and I covered her fingers with mine. Together, we grasped the bars.

The steps grew closer, and I squeezed my eyes shut. The sudden pain of realizing I could lose her surged through my blood—the agony like a raging riptide splashing against my bones. My fists tightened around hers, and I hunched over, my front against her back, my head beside hers, training my thoughts on two heartbeats that were becoming one.

One solid beat.

Each thump vibrated my core and waved like an electrical current through me. And then we were surrounded by silver light. Everything was slow motion. So slow that time stopped. The heartbeat was a heavy, solid beat, drawn out like a bass. A bubble around us locked us in this halted time.

A force snapped, and we were plunged forward to the other side.

I toppled over Fallon to the ground. It took me a moment to gather myself. I rolled off her with a grunt onto my back. My leg jolted in an electric spasm. My thoughts were all over the place, and panic coiled around me in a tight fist. *Fallon.*

I popped up to my feet and pushed a blanket of white hair from her face. "Fallon, hey. Are you okay?" My head cocked to the side, trying to piece together what just happened. The steel gate was still intact, and we were on the other side. We went through steel bars. "Fallon!"

She gasped for air and blinked her eyes open.

I helped her to her feet. "You okay?"

"What happened?"

I laughed, still amazed. We went through steel bars. *My Spirit element.* "I'm not sure, but we don't have time to figure that out. We have to move."

I scooped her up into my arms, knowing she wouldn't be able to run in the dress, and sprinted the rest of the way to Sacred Sea's chamber.

The trinity Celtic knot symbol, three interconnected leaves, was engraved in the arched wooden door. I set her down, opened the door, and we slipped inside the small room.

To my right, an entire wall was made up of glass, on the other side of the glass, the forbidden underground springs.

"What is this place?" Fallon whispered, grazing her fingertips along the glass wall. The glimmering blue hue of the waters lit up her pale features.

"Sacred Sea's chamber." I had to force my gaze away from her and looked about the room for a sign of the books. "There's an old tale about the color of the underground springs. The Forbidden Girl of the Caverns," I started to say, approaching the bookshelf. "The forbidden girl was a wife to one, a mistress to another. She used these tunnels to sneak back and forth to see her lover, who was her father's enemy. The story goes, she was planning on running away with him. But when her father discovered the truth of her infidelity, he'd hid her away somewhere in these caverns, ashamed of her treachery. Some say her father even drowned her in those waters. Her spirit has been haunting the tunnels and springs, waiting, to this day, for her lover to rescue her. Those waters have been that color ever since. Some say when her lover returns to the tunnels to save her spirit, her reincarnated soul will be complete again, and the water will run clear."

"That's ... really sad. What was her name?"

I shrugged and felt my way around to the back of the bookshelf. "The books never named her. They just called her The Forbidden Girl. This town runs on many tales. Some true, some I believe to keep us in line." I found a fault in the wall. "For a witch, not being able to reincarnate with our entire soul is our hell."

My dress shoes slipped on the slick and solid ground as I searched for grip, pushing the bookshelf along the side of the wall. The wooden bookcase creaked and moaned as it inched out of the way. Fallon approached me from behind.

"I think this is it." I removed loose stones from the wall, handing them off to Fallon. In the pocket of the wall laid the three missing books. I let go of a breath, feeling a tight emotion spiral up my chest. "I can't believe it."

One by one, I grabbed the books and stacked them in my arms.

Book of Cantini. Book of Danvers. Book of Blackwell.

Every Heathen before you tried, and every Heathen failed, Goody's words rang. I fell back against the wall with a smile and let go of a relieved breath.

I met eyes with Fallon. "LET'S GET OUT OF *HERE*."

JULIAN
chapter forty six

A MALEFIC HUSH HAD FALLEN OVER THE WOODS. Languorous shadows, urged by the night's tale, twisted around me as fire blazed at my feet. Fallon was inside showering. She'd never once asked me why we'd broken into the Sacred Sea chambers and stolen books from the room. On the way to the exit at the cemetery on the other side of town, we'd talked of everything else, both avoiding the things we'd left behind us.

I picked up the Book of Cantini and flipped through pages until my sight latched on to the crescent moon birthmark sketched onto the aged papyrus paper. I tore out the pages, crumbled them in my fist, and tossed them into the fire. I did the same with pages from the Book of Danvers. Once Clarice Danvers had found out how to break the curse, she'd stolen these journals and written the answers into the Book of Danvers before Matteo Cantini confiscated them—just before he'd cast her out of Weeping Hollow.

She'd taken on the identity of Carrie Driscoll, waiting over a hundred years for the perfect opportunity to finish the job of murdering the moon girl.

The moment was so bittersweet. For almost two centuries, the Hollow

Heathens searched and searched for the same truths I'd discovered. And I threw it all away for love. I wondered what my ancestors would think of me, and if they'd be disappointed. If they'd curse my soul for eternity, casting me into a witch's hell with the inability to reincarnate fully like the Forbidden Girl.

I wondered what my brothers would think if they knew all the things I'd done. If they could one day understand that … I, Julian Blackwell, had found a love that was deeper than love, and I loved in a way as if it were all that I'd known.

The fire crackled, and a raven called out to me in the distance when I reached for the Book of Blackwell. I'd never held my family book in my hands, and the fire's flames reflected off the silver foil under a pitch-black sky. A drowsy terror stole through the woods.

Why had everything felt right until this moment? Why had the Blackwell book been taken to begin with? Had my family always known the answers to the curse too?

The thought paralyzed me. I couldn't bring myself to do it.

I couldn't destroy the pages of my book. Not yet.

The raven called again, and I nodded as if I understood what it was trying to tell me.

Once I returned inside, I hid the books under a cushion of the couch. But not the Book of Blackwell. It screamed in the palm of my hand. I straightened my back and walked to the fireplace, pressing my foot to search for the loose floorboard. The wood creaked, and I crouched down, removed the plank, and wedged the book inside the tight space. The plank slid back into place, and I walked to my bedroom, where Fallon was standing. Her hair was damp. She was wearing one of my shirts.

Fallon had only been in my bedroom once before, and it was brief. She had been upset and probably didn't get a chance to get a good look around, not in the way she was doing now. There wasn't much to see.

A full-sized bed was pushed into the corner of the room under a window, where moonlight cast a single beam between us. A lantern rested on the sill. All my blankets were hand-made by Mrs. Edwin. A nightstand Phoenix had built, along with a chest against the opposite wall. No pictures. The only décor was the dreamcatcher Jolie had made me, hanging from my wooden headboard, which never caught dreams. My cherished *Frankenstein* laid on my nightstand. Her gaze returned to me.

The way she looked at me had my heart stripping off its armor from the night's events. I swallowed and cleared my throat.

I turned to close the door. Then pinned my back against it. "Take off your clothes. All of them."

The witching hour was long gone. The sun would soon rise. While the pre-morning dark was on, I needed to be with her in the way the night was with the moon.

Fallon watched me watching her undress.

Shame, guilt, fear, none of that lived here with us. Only something else. Something immortal. Some ferocious thing that tasted like deathless devotion on the tip of my tongue.

She peeled off my shirt from her body, and my gaze followed the way her stomach slightly rose when she stole a breath. White hair fell around her shoulders as she slipped out of her panties. Her spine erected, facing me again. My mouth parted behind my mask as my eyes followed her curves in slow motion, her dips and valleys and uncharted places my mouth hadn't traveled.

Under the necklace I'd gifted her, her breasts rose and fell when her eyes locked on mine. I tore my gaze away and dropped them down her body, settling them on the dip of her hip bone. I closed my eyes. Opened them again. My vision was blurry but still burned by the patch on her hip.

And what laid behind it.

I took a step closer and stood before her. Then I dropped to my knees. Fallon tensed when I peeled off the patch. And under it, the dark shape of a crescent moon marked her pale skin.

The truth slammed into me all over again, a reminder that everything I'd done tonight was for her. I could never tell her. I could never tell anyone.

Breaking the curse did not come first. Fallon came first. And they would kill me if they ever found out I was keeping the truth from them. Over and over, I'd do it again and again.

Fallon fell back and sat on the edge of the bed, taking my head into her lap, and she pushed her fingers through my hair. I kissed her birthmark, both hating and loving it. Wanting to rid her of it, and wanting to cherish it. It was a peculiar feeling. One that was inescapable. It was the very thing that made me see so clearly. Made everything hurt like hell.

My thoughts tortured me. I'd blurted out words, moved fast and slow. My mind was everywhere, digging fingers into Fallon's pale skin, kissing her softly before sinking my teeth into her. I couldn't make sense of anything. She gripped my hair as I fought with myself.

Fallon told me she was here with me. She spoke words, something about me being good. She trusted me. She believed in me. She loved me. We were both unhinged for different reasons, and she had no idea.

"Julian," she whispered, unbuttoning my dress shirt, her voice brushing my skin. Then I was out of it, kneeling between her legs and looking up at her. My gaze moved back and forth between hers, my palms sliding up her back. "I'm right here," Fallon insisted, studying me, soothing me. "What's wrong—"

I grabbed the back of her neck and pulled her close until her eyes fluttered closed. Then I lifted my mask and slipped my tongue inside her mouth. I tasted something that felt like a combination of running and screaming and letting go.

A moan rattled in my throat. I pulled back, my thumbs brushing her closed lashes as I admired her parted mouth. My tongue darted out to stroke her delicate lips before I filled her mouth again. My cock swelled inside my pants from her taste. Everything was sensitive, like an open scar.

Rising to my feet, I leaned over her. She undid my button and zipper and slid my pants off my hips. Her fingers brushed across the lesions that were slowly healing.

She pulled away with sadness in her eyes, but I grabbed her face.

"It's okay," I whispered, shaking my head, keeping her in this kiss.

Fallon pulled away. "No, Julian, it's not okay. Who did this to you?"

I hung my head and drew in a breath. "My coven needed me."

"Your coven did this to you? Why? And don't give me some vague answer either. For once, just be honest with me."

I tried to hold off for as long as possible. I didn't want to tell her what they did to me. What they always did to me. What I'd let them do to me. Fallon rose from the bed to get closer. I pinned her flush against me, leaving no space between us, searching for the right words to help her understand.

"Because a fourteen-year-old girl was dying, and they needed our magic to save her. You have to understand that I wanted to save her. This is what I am. A host for magic."

"No," Fallon shook her head, her fingers drifting across old scars and new wounds. "You're so much more than that."

Silencing her, I turned her around and nailed her back to my chest. Her throat was a fragile thing in my palm, her collarbone carved and delicate. I kissed her shoulder and neck. Both of her hands squeezed my naked thighs before she found my hands. She guided them, dragging one across her stomach, the other cupping her breast. She wanted me now. Her arms wrapped around my neck, giving me access to touch her freely.

White hair covered my vision when her head fell back against me. I hung my head and watched my hands slide across her shuddering skin. These same hands I'd used to murder were capable of holding her together in my arms. But that was never me. *This is me.*

My palm glided up to her breasts and cupped them, a gentle squeeze. The other dipped down and covered her sex, and I swiped a finger through her heated slit. Fallon moaned so lightly. I watched her pull her bottom lip between her teeth.

The small gesture was enough to provoke all five senses. An eagerness spurred my movements. I held my breath, dipped down, and plunged my cock inside her. The instant and electric connection almost took me off my feet, and I choked on my words as her tight warm pussy clenched around me. "Fallon—I'm—fuck..."

She was on her toes now, digging her fingers into my neck for leverage. I wrapped my arm around the front of her and palmed her sex, slamming my cock deeper, feeling her ridges grip everywhere from my tip to the base. I felt it throughout my entire body. Fallon whimpered, and I cursed, and this was us.

Connected, I crossed my hand across her chest and palmed her breast, the other stroking her clit as I lost myself in the grind. The friction made me dizzy and drove me crazy. *My gods*, her fairytale scent was swelling the room and soaking into my skin.

My moans were broken. Her whimpers were shattered. I tilted her head until my mouth crushed hers, and my tongue swept between her sweet lips before we both fell forward onto the bed.

Lifetimes pressed into ten fingers rewrote our new story on our bodies. We found ourselves tangled with the bedsheets.

She whispered sweet nothings in my ear.

The night held us in its hands.

Mouths alive, palms pressed to palms, fingers woven, breasts sliding against my chest, and submerged deep inside her was when her orgasm gripped mine, and my own began to pulse. The vibrations started in my bones, and I felt the change shift in my veins. It felt like an injection of rapture straight into my blood, an endless and enduring climax.

Then my magic expelled a silver aurora around us, protecting us. It had never happened like this before, and I pulled my hand over her eyes and looked around the illuminating room. It seemed as if the galaxy had fallen around us. Or the world had been turned upside down, and we were hanging in a star-filled sky. My heart was calm, but my body was spent, tipsy, and spinning.

"This can't be real," I breathed out, my soul drunk from it. I dropped my head, watching Fallon pull her bottom lip between her teeth. Then she parted her trembling lips before I filled her with my kiss once more, losing ourselves all over again.

FALLON

THE LARGE AWNING WINDOW STRETCHED ACROSS THE WALL OVER HIS bed. There were no curtains. No blinds. Nothing but a backdrop of the woods. The cold, fresh morning air slipped through the opened window from the bottom because he'd cracked it before we'd fallen asleep. It was so cold in his bedroom, but I felt at home here, lying bare between his warm sheets. Julian slept with his turned head under a pillow and on his back, one hand above his head, the other laying naturally across my hip.

Julian had always disappeared before morning came, and I'd never seen him sleep when the sun rose. It was fascinating, watching as his chest and stomach filled and fell in a soothing cadence. All these things inside him working together so beautifully without effort.

I sat up against his headboard, pulled the blanket up to my chest, and looked around the bare room. I picked up a book from the nightstand. *Frankenstein*. There were coffee rings on the cover. The book was treated like a favorite childhood blanket or stuffed animal. I opened the book and flipped through it. Julian's handwriting filled the margins. Black ink had sentences underlined, and pages were creased at the corners. It was fascinating.

Julian stretched beside me. He rubbed his chest, slid his palm down his stomach and under the blanket, and grabbed himself. His other hand that was laying on me moved too, and his fingers mapped my skin, recognizing everywhere he'd journeyed through the night.

"Are you awake?" he asked from under the pillow, squeezing my thigh.

"Yeah." I quickly closed the book and held it close to my chest.

"In the drawer of my nightstand, there's a mask. Hand me one?"

The drawer slid out smoothly, and inside were a collection of plain black masks. I grabbed one and reached behind me to drop it on his chest.

I faced the doorway when I felt the bed shift as he rose. "Okay," he said, and I turned back and laid against the headboard beside him.

Julian pushed his fingers over his eyes and through his hair. Then he looked at me. And I wished I knew what was going through his head. He looked at me like he'd never seen anything like me before. He looked at me like he was seeing me for the first time, each time.

"Have you read it before?" he asked.

Read it before? And Julian's eyes fell to the thing clutched to my chest. "Oh," I said, then looked down at the book's cover. "No. I mean, I know the story, but never actually read the book."

"Then how do you know the story?"

I tucked my smile into a straight line. "Everyone knows the story of Frankenstein."

Julian shook his head. "The story could be different depending on who you heard it from. Filmmakers, critics, people who've read it, they all retell *their* versions, their perception of the story, but you have to read the book for yourself to find *your* story."

I raised a brow. "I didn't know you liked to read."

Julian laughed lightly. "I don't, actually. I just like this one book. I've memorized it."

"You've memorized it." It was a statement. An incredulous statement.

"You're doubting me."

"No, I'd never doubt you."

"Choose a page number," he challenged, and I smiled. "Go on, I'm not kidding."

My smile was burning my face, and I flipped through the book, feeling Julian's eyes on me. Then I turned to face him so he couldn't see the words or cheat. "Page forty."

Julian thought for a moment, his gaze turning solemn. He looked at me, and his silver eyes filled with a field of emotion. *"Learn from me, if not by my precepts, at least by my example, how dangerous is the acquirement of knowledge, and how much happier that man is who believes his native town to be the world, than he who aspires to become greater than his nature will allow."* He said the words so fluidly. There was no smile in his eyes, only that of something he'd lost. Then he added, "I want you to have it."

"Have what?"

He tapped his finger on the page. "The book. I want you to have it."

"Julian, you love this book."

"I know." He took the book, closed it, and set it down. He pulled me to his chest and back under the covers where our bodies were warm, and our faces were cool from the early morning chill. He twisted a lock of hair around his finger. "Because I—"

A sound echoed through the cabin and shook the walls. It sounded like someone broke through the front door.

My eyes widened, seeing into Julian's terrified ones.

"They're here," he stated.

Time slowed, passed by the counts of my slamming heart. He dragged in a breath. Held it. He lurched forward, over me, grabbed a shirt from the floor, pushed it over my head.

"You have to do something for me," he started to say.

My eyes darted around as footsteps echoed within the cabin. Obscured deep voices bounced just outside his bedroom door. My heart was in my throat, my stomach twisted. A state of panic froze me still. Julian was fast, grabbing a pair of pants, throwing them into my chest to put on.

"If anything happens to me, under no circumstance do you fight for me. Don't go to the Order. Don't go to the woods. Don't tell anyone about anything. Fallon, you keep your mouth shut. You have to let them take me. You have to let me go."

"What? No!" The words had come out so fast, as I was tripping over the pants. Julian was naked, not worrying about himself, only helping me dress.

Crashes! and *bangs!* and *booms!* filled the cabin as his things were being destroyed.

"Julian, you're scaring me," I cried. "Does this have anything to do with what we did last night?" My eyes bounced between his panicked ones. He stayed silent and grabbed *Frankenstein* from the bed, then tucked it into my waistband.

"I'm so sorry, but just know if anything happens to me, I did it all because…"

"Because what?" My mind was in chaos. Julian's eyes were wild and desperate. "What did you do?!"

"Fallon, I—I—" he dragged in a deep breath.

And the bedroom door was kicked in. Three Heathens barged into the room. Zephyr was slinging one of my heels around his finger. Phoenix was holding two books we stole hours before. Beck's blue eyes instantly hit me, and he threw himself between Julian and me to box me out.

I stumbled backward against the wall.

There was no exchanging of words.

A million emotions passed through Julian's eyes before Zephyr kicked the backs of his legs and forced him on his knees. Julian cut one last apologetic gaze to me just as Phoenix shoved a burlap sack over his head. They bound his wrists together. But Julian didn't fight. Why wasn't he fighting?

"He didn't do anything," I screamed out.

I tried to get to Julian, but Beck shifted like a sliding brick wall, not allowing me to pass.

Zephyr held the back of Julian's head and slammed his knee into his ribcage. A *crack!* rang in the room and tears pushed through my eyes, heat enveloping me. Hot rage rushed through my veins. I lunged at Beck, trying to get to Julian. But I couldn't get to him.

"No! Let him go," I screamed, but no one looked at me.

No one paid me any attention. No one said a word. Julian was hunched forward on his knees *naked* as they beat into him. And I was screaming for someone to stop, anyone!

"Beck, please," I cried, but he never let me pass. "Let him go!"

Phoenix grabbed Julian's arms and lifted him to his feet.

Then they dragged him out of the room.

Beck hung back and stood by the door with his arms behind his back. No matter how many times I pushed and shoved and beat against him, he stood like an invincible statue.

I didn't know how much time had passed, as I was crying and screaming and throat raw with pain.

Eventually, Beck took off, leaving me in the hallway all alone.

And Julian was *long* GONE.

JULIAN
chapter forty seven

I LOVED HER, AND PERHAPS IT WAS A KIND OF LOVE that wasn't normal. Perhaps love wasn't supposed to move something like her, quiet and gentle. Or maybe it wasn't supposed to move something like me, cruel and unusual. Ours was different—*a strange love*. A mixture of us. Quiet *and* cruel, hiding in the depths of darkness before plunging a sharp blade into our hearts.

The kind of strange love to be murdered by.

THIN SLICES OF DAYLIGHT SHONE BETWEEN THE WOODEN SHEETS OF THE barn. I lifted my head enough to see Phoenix, Zephyr, and Beck off to the side, their voices hushed. My skull pounded. I pinched my eyes closed, then squinted. The positioning of the sun told me it wasn't noon yet. It was still the first day of Samhain.

"He's awake," Phoenix said. The three approached me. I tried to free myself from my restraints and froze when Phoenix squeezed my shoulder. "You're not going anywhere."

I settled my eyes on Zephyr, who stood before me with his arms crossed over his chest. He dropped his gaze to the books stacked at my feet.

"Found these in the cabin. I expected something like this from Nix, but not you."

Phoenix grunted. My teeth ground together behind my mask, having everything and nothing to say.

Zephyr nodded. "What makes you think you are of a higher power? That you're better than any of us? I'm confused, truly. You speak of loyalty, honesty, this so-called change within the coven, yet where is the loyalty?" Zeph took a step forward and gripped my wrist. Inside my palm was my oath. A scar from my middle finger down to my wrist. Then he whispered in my ear through gnashed teeth, "I will get the answers out of you. Even if it means toying with your little freak."

"You will not touch the girl," Beck stated from behind. "Let's wait until Clarence arrives."

"This is pointless." Phoenix kicked a crate, and it flew across the barn. He stormed at me and pressed his forehead to mine. "Where are the missing pages?" he screamed, spit flying, our heads connected. Phoenix Wildes, the wildcard built from ashes of psychedelic gold. My eyes bounced between his, noticing the same desperation I'd come to know, and I hadn't realized it until now. Perhaps only those who knew Love's wrath could see it in others. Phoenix Wildes had something to lose too. *"WHAT DID YOU DO WITH THEM?"*

"Stand back, Wildes," Clarence's harsh yet steady voice filled the barn. Phoenix's chest heaved, and after a moment, he obeyed, stepping back. "I can appreciate the audacity, Blackwell, but I will not stand for it. You and I both are the same as we don't play games. I will not threaten you, coerce you, or beat it out of you. You have one chance to tell me what I need to know about breaking the curse before I take you to the Order. Pruitt is aware someone broke into the Sacred Sea chamber." He looked around the room at the Heathens. "We have no choice but to turn him in."

Beck cocked his head, surprised. "And his spirit element? You would sever it?"

"For the sake of the coven, yes. Pruitt wants the traitor, and we cannot admit Norse Woods' involvement and risk all of you. We can say Julian acted alone, which isn't far from the truth. We've survived this long without the Danvers bloodline. And, to be honest, I'm sick and tired of the

Blackwells. They have been a disgrace to our coven. I'm certain we can survive without Spirit. At least their shadow-blood wouldn't be able to take any more lives," he spat.

Beck rose to his feet. "It was Carrie, and you know that. It was never Julian who did all those things. We found balance when we burned her body at The Wicker Man. You cannot condemn him for those acts any longer."

"If you turn him over to the Order, we'll never get the answers," Phoenix added.

"My question is why Carrie would go through such lengths to use the Blackwells? Something tells me Julian knows more than he's leading on and cannot be trusted." Goody clasped his hands in front of him. "He has ten seconds to tell us what he knows. If he doesn't speak now, I'm sure it is something he planned to take to his grave." His formidable green eyes settled on mine. "Here's your chance, Julian. If you give me information that could help, I can use it in your favor and lessen your charges. Your ten seconds start now."

Tilting my head back, I closed my eyes.

"So ... are you ... the type ... of runner ... that doesn't ... talk?" Fallon *called out from behind me as I leaped over the dip in the earth. I turned, making sure she was following me as we ran through the woods to my cabin.*

"What do you want to talk about?" I called back with a smile, noticing her shortness of breath.

"For starters ..." she appeared beside me, and we fell into a rhythm, "free will versus fate."

"Wow, right *to the gut."*

I ducked under a branch and dipped around a bend as the debate sank in. At the academy, we'd discussed free will. One professor had posed the question of whether our free will had been manipulated by cause and effect and previous occurrences entirely out of our control. Begging the question, had I ever decided anything about my current life or was it all forced upon me by years and years of circumstance and gradual guidance? And if so, if outside forces influenced my every moment and decision, then did I ever really have free will to begin with as our belief stated? Did any of us? Was this very moment the result of rebellion? If I'd never been turned into a cursed monster, would I still be here, running in the woods with Fallon?

"Free will is a delusion from the moment we're born."

"How so?" Fallon was keeping up in her dress.

I ran faster. Challenged her. Pushed her limits.

"Our families, professors, the coven, the town, they all feed us bias information to lean one way instead of educating from all perspectives and allowing us to think for ourselves." I looked over, making sure she was keeping up as I clutched the books under my arm. "Answer me this, was it your free will to come to Weeping Hollow?"

"Yes," she answered in a keen cutting whisper.

I cocked my head. "Really?" I asked, incredulously. "Stop lying to yourself. You were manipulated, no? Pressured? Be honest, if you never received the letter, you would have never come. Even after having knowledge of Weeping Hollow. We would have never met. The seed was planted in your mailbox. How is that free will when a circumstance came that was beyond your control?"

Fallon's expression pinched together in thought while her body bobbed beside me. She shrugged. "I ... beg ... to differ."

I laughed. "How so?"

"Everyone told you to stay away, but you didn't. You went ... against ... the Order. And you still came for me. How ... is that ... not free will?"

"That's cute," I told her. "You thinking I have any sort of power."

Her eyes darted between me and the trees in our path. "What ... are ... you saying?"

"I'm saying, when it comes to you, I have no will. You have complete control over me. What's cute is that you are oblivious to it."

Silence fell so comfortably around us. Free will versus fate, my mind wondered, transporting back to long discussions with Beck around the fire. Beck's weakness was knowing what the future held, and it was a weakness because he was the only one to bear that burden. He'd told me once that fate could not be changed, but if I'd known of what lay ahead, the journey to the destination would be altered, and it would cause more harm than good. Beck only told me what I needed to know, when I needed to know it. His mind was in constant torment. Either way, fate may have turned me into this, but Fallon was my choice—my free will.

I refused to believe otherwise.

"So, fate," Fallon said, interrupting my thoughts.

I cut around a tree. "A justification."

"Julian," she groaned, "You don't believe in free will or fate?"

"Do you?" I asked, and her silence called upon my gaze. "If you believe in fate, Fallon, you're telling me that whatever may happen to you has been pre-determined and cannot be changed."

"You're confusing me."

I wanted to stop and face her, but we were almost there, and my eagerness to show her why I found such freedom in running was steadfast. "I'm giving you arguments from both sides, which is what you deserve, isn't it? What we all deserve? You have to decide what you believe in."

"What do you believe in?"

"I'm still trying to figure that out." I felt it coming, the strain in my legs, the ache in my chest. "How are you feeling over there?"

"Like … I'm … dying," she pushed out.

I cut my eye to her, seeing her hanging on by a thread. "Good, because it's coming."

"What's coming?"

"The living part." I pushed past her, ran faster.

I ran until my legs almost buckled. I ran until my sight became hazy. I filled my lungs with as much air as they could handle as I ran past the pain, unafraid of what was on the other side. Fallon ran beside me—my girl, both stubborn and relentless. And after a few minutes, we broke through to our second wind. I knew she felt it too when a smile stretched across her face.

"This is what I believe in."

Goody clapped his hands. "Times up, Blackwell."

Barefoot and bare-chested and in tattered slacks, I was escorted the two miles from Goody Plantation and through the tunnels to the Chambers. Every step of the Heathens was in solidified cadence, the heartbeat of their march echoing in the damp and cold tunnel as we walked in a single file line. I kept my eyes forward, thinking of the mistakes I'd made to get me here. Perhaps I could have been honest with Fallon from the beginning, told her I loved her, maybe realized I loved her *sooner*.

Woke up sooner. Found myself sooner. I didn't want to wait until my next lifetime. I wanted this one. We deserved this one too.

"We meet again, and so soon," Augustine Pruitt stated, hands clasped firmly in front of him as Clarence Goody took his seat, joining Viola

Cantini and Agatha at the table. "Clarence tells me you have acted alone in breaking into my chamber. Is this true?"

"I have—" I started to say when Clarence interrupted, "Yes, Norse Woods took no part in his schemes."

I cut my eyes to him.

"Now, Goody, let the man speak for himself," Viola insisted, gesturing for me to continue.

Clarence cleared his throat, and Agatha's expression remained stoic, eyes unblinking.

"Yes, I've acted alone to retrieve the books from a place they do not belong, as they belong in the bibliotheca. May I ask what you were doing with the Book of Danvers and Blackwell? My family's book?" Pruitt's eyes widened, and Viola looked to Pruitt. "What use is my family book to you, and why can't I have access to it?"

"I was told it was only the Cantini book," Viola asked Pruitt in a whisper.

"It was two Norse Woods' books and yours," I answered for him honestly.

"It doesn't matter. You trespassed into our chamber," Pruitt snapped.

"With the Morgan girl," Clarence added, and my chest tightened.

I glanced back to see Zephyr, Phoenix, and Beck standing at the far wall, backs straight and eyes cold.

"Yes, Fallon Grimaldi was with me," I returned my gaze and swallowed the dryness in my throat. I didn't want Fallon to be involved, and now she was. "I forced her to join me. I needed someone to take the blame. It seems my plan didn't play out so well."

"No, it certainly did not. The truth always comes to light," Clarence stated.

I squared my shoulders. "Except one. I still don't know what you wanted with the Book of Blackwell or the Book of Danvers."

"Pruitt?" Viola asked him, the keeper of secrets, the demander of truths.

Augustine Pruitt sucked on his teeth before saying, "I didn't take their damn books."

"Someone did," Agatha pointed out. "Someone who has access to your chamber. A house guest perhaps? Someone who has been staying with you?"

"Are you insinuating that Carrie Driscoll stole books from the bibliotheca?" Pruitt asked, but it came out as a statement. "Carrie is innocent—"

"We will discuss Carrie later," Viola cut in, knowingly. "This meeting is about you, Julian Blackwell. Why would you risk your life over a few books?"

"Risk my life? With all due respect, don't play down what is right in front of you. It's obvious, isn't it? After everything my coven has endured, the lives we lost, Beck's mother, Phoenix's parents, little Johnny, your wife, Clarence! We cannot go on like this! If only you understood what it has done to us. I have no doubt any one of you in Sacred Sea would have done the same," I said, trying to manage a steady voice. "Don't be so surprised at how far any of us are willing to go to save our coven."

Clarence cast his eyes away.

"The facts remain," Pruitt stated. "We can no longer trust a rogue and cursed Heathen. I gave you an opportunity, welcomed you into my home, and you have only shown your true character. Who knows what you will do next?"

"Norse Woods can't trust him either," Clarence muttered.

Viola nodded. "I agree."

Agatha's eyes widened, frightened with the direction of where my fate was heading. "But what if he *can* break the curse? What if he has found the answers? If we can break the curse, the town won't live in fear of them any longer. No more lives would be endangered." She turned to Mina Mae, who had been seated quietly in the corner as always, desperately searching for any last chance of hope to save me. "The flatlanders would be safe—"

"Agatha—" I tried to say, but she cut me off.

"Augustine, listen to me. Give us a little more time. Julian can do this. I know he can—"

"Agatha!" I ordered again, trying to stop her from making a fool of herself.

She ignored me, adamant. "Everyone has suffered, not just Norse Woods. Sacred Sea has lost people. Flatlanders have died. This curse has put a black cloud over our heads since the beginning! Please, we need more—"

"*MOM!*" I shouted, silencing her as a tear slipped from my eye.

And the room went silent as well. Glances exchanged, and I turned my head for a moment to contain myself. Even though I had all the answers to break the curse, I would never let anyone hurt Fallon. Agatha was only prolonging the inevitable, and though I couldn't stand to see her like this, filled with so much hope, I was in love with the moon child. Enough to sacrifice myself before I let anything happened to her.

Pruitt cleared his throat, disrupting the awkward emotions filling the room. "If Julian breaks the curse, he is free, but we will not allow him to roam freely within the town."

"No," Agatha whispered in a shaky breath, her hand trembling as it reached for her chest. Pruitt continued, "I'm sentencing Julian Jai Blackwell to The Wicker Man after seven days in the Wiccan Cell. If the curse is not broken within the next seven days, Julian Blackwell shall burn."

"*NO!*" Agatha wailed out a harrowing cry, one that pierced my chest when Pruitt slammed down his gavel.

As I walked out of the Chambers, the Heathen's remained aloof, trained beasts to withhold objection before the Order. I didn't blame my brothers for turning me in. We were wretched Heathens, after all. And all wretched things had a creator. The curse was ours—the only real monster existing inside all of us. In their eyes, I'd burnt our last hope to ash. Our freedom now at rest, lying at the bottom of our fire pit we'd spent so many nights together.

What was worse, I felt no remorse for what I'd done.

I knew this day would come.

IN THE PRISON CELL, THERE WAS NO SUN, NO MOON, NO STARS, NO SKY. There was no ocean, no woods. There was only me and my solitude. Dark, dreadful solitude. A waiting game. For the first hour, I'd walked along the wall of iron-like bars separating me from a former life that seemed centuries away. The bars contained a magic I couldn't get through. I knew because I'd tried, burned layers of my flesh in the process.

I'd spent my second hour finding sleep, but it would never come. There would be seven days of this. Sweet, deathlike solitude for seven days. My back hit the wall, and I slid to the ground...

Our chests heaved as we collapsed under the polar moon after our run, the cabin only feet away, the books we'd stolen at my side. For a while, we stared up at the stars inside the deep Norse Woods, the place where all the wild things were. I turned my head to Fallon, watching her chest rise and fall, her stomach dip, her lashes flutter, her mouth part.

"Do you think they know we're looking at them?" she asked, keeping her gaze in the sky. "You know, the stars?"

I couldn't stop staring at her. Her mind held a universe of questions, most of which she already had the answers to. It was unnerving and nostalgic at once, the way her unceasing willfulness spoke to mine. If I didn't know better, I'd say she'd even question the significance of my black, rotten heart even after ripping it out of my chest and showing it to her, proving it was a useless thing.

"I think the stars are probably asking themselves the same question," I told her, tapping my fingers along her wrist, feeling her pulse kick.

"What do you mean?"

"You believe you're gazing at the stars, when, in all reality, the entire galaxy is gazing at you." I squeezed her hand, unsure of why I couldn't just say I loved her. Why I couldn't tell her something so real and true. I'd never been good at anything, but I'd always been good with her in my own, strange way. Fallon's blush crawled from her cheeks down to her chest. It was a sight to see, especially knowing it was I who could inflict that kind of reaction. "How was that feeling, Fallon?"

"Liberating." She rolled over and threw herself on top of me. "What was that?"

"A second wind. The reason I run. One of the few moments we experience when our body rejects what our mind is thinking, proving it wrong. A phenomenon that doesn't happen very often, and one that comes when you least expect it. It's one of those unexplainable feelings that you have to experience for yourself. Proof that we are so much stronger than we believe."

FALLON
chapter forty eight

I F TEARS COULD TALK, I WONDERED THE WORDS THEY WOULD FORM. Maybe a certain name they would spell across his hallway floor.

I didn't know how long I'd been lying here. At one point, I'd forced myself to stop crying, seeing if by holding back my tears, my heart wouldn't know it was breaking. It was no use. I was a lost cause, clutching a book close to my chest as the sun descended into the woods through the window.

A brief sense of serenity had gripped me in sweet, sporadic moments of sleep. Julian was there too. Because he was always everywhere and nowhere … And I hated him for it, for what he did to me. For what he did to us. For not fighting harder.

Where could they have taken him? What could they have done with him? Nothing made sense, and I couldn't understand why his friends—the only three people who were supposed to understand—beat him while he was naked on his bedroom floor. It broke my fucking heart, and there was nothing I could do.

I found myself crazy—*maddened*—screaming, crying, shaking then utterly still. Highs and lows and hollows, again, on repeat, all for him. All for a human who couldn't learn to love himself the way I loved him. One who couldn't fight back at all.

It took everything—*everything*—not to rip out every page from the spine of this book he left with me, and instead, I pitched it across the cabin against a wall. I gripped my hair. He didn't fight. And now I was left fighting with myself enough for the both of us. All he had done was steal books, though was it worth taking him like that? Would they take his *life* too? The unknowns were slowly killing me. I knew nothing anymore. Then after another insane spell, I fell into stillness once again.

Time had passed, and the front door to the cabin creaked open.

I didn't bother lifting my head to look.

The footsteps grew nearer, louder.

A hand lay on my shoulder.

"Fallon, what are you doing here?" The voice did not belong to Julian. I no longer cared who it belonged to or what they would do to me. Whoever it was circled me, crouched down. My gaze stayed paralyzed on the same spot where the wall used to be. Only faded denim now. "Why don't you let me take you home?"

"And where is that? Home?" I whispered, recognizing that it was Jonah. There was a long stretch of silence, a big aching void in the air. I curled deeper into the hardwood floors, if that were at all possible. Jonah rubbed my arm, and I yanked it away. "I want to be here for when he comes back."

"Julian's not coming back," he said, and his words sliced into me. I squeezed my eyes shut, forcing my tears not to believe it. I squeezed my heart, rejecting my heart to receive it. I squeezed my mind, wanting to forget it. "He's in the cell. In the tunnels."

"Then I suppose we are both imprisoned in this pain. Good. He deserves it." I didn't mean it, but I couldn't contain my anger either. Julian could have fought against them. At least tried. If not for himself, at least for me.

"Then you would also be pleased to know he will be sentenced to The Wicker Man in seven days. If you honestly mean that, you will come with me and let me take you home so you can be safe. It's the first day of Samhain and a full moon tonight. You never know what kind of mischief the flatlanders have in store." He paused, gathering a breath. "Then you can say your goodbyes to the town's *monster* when the time comes. He'll want to see you." *Monster.* He'd said it with such distaste as if to test my adoration, to get a rise out of me.

And I whispered, "All men are monsters in some way or another." I dragged my gaze to his and narrowed my eyes. "If Julian wants to see me, he'll have to either break out of that cell or haunt me. And if he doesn't get out, and you happen to see him, tell him I said he's nothing but a bitch-bitch." I lowered my gaze. "You'll have to say bitch twice because he's being extra weak."

Jonah waited for quite some time, and without movement from me, he expelled a heavy sigh, slapped his palms against his thighs, and stood. My gaze returned to the same spot on the wooden wall. My heart rate seemed to return to normal, too, as if now that Jonah was gone, Julian was not in the cell. He was only hiding somewhere in the shadows where this town had put him—possibly running in the woods.

In the short distance, I heard the shuffling of a floorboard. Then a click. Then footfalls. A pause. And a door open. Then close.

Minutes ticked by, and the wind howled through the cracked window casement above the bed where we had slept less than twenty-four hours earlier, wrestling its way into the cabin, into my heart. A soft cry ebbed and flowed, intertwining with the coming night. A cry that wasn't my own. I sniffled, rolling my body onto my back then my side to face the sound. Julian's sheets were still disheveled just as we left them. The hinge of the window moaned as the casement swung slightly.

The cry continued, and I pulled myself onto my feet and walked with caution. It was Samhain, the one time during the entire year where the veil was the thinnest. My knees hit the edge of the mattress, and I crawled across the bed, peeking out the window, anticipating to see more than trees within the woods. But that was all there was, and a gust of wind raked through their branches, bending their tips. I clutched the seal of the window, feeling the ethereal cold trapped in this spot. I pulled my hand back, my nerves thundering.

And the cry came again.

Below the window, there was a bone-white ball of fur.

"*Casper*," I whispered. "Where have you been?"

Casper cried again, and a slice of life sparked inside me. "Hold on, I'm coming."

I shuffled off the bed, grabbed the molding around the door frame, and swung into the hallway to the back door. On my way, I paused, staring at the opened book Julian left with me. I bent down and scooped it up before slipping out into the cold behind the house.

One green eye and one blue eye stared at me from the ground beneath Julian's window. We locked eyes for a moment, and then Casper took off around the cabin. I was still wearing Julian's tee and a pair of his plaid pajama pants as my bare feet moved quickly through the woods, muddying the bottoms.

Casper darted south. I was a good fifteen feet behind him and could hear the rising wind whistle through the trees' branches as we swept through the woods.

It grew colder and colder, and my eyes stayed trained on the powdery-white form leaping over roots and ruts in the ground. I called out for Casper, but he didn't slow. He was on a mission. Possibly trying to tell me something or lead me somewhere.

It hadn't occurred to me until after some time that we were heading in the direction of the funeral home. In the distance, torches and candles blanketed the cemetery, townspeople dressed in all white, bathing in the soft yellow moonlight. Trees thinned out around me until canopies turned into the velvety night sky.

Tonight, it seemed as if all the stars had fallen from the sky and were dancing over the graveyard. They were here to celebrate the lives of loved ones stuck on the other side, possibly even be able to visit them on this night. The mere beauty lit a fire inside my chest, and I slowed to a half jog, half walk.

Casper meowed in front of me, steering me to the corner beside the building where it was dark and empty. He circled in place then sat beside a headstone that was alone in front of a beech tree. Branches loomed over me, and my gaze settled on the carved rock that read:

FREYA DELIA GRIMALDI MORGAN

"THE LONE LUNA"

JULY 10th 1968- JULY 1st 1996

BELOVED MOTHER, WIFE, FRIEND

& my moon

My moon seemed as if it were carved after the fact.

And my eyes glossed over, but I couldn't blink the tears away. They froze there, in my eyes, blurring the headstone, distorting the words. I was cold but not shivering. I could hear the townspeople's hushed voices in the distance, but nothing seemed to sink in. It felt wrong to be standing here, at her grave. She'd died giving me life, and all I'd brought her was death.

"I've been waiting a long time to meet you, Fallon."

The voice was familiar and like a song in the wind. Coming from the shadow, and beside the tree, stood the woman from a picture I'd seen before. Her hair was twisted masses of white with eyes like pale sapphires. I recognized her face, and not from a picture, but a mirror.

Small differences. My hair was straight, hers wavy. My nose was smaller, pert. Same lips. But it was as if I already knew her, the instant recollection like a dreamy pastime. I was nervous, yet my nerves settled as if remembering where to lay their heads.

My mother was here, standing in front of me. My eyes blinked, and the tears were warm as they slipped down my cheeks.

"Oh, baby, please don't cry."

She said *baby*, and I shook my head as tears tumbled, one chasing the other. For twenty-four years, I longed to hear my mother's voice call out to me with *any* given name. I'd imagined what it would sound like. If I had the kind of mother who would raise her voice when she was mad, sing me to sleep, whisper stories like Marietta used to do, had a musical melody in her laugh. Oh, how I envied all those who had a mom at all, who I'd overhear complain about groundings and overprotectiveness and rules and curfews. I'd stood on the sidelines, wishing to trade places with them. Yearning for someone to ground me, to shelter me, to *yell* at me.

I killed her, and she was calling me *baby*.

If I wasn't frozen in place, I feared I'd fall. But she kept her chin up and held my gaze though we both had tears in our eyes.

"I'm so sorry," I cried as she walked nearer.

"It's not your fault, Fallon. None of this is your fault."

"You died because of me."

She smiled. "You have it all wrong. I died so you could live."

"I don't understand." Another wave of tears washed over my face, and I didn't want to wipe my eyes, afraid it would wipe away the vision of her. "Gramps died, and it was all my fault," I told her in case she didn't already know. "I couldn't help him. I failed him. And Dad's dead too. Marietta's dead, you're dead. And now… Julian … and I love him. I love him so much that it hurts … and maybe it's because of me. Because death surrounds *me*."

"But that is why I'm here. You must listen to me, Fallon. The birthmark on your skin links you to a bloodline of the moonchildren, a type of witch who originally found power through love and misery. It's your duty now to keep our magic alive."

"Magic? I have no magic." I shook my head, hearing the same story and still unable to believe it. "They tried. Dad's coven tried to pull it out of me and force me to become one of them. They tried! I've been bullied and betrayed and lied to, and no matter how far they push me, there was nothing I could do to stop them. There's nothing. No magic. I can't do anything. I'm just a girl."

"You are not *just* a girl. And if no one can see that, be your own lover. Moonchildren were never meant to be in a coven because we are our own breed," she tsked, "stubborn and wild and unchained. Tell me I'm wrong, Fallon. Tell me you have no interest in guiding the spirits who seek you or wander under the moon's phases when I know you do. Tell me you're not insecure yet love intensely because when we love, it's rare. But your heart is a wild beast all on its own. A love so fierce and a hate so raw, which is your curse, moonchild. You're not just a girl, but if you don't rise up and tell them who it is you are, they will do it for you."

"The Lone Luna," I whispered, staring at her.

She understood how it was to be like me. I had so many questions, but she could leave at any moment, and there was not enough time. There had to be a way to break Julian free, and maybe she had all the answers.

I took a step forward with anxiety rising in my chest. "They took Julian, and he'll die if I can't do anything to stop it."

She took a step back and grasped the tree. "There's something else I came here to tell you."

"Then tell me. If it's about Julian, I need to know."

"The Curse of the Hollow Heathens is passed on through our bloodline. As long as we're living, so is their curse. If anything happens to you before you have a child, their curse will end, but so will our magic. It is your responsibility to make sure you stay alive. You cannot trust anyone."

"I *can* trust him," I assured her. "He loves me, I know he does."

"Of course, he loves you. Each and every time," she whispered, her spirit beginning to falter, fade. Her words weren't making sense as if she was speaking to herself. "I don't have much time, but remember, Fallon, he may love you, but he will never choose you. He will always choose the coven. Let him go, baby. You must choose yourself. When you find your magic, protect it and pass it on to your daughter as I did. One day, it will be needed." The tree appeared behind her, and her spirit was slipping with the nighttime breeze.

"You're wrong," I told her, panic bubbling inside of me.

"You'll do what is right, I know you will," her voice turned into a whisper, and I forced my feet forward to wrap my arms around her, to keep her longer, to convince her. "I love you, Fallon."

Then she was gone, her afterword like mist in her wake as I clasped onto air, my arms holding nothing. I stumbled forward until my palms hit the tree, breaking my fall. I whipped my head to my left, to my right, behind me, searching for her. But she was gone, and she wasn't coming back.

Casper meowed, arching his spine and rubbing against my leg, letting me know he was still here. I wrapped my arms around my waist with Julian's book tucked inside, wishing her visit would have given me more answers than questions.

Freya couldn't know Julian as I knew him. When I'd needed words of comfort and support, my mother only told me the same things as the rest of the town.

This was why Carrie Driscoll wanted me dead. She wanted to break the Heathens' curse. And she was trying to use Julian to kill me. The cold was stinging me everywhere, but my insides were numb to the sensations. I kept my head down, staring at the graves my feet passed as I walked through the cemetery, replaying the last few days. Julian knew this and it was why he had acted alone without the other Heathens. Julian did know nicole fiorina

how to break the curse, and he'd done all this to make sure no one else did.

Julian was trying to protect me.

I didn't know whether to walk back to Julian's or Gramps'. Without a sense of direction, I stumbled across a bench in the cemetery and lay my head. Soft glows from candles and torches swayed in the distance, the town finding spots and laying out blankets to spend the night in the cemetery to be rejoined with their loved ones.

Julian Blackwell was in a cell. He went against everyone to protect me.

"Oh, Fallon," a familiar voice filled the cold air. "You're shivering," it said. I knew there was a hand caressing my skin, but I made no effort to move. "You'll get yourself sick if you stay out here all night without a coat."

"He's an asshole," I think I cried out, and I only knew I was crying again because I tasted the salt upon my lips. I was on my feet now, staring into soft brown eyes. "I hate him, Kioni. I want to kill him myself for this. Who does he think he is? Thinking he could be some kind of hero?" Air pushed out between my lips, and I shook my head, "So that's what this is?"—I nodded, trying to sort through my thoughts—"He thinks he can die and leave me like *this*. He's selfish, and I won't have it. And she's wrong, you know." I looked at Kioni, who had her fingers clutching my arm, pulling me to a car.

"Who's wrong?"

I huffed. "My *mother*." Kioni's brows spiked. "That's right, I talked to the *Lone Luna*. Not all it's cracked up to be either."

"You're talking nonsense right now. You don't mean that."

"I mean every word." I turned and screamed into the air. "You hear that, *Mother*? You don't know anything!"

"Fallon, you've officially lost your mind, now get in the car." She opened the door and may as well have pushed me into the passenger seat. Then she shut me inside.

It seemed like forever in this stagnant silence until the driver's side door opened, and Kioni slid into the driver seat beside me. She rubbed her hands together and blew hot air into her palms. "Okay, now let's just hope I don't kill us on the way to Benny's."

"What are you doing here, anyway?" I asked, digging my fingers into the book and looking out through the windshield, but images of Julian being locked and alone inside the tunnels consumed my mind.

"Because, unfortunately for me right now, I'm your keeper, and I have to make sure you don't do anything stupid."

My laugh was empty. "*Of course*, you are."

KIONI FACED ME AS WE LAY THERE IN THE DARK IN MY BEDROOM. SHE hadn't left my side. Even forced me to stand inside the bathroom with her. I hadn't changed out of Julian's clothes. I hadn't set the book down. Casper had returned to the house and curled into a ball atop the blanket over my feet. Kioni's eyes were closed, but I knew she was awake. "I have to die for the curse to be broken?" I asked aloud. "That's what Freya told me. That the only way to break the curse for the Hollow Heathens is for me to die."

"It's true," Kioni whispered, not opening her eyes. "If Norse Woods finds out, they will kill you. If Sacred Sea finds out, they will use it against Norse Woods. Your dad, Marietta, Benny, me, one of us would have eventually told you before you had your first child. But then everyone started dying ... There's something about knowing the truth that could be dangerous before then."

"A burden."

"Exactly."

"I wouldn't want my baby to have to go through this."

"Exactly," Kioni said again. "Then maybe you would have avoided getting pregnant or falling in love period. Or on the flip side, you could have lived here and found a hatred toward Norse Woods for something and told Sacred Sea the secret. It could have worked either way, and there is no reason for the moon girl to know until she's pregnant. That way, every decision you made was because you wanted to make it. Not because of the curse."

"The books Julian stole ... they were in Sacred Sea possession. You think they knew this whole time?"

A sigh fell from her lips. "No, even the books are cryptic. The Cantinis know, yes, but they are the Keepers of Secrets. Sacred Sea should have never had the books to begin with, and Viola Cantini would never reveal a secret to anyone, not even her coven."

"So, Julian's in a cell because he stole books from a coven who should have never had them in the first place."

"Julian's in a cell because he betrayed his coven and broke into the Sacred Sea chamber. It's a breach in the peace treaty between the two covens. Julian has lost all integrity. He's a cursed Hollow Heathen, and in order for Norse Woods to keep credibility, Julian has to be sacrificed."

"A human in exchange for breaking and entering is not fair."

Her eyes sprang open. "In this town, it is."

I shifted closer to Kioni, slid my eyes between hers. "Tell me the truth. Tell me, how do I save him?"

For a moment, Kioni stayed silent as if to choose her words carefully. Then, "You can't. The only way to save Julian is by some kind of miracle, and miracles don't happen in Weeping Hollow."

"A miracle, something that's never been done," I whispered, locking eyes on her with my hollow heart shaking inside my chest.

Breaking the curse has never been done before. It was the only way to end the cycle once and for all. I had to sacrifice myself. It was risky, but if Julian died, I had nothing left to lose. Kioni's eyes hardened as if to recognize my revelation.

BUT MY HEART MADE UP ITS *mind.*

JULIAN
chapter forty nine

D ID YOU BRING IT?" I ASKED, CLIMBING TO MY FEET AND approaching the prison bars. I gripped them, my impatient gaze frisking Jonah for the Book of Blackwell. The magic coating the bars sizzled my flesh, and I yanked them back, seeing the poison eating another layer from my skin.

"*Ah shit,*" I hissed, then dug my teeth into my lip to fight the burn.

I glanced at my palms, blisters already forming.

"It's only an herb. Heathen up," Jonah said, fanning my family book in front of him. "It was right where you said it was." He passed the book through the bars to me. "There was something else inside your cabin I wasn't expecting."

My body tensed in a hopeful grip. "Fallon? Is she okay?"

Jonah's face turned somber, and he averted his eyes. "She'll be fine."

I fell back against the wall and collapsed to the floor. For hours, I'd depleted all magic inside me, waited for it to restore, and used it up again to get back to her. I did this over and over and my legs could hardly bend at the knee anymore. My head couldn't lift on its own. I was surprised I could stand at all once Jonah arrived, but now my body was being reminded.

"Don't lie to me. I know her as I know myself. I'm afraid of what she might do if she finds out the truth. At least death will take me, but her? I know her, Jonah. She'll do something as stupid and desperate as I did." I looked down at the book in my hands, wishing I were holding Fallon instead. "I thought I had one more day with her. The things I would do for one more day."

"She wanted me to tell you that you're a bitch-bitch," Jonah muttered.

My head fell back against the wall, a small laugh pushed through my misery. "A bitch-bitch?" I shook my head, knowing Fallon rarely cursed. If she was cursing, she was either angry, frustrated, or utterly helpless. "You have to be a keeper to her as you were to me. She's a Blackwell, Jonah. She's the one I committed myself to, so you have no choice but to protect her now." I slid my gaze to Jonah, who was crouching down to level with my eyes with the hexed bars between us. "If you don't … my death will take us both, I know it. Then all this will be for nothing."

"Are you ready to die?"

I shook my head. "No." And the word shook the thing in my chest. There was not another stable breath after as they were all broken now. Each one of them. All I could do was hang my head, no longer having the energy to try and lift it. I cut my eyes to Jonah with emotion bottling in my throat. I couldn't look him in the eye, so my gaze rested on the ring on his finger that was hanging off his knee. "I thought I was, but I'm not ready to die. I want to live. But only if it means living with her." I inhaled in a shaky breath and used all my strength to keep my body upright. "When will she come see me?"

"She's not."

I squeezed my eyes shut. "She's not coming," I repeated, but the words were not registering.

"No, she says if you want to see her, you'll have to go to her."

"Why is she so fucking stubborn?" My head bobbed, no will to yell. "And she knows I'm locked in here? I do all this for her, and she can't say goodbye?" Jonah didn't respond. It went silent. My fingers dug into the Book of Blackwell. All the things I should have said swirled in my mind. "I didn't even tell her—" I stopped there and pinched my eyes shut.

"Then I guess your soul will have to live with—" he paused and sucked in a breath. "Look, Julian. I'm sorry I couldn't protect you the way I should have. I'm sorry I couldn't do more for your family."

"Stop. You did good. You did everything in you power. None of this is your fault. I would have fought against you every step of the way on this."

"I know. But I still wanted to tell you that it was a wild ride. You definitely kept me on my toes. Without another Blackwell, I don't know what this means for the St. Christophers. I don't want to end up like Ocean." He laughed a nervous laugh.

I side-eyed him. "Live your life for you for once. Find a girl."

"A girl in this town?" He sighed and patted his knees before standing. "You have three more days, Julian Jai. At the next end of watch, I'll make a visit so we can say our goodbyes. Read your family book, find reprieve for your soul." He hung back for a few more beats, unsaid words hanging in the air between us.

Then his footfalls echoed inside the tunnels, and I watched his boots as he walked away, promising myself to inform Jonah of Stone Danvers, and where he could find him, before I would be burned. Without me, the coven would need Stone. That was, if he was still alive.

I'D BEEN TORTURED BEFORE—NUMEROUS TIMES—BUT NOTHING HAD prepared me for what I'd been experiencing these past four days. When I was at the academy, I'd read about a man who lost his arm at sea. It had tangled with the pot warp while lobstering, cutting off blood circulation for far too long. His arm had to be amputated. Years had gone by without his arm, and still, he felt the presence of the missing limb. He could even feel pain in the arm that was no longer there.

The *Phantom Limb Phenomenon*. Another unexplainable mystery.

And now I understood what it felt like to feel something that was no longer here. The sensations my body remembered, the pain it now endured even though parts of me were missing. Perhaps they were missing before her too. And the phantom of her touch would always be there, haunting my soul.

I had to force my eyes to stay open to read. Pages flipped between my fingers as I spent my last days losing myself inside the Book of Blackwell. I read about the journey from their old home. The five Heathens were once men the coven respected, loved, looked up to. Honored. The five carried their coven through bitter winters, refusing to stop or quit until safety was found. They'd sacrificed food so the others could eat. They carried those who were weak, made cots for the dead, leaving no one behind. The five had to swallow their emotions for the sake of the others because it was the rest of the coven who depended on them, looked to *them* for strength.

I'd read, through the eyes of Horace Blackwell, and how he'd discovered the land before it had become Weeping Hollow. He'd written about the Order, and how it came to be on the year's coldest night. He'd written about the first time he cried when the first baby of Weeping Hollow was born. Bellamy Blackwell. His son.

Woven in every page, in every line, I read of nothing but unconditional love and the lengths he'd gone for his son to protect him and the coven. I didn't stop reading, discovering how our coven used to be, the vision I'd always imagined it should have been.

Eventually, the book's narrative had changed from Horace to Bellamy, and Bellamy reminded me much of myself. His defiance, his loyalty, his misunderstood love for the woods. It was as if I were reading myself, and I couldn't find the will to stop.

I became immersed in the story of Bellamy and Sirius, and how their relationship unfolded. The secrecy, the unrequited acceptance by no other, but the very thing they had found in each other. I recognized the mistakes they had made, their folly, their desperation.

But it wasn't until after Sirius died, I came upon Bellamy Blackwell's last journal entry when everything made sense. It wasn't until then that everything clicked. I didn't have to read the rest of the book to know what I had to do. What I needed to do. What Bellamy should have done.

The revelation hit me like a storm.

After closing the book, I sat there in a blank daze, my eyes bouncing back and forth as I tried to comprehend it all. My heart hammered inside my chest. My muscles were flexing under my skin, wanting to run. The burning need to scream lodged in all my hollow places—my lungs, my chest, my throat, my head.

I was wrong all along. Clarice Danvers was wrong. Everyone was wrong.

I had the answer, and it was here, in the Book of Blackwell the entire time. Bellamy had always known, but no one would have been able to figure it out without experiencing a love like ours for themselves—

"Julian!" My name tumbled through the tunnels, and I snapped my gaze to the sound, seeing Kioni running toward my cell. Her eyes were big and wild and scared. "Julian!" She was out of breath, clutching her side.

The Book of Blackwell fell from my lap as I jumped to my feet. A guard grabbed her by the arm and began pulling her away.

"Kioni, what happened?" I shouted, every cell in my blood turning into a pulse and slamming inside me as I waited for a reply. *Please, do not let it be Fallon.* "Answer me!"

"I woke up this morning, and she was gone. *She's gone, Julian!* She knows. *She knows about everything.* I can't find her anywhere. You have to find her," she cried out, thrashing against the guards to break free. *"Julian, you have to … or she's … to break the curse!"* Her screams muffled, and panic enveloped me when another one of her pleas echoed throughout the tunnel. *"HURRY … FALLON IS GOING TO DIE!"*

My hands were gripping the poisonous bars, but I couldn't feel the burn. My entire body was on fire by each one of Kioni's blood-curdling cries. Fallon knew, and a thunder ruptured inside me. Fallon knew everything, and a scream rolled throughout the tunnels in a deafening tidal wave.

Fallon was going to break the curse all on her own.

My chest burned, and my scream's force took Kioni and the guard to the ground, knocking them out. It was as if I'd gotten hit by lightning, and the lightning had come from within me—an amplified power bursting from my chest.

And it all happened so fast.

My second wind had come.

My body vibrated, a fierce hum inside this silver pocket of space I'd created.

With my body locked inside this halted time, my clenched fists moved through the bars. On the inside, my body felt like a million frayed wires that had come alive, a beam of silver light twisting, turning, and jumping with the most intense sensations. But on the outside, it was as if I was wearing my soul as my skin, able to pass through anything.

Taking a step forward, I passed through the bars as the tunnels still pulsed in my ear-splitting scream. I couldn't hear it, but I felt the buzzing of it all around me, the drawn-out boom inside me.

I moved so strangely on a different wavelength than the rest of the world.

And I took off running, knowing exactly where my girl was, and what she was about to do.

I JUST HOPED I COULD GET TO HER IN *TIME.*

the dawn of
JULIAN

When a great love dies, a billion hearts stall. It amazes me that every single one of those hearts live within my own. It feels as if I have an endless number of lifetimes pressed into every pulse. Every second without her, an excruciating reminder. Some may say I have even become melodramatic in my misery. However, this is my misery and my misery alone. How dare anyone tell me the extent of my pain. How I should feel or continue to go on, when going on feels like torture to me. Any thoughts you spend on your beloved, for I spend a thousand times more on mine. Tell me I am wrong, and I will offer my chest for you to rip my heart from my bones so you can see. While you have it, go on and cut into it, grant me the freedom of this heartache. I dare you. Then be gone with your self-righteous notions about how I should feel during a time I wish to feel nothing.

Half of me has filled with hatred toward my father. I can hardly stand to look at him, and I cannot leave either, as I have tried. The other half of me is gone. Nothing is there anymore. All I can do is waste my sleepless nights lying at her grave, where her ashes are all that remain. From dusk to dawn, I am awake and talking to the moon like a madman. And my days, I am the very monster her death has made me become.

My love for her is unconditional, and I will hold on to it for as long as I can so that the darkness cannot take me completely, but I feel as if I am losing myself. I am slipping into the comfort of the shadows and the blackest depths of the earth. Nothing can warm me, not even the sun. The regret I live with is for not trying harder, not fighting harder. Oh, if I could go back in time and choose her over everything. If I could reverse time, I would have seen our love from an artist's point of view as I should have all along.

Father says her last words were of a curse, and to that, I say, I am already cursed. I am cursed for the rest of my days because I should have broken every chain to get to her. I should have burned with her at her side. To know she died believing I have given up on us or have chosen a different path haunts me. And it will only continue to do so past this lifetime and in every single one hereafter. If only she knew, the entire world could not love as much in an eternity as I love her in a day.

It is deep down inside me where the curse lives. I can feel it woven in with my shadow-blood. It will live there and pass along to every son, I am sure. The only way to rid us of our curse is to choose love, yet how can it be when my love is not here? You are not given love, for it is not a right. Love is a privilege, and what have any of us done to deserve it? It is my hope the curse is as real as my pain, and it inflicts on every Heathen hereafter, and I want no one to escape it.

They are of formidable beauty, both love and death. Within them lies their immortality. Therefore, there will be no cure for the curse, none that a loveless creature can see. They do not know that the moon in my black sky has died all alone, and the only way was for us to live as one, or decease together.

They do not know that the cure also lies within me.

JULIAN
chapter fifty

TWENTY FEET AWAY, FALLON WAS STANDING THERE, facing the sunrise at the cliff's edge, looking at it differently than all the other times I'd seen her look at it. And the sun was rising differently this morning too. Its pale purple and pink shades spilled into the sky and bathed us in its colors.

In Weeping Hollow, no two sunrises were the same. No two sunsets either. But on this morning, there seemed to be more than one sunrise in the same sky. A lavender and pink one above us, and then just below it, another with a heartbeat—one that was alive, breathing, and bleeding across the horizon, covering the town in its bloodshed. The sky was so big and forever changing that sometimes it was hard to believe it wasn't a painting.

And then there was Fallon. My only sunrise. I stood behind her, off to the side, looking at her the same way she was looking at the sky. White hair. Pearly skin. Dusty pink lips. The winter season in her eyes. She was cold-blooded, but, *my gods*, she was a nocturnal rainbow.

Above us, gulls circled, searching for scraps. Around us, the wind whistled in our ears. I kept my attention on her, my throat thick with fear, and my heart going a million miles per second.

Fallon took a step forward, and my muscles flexed under my skin.

I took a step forward, too, calling out to stop her. "A bitch-bitch?" I tried to keep my nerves at bay, this intruding emotion building in my chest.

Fallon whipped around, her eyes wide. I wanted to take another step to her, but I didn't want to press her further.

Keeping our twenty-foot separation between us, I continued, "That's what you were going to leave me with? Do you realize the lengths I've gone to get here? I went against my coven and broke into Sacred Sea's chamber. I was fucking de-humanized. Then I had to be locked in a cell for six days to find out you couldn't just let it go, could you?"

Fallon stood frozen at the edge of the cliff. Seconds stretched out with the sound of the waves crashing against rock at the bottom. I wanted to run to her, but I was so afraid of what she would do.

Instead, I held my arms up at my sides. "If I knew it was going to come to this, I would have just told you everything to avoid all the shit I've been through. We could have ended up here together days ago, Fallon!" I was screaming now, my chest aching at the thought of her willing to sacrifice herself for *me*—a *monster*.

And she still hadn't moved. She just stood there, staring at me as her white hair blew around her. I dropped my arms, gripped my sides, and gathered a breath. I ran my agitated fingers through my hair, unable to think straight, trying to hold back these tears threatening to explode. All my senses were on fire, and I didn't know how much more I could bear.

I pointed at her, taking another hesitant step forward. "You're the only thing I'm good at. And protecting you was the *one* thing I could do to show you—" I stopped, words caught in my throat. Saying them felt like a goodbye. I never wanted to say goodbye. My hand dropped, my arm now hanging at my side. I was looking at her, terrified.

She was looking at me, still surprised I was here.

"To show me what?" she asked in a shaky whisper.

Our glances battled back and forth, until tears arose, and we found ourselves crying. "To show you that I *chose* you. That I fucking love *you!*" I snapped, a blur in my gaze as I latched on to her glassy eyes. My chest was heaving, feeling the end near, the pressure weighing heavier. I slapped the back of my hand with my other palm. "*My god*, Fallon, I'm in love with you. Always have been. And I'm certain that I loved you a thousand times before as I do now, and I hope to love you a thousand times again. That's it. That's all there is to it." I threw my hands up at my sides, taking another step forward. "Because that's the point of us, isn't it?"

"No, Julian, stay back." Her tear-streaked face shook back and forth.

I took another step forward. "You don't have to do this. It's not the way."

"Yes, I do," she cried, nodding and sniffling. "I have to end this. They're going to burn you tomorrow. And if this is not enough to save you before then, at least the curse will be broken, and the Heathens won't be seen as monsters any more. If I don't do this, the town will always live in fear. It will never end, Julian. Never. Not unless I do something about it, and after you're gone, I have nothing left to lose. Let me fix this. I have to fix this!"

Tears wouldn't stop falling from my eyes, but I was too scared to wipe them away. To think the moment I so much as blinked, she'd fall off the edge without me. I took another step forward, needing to be closer. "If you jump off that cliff, Fallon, I'm jumping with you."

Men and women of the town approached from behind, calling out to me, threatening me if I hurt her. They had no idea what she meant to me. They cursed me, called me names, and demanded to take me to The Wicker Man *now*. I heard them all, and Fallon's terrified gaze darted from me to what was going on behind me. I shook my head, caught her attention, kept it with mine.

Neither one of us needed to explain ourselves. To anyone.

"Don't listen to them, Fallon. They're all liars, but we're not," I whispered, less than fifteen feet away from her.

Fallon's toes were at the edge of the cliff, her opened sweater being pulled with the harsh breeze. My muscles tensed. I either had to save her, or die with her. *Live as one or decease together*, Bellamy had said.

But how do I save her?

Fallon looked to me, and I saw the shift in her expression instantly.

The finality.

Then she tore her eyes from mine and looked down.

"I'll find you," she said, but I couldn't make sense of the things she was saying when my heart was beating out of my chest.

"Fallon, no," I threw my palms out in front of me, and she took a single step back. "Fallon, stop!" She lunged forward, bent her knees. *"NO!"*

She was jumping, and I was sprinting after her, not stopping until there was no ground beneath me and all of me was in the air. Then I was holding her, twisting with her in my arms until my back hit the hard surface of the ocean. All air knocked from my lungs. A fierce cold shocked me, an instant sting from my flesh to my marrow, freezing me still.

Everywhere, the waters of the Atlantic consumed me. And Fallon wasn't in my arms. My arms registered before my brain did.

Fallon wasn't in my arms.

FALLON

I FELT MYSELF DRIFTING, AND IT MADE ME FEEL *WEIGHTLESS*.

I was weightless, and all around me was black except for above me. At the surface, Julian was splashing and twisting in place under the sun, his legs kicking out from under him. As long as he was at the surface.

This dark and cold ocean was my funeral. My final resting place. And maybe because the curse would be broken, Julian would live. It was all I ever wanted as I was drifting, drifting, *drifting*.

The sun had these streaks that glinted off the surface of the water. They looked like stars from down here. I wondered if anyone knew the ocean had its own sky, one where Julian was. I was sure above was warmer than down here, because down here, the cold had already frozen me, but I was prepared this time. I didn't fight the cold when I wanted death to take me.

And death was so quiet, cold, and fierce, like Julian.

Then Julian flipped around and dipped under the waterline. His head shifted back and forth as he searched the bottom. That was when my calm heart stopped being calm. His wild and panicked eyes locked on mine, and he pushed his arms against the water, swimming down to me. I shook my head, pointing to the surface, trying to tell him to stop and leave me be.

I tried to move, sink faster, to put more distance between us. Julian gripped my shirt and yanked me up to him until he had me in his arms. I struggled against him, water bubbles exploding from my mouth. The sea slipped between my lips, filling my chest and lungs.

His eyes were strained and desperate as he fought against me, struggling to lift me from the depths before running out of oxygen. His fingers dug into my flesh to keep me one with him, but I pushed back against his chest.

Julian grasped the back of my head, and our desperate and defeated eyes met. His eyes said so many things at that moment. But once he knew I wasn't going to go with him, that I would fight him every second of the way, his eyes calmed, saying: *Okay, I'm not leaving you. We're going to die. Together.*

Then they said, *I love you, Fallon.*

I shook my head, begging for him to let me go and save himself. In a last-ditch effort as my body jerked for air, I tried to pry his body from mine. Julian refused to let go. He only held me tighter.

Then he slipped down his mask, and he pressed his mouth to mine, breathing all of his last breath of warm air into me.

Together, we were sinking, just like every other time we kissed.

He never stopped fighting.

The thought of it all changed something inside me.

Instead of slowing, it felt as if everything was reversing, heightening, pacing. My blood felt like beams of moonlight. A glacier rushed through my veins. Around me, it was no longer a black abyss but a soft-white glow lighting up the tinted sea. The bottom of the ocean stirred, creating a sandstorm on the floor. Shells, seaweed, and sand sifted up and clouded the waters. Julian's eyes sprang open and darted around. It wasn't him. It was all coming from me, and a fierce energy was humming inside me.

Something was happening to me. Something magical.

I pulled Julian closer, laid my palms against his chest, and I shoved him with every bit of strength I had until he rocketed up through the waters and broke through the surface above. The blur of his shadow was the last thing I saw.

Julian's muffled scream reached me from the surface.

I *did* have magic inside me, and it saved him.

I was going to break the curse, and Julian was going to live long enough to make a change for his coven. What he'd always wanted.

Relief settled in my heart as I closed my eyes and surrendered to Death's gentle embrace.

JULIAN

SALTWATER STUNG MY EYES. ENDLESS WAVES CRASHED AGAINST MY FACE. My muscles were spent but my heart was still strong. I couldn't see anything as I dove back down, but an invisible force kept pulling me back. I screamed underwater, a fire in my chest. I couldn't see her!

Then the sandstorm settled.

The force snapped.

Swimming against the ocean was like swimming through mud. Pressure built in my ears the farther I descended. Though the salt was burning my eyes, I forced them open and waved my arms around to connect with her. I couldn't hear her heart beating anymore. I couldn't think. It was black down here, but I could see in the dark. And now, I could see her.

Fallon's eyes were closed. Her lips were blue. Her body swayed with the sea as if she were a part of it. My chest tightened, my lungs ached, telling me I didn't have any oxygen left. I grabbed her limp body and kicked off the ocean floor, lunging for the surface.

I will never stop fighting, Fallon. That was the point of us. Our love was a tenacious thing buried in deep, dark places. And I would *never* stop.

We were both onshore now. I could barely walk. I could barely see anything. I didn't know how I was able to get us to the beach, but I somehow did.

Fallon was in my arms, not breathing. Tears plummeted from my eyes. My hands shook, her white hair tangled in my fingers.

"No, no, no," I laid her on the sand and crawled over her body as sand shuffled around me. I pressed my ear to her chest, hearing nothing. "No!"

It wasn't supposed to happen like this. I dropped Fallon's head back and pushed air into her lungs. I beat against her chest. *I was supposed to die with you. Come back!*

"Fallon," I cried, pumping my palms against her chest. My arms were locked. My soul, my heart, my screams were all desperate for her to come back to me. "Please, come back to me." I held her nose, and pushed air down her throat again. It was as if I'd left my body, watching myself from the outside, remembering this moment. As if we'd been here before.

"FALLON!" Take me with you.

People were trying to pull me away, ripping at my wet clothes from behind, and a monstrous scream barreled through my windpipe as I slammed my fist down against her chest one last time.

Then Fallon gasped.

She *gasped* and her heartbeat pounded in my ears at the same time a single *boom!* shook our souls. It was an echo. And an invisible, fierce wave slammed against my chest and took me in the air. My back hit the cliff. Then the echo rolled throughout Weeping Hollow like a bright beam of pearlescent light.

For a brief moment, it was as if our hearts had been restarted.

A quietness swept across the beach, not even the waves that were crashing made a sound. It was so calm, so peaceful.

As I looked back, the town's panicked eyes surrounded me, and there was a collection of gathered breaths. But all I wanted to see, hear, feel was Fallon. Instinct engaged, and I shuffled back through the sand, rolling her on to her side.

"Fallon, b-b-breathe," I said through shaking lips, pushing my palm up her spine as she spewed the wicked sea.

Fallon's chest heaved, and every muscle inside me collapsed with relief as I took her cold and trembling body into my arms. I dropped my head into her neck and squeezed my burning eyes together as my knees dug into the sand.

And I held her for a while, feeling her heartbeat tap against my fingers, her chest hitting mine, never wanting to let her go. She was alive. I was alive. We were here, together for the time being, and it was all that mattered.

She whispered my name, pulling away and taking my head into her hands. Fallon's gaze swept across my face before her eyes hit mine again. And the way she looked at me was as if *she* found *me*, and we didn't need to be lost again.

"Julian, you did it," she cried out, gripping the back of my head and cradling my head in her palm. Her hands were everywhere, touching all over my face. New tears rolled down her cheeks, and her smile was faint but real.

I shook my head, my eyes sliding between hers when it hit me.

My mask was gone, and she was looking at me, smiling.

I touched my cheeks and mouth. I pushed my hand down my face.

"No," I whispered with shock, unable to believe it.

Fallon's smile lit her up as she nodded.

"It can't be—"

"Yes!" she laughed, and a new wave of emotion roared through me, one that I could not control. I buried my face into her neck, and my tired body shook as I cried, clutching on to her wet clothes.

Fallon held my face and pulled me up until our mouths crashed.

As soon as my tongue hit hers, my entire being relaxed, feeling a weight of two centuries and countless deaths slide off me.

"*The curse is broken!*" someone shouted behind me, and the entire beach went up in a roar as Fallon and I lost ourselves to each other. "*The curse is fucking broken!*"

"You did it!"

"JULIAN!"

"What just happened?"

"The Hollow Heathens are free!"

The town surrounded us, but all I saw was her. My girl.

Fallon kissed my forehead, my cheek, my nose, my lips, my neck, until she dropped her face into my chest, her shoulders shaking as she found herself crying too. I held her tighter, unable to stop the dawn of my smile.

Bellamy was right. It took the both of us. It took never giving up on each other. It took our unwavering and unselfish love. It took fighting for her—saving her—to break the curse.

I didn't know what that meant for our coven going forward, but there was one thing I was certain of: we were together, and it was all I ever wanted. We had this lifetime and every single one hereafter.

Perhaps it was true, there were cold spots in the hearts of monsters that could not be touched without a death-defying love.

So, for a while, we held each other in the sand, in the way our stories were connected, our love, our pasts that made this moment possible, with all of Weeping Hollow around us.

And my head dropped back as the warm sun embraced my face for the

very FIRST TIME.

the moon & the
BLACK NIGHT

At 3:03 a.m. on a hot summer night, Fallon Grimaldi Morgan was born under a full Thunder Moon. Outside, a fierce storm howled, struck, and shook the small cottage.

And in the dark corner, a heart-splitting cry from the wooden bassinet filled the room. But these cries were not of Fallon as they were coming from another.

Hot rain blew in from the open window casements as Freya held out her arms for her daughter, Fallon.

"She isn't crying," alarm laced Freya's voice, her eyes panicked, "Why isn't she crying? Is she okay?"

"She's a Moonchild," Marietta whispered so Agatha Blackwell could not hear, admiring the birthmark before swaddling the infant in a blanket. Baby Fallon was carried to Freya and placed in her arms. Marietta sat beside the cot and pressed a cold rag to the mother's forehead. "Do not worry, your daughter is all right. Look at her, she is perfect." Marietta leaned over, looked into Freya's eyes, and whispered, "For as long as I am here, I will protect her. Now there is not much time." The screaming continued from the corner of the room, and Marietta's face pinched as she cut her gaze to the shadow where baby Julian Jai laid. "Agatha, please, do something for him!"

"I can't," Agatha said with defeat. "He screams and screams and screams. I'm so sorry. There is nothing I can ever do."

Freya gripped Marietta's hand, using every last bit of strength. "Promise me, you and Tobias will take her far away from here," she whispered, clutching her baby close to her chest. "Tell her the stories so she will always know who she is, but never bring her back. Promise me, you are my keeper, and now hers. You will *do this for me!"*

"The Cantini family agreed to help with our escape. They are waiting with Tobias at the grounds now. I promise everything will be all right," Marietta assured. From the corner of the room, Agatha rocked her son, but nothing would calm the cries. The storm was only worsening outside, the winds roaring, the thunder continuing to rattle the small cottage inside the hill. Marietta called Agatha over for a picture, but Agatha didn't know it would be her and Freya's last. So, Agatha lay her screaming baby once more in the bassinet before appearing at Freya's side.

The camera clicked! and afterward, Marietta noticed Freya's eyes rolling to the back of her head.

"What's happening?" Agatha asked. Marietta ignored her and rushed to Freya, scooping baby Fallon into her arms before Freya's heart gave out. "Oh, god, no! Marietta, do something! Quick!" Agatha cried out, clutching Freya's head into her hands. Marietta hurried, placing the newborn into the bassinet beside Julian, then returned to Freya.

A new wave of cries filled the room as Agatha performed heart compressions, trying to bring her best friend back. Marietta wept beside the cot, knowing the time had come, and there was no way to reverse it. Lightning struck outside the window, painting the sky in purple as rain pounded glass. The wind turned forceful, pushing the window open and slamming it back and forth against the wall. Chaos seemed to swirl inside the room, except not entirely.

During all the commotion, in the dark corner of the room where the bassinet stood, Julian Jai looked into the moonchild's bright eyes.

And, at last, his screaming fell silent.

the
END

ACKNOWLEDGMENTS

My daughter, Gracie. *Grace-face. Gracie-girl.* Thank you for always being my number one fan. Thank you for your excitement for Hollow Heathens. Thank you for our many nights sitting on the kitchen counters, drinking vanilla Coke & Root Beer, going over the plot, characters, covens, ghosts, & superstitions, etc., making the book what it is. Thank you for curling up next to me at night while we read chapters of the book to each other. Thank you for loving this book and inspiring me to build this world for you. I couldn't have done this one without you, baby. My love for you is an infinite sky, a deep blue thing. To the moon & past every galaxy!

To the readers, thank you for giving this book a chance, especially those who stepped outside their comfort zone and genre to do so. I'll always be grateful for you, your time, and getting lost inside these pages. If you ever have time, please contact me. I always love to hear what you think! ☺

To the NF Gang, I wish I could hug each one of you. We've been together for over a year now. Can you believe it? First with *Stay with Me*, and now the beginning of Tales of *Weeping Hollow*. I hope you all enjoyed what I've put together, and if it weren't for you guys making me smile during my stressful days, I couldn't have finished this. I'm serious. You all keep me motivated, grounded, and inspired to keep publishing. I love you all!

To Kassy, K. Dosal McLendon. Thank you for always being real with me. Thank you for your honesty with this story and falling in love with Julian. I've written you three love letters now in my acknowledgements. This will be the fourth. And still, you're support and friendship has only strengthened. Thank you for all your knowledge with Young Adult, and helping me convert this book for my daughter. You are my sister now. You are my family. I love you. Xoxo

Thank you, Shaley. You always know what to do and when to do it, and ALWAYS manage to get things done. Thank you for continuing to take care of the Street Team, posts, and always checking in on me and *trying* to keep me organized. (We both know it's a work-in-progress with me, lol). I love you, girl xoxo

Thank you, Giovanna, for always supporting, promoting, and loving my work. Thank you for loving these characters before ever reading about them. You trust me blindly, and I am so grateful. Thank you for all your amazing graphics and edits you do. You will always have a place in my heart!

Thank you, Christy L., for beta reading this one and catching things! I'm so grateful for your time and having you a part of *Hollow Heathens*.

Thank you, Nyla and Lisa, for proofreading Hollow Heathens. I know it was a difficult one, and I appreciate both your time and hard work.

Thank you, Surovi for illustrating this book, and bringing this story to life. I cannot wait to work with you more in the future. It's been a pleasure!

Michael *&* Christian, my husband *&* son. Thank you both for taking care of me. For listening to me complain, picking up my slack, and understanding my anxiety through Hollow Heathens.

Michael, as a Harry Potter fan, I hope you read this one. And if you do, and you don't like it, don't tell me. I love you. Xoxo.

Christian, thank you for always going back and forth to the fridge for me for a fresh, ice-cold Red Bull. I love you, bud.

Thank you, Mom. After everything we went through this year, you always put my sisters and me first before yourself. You are the strongest person I know, and you can get through anything. I love you, *&* I'll be by your side every step of the way. xoxo

Thank you, Auntie Sherri, for always supporting me and asking about my books. You are one of the most courageous and motivating woman I know, and I'm grateful to have you in my life, even more ... I get to call you Auntie. I'm one lucky girl. I love you *&* hope you enjoyed this one.

Thank you to the greatest inspirations for this story, Stephen King and Mary Shelley's *Frankenstein.*

There were many, many nights I'd stayed up, watching King's motivational videos on YouTube. He's truly inspiring and I recommend everyone, writer or not, watch him. Mr. King, if you are reading this, I hope you found all my small tokens of appreciation for you within this story (all 78 of them).

And *Frankenstein,* the horror book that moved me in so many ways. I hope I've done this book justice, sprinkling the archaic style I've recognized, obsess over, and appreciate. Thank you for the inspiration.

To my family and friends across the globe, Thank you!
From the bottom to the top of my chaotic heart.

topics and questions for DISCUSSION

1. In the book, Julian would only refer to Fallon as Fallon Grimaldi, and not Fallon Morgan. Do you think he refuses to see her connected to Sacred Sea in any way, or is it because of something else entirely?

2. Fallon's magic never ascended during the Sacred Sea initiation ritual at the cemetery, but it materialized during her attempt to sacrifice herself in the Atlantic Ocean. Why do you think that is?

3. During a heated argument, Agatha calls Julian a *monster*. Does she truly believe he is a monster and has held on to anger for his part in the deaths of her husband and son, or is she terrified of suffering another loss and taking it out on Julian?

4. Zephyr, Phoenix, and Beck broke into Julian's home, beat him, and took him to the barn after Julian worked without them to steal the books during the Pruitt Ball. On a separate occasion, Zephyr, Phoenix, and Beck took Clarice Danver's body to The Wicker Man and burned her body to return balance to the town because Julian was unable to do so since he was bound to the woods. Do the Hollow Heathens make decisions based on what is right for their coven and town, regardless of who stands in the way (Julian)? Do you believe the three other Heathens would have been emotionally impacted by the loss of Julian, or has the way they were raised impacted their ability to love?

5. Hollow Heathens shifts between Bellamy and Siri's story and the present. How did this structure impact your reading and your perspective on the various characters? What is gained by switching

back and forth between time periods?

6. Fallon lacks experience with friends, love, and intimacy, but on the other hand, she doesn't fail to stand up for herself when needed. Though she internally questions her actions, has insecurities, and self-doubt, do you see Fallon as being a weak character? Where do you find the most growth of Fallon throughout the story?

7. What do you think will happen to the characters now that the first book in the interconnected series is over? How do you think breaking the curse will impact each of them in their lives and relationships going forward? How will it impact the town?

8. Julian mentioned he would not tell a soul about Stone Danvers, in fear of Stone's knowledge of how to break the curse. Now that the curse is broken, do you think Julian will now go to Bone Island to find the fifth Hollow Heathen that has been gone for almost two centuries?

Enhance your Book Club

• Have a themed monthly read and dress up for your get-togethers! Make things fun with themed cocktails and games related to the book.

• If you're not too scared, turn the lights out and bring out your flashlights (or Ouija boards)!

MORE BOOKS
by nicole fiorina

STAY WITH ME SERIES

This trilogy is **for the poetry lovers, dreamers, and those who love emotional rollercoasters and suspense.** This trilogy is known to be a tear-jerker, with dark, broken, and beautiful themes. All three books are complete and available on Amazon's Kindle Unlimited and also available in audio! Check out the reading order below:

Stay with Me
Even When I'm Gone
Now Open Your Eyes

TALES OF WEEPING HOLLOW

For the reader who adores century-old curses, midnight tales, & magic. Inspired by classic horror novels, gothic romance, and the supernatural. Timeless, forbidden, and haunting. Available on Kindle Unlimited. Young Adult edition available only at nicolefiorina.com

Hollow Heathens: Book of Blackwell
Bone Island: Book of Danvers

THE HENDRIX BROTHERS

LINC & LO
A rockstar at rock bottom, a notorious party girl, and a Chevy C10.
What happens when two stars collide?

For the reader who adores guitar players with a lip ring, a kick-ass heroine, and tacos. Meet rockstar, Lincoln Hendrix, and notorious party girl, Harlow St. James in Going Going Gone, a rockstar romance set in California. Going Going Gone is a short story prequel, with a standalone to follow. Check out the reading order below:

Going Going Gone
City of Angels

TY & KATE
A rap god and his SoHo Daydream.

For the reader who loves tortured musicians, steam, and characters with an empire state of mind! The 12-hour soul-searching journey starts in What If, a short story prequel set in New York City (ends in happy for now!). The full-length novel is expected to release in 2023. What If is currently on Amazon's Kindle Unlimited!

What If
In Too Deep

For more information, visit:
w w w . n i c o l e f i o r i n a . c o m

about the AUTHOR

Nicole is the author of the Stay with Me series and Amazon's #1 Best Selling Author in Poetry & Gothic Romance, for her debut in Urban Fantasy, Hollow Heathens. She lives in Florida with her husband, two kids, two cats (one with a mustache) and lazy Great Dane, Winston.

Her writing style is "insanely romantic" and "wildly addicting," striving to push hearts and limits. When She's not writing, she's either listening to crime podcasts, watching horror flicks with her kids, traveling, or planning her next book adventure—with one hand on her laptop and the other balancing a starbies.

Keep up with Nicole:
Instagram: @authornicolefiorina
Facebook: @nicolefiorinabooks
TikTok: @nicolefiorinabooks

For more information, visit:
w w w . n i c o l e f i o r i n a . c o m

Made in the USA
Middletown, DE
15 October 2023

40803994R00309